Deep in a Forbidden Netherworld of the
Andes Mountains, DIRK PITT®
Uncovers an Empire of Evil Pursuing an
Untold Fortune in . . .

INCA GOLD

Now available for the first time
in an Archway edition.

DIRK PITT

He is a man of action who lives by the moment
and for the moment . . . without regret. A graduate of the Air Force Academy, son of a United
States Senator, and Special Projects Director for
the U.S. National Underwater and Marine Agency (NUMA), he is cool, courageous and resource-
ful—a man of complete honor at all times and of
absolute ruthlessness whenever necessary. Pitt
answers to no one but Admiral James Sandecker,
the wily commander of NUMA, and trusts no one
but the shrewd, street-smart Al Giordino, a friend
since childhood and his partner in undersea adventure for twenty years.

Dr. Shannon Kelsey: A respected archaeologist, a woman of fierce independence and beauty, her passion for the great ancient mysteries has brought her to the mountains of Peru, where she stands on the threshold of an astounding discovery . . . and on the verge of death.

Joseph Zolar: Within a labyrinth of legitimate business enterprises he has created a vast international empire built on illegal trade in antiquities. Now he has set his sights on the ultimate prize—golden antiquities worth almost a billion dollars—and from his lavish headquarters he coolly signs the death warrant of anyone who dares to challenge him.

Cyrus Sarason: Zolar's brother and partner, he takes a more personal, up-close approach to the family business. And when fortunes are at stake, he prefers to get his hands dirty—often putting them to lethal use.

Tupac Amaru: Feared as a revolutionary but driven by greed, he has cut a swath of destruction throughout the hill country of the Amazonas, his cruel black eyes as empty as his heart. But after a savage encounter with DIRK PITT, Amaru dreams only of vengeance.

David Gaskill: An agent for U.S. Customs, he specializes in tracking down smugglers of art and artifacts. He loves the game and the intrigue . . . and now the opportunity of a lifetime: a chance to penetrate and smash a powerful crime family.

Congresswoman Loren Smith: Stylish, with knockout violet eyes, she is friend and confidante to DIRK PITT. But she becomes hostage to Zolar's greedy scheme, a pawn in a brutal game that threatens to turn deadly.

Books by Clive Cussler

INCA GOLD
SHOCK WAVE

Available from Archway Paperbacks
Published by Pocket Books

Clive Cussler
Inca Gold

A DIRK PITT® ADVENTURE

AN ARCHWAY PAPERBACK
Published by POCKET BOOKS
New York   London   Toronto   Sydney   Tokyo   Singapore

This book is a work of fiction. Names, characters, places and incidents are products of the author's imagination or are used fictitiously. Any resemblance to actual events or locales or persons, living or dead, is entirely coincidental.

This is an abridged version of *Inca Gold*, first published in hardcover by Simon & Schuster Inc.

An Archway Paperback published by
POCKET BOOKS, a division of Simon & Schuster Inc.
1230 Avenue of the Americas, New York, NY 10020

ISBN: 0-671-02056-0

First Archway Paperback printing October 1998

10 9 8 7 6 5 4 3 2

Front cover illustration by Franco Accornero

Printed in the U.S.A.

IL 5+

Contents

PROLOGUE

THE MYSTERIOUS INTRUDERS

INCA SEAGOING VESSEL

A.D. 1533
A Forgotten Sea

THEY CAME FROM THE SOUTH WITH THE MORNING SUN, shimmering like ghosts in a desert mirage as they slipped across the sun-sparkled water. No commands were spoken as the crews dipped and pulled their paddles in eerie silence. Overhead, a hawk swooped and soared as if guiding the steersmen toward a barren island that rose from the center of the inland sea.

The rafts were constructed of reed bundles bound and turned up at both ends. The raised prow and stern were shaped like serpents with dog heads.

The lord in command of the fleet sat on a thronelike chair perched on the pointed bow of the lead raft. His head was covered with a plumed helmet and a face mask of gold. Ear ornaments, a massive necklace, and arm bracelets also gleamed yellow under the sun. Even his shoes were fashioned from gold. What made the sight even more astonishing was that the crew members were adorned just as magnificently.

Along the shoreline of the fertile land surrounding the sea, the local native society watched in fear and wonder as the foreign fleet intruded into their waters. There were no attempts at defending their territory against invaders. They were simple hunters and foragers who trapped rabbits, caught fish, and harvested a few seeded plants and nuts. Theirs was an archaic culture, unlike their neighbors to the east and south who built widespread empires. As one mind they saw the fleet as a miraculous appearance of warrior gods from the spirit world.

The mysterious strangers took no notice of the people crowding the shore and continued paddling toward their destination. They were on a mission and ignored all distractions. They headed straight for the steep, rock-blanketed slopes of a small mountain making up an island that rose 200 meters (656 feet) from the surface of the sea. It was uninhabited and mostly barren of plant life.

Soon the lustrously attired crewmen grounded their rafts on a small pebble-strewn beach that opened into a narrow canyon. They lowered their sails, woven with huge figures of supernatural animals, and began unloading large reed baskets and ceramic jars onto the beach.

Throughout the long day, the cargo was stacked in an immense but orderly pile. In the evening, as the sun fell to the west, all view of the island from the shore was cut off. In the dawn of the new day, the fleet was still snug on shore and the great mound of cargo was unmoved.

On top of the island mountain much labor was being expended by stone workers assaulting a huge rock. Over the next six days and nights, using bronze bars and chisels, they laboriously pecked and hammered the stone until it slowly took on the shape of a fierce, winged jaguar with the head of a serpent.

Then one morning the inhabitants looked across the water at the island and found it empty of life. The enigmatic people from the south, along with their fleet of rafts, had disappeared, having sailed away under cover of darkness.

Curiosity quickly outweighed fear. The next afternoon, four men from the main village along the coast of
the inland sea pushed off in a dugout canoe and paddled
across the water to the island to investigate. After
landing on the little beach, they were observed entering
the narrow canyon leading inside the mountain. All day
and into the next their friends and relatives anxiously
awaited their return. But the men were never seen again.
Even their canoe vanished.

The primitive fear of the local people increased when a
great storm swept the sea and turned it into a raging
tempest. The natives were certain the gods of the sky and
darkness were led by the jaguar/serpent to punish them
for their intrusion. They whispered of a curse against
those who dared trespass on the island.

Then as abruptly as it came, the storm passed over the
horizon and the wind died to a baffling stillness. Then
gulls appeared and wheeled in a circle above an object
that had been washed onto the sandy beach of the
eastern seashore. When the people saw the unmoving
form lying in the tide line, they approached warily and
stopped. They gasped as they realized it was the dead
body of one of the strangers from the south. He wore
only an ornate, embroidered tunic. All trace of golden
face mask, helmet, and bracelets was gone.

Unlike the dark-skinned natives with their jet black
hair, the dead man had white skin and blond hair. His
eyes were staring sightless and blue. If standing, he
would have stood a good half-head taller than the
astonished people studying him.

Trembling with fear, they tenderly carried him to a
canoe and gently lowered him inside. Then two of the
bravest men were chosen to transport the body to the
island. Upon reaching the beach they quickly laid him
on the sand and paddled furiously back to shore. Years
after those who witnessed the remarkable event had

died, the bleached skeleton could still be observed partly embedded in the sand as a warning to stay off the island.

It was whispered the golden warriors' guardian, the winged jaguar/serpent, had devoured the inquisitive men who trespassed its sanctuary, and no one dared risk its wrath by setting foot on the island ever again.

CATACLYSM

March 1, 1578
West Coast of Peru

CAPTAIN JUAN DE ANTON, A BROODING MAN WITH CASTILIAN green eyes and a precisely trimmed black beard, peered through his spyglass at the strange ship following in his wake and raised his eyebrows in surprise. "What do you make of her, Luis?" he asked his second-in-command and chief pilot, Luis Torres.

Torres shrugged. "Too small for a bullion galleon. I judge her to be a wine merchantman out of Valparaiso heading for port in Panama the same as we."

"You do not think there is a possibility she might be an enemy of Spain?"

"Impossible. No enemy ships have ever dared attempt the passage through the treacherous labyrinth of the Magellan Strait around South America."

Reassured, de Anton nodded. "Since we have no fear of them being French or English, let us put about and greet them."

Torres gave the order to the steersman, who manhandled a vertical pole that pivoted on a long shaft that turned the rudder. The *Nuestra Señora de la Concepción*, the largest and most regal of the Pacific armada treasure galleons, leaned onto her port side and came around on a reverse course to the southwest.

9

Captain de Anton casually sat on a small stool and resumed peering through his spyglass at the rapidly approaching ship. It never occurred to him to alert his crew for battle just to be on the safe side.

He had no certain foreknowledge, not even a vague premonition that the ship he had turned to meet was the *Golden Hind,* captained by England's indefatigable sea-dog, Francis Drake, who stood on his quarterdeck and calmly stared back at de Anton through a telescope, with the cold eye of a shark following a trail of blood.

"Considerate of him to come about and meet us," muttered Drake, a beady-eyed man with a light sandy beard that tapered to a sharp point under a long swooping moustache.

"The very least he could do after we've chased his wake for the past two weeks," replied Thomas Cuttill, sailing master of the *Golden Hind.*

"Aye, but she's a prize worth chasing."

Already laden with gold and silver bullion, a small chest of precious stones, and valuable linens and silks after capturing a score of Spanish ships since becoming the first English vessel to sail into the Pacific, the *Golden Hind,* formerly named the *Pelican,* pounded through the waves like a beagle after a fox.

Drake pointed at the unsuspecting ship approaching bow on. "They don't know it yet, but they're sailing into a trap of their own making."

Except for a few crew members who were dressed as Spanish sailors, Drake had hidden the mass of his men below decks and armed them with protective coats of mail and an arsenal of pikes, pistols, muskets, and cutlasses. Grappling hooks attached to stout ropes were stowed along the bulwarks on the top deck. Crossbowmen were secretly stationed in the fighting tops above the mainyards of the masts.

* * *

From his view, de Anton saw no unusual activity on the decks of the seemingly friendly and businesslike ship. The crew looked to be going about their duties without undue curiosity toward the *Concepción*. The captain, he observed, leaned casually against the railing of the quarterdeck and saluted de Anton.

When the gap between the two ships had narrowed to 30 meters (97 feet), Drake gave an almost imperceptible nod, and his ship's finest sharpshooter, who lay concealed on the gun deck, fired his musket and struck the *Concepción*'s steersman in the chest.

As the ships crushed together and their beams and planking groaned in protest, Drake roared out, "Win her for good Queen Bess and England, my boys!"

Grappling hooks soared across the railings, clattered and caught on the *Concepción*'s bulwarks and rigging, binding the two vessels together in a death grip. Drake's crew poured onto the galleon's deck, screaming like banshees. His bandsmen added to the terror by beating on drums and blaring away on trumpets. Musket balls and arrows showered the dumbfounded Spanish crew as they stood frozen in shock.

It was over minutes after it began. A third of the galleon's crew fell dead or wounded without firing a shot in their defense. Stunned by confusion and fear they dropped to their knees in submission as Drake's crew of boarders brushed them aside and charged below decks.

Drake rushed up to Captain de Anton, pistol in one hand, cutlass in the other. "Yield in the name of Her Majesty Queen Elizabeth of England!" he bellowed above the din.

Dazed and incredulous, de Anton surrendered his ship. "I yield," he shouted back. "Take mercy on my crew."

"I do not deal in atrocities," Drake informed him.

As the English took control of the galleon, the dead were thrown overboard and the surviving crew and their wounded were confined in a hold. Captain de Anton and his officers were escorted across a plank laid between the two ships onto the deck of the *Golden Hind*. Then, with the characteristic courtesy that Drake always displayed toward his captives, he gave Captain de Anton a personally guided tour of the *Golden Hind*. Afterward he treated all the galleon's officers to a gala dinner, complete with musicians playing stringed instruments and solid silver tableware.

The next four days were spent transferring the fantastic treasure trove from the cargo holds of the *Concepción* to the *Golden Hind*. The vast plunder included thirteen chests of royal silver plate and coins, eighty pounds of gold, twenty-six tons of silver bullion, hundreds of boxes containing pearls and jewels, and a great quantity of food stores such as fruits and sugar. The catch was to be the richest prize taken by a privateer for several decades.

There was also a hold full of precious and exotic Inca artifacts that were being transported to Madrid for the personal pleasure of His Catholic Majesty, Philip II, the King of Spain. Drake studied the artifacts with great astonishment. He had never seen anything like them. Oddly, the item that interested him most was not a masterwork of three-dimensional art inlaid with precious stones but rather a simple box carved from jade with the mask of a man for a lid. The masked lid sealed so perfectly the interior was nearly airtight. Inside was a multicolored tangle of long cords of different thicknesses with over a hundred knots.

Drake took the box back to his cabin and spent the better part of a day studying the intricate display of cords tied to lesser cords in vibrantly dyed colors with the knots tied at strategic intervals. A gifted navigator and an amateur artist, Drake realized that it was either a mathematical instrument or a method of recording dates as a calendar. He wrapped the jade box in linen. Then he called for Cuttill.

"The Spaniard rides higher in the water with most of her riches relieved," Cuttill announced jovially as he entered the captain's cabin.

"You have not touched the artworks?" Drake asked.

"As you ordered, they remain in the galleon's hold."

Drake rose from his worktable and walked over to the large window and stared at the *Concepción.* "The art treasures were meant for King Philip," he said. "Better they should go to England and be presented to Queen Bess."

"The *Hind* is already dangerously overladen," Cuttill protested. "By the time another five tons are loaded aboard, she'll founder sure as heaven if we take her back through the tempest of Magellan Strait."

"I don't intend to return through the strait," said Drake. "My plan is to head north in search of a northwest passage to England. If that is not successful, I'll follow in Magellan's wake across the Pacific and around Africa."

"The *Hind* will never see England, not with her cargo holds busting their seams."

"We'll jettison the bulk of the silver on Cano Island off Ecuador, where we can salvage it on a later voyage. You, Thomas, will take ten men from the *Hind* and sail the *Concepción* to Plymouth."

Cuttill spread his hands in anguish. "I can't possibly sail a vessel her size with only ten men, not through heavy seas."

Drake walked back to his worktable and tapped a pair of brass dividers on a circle marked on a chart. "On charts I found in Captain de Anton's cabin I've indicated a small bay on the coast north of here that should be free of Spaniards. You will sail there and cast off the Spanish officers and all wounded crewmen. Impress twenty of the remaining able-bodied seamen to man the vessel. I'll see you're supplied with more than enough weapons to preserve command and prevent any attempt to wrest control of the ship."

Cuttill knew it was useless to object. Debating with a stubborn man like Drake was a lost cause. He accepted his assignment with a resigned shrug.

At sunrise the following morning Cuttill ordered the crewmen to cast off the lines binding the two ships. Safely tucked under one arm was the linen-wrapped box that Drake had directed him to personally give to the queen. He carried it to the captain's cabin and locked it inside a cabinet in the captain's quarters. Then he returned to deck and took command of the *Nuestra Señora de la Concepción* as she drifted away from the *Golden Hind*.

Drake and Cuttill exchanged final waves as the *Golden Hind* set a course to the northeast. Cuttill watched the smaller ship until she was hull down over the horizon. A deep feeling of foreboding settled in the pit of his stomach.

The *Concepción* tacked and headed due east, making landfall and reaching the bay marked on the Spanish chart by Drake sometime late the next evening. The anchor was dropped and the watch lights set.

Daylight brought the sun shining down over the Andes as Cuttill and his crew discovered a large native village of more than a thousand inhabitants, surrounded by a large bay. Without wasting time, he ordered his men to begin ferrying the Spanish officers and their wounded to shore. Twenty of the best seamen among the survivors were offered ten times their Spanish pay to help sail the galleon to England where they were promised to be set free upon landing. All twenty gladly signed on.

Cuttill was standing on the gun deck overseeing the landing operation just after midday when the ship began to vibrate as though a giant hand were rocking it. Every eye turned to shore where a great cloud of dust rose from the base of the Andes and appeared to be moving toward the sea. A frightening thundering sound increased to deafening proportions along with a tremendous convulsion of the earth. As the crew gawked in stunned fascination, the hills east of the village seemed to rise and fall like breakers rolling on a shallow shore.

The dust cloud descended on the village and swallowed it. Above the uproar came the screams and cries of the villagers and the crashing sounds of their rock and adobe mud houses as they shook apart and crumbled into ruin. None of the crew had ever experienced an earthquake, and few were even aware of such a phenomenon. Half the Protestant English and every one of the Catholic Spaniards on the galleon dropped to their knees and began praying fervently to God for deliverance.

In minutes the dust cloud passed over the ship and dispersed out to sea. They all stared uncomprehendingly at what had been a thriving village bustling with activity. Now it was nothing but flattened ruins. Cries came from those trapped under the debris. A later estimate would show that less than fifty of the local inhabitants survived.

Suddenly desperate to escape the cataclysm on shore, Cuttill began shouting orders to get the galleon underway. The Spanish prisoners cooperated wholeheartedly, working alongside the English to unfurl the sails and pull in the anchor.

Suddenly, another earthquake shook the land, accompanied by an even more thunderous roar. The terrain began to undulate as if some monster were shaking a giant carpet. A constant flow of tremors moved the earth as the submarine quake caused crustal fracturing, collapsing the seafloor and creating a vast depression. Then it was the sea's turn to go crazy as it swept in from all sides to fill the hole. The water piled up in a gigantic counter-surge with incredible speed. Millions of tons of pure destruction rose higher and higher until its crest reached 40 meters (157 feet) high, a phenomenon that would later become known as a tsunami.

Paralyzed and speechless in fear of the green and froth-white mountain of water rising before their eyes, the men could only stand and watch it rush toward them. Only Cuttill had the presence of mind to run under the protecting deck over the tiller and wrap his limbs around its long wooden shaft.

Bow on to the colossal wall of water, the *Concepción* arched and soared vertically toward the curling crest. Moments later she was engulfed in a boiling turbulence as nature ran berserk.

Now that the mighty torrent had the *Concepción* in its grasp, it hurled the galleon toward the devastated shore at tremendous speed. The violent surge totally erased what was left of the village. The few drenched men who somehow remained alive on the battered *Concepción* were even further terrorized by the sight of centuries-dead mummies of the ancient Incas rising to the surface and surrounding the ship.

The mad swirl of the tidal current caused a vortex that spun the galleon with such force the masts went crashing over the sides and the two guns broke their lashings and tumbled about the deck in a wild dance of destruction. One by one the fear-crazed seamen were swept away by the gyrating avalanche of water until only Cuttill was left.

Cuttill felt the galleon become motionless. For nearly an hour he huddled under the tiller, fearing a return of the murderous wave, but the ship remained still and silent. Slowly, stiffly, he made his way to the top of the quarterdeck and surveyed the scene of devastation.

Astoundingly, the *Concepción* sat upright, high and dry in a flattened jungle. Cuttill judged her to be almost three leagues from the nearest water. Her survival was due to her rugged construction and the fact she was sailing into the wave when it struck. She had endured, but she was a wreck that would never feel the sea beneath her keel again.

Cuttill decided his only course, one with little probability of success, was to trek over the Andes and work east. Once he reached the Brazilian coast there was always the possibility of meeting up with an English marauder that was raiding Portuguese shipping.

The following morning he made a litter for his sea chest and filled it with food and water from the ship's galley, bedding, two pistols, a pound of gunpowder, a supply of shot, flint, and steel, a sack of tobacco, a knife, and a Spanish Bible. Then with nothing else but the clothes on his back, Cuttill set off with his litter for the mists hovering over the peaks of the Andes, taking one final look at the forlorn *Concepción* and wondering if perhaps the gods of the Incas were somehow responsible for the catastrophe.

Now they had their sacred relics back, he thought, and they were welcome to them. The antique jade box with its strange lid came to mind, and he did not envy the next men who came to steal it.

Drake returned triumphantly to England, arriving at Plymouth on September 26, 1580, with the *Golden Hind*'s holds bulging with spoils. But he found no sign of Thomas Cuttill and the *Nuestra Señora de la Concepción*. His backers received a 4700 percent profit on their investment and the queen's share became the foundation for future British expansion. During a lavish party on board the *Hind* at Greenwich, Queen Elizabeth conferred knighthood on Drake.

Sir Francis Drake continued his exploits for another sixteen years. On a later voyage, he seized the city ports of Santo Domingo and Cartagena and became Her Majesty's Admiral-of-the-Seas. He also served as mayor of Plymouth and a member of Parliament. And then there was his bold attack on the great Spanish Armada in 1588. His end came during an expedition to plunder ports and shipping on the Spanish Main in 1596. After succumbing to dysentery he was sealed in a lead coffin and dropped in the sea near Portobelo, Panama.

Before his death, hardly a day passed when Drake didn't puzzle over the disappearance of the *Concepción* and the enigma of the mysterious jade box and its knotted cords.

PART I

BONES AND THRONES

October 10, 2005
Andes Mountains of Peru

1

THE SKELETON RECLINED IN THE SEDIMENT OF THE DEEP POOL as if resting on a soft mattress, the cold unwinking eye sockets of the skull staring upward through the liquid gloom toward the surface 36 meters (120 feet) away. One arm was held in an upright position, the bony fingers of the hand as if beckoning the unwary.

From the bottom of the pool to the sun above, the water gradually lightened from a dismal gray-brown to a pea-soup green from the pond scum that flourished under the tropical heat. The circular rim stretched 30 meters (98 feet) across and the sheer walls dropped 15 meters (49 feet) to the water. Once in, there was no way a human or animal could escape without help from above.

.The place was more than a sacred well where men, women, and children had been thrown alive into the dark waters as sacrifices during times of drought and harsh storms. Ancient legends and myths called it a house of evil gods where strange and unspeakable events occurred. There were also tales of rare artifacts, hand-crafted and sculpted, along with jade, gold, and precious gemstones, that were said to have been cast into the forbidding pool to appease the evil gods who were inflicting bad weather. In 1964 two divers entered the depths of the sinkhole and never returned. No attempt had been made to recover their bodies.

A great deal of unresolved controversy had surrounded the sacred pool since then, and now archaeologists had finally gathered to dive and retrieve artifacts from its enigmatic depths. The ancient site was located on a western slope beneath a high ridge of the Peruvian Andes near a great ruined city. The nearby stone structures had been part of a vast confederation of city-states, known as the Chachapoyas, that was conquered by the renowned Inca empire around A.D. 1480.

As she stared down at the stagnant water through big, wide, hazel eyes under raised dark brows, Dr. Shannon Kelsey was too excited to feel the cold touch of fear. Her hair was straight and soft blond and tied in a ponytail by a red bandanna, and the skin that showed on her face, arms, and legs was richly tanned.

Dr. Kelsey had enjoyed a ten-year fascination with the Chachapoyan cultures. To work where an enigmatic and obscure people had flourished and died was a dream made possible by a grant from the Archaeology Department of Arizona State University.

"Useless to carry a video camera unless the visibility opens up below the first two meters," said Miles Rodgers, the photographer who was filming the project.

"Then shoot stills," Shannon said firmly. "I want every dive recorded whether we can see past our noses or not."

Rodgers was an old pro at underwater photography. He was in demand by all the major science and travel publications to shoot below-the-sea photos of fish and coral reefs. His extraordinary pictures of World War II shipwrecks in the South Pacific and ancient submerged seaports throughout the Mediterranean had won him numerous awards and the respect of his peers.

A tall, slender man in his sixties, with a silver gray beard that covered half his face, held up Shannon's air tank so she could slip her arms through the straps of the backpack. "I wish you'd put a hold on this until we've finished constructing the dive raft."

Shannon smiled at her colleague, Dr. Steve Miller from the University of Pennsylvania. "That's two days away. By doing a preliminary survey now we can get a head start."

"Then at least wait for the rest of the dive team to arrive from the university. If you and Miles get into trouble, we have no backup."

"Not to worry," Shannon said. "Miles and I will only do a bounce dive to test depth and water conditions. We won't run our dive time past thirty minutes."

Shannon spit into her face mask, smearing the saliva around the inside of the lens to keep it from misting. Next she rinsed the mask from a canteen of water. After adjusting her buoyancy compensator and cinching her weight belt, she and Rodgers made a final check of each other's equipment. Satisfied everything was in place and their digital dive computers properly programmed, Shannon smiled at Miller.

"See you soon, Doc."

The anthropologist looped under their arms a wide strap that was attached to long nylon lines, gripped tightly by a team of ten Peruvian graduate students of the university's archaeology program, who had volunteered to join the project. "Lower away, kids," Miller ordered.

Hand over hand the lines were paid out as the divers began their descent into the ominous pool below. Shannon and Rodgers extended their legs and used the tips of their dive fins as bumpers to keep from scraping against the rough limestone walls. They could clearly see the coating of slime covering the surface of the water. The aroma of decay and stagnation was overwhelming. To Shannon the thrill of the unknown abruptly changed to a feeling of deep apprehension.

When they were within 1 meter (about 3 feet) of the surface, they both inserted their air regulator mouthpieces between their teeth and signaled to the anxious faces staring from above. Then Shannon and Miles slipped out of their harnesses and dropped out of sight into the odious slime.

Miller nervously paced the rim of the sinkhole, glancing at his watch every other minute while the students peered in fascination at the green slime below. Fifteen minutes passed with no sign of the divers. Suddenly, the exhaust bubbles from their air regulators disappeared.

Frantically Miller ran along the edge of the well. Had they found a cave and entered it? He waited ten minutes, then ran over to a nearby tent and rushed inside. Almost feverishly he picked up a portable radio and began hailing the project's headquarters and supply unit in the small town of Chachapoyas, 90 kilometers (56 miles) to the south. The voice of Juan Chaco, inspector general of Peruvian archaeology and director of the Museo de la Nación in Lima, answered almost immediately.

"Juan here. That you, Doc? What can I do for you?"

"Dr. Kelsey and Miles Rodgers insisted on making a preliminary dive into the sacrificial well," replied Miller. "I think we may have an emergency."

"They went into that cesspool without waiting for the dive team from the university?" Chaco asked in a strangely indifferent tone.

"I tried to talk them out of it."

"When did they enter the water?"

Miller checked his watch again. "Twenty-seven minutes ago."

"How long did they plan to stay down?"

"They planned to resurface after thirty minutes."

"It's still early." Chaco sighed. "So what's the problem?"

"We've seen no sign of their air bubbles for the last ten minutes."

Chaco caught his breath, closed his eyes for a second. "Doesn't sound good, my friend. This is not what we planned."

"Can you send the dive team ahead by helicopter?" asked Miller.

"Not possible," Chaco replied helplessly. "They're still in transit from Miami. Their plane isn't scheduled to land in Lima for another four hours."

"We can't afford government meddling. Certainly not now. Can you arrange to have a dive rescue team rushed to the sinkhole?"

"The nearest naval facility is at Trujillo. I'll alert the base commander and go from there."

"Good luck to you, Juan. I'll stand by the radio at this end."

"Keep me informed of any new developments."

"I will, I promise you," Miller said grimly.

In Chachapoyas, Chaco pulled out a handkerchief and mopped his face. He was a man of order. Unforeseen obstacles or problems irritated him. If the two stupid Americans drowned themselves, there would be a government inquiry. Despite Chaco's influence, the Peruvian news media were bound to make an overblown incident out of it. The consequences might very well prove to be nothing less than disastrous.

"All we need now," he muttered to himself, "are two dead archaeologists in the pool."

Then with shaking hands he gripped the radio transmitter and began sending out an urgent call for help.

2

ONE HOUR AND FORTY-FIVE MINUTES HAD PASSED SINCE Shannon and Miles had entered the sacrificial pool. Nothing could save them now. They had to be dead, their air used up long ago. Two more victims added to the countless number who had disappeared into the morbid waters through the centuries.

In a voice frantic with desperation, Chaco had informed Dr. Miller that the Peruvian navy was caught unprepared for an emergency. Their water escape and recovery team was on a training mission far to the south of Peru near the Chilean border.

One of the female students heard the sound first. She cupped her hands to her ears and turned back and forth like a radar antenna. "A helicopter!" she announced excitedly, pointing in a westerly direction through the tops of the trees.

In an expectant hush everyone around the rim of the pool listened. The faint thumping sound of a rotor blade beating the air came toward them, growing louder with each passing moment. A minute later a turquoise helicopter with the letters NUMA painted on its sides swept into view.

Where had it come from? Miller wondered, his spirits

rising. It obviously didn't have the markings of the Peruvian navy. It had to be a civilian craft.

The tops of the surrounding trees were whipped into a frenzy as the helicopter began its descent into a small clearing beside the sinkhole. The landing skids were still in the air when the fuselage door opened and a tall man with wavy black hair made an agile leap to the ground. He was dressed in a thin, shorty wet suit for diving in warm waters. Ignoring the younger people, he walked directly up to the anthropologist.

"Dr. Miller?"

"Yes, I'm Miller."

The stranger, a warm smile arched across his face, shoved out a calloused hand. "I'm sorry we couldn't have arrived sooner."

"Who *are* you?"

"My name is Dirk Pitt."

"You're American," Miller stated, staring into a craggy face with eyes that seemed to smile.

"Special Projects Director for the U.S. National Underwater and Marine Agency. As I understand it, two of your divers are missing in an underwater cave."

"A sinkhole," Miller corrected him. "Dr. Shannon Kelsey and Miles Rodgers entered the water almost two hours ago and have failed to resurface."

Pitt walked over to the edge of the pool, stared down at the stagnant water, and quickly determined that diving conditions were rotten. The pool went from slime green at the outer edges to pitch black in the center, giving the impression of great depth. There was nothing to indicate that the operation would prove to be anything more than a body recovery. "Not too inviting," he mused.

"Where did you come from?" queried Miller.

"NUMA is conducting an underwater geological survey off the coast due west of here. The Peruvian naval

27

headquarters radioed a request to send divers on a rescue mission and we responded. Apparently we're the first to arrive on-site."

"How can oceanographic scientists carry out a rescue and recovery operation in a hellhole?" Miller snapped.

"Our research ship contained the necessary diving equipment," Pitt explained. "I'm not a scientist but a marine engineer. I've only had a few training sessions in underwater recovery, but I'm a reasonably good diver."

Before a discouraged Miller could reply, the helicopter's engine died as the rotor blades slowly swung to a stop, and a short man with the broad shoulders and barrel chest of a dock worker squeezed through the exit door and approached. He looked the complete opposite of the tall, lean Pitt.

"My friend and associate, Al Giordino," Pitt said, introducing him.

Giordino nodded under a mass of dark, curly hair and said simply, "Hello."

Miller looked behind them through the windshield of the aircraft, and seeing the interior held no other passengers, groaned in despair. "Two of you, only two of you. It will take at least a dozen men to bring them out."

"Trust me, Doc," Pitt said in a tone that stopped any further argument. "Al and I can do the job."

Within minutes, after a brief planning session, Pitt was ready to be lowered into the pool. He was wearing a full EXO-26 face mask from Diving Systems International with an exothermic air regulator good for polluted water applications. The earphone sockets were connected to an MK1-DCI Ocean Technology Systems diver radio. He carried twin 100-cubic-foot air tanks on his back and wore a buoyancy compensator with an array of instruments indicating depth, air pressure, and compass direction.

As Pitt geared up, Giordino connected a thick nylon

Kermantle communications and safety line to Pitt's earphone and an emergency release buckle on a strap cinched around Pitt's waist. The remainder of the safety line wound around a large reel mounted inside the helicopter and connected to an outside amplifier. After a final check of Pitt's equipment, Giordino patted him on the head and spoke into the communication system's microphone.

"Looking good. Do you read?"

"As though you were inside my head," Pitt answered, his voice audible to everyone through an amplifier. "How about me?"

Giordino nodded. "Clear and distinct. I'll monitor your decompression schedule and dive time from here."

"Understood."

"I'm counting on you to give me a running account of your situation and depth."

Pitt wrapped the safety line around one arm and gripped it with both hands. He gave Giordino a wink from behind the lens of the face mask. "Okay, let's open the show."

Giordino motioned to four of Miller's students who began unwinding the reel. Unlike Shannon and Miles who bounced their way down along the sinkhole walls, Giordino had strung the nylon line over the end of a dead tree trunk that hung 2 meters (over 6 feet) beyond the edge of the vertical precipice, allowing Pitt to drop without scraping against the limestone.

For a man who was conceivably sending his friend to an untimely death, Miller thought, Giordino appeared incredibly calm and efficient. He did not know Pitt and Giordino, had never heard of the legendary pair. He could not know they were extraordinary men with almost twenty years of adventuring under the seas who had developed an unerring sense for assessing the odds of survival. He could only stand by in frustration at what he was certain was an exercise in futility. He leaned over the brink and watched intently as Pitt neared the green surface scum of the water.

"How's it look?" asked Giordino over the phone.

"Like my grandmother's split pea soup," replied Pitt. "I don't advise sampling it."

"The thought never entered my mind."

No further words were spoken as Pitt's feet entered the liquid slime. When it closed over his head, Giordino slackened the safety line to give him freedom of movement. Pitt began breathing through his regulator, rolled over, kicked his fins, and dove down into the murky world of death. The increasing water pressure squeezed his eardrums and he snorted inside his mask to equalize the force. He switched on a Birns Oceanographics Snooper light, but the hand-held beam could barely penetrate the gloom.

Then, abruptly, he passed through the dense murk into a yawning chasm of crystal clear water. Instead of the light beam reflecting off the algae into his face, it suddenly shot into the distance. The instant transformation below the layer of slime stunned him for a moment. He felt as if he were swimming in air. "I have clear visibility at a depth of four meters," he reported topside.

"Any sign of the other divers?"

Pitt slowly swam in a 360-degree circle. "No, nothing."

"Can you make out details of the bottom?"

"Fairly well," replied Pitt. "The water is transparent as glass but quite dark. The scum on the surface cuts the sunlight on the bottom by seventy percent. It's a bit dark around the walls so I'll have to swim a search pattern so I won't miss the bodies."

For the next twelve minutes Pitt circled the steep walls of the sinkhole, probing every cavity, descending as if revolving around a giant corkscrew. He planed horizontally and swam in slow motion, sweeping the beam of light back and forth in front of him. The illusion of soaring over a bottomless pit was overwhelming.

Finally, he leveled out over the floor of the sacrificial pool. No firm sand or plant life, just one uneven patch of ugly brown silt broken by clusters of grayish rock. "I have the bottom at slightly over thirty-six meters. Still no sign of Kelsey or Rodgers."

Far above the pool, Miller gave Giordino a dazed look. "They *must* be down there. Impossible for them to simply vanish."

Far below, Pitt kicked slowly across the bottom, careful to stay a good meter above the rocks and especially the silt, which might billow into a blinding cloud and reduce his visibility to zero within seconds.

Giordino's voice broke through his earphones. "Speak to me."

"Depth thirty-seven meters," Pitt answered.

"Still no sign of bodies?"

"Not yet."

Pitt began to feel an icy finger trail up the nape of his neck as he spotted a skeleton with a bony hand pointing into the gloom. Beside the rib cage was a rusty breastplate, while the skull was still encased in what he guessed was a sixteenth-century Spanish helmet.

Pitt reported the sighting to Giordino. "Tell Doc Miller I've found a long-dead Spaniard complete with helmet and breastplate down here." Then, as if drawn by an unseen force, his eyes followed in the direction a curled finger of the hand pointed.

There was another body, one that had died more recently. It appeared to be a male with the legs drawn up and the head tilted back. The expensive hiking boots, a red silk scarf knotted around the neck, and a Navajo silver belt buckle inlaid with turquoise stones made it easy for Pitt to recognize someone who was not a local peasant. Whoever he was, he was not young. Strands of long silver hair and beard swayed with the current from

Pitt's movements. A wide gash in the neck also showed how he had died.

A thick gold ring with a large yellow stone flashed under the beam of the dive light. The thought occurred to Pitt that the ring might come in handy for identifying the body. Disagreeable as the job was, he removed the ring, swished it through the silt to clean off any remnant of its former owner, and then slipped it onto one of his own fingers so he wouldn't lose it.

"I have another one," he notified Giordino.

"One of the divers or an old Spaniard?"

"Neither. This one looks to be a few months to a year old."

"Do you want to retrieve it?" asked Giordino.

"Not yet. We'll wait until after we find Doc Miller's people—" Pitt suddenly broke off as he was struck by an enormous force of water that surged into the pool from an unseen passage on the opposite wall and churned up the silt like dust whirling around a tornado. He would have tumbled out of control like a leaf in the wind by the unexpected energy of the turbulence but for his safety line. As it was he barely kept a firm grip on his dive light.

"That was quite a jerk," said Giordino with concern. "What's going on?"

"Feels like I'm being pulled into a narrow tunnel feet first. I can touch the walls closing around me. Lucky I have a safety line. Impossible to swim against the surge."

Pitt felt as though he was being sucked through the narrow slot for an hour when it was only twenty seconds. The silt cloud had faded slightly, most of it remaining in the deep pool behind. He began to see his surroundings more clearly. His compass showed he was being carried in a southeasterly direction. Then the walls suddenly opened out into one enormous, flooded room. To his right and below he caught the momentary flash of something glinting in the murk. Something metallic vaguely reflecting the silt-dimmed beam of his dive light.

It was an abandoned air tank. Nearby was a second one. He swam over and peered at their pressure gauges. The needles were pegged on empty. He angled his dive light around in a circle, expecting to see dead bodies floating in the darkness like phantom demons.

He mentally sharpened his senses and forced himself to be alert. If the bodies were swept into a side passage, he thought, he could easily pass them by and never notice. But a quick search turned up nothing but a pair of discarded swim fins. Pitt aimed the dive light upward and saw the reflective glitter of surface water that indicated the upper dome of the chamber contained an air pocket.

He also glimpsed a pair of white feet.

3

RODGERS, FOR ALL HIS GUTS, WAS IN A BAD WAY, AND Shannon was just hanging on by a thread when suddenly she noticed a flickering light in the forbidding water below. Then it became a bright, yellow beam stabbing the blackness in her direction. Was her numbed mind playing tricks? Did she dare entertain a glimmer of hope?

"They've found us," she gasped to Rodgers as the light moved toward her.

Shannon felt a hand grab her foot, and then a head popped out of the water less than an arm's length away. The dive light was beamed into her eyes, momentarily blinding her. Then it moved onto Rodgers's face. Instantly recognizing that Rodgers was the worse off, Pitt reached under one arm and took hold of an auxiliary air regulator. He quickly slipped the mouthpiece between Rodgers's lips. Then he passed Shannon a reserve pony bottle and air regulator that was attached to his waist belt.

Several deep breaths later, the revival in mood and physical well-being was nothing short of miraculous. Shannon gave Pitt a big bear hug as a renewed Rodgers pumped his hand so vigorously he nearly sprained Pitt's wrist. There were moments of speechless joy as all three were swept away in a euphoria of relief and excitement.

Only when Pitt realized that Giordino was shouting through his earphones, demanding a situation report, did he announce, "Tell Doc Miller they are alive, repeat, they are alive and well."

"You have them?" Giordino burst through Pitt's earphones. "The Doc wants to know how they stayed alive."

"The current swept them into a chamber with an air pocket in its dome. Lucky I arrived when I did. They were minutes away from using up the oxygen."

Since the lost divers had dropped all of their useless dive gear, except for face masks and buoyancy compensators, Pitt felt confident the three of them could be pulled back through the narrow shaft against the current and into the main pool by his phone and safety line without complications.

He signaled Shannon to wrap one leg and one arm around the line and lead off, breathing through her pony bottle. Rodgers would repeat the step and follow, with Pitt bringing up the rear close enough for the spare regulator to reach Rodgers's mouth. When Pitt was sure they were stable and breathing easy, he alerted Giordino.

"We're positioned and ready for escape."

Giordino paused and stared at the young archaeology students, their hands gripping the safety line, poised as if ready for a tug-of-war. "Stand by. Give me your depth."

"I read slightly over seventeen meters. Much higher than the bottom of the sinkhole. We were sucked into a passage that sloped upward for twenty meters."

"You're borderline," Giordino informed him, "but the others have exceeded their time and pressure limits. I'll compute and advise you of decompression stops."

"Don't make them too long. Once the pony bottle is empty, it won't take long for the three of us to use up what air I have left in my twin tanks."

Giordino held up his hand as a signal for the students to begin pulling. "Here we go."

The safety line became taut and the long, slow haul began. The rush of the surge through the shaft was matched by the gurgling of their exhaust bubbles from the air regulators.

With nothing to do now but grip the line, Pitt relaxed and went limp, allowing his body to be drawn against the flow of the underground current that gushed through the narrow slot. The lighter silt-clouded water in the pool at the end of the passage seemed miles away. Time had no meaning, and he felt as if he'd been immersed for an age. Only Giordino's steady voice helped Pitt keep his grip on reality.

"Cry out if we haul too fast," ordered Giordino.

"Looking good," Pitt replied, hearing his air tanks grinding against the ceiling of the shaft. "Six more meters and we're out of here," Pitt informed him.

And then a minute, probably a minute and a half, struggling to hold on to the safety line as they were buffeted by the diminishing force of the torrent, and they broke free of the shaft into the cloud of silt swirling around the floor of the sacrificial pool. Another minute and they were pulled upward and clear from the drag of the current and into transparent, unclouded water. Pitt looked up, saw the light filtering through the green slime, and felt a wondrous sense of relief.

Giordino ordered a halt to the ascent operation as he rechecked his decompression data on a laptop computer. One stop of eight minutes would take Pitt out of any danger of decompression sickness, but the archaeology project divers would need stops of far longer duration.

Finally, Giordino set aside the computer and called Pitt. "Bad news. There isn't enough air left in your tanks for the lady and her friend to make the necessary decompression stops."

"Tell me something I don't know," Pitt came back. "What about backup tanks in the chopper?"

"No such luck," moaned Giordino. "In our rush to leave the ship the crew threw on an air compressor but forgot to load extra air tanks."

"The manifold valves on my air tanks," Pitt said hastily. "They're the new prototypes NUMA is testing. I can shut off one independently of the other and then remove it from the manifold without expelling air from the opposite tank."

"I read you, pal," said an enlightened Giordino. "You disconnect one of your twin tanks and breathe off the other. I pull up the empty and refill it with the compressor. Then we repeat the process until we satisfy the decompression schedule. I just hope your plan works."

"Never a doubt." Pitt's confidence seemed genuine. "When I step onto firm ground again, I'll expect a Dixieland band playing 'Waiting for the Robert E. Lee.'"

"Spare me," Giordino groaned.

As Giordino ran toward the helicopter, he was confronted by Miller.

"Why did you stop?" the anthropologist demanded. "What are you waiting for? Pull them up!"

Giordino fixed the anthropologist with an icy stare. "Pull them to the surface now and they die."

Miller looked blank. "Die?"

"The bends, Doc, ever hear of it?"

A look of understanding crossed Miller's face, and he slowly nodded. "I'm sorry. I won't trouble you again."

Giordino smiled sympathetically. He continued to the helicopter and climbed inside, never suspecting that Miller's words were as prophetic as a lead dime.

The tool kit was tied loosely to the safety line by a bowline knot and lowered by a small cord. Once the tools were in Pitt's hands he gripped the air tank pack between his knees. Next he shut off one valve and unthreaded it from the manifold with a wrench. When one air tank came free, he attached it to the cord.

"Cargo up," Pitt announced.

In less than four minutes, the tank was raised by willing hands on the secondary cord, connected to the throbbing gas-engine compressor and taking on purified air. Giordino cut off the compressor when the pressure reached 2500 and wasted no time in sending the tank back down into the sinkhole. The process was repeated three more times after Pitt and the other divers moved to their next decompression stop at three meters, which meant they had to endure several minutes in the slime. The whole procedure went off without a hitch.

Giordino allowed an ample safety margin. He let nearly forty minutes pass before he pronounced it safe for Shannon and Rodgers to surface and be lifted to the brink of the sacrificial pool. It was a measure of his complete confidence in his friend that Pitt didn't even bother to question the accuracy of Giordino's calculations. Ladies went first as Pitt encircled Shannon's waist with the strap and buckle that was attached to the safety and communications line. He waved to the faces peering over the edge and Shannon was on her way to dry land.

Rodgers was next. His utter exhaustion after his narrow brush with death was forgotten at the sheer exhilaration of being lifted out of the godforsaken pool of death and slime, never, he swore, to return. A gnawing hunger and a great thirst mushroomed inside him. He was high enough now to see the faces of Dr. Miller and the Peruvian archaeology students. He had never been as happy to see anyone in his life. He was too overjoyed to notice that none of them was smiling.

Then, as he was hoisted over the edge of the sinkhole, he saw to his astonishment and horror a sight that was completely unexpected.

Dr. Miller, Shannon, and the Peruvian university students stepped back once Rodgers was on solid ground. As soon as he had unbuckled the safety line he saw that they all stood somberly with their hands clasped behind their necks.

There were six in all, Chinese-manufactured Type 56-1 assault rifles gripped ominously by six pairs of steady hands. The six men were strung out in a rough semicircle around the archaeologists, small, blank-faced, silent men dressed in wool ponchos, sandals, and felt hats. Their furtive dark eyes darted from the captured group to Rodgers.

To Shannon, these men were not simple hill-folk bandits supplementing their meager incomes by robbing visitors of food and material goods that could be hawked in public markets, they had to be hardened killers of the *Sendero Luminoso* ("Shining Path"), a revolutionary group that had terrorized Peru since 1981 by murdering thousands of innocent victims. She was suddenly gripped by terror. The Shining Path killers were notorious for attaching explosives to their victims and blasting them to pieces.

The guerrillas stood around their captives, alert and watchful, with sadistic anticipation in their eyes. One of them, an older man with an immense sweeping moustache, motioned for Rodgers to join the other captives. "Are there more people down there?" he asked in English with the barest trace of a Spanish accent.

Miller hesitated and cast a side glance at Giordino.

Giordino nodded at Rodgers. "That man is the last," he snapped in a tone filled with defiance. "He and the lady were the only divers."

The rebel guerrilla gazed at Giordino through lifeless, carbon black eyes. Then he stepped to the sheer drop of the sacrificial pool and peered downward. He saw a head floating in the middle of green slime. "That is good," he said in a sinister tone.

He picked up the safety line that descended into the water, took a machete from his belt and brought it down in a deft swing, severing the line from the reel. Then the expressionless face smiled a morbid smile as he casually held the end of the line over the edge for a moment before dropping it into the unescapable sinkhole.

4

HOLDING UP THE SEVERED END OF THE SAFETY AND COMMU-
nications line, Pitt stared at it, incredulous. Besides
having his means of escape dropped around his head, he
had lost all contact with Giordino.

Pitt was half a second away from shouting for help
when a roaring blast of gunfire reverberated around the
limestone walls of the sinkhole. What was happening up
there? He became increasingly apprehensive with each
passing moment. He didn't need a manual on mountain
climbing to tell him it was impossible to climb the sheer
ninety-degree walls without proper equipment or help
from above.

Giordino would never have deserted him, he thought
bleakly. Never—unless his friend was injured or unconscious. He didn't allow himself to dwell on the unthink-
able possibility that Giordino was dead. He would have
to climb out alone. He looked up at the sky. There was
less than two hours of daylight left. If he was to save
himself, he had to start now.

He floated on his back and examined the walls that
surrounded him. The limestone was pockmarked with
small hollow cavities and lined with tiny edges. He swam
around the circular walls until he was under a small
outcropping that protruded from the side about halfway

41

to the top. He removed his air tank pack and the rest of his diving gear, except for the accessory belt, and let it drop to the floor of the sinkhole. All he kept were the pliers and the geologist's pick hammer from the tool kit.

First, he pulled a dive knife from a sheath strapped to his leg and cut off two lengths of safety line. He tied one section of the line tightly to the narrow section of the pick hammer's handle close to the head so it wouldn't slip over the wider base. Then he tied a step-in loop at the free end of the line.

Next he rigged a hook from the buckle of his accessory belt, bending it with the pliers until it resembled a C. He then fastened the second section of line to the hook with another step-in loop. When he was finished, he had functional, though rudimentary, climbing tools.

Now came the tough part.

With a commitment bred of desperation, he reached up and stuck the belt hook into a small protruding edge of limestone. He then stepped into the loop, grasped the upper end of the line and pulled himself out of the water.

Now he lifted the hammer as high as he could reach, slightly off to one side, and rapped the pick end of the hammer into a limestone pocket. Then he placed his free foot in the loop and pulled himself to a higher stance up the limestone wall.

Breathing heavily, he rested until his aching muscles stopped protesting. He sat there hugging the sheer side of the sinkhole wall for almost ten minutes. He felt like sitting there for another hour, but time was passing. The surrounding jungle was quickly turning dark once the sun was gone.

He had expected the darkness to shroud his vision, forcing him to scale the limestone by feel only. But a strange light was forming below him. He turned and stared down into the water.

The pool was emitting an eerie phosphorescent green light. No chemist, Pitt could only assume the strange emission was caused by some sort of chemical reaction from the decaying slime. Thankful for the illumination, however dim, he continued his grueling climb upward.

The last 3 meters (10 feet) were the worst. So near, yet so far. The brink of the sinkhole seemed close enough to touch with his outstretched fingertips. Three meters, no more. Just ten feet. It might as well have been the summit of Mount Everest.

Then, when he was within reach of the sinkhole's edge, he dropped the loop attached to the C hook. One moment stiffening fingers were tugging it from the limestone, the next it was falling toward the water where it entered the weirdly glowing algae layer with hardly a splash to mark its entry. In combination with the pick hammer, he began using the pockets of limestone as toe- and handholds. Near the top he swung the hammer in a circle above his head and hurled it over the edge of the sinkhole in an attempt to implant the pick end into soft soil.

It took four tries before the sharp point dug in and remained firm. With the final reserve of his strength, he took the line in both hands and pulled his body up until he could see flat ground before him in the growing darkness. He lay quiet and studied his surroundings. The dank rain forest seemed to close in around him. It was dark now and the only light came from the few stars and a crescent moon. The dim light that filtered down illuminated the ancient ruins with a ghostly quality. The eerie scene was enhanced by the almost complete silence. Pitt half expected to see weird stirring and hear ominous rustling in the darkness, but he saw no lights or moving shadows nor heard voices. The only sound came from the faint splatter of a sudden light rain on the leaves as Pitt moved away from the sinkhole as fleetingly as a phantom.

The campsite was deserted. The tents he'd observed before being lowered into the sacrificial well were intact and empty. He approached the clearing where Giordino had landed the NUMA helicopter. It was riddled from bow to tail by bullets. Using it to fly for help was a dashed hope. No amount of repair would put it in the sky again.

The shattered rotor blades hung down like distorted arms twisted at the elbow. It was too painfully obvious that a group of bandits or rebels had attacked the camp and blasted the craft into scrap.

He pushed aside the entry door that sagged on one hinge and entered, making his way to the cockpit. He groped under the pilot's seat until he found a long pocket and retrieved a flashlight. The battery case felt undamaged. He held his breath and flicked on the switch. The beam flashed on and lit up the cockpit.

"Score one for the home team," he muttered to himself.

Pitt carefully made his way into the cargo compartment. He found his nylon carry bag and pulled out the contents. His shirt and sneakers had escaped unscathed but a bullet had pierced the knee of his pants. Removing the shorty wet suit, he found a towel and gave his body a vigorous rubdown to remove the sinkhole's slime from his skin. After pulling on his clothes and sneakers, he then rummaged around until he came upon the box lunches packed by the chef on board their research ship. Pitt wolfed down a peanut butter sandwich and a dill pickle and drained a can of root beer. Now, he felt almost human again.

Back in the cockpit, he unlatched a panel door to a small compartment and pulled out a leather holster containing an old .45-caliber automatic Colt pistol. His father, Senator George Pitt, had carried it from Normandy to the Elbe River during World War II and then presented it to Dirk when he graduated from the Air Force Academy. The weapon had saved Pitt's life at least twice in the ensuing years. He ran his belt through the loops of the holster and buckled it around his waist along with the sheath of the dive knife.

He fashioned a small shade to contain the beam of the flashlight and searched the campsite. Unlike the helicopter, there was no sign of gunfire except spent shells on the ground, but the tents had been ransacked and any useful equipment or supplies that could be carried away were gone. A quick survey of the soft ground showed what direction the exodus had taken. A path that had been hacked out by machetes angled off through the dense thickets before vanishing in the darkness.

The forest looked forbidding and impenetrable. This was not an expedition he would have ever considered or undertaken in daylight, much less nighttime. He was at the mercy of the insects and animals that found humans fair game in the rain forest. He recalled hearing of boa constrictors and anacondas reaching lengths of 24 meters (80 feet). But it was the deadly poisonous snakes like the bushmaster, the cascabel, or the nasty fer-de-lance, or lance-head, that caused Pitt a high degree of trepidation. Low sneakers and light fabric pants offered no protection against a viper with a mean streak.

Beneath great stone faces staring menacingly down at him from the walls of the ruined city, Pitt set off at a steady pace, following the trail of footprints under the narrow beam of the flashlight. He turned and took a last look at the unearthly green glow coming from the bottom of the sinkhole. Then he entered the jungle.

Within four paces the thick foliage swallowed him as if he'd never been.

5

SOAKED BY A CONSTANT DRIZZLE, THE PRISONERS WERE
herded through a moss-blanketed forest until the trail
ended at a deep ravine. Their captors drove them across
a fallen log that served as a bridge to the other side where
they followed the remains of an ancient stone road that
wound up the mountains. The leader of the terrorist
band set a fast pace, and Doc Miller was particularly
hard-pressed to keep up. His clothes were so wet it was
impossible to tell where the sweat left off and the damp
from the rain began. The guards prodded him unmerci-
fully with the muzzles of their guns whenever he
dropped back. Giordino stepped beside the old man,
propped one of Miller's arms over his shoulder, and
helped him along, seeming oblivious to the pummeling
provided by the sadistic guards against his defenseless
back and shoulders.

"Keep that gun off him," Shannon snapped at the
bandit in Spanish. She took Miller's other arm and hung
it around her neck so that both she and Giordino could
support the older man.

Giordino found himself smiling at Shannon, wondering at her spirit and grit and untiring fortitude. He was
also conscious of an overwhelming sense of cowardice
for deserting his old friend without a fight. He'd thought

of snatching a guard's gun at least twenty times since being forced away from the sinkhole. But that would only have gotten him killed and solved nothing. As long as he somehow stayed alive there was a chance.

For hours they fought for breath in the thin Andes air as they struggled to an altitude of 3400 meters (11,000 feet). Everyone suffered from the cold. Although it soared under a blazing sun during the day, the temperature dropped to near freezing in the early hours of morning. Dawn found them still ascending along an ancient avenue of ruined white limestone buildings, high walls, and agricultural terraced hills that Shannon never dreamed existed.

As the stone road followed along raised walls that reached almost into the mists rolling in from the mountain peaks above, Shannon was astounded by the thousands of stone carvings of a very different ornamentation than she had ever seen. Great dragonlike birds and serpent-shaped fish mingled with stylized panthers and monkeys.

The sun was showing when the bedraggled party emerged from a narrow pass into a small valley with mountains soaring on all sides. They saw ahead a lofty stone block building rising a good twelve stories high. Unlike the Mayan pyramids of México, this structure had a rounder, more conical shape that was cut off at the top. It had ornate heads of animals and birds carved into the walls. Shannon recognized it as a ceremonial temple of the dead. An edifice on the top of the building, flanked with two large sculptures of a feathered jaguar with wings, she tentatively identified as a palace of the death gods. It was sitting in a small city with over a hundred buildings painstakingly constructed and lavishly decorated. The variety of architecture was astonishing. Some structures were built on top of high towers surrounded by graceful balconies. Most were completely circular while others sat on rectangular bases.

Shannon was speechless. For a few moments the immensity of the sight overwhelmed her. The identity of the great complex of structures became immediately apparent. If what she saw before her was to be believed, the Shining Path terrorists had discovered an incredible lost city—the lost City of the Dead, whose mythical riches went beyond those in the Valley of the Kings in ancient Egypt.

Shannon gripped Rodgers tightly about one arm. "The lost Pueblo de los Muertos," she whispered.

After a short walk over a broad stone street, they approached the circular structure that towered over the surrounding ceremonial complex. They toiled up several flights of an extraordinary switchback stairway decorated with mosaics of winged humans set in stone, designs Shannon had never seen before. On the upper landing, beyond a great arched entrance, they entered a high-ceilinged room with geometric motifs cut into the stone walls. The center of the floor was crammed with intricately carved stone sculptures of every size and description. Ceramic effigy jars and elegant ornately painted vessels were stacked in chambers leading off the main room. One of these chambers was piled high with beautifully preserved textiles in every imaginable design and color.

The archaeologists were stunned to see such an extensive cache of artifacts. To them it was like entering King Tut's tomb in Egypt's Valley of the Kings before the treasures were removed by famed archaeologist Howard Carter and put on display in the national museum in Cairo.

There was little time to study the treasure trove of artifacts. The terrorists quickly led the Peruvian students down an interior stairway and imprisoned them in a cell deep beneath the upper temple. Giordino and the rest were roughly thrown into a side room and guarded by two surly rebels who eyed them like exterminators contemplating a spider's nest. Everyone except Giordino sank gratefully to the hard, cold floor, fatigue etched in their drawn faces.

Giordino pounded his fist against the stone wall in frustration. During the forced march, he had watched intently for a chance to fade into the jungle and make his way back to the sinkhole, but with at least three guards taking turns training their automatic weapons at his back with cold steadiness the entire trip, the opportunity for escape never materialized. Any hope of reaching Pitt now was slim indeed. During the march he had smothered his characteristic defiance and acted meek and subjugated. Except for a valiant display of concern for Doc Miller, he did nothing to invite a torrent of bullets to the gut. He had to stay alive. In his mind, if he died, Pitt died.

With the flashlight carefully hooded to prevent being seen by the terrorists, and its beam angled down at the indentations in the compost covering the soft earth that traveled into the darkness, Pitt plunged through the rain forest. Time meant nothing. Not once did he glance at the luminous dial of his watch. Only when the morning sky began to brighten and he could put away the flashlight did his spirits take a turn for the better.

When he began his pursuit, the terrorists had more than a three-hour start. But he had closed the gap, walking at a steady gait when the trail ran steeply upward, jogging on the rare stretches where it leveled briefly. He never broke his stride, never once stopped to rest. When he came on the ancient stone road and the going became easier, he actually increased his pace.

He rushed on, now in daylight and on open ground, making little or no attempt at concealment. He spotted the huge temple against the steep cliff approximately a half kilometer (a third of a mile) distant. One tiny figure sat at the top of the long stairway, hunched over with his back against a wide archway. There was no doubt in Pitt's mind this was where the terrorists had taken their hostages.

He moved in closer, using the fallen walls of old residential homes around the temple as cover. He crouched and ran soundlessly from one shelter to the next until he crawled behind a large stone figure. He paused and stared up at the entrance to the temple. The long stairway leading to the entrance presented a formidable obstacle. Unless he somehow possessed the power of invisibility, Pitt would be shot down before he was a quarter of the way up the steps.

Then providence laid a benevolent hand on his shoulder. The problem of creeping up the stairs unseen was erased when Pitt observed that the terrorist who was guarding the entrance to the temple had fallen hard asleep. Inhaling and exhaling a deep breath, Pitt stealthily crept toward the stairway.

Tupac Amaru was a smooth but dangerous character, and he looked it. Having taken the name of the last king of the Incas to be tortured and killed by the Spanish, he was short, narrow-shouldered, with a vacant, brown face devoid of expression: he looked as though he never learned how to express the least hint of compassion. Unlike most of the hill-country people whose broad faces were smooth and hairless, Amaru wore a huge moustache and long sideburns that stretched from a thick mass of straight hair that was as black as his empty eyes.

His band of cutthroats was responsible for the disappearance of several explorers, government archaeologists, and army patrols that had entered the region and were never seen again. Amaru couldn't have cared less about revolution or improving the lot of the abysmally poor Indians of the Peruvian hinterlands, most of whom worked tiny plots to eke out a bare existence. Amaru had other reasons for controlling the region and keeping the superstitious natives under his domination.

He stood in the doorway of the chamber, staring stonily at the three men and one woman before him as if for the first time, relishing the defeat in their eyes, the weariness in their bodies, exactly the state he wanted them.

"I regret the inconvenience," he said, speaking for the first time since the abduction. "It is good that you offered no resistance or you would have surely been shot."

"You speak pretty good English for a highlands guerrilla," Rodgers acknowledged, "Mr.—?"

"Tupac Amaru. I attended the University of Texas at Austin."

"Why have you kidnapped us?" Shannon whispered in a voice hushed with fear and fatigue.

"For ransom, what else?" replied Amaru. "The Peruvian government will pay well for the return of such respected American scientists, not to mention their brilliant archaeology students, many of whom have rich and respected parents. The money will help us continue our fight against repression of the masses."

Shannon glared at Amaru, the pale fear in her face replaced with red anger. "You're a fraud," Shannon stated firmly.

Amaru looked at her with a bemused expression. "And what brings you to that curious conclusion, Dr. Kelsey?"

"You know my name?"

"My agent in the United States alerted me of your latest project to explore the mountains before you and your friends left the airport in Phoenix, Arizona."

"Informant, you mean."

Amaru shrugged. "Semantics mean little."

"A fraud and a charlatan," Shannon continued. "You and your men aren't Shining Path revolutionaries. Far from it. You're nothing more than *huaqueros*, thieving tomb robbers."

"She's right," Rodgers said, backing her up. "It's obvious; you're running an elaborate artifact theft ring that has to be a full-time operation."

Amaru looked at his prisoners in mocking speculation. "Since the fact must be patently apparent to everyone in the room, I won't bother to deny it."

A few seconds passed in silence, then Doc Miller rose unsteadily to his feet and stared Amaru directly in the eye. "You thieving scum," he rasped. "Pillager, ravager of antiquities. If it was in my power, I'd have you and your band of looters shot down like—"

Miller broke off suddenly as Amaru, his features utterly lacking the least display of emotion and his black eyes venting evil, removed a Heckler & Koch nine-millimeter automatic from a hip holster. With the paralyzing inevitability of a dream, he calmly, precisely, shot Doc Miller in the chest. The reverberating blast echoed through the temple, deafening all ears. One shot was all that was required. Doc Miller jerked backward against the stone wall for one shocking moment, and then dropped forward onto his stomach without a sound.

The captives all reflected different reactions. Rodgers stood like a statue frozen in time, eyes wide with shock and disbelief, while Shannon instinctively screamed. No stranger to violent death, Giordino clenched his hands at his sides. There was no doubt in his mind, in anybody's mind, that Amaru intended to kill them all. With nothing to lose, Giordino tensed to leap at the killer and tear out his throat before he received the inevitable bullet through the head.

"Do not try it," said Amaru, reading Giordino's thoughts. He inclined his head toward the guards, who stood with guns level and ready, and gave them orders in Spanish. Then he stepped aside as one of the guards grabbed Miller around the ankles, and dragged his body out of sight into the main room of the temple, leaving a trail of blood across the stone floor.

Shannon's scream had given way to uncontrollable sobbing as she sagged to her knees in shock and buried her face in her hands. "He couldn't harm you. How could you shoot down a kindly old man?"

Giordino stared at Amaru. "For him, it was easy."

Amaru's flat, cold eyes crawled to Giordino's face. "You would do well to keep your mouth closed, little man. The good doctor was supposed to be a lesson that apparently you did not comprehend."

No one took notice of the return of the guard who had dragged away Miller's body. No one except Giordino. He caught the hat pulled down over the eyes, the hands concealed within the poncho. He flicked a glance at the second guard who slouched casually against the doorway, his gun now slung loosely over one shoulder, the muzzle pointing at no one in particular. Only two meters separated them. Giordino figured he could be all over the guard before he knew what hit him. But there was still the Heckler & Koch tightly gripped in Amaru's hand.

When Giordino spoke, his voice wore a cold edge. "You are going to die, Amaru. You are surely going to die as violently as all the innocent people you've murdered in cold blood."

Amaru didn't catch the millimetric curl of Giordino's lips, the slight squint of the eyes. His expression turned curious, then the teeth flashed and he laughed. "So? You think I'm going to die, do you? Will you be my executioner? Or will the proud young lady do me the honor?"

He leaned down and savagely jerked Shannon to her feet, took hold of her ponytail, and viciously pulled her head backward until she was staring from wide, terrified eyes into his leering face.

"Please, no," Shannon moaned.

A brawny arm tightened around his throat and choked off his words. "This is for all the people you made suffer," said Pitt, a macabre look in his intense green eyes, as he cast aside the poncho, aimed the barrel of the .45 Colt at Amaru's right knee, and pulled the trigger.

6

FOR THE SECOND TIME THE SMALL CONFINES OF THE ROOM echoed with the deafening sound of gunfire. Giordino hurled himself forward, his head and shoulder driving into the startled guard, crushing him against the hard wall, causing an explosive gasp of pain. He caught the distorted look of horror and agony on Amaru's face, the bulging eyes, his mouth open in a silent scream. And then Giordino punched the guard in the teeth and tore the automatic rifle from his hands in almost the same movement. He swung around in a crouched firing position, muzzle aimed through the doorway.

This time Shannon didn't scream. Instead, she crawled into a corner of the room and sat motionless, staring dumbly at Amaru's blood splattered over her bare arms and legs. If she had been terrified earlier, she was now merely numb with shock. Then she stared up at Pitt, lips taut, face pale.

Rodgers was staring at Pitt too, with an expression of astonishment. "You're the diver from the cave," he said dazedly.

Pitt nodded. "One and the same."

"You're supposed to be back in the well," Shannon murmured in a trembling voice.

"Sir Edmund Hillary has nothing on me." Pitt grinned

slyly. "I scramble up and down the walls of sinkholes like a human fly." He shoved a horrified Amaru to the floor and placed a hand on Giordino's shoulder. "You can relax, Al. The other guards have seen the light of decency and virtue."

Giordino, with a smile as wide as an open drawbridge, laid aside the automatic rifle and embraced Pitt. "I never thought I'd see your gargoyle face again."

"The things you put me through. I can't go away for half an hour without you involving me in a local crime wave."

"Why the delay?" asked Giordino, not to be outdone. "We expected you hours ago."

"I missed my bus. Which reminds me, where is my Dixieland band?"

"They don't play sinkholes. Seriously, how did you climb a sheer wall and trail us through the jungle?"

"Not exactly a fun-filled feat, believe me. I'll tell you another time."

"And the guards, what happened to the other four guards?"

Pitt gave a shrug. "Their attention wandered and they all met with unfortunate accidents, mostly concussions or possible skull fractures." Then his face turned grim. "I ran into one pulling Doc Miller's body through the main entrance. Who carried out the execution?"

Giordino nodded at Amaru. "Our friend here shot him in the heart for no good reason. He's also the guy who dropped the safety line down around your head."

"Then I won't bother myself with remorse," Pitt said, staring down at Amaru, who was clutching his right knee and moaning in agony. "Does he have a name?"

"Calls himself Tupac Amaru," answered Shannon. "The name of the last Inca king. Probably took it to impress the hill people."

"The Peruvian students," Giordino said, remembering. "They were herded down a stairway underneath the temple."

"I've already released them. Brave kids. By now they should have the guerrillas tied up and neatly packaged until the government authorities arrive."

"Not guerrillas, and hardly dedicated revolutionaries. More like professional artifact looters masquerading as Shining Path terrorists. They pillage precious antiquities to sell through international underground markets."

"Amaru is only the base of a totem pole," added Rodgers. "His clients are the distributors who make the bulk of the profits."

"They have good taste," observed Pitt. "From what I glimpsed, there must be enough prime merchandise stashed here to satisfy half the museums and private collectors in the world."

"Thank goodness you got here when you did," said Shannon with a shiver. "You saved our lives. Thank you."

"Not once but twice," Rodgers added, pumping Pitt's hand.

"A lot of luck was involved," Pitt said with uncharacteristic embarrassment. "I deeply regret I was too late to save Doc Miller."

"Where have they taken him?" asked Rodgers.

"I stopped the scum who was disposing of the body just outside the temple entrance. Doc is lying on the landing above the steps."

Giordino gazed at Pitt, inspecting him from head to toe, observing the multitude of cuts and scratches on his friend's face and arms from his race through the jungle in the dark. "You look like you just finished a triathlon and then fell on a roll of barbed wire."

"I look worse than I feel," Pitt said cheerfully. "Besides, I don't have the slightest inclination to play Tarzan again. I'm taking the next flight out of here."

"Do you really think we can fly out of here?" inquired Shannon skeptically.

"Absolutely," Pitt said. "In fact I guarantee it."

Rodgers stared at him. "Only a helicopter could come in and out of the valley."

Pitt grinned. "I wouldn't have it any other way. How else do you think Amaru, or whatever his name is, transports his stolen goods to a coastal port for shipment out of the country? That calls for a communications system, so there must be a radio around we can appropriate to send out a call for help."

Giordino gave an approving nod. "Makes sense, providing we can find it. A portable radio could be hidden anywhere in one of the surrounding ruins. We could spend days looking for it."

Pitt stared down at Amaru, his face expressionless. "He knows where it is."

Amaru fought off the pain and stared back at Pitt with black malignant eyes. "We have no radio," he hissed through clenched teeth.

"Forgive me if I don't take you at your word. Where do you keep it?"

"I will tell you nothing." Amaru's mouth twisted as he spoke.

"Would you rather die?" Pitt queried dryly.

"You would do me a service by killing me."

Pitt's green eyes were as cold as a lake above timberline. "You're only kidding yourself." Pitt took the Colt .45 and placed the muzzle against the side of Amaru's face. "Kill you? I fail to see the percentage in that. One shot through both eyes would be more appropriate. You'll still live, but along with your other recent impairment you'll also be blind."

Amaru put on a show of arrogance, but there was unmistakable fear in his dead eyes, and there was a noticeable trembling of his lips. "You're bluffing."

"After the eyes, then the ears next, or better yet the nose. If I were you, I'd quit while I was ahead."

Seeing that Pitt was stone-cold serious, and realizing he was at a dead end, Amaru caved in. "You'll find what you're looking for inside a round building fifty meters west of the temple. There is a monkey carved above the doorway."

Pitt turned to Giordino. "Take one of the students with you to translate. Contact the nearest Peruvian authorities. Give our location and report our situation. Then request they send in an army unit. There may be more of these characters lurking in the ruins."

Giordino looked thoughtfully at Amaru. "If I send a Mayday over an open frequency, this homicidal maniac's pals in Lima might very well pick it up and send in a force of goons ahead of the army."

"Trusting the army can be touch-and-go," added Shannon. "One or more of their high-ranking officers could be in on this. We can use our own frequency and contact Juan," suggested Shannon.

"Juan?"

"Juan Chaco, the Peruvian government coordinator for our project. He's in charge of our supply headquarters at the nearest city."

"Can he be trusted?"

"I believe so," Shannon replied without hesitation. "Juan is one of the most respected archaeologists in South America, and a leading scholar on Andean cultures. He's also the government watchdog on illegal diggings and smuggling of antiquities."

"Sounds like our man," Pitt said to Giordino. "Find the radio, call him up and ask for a chopper to airlift us the hell back to our ship."

"What about Doc's body?" asked Rodgers.

"Bring him inside the temple out of the sun and wrap him in some blankets until he can be airlifted to the nearest coroner," Pitt said.

"Leave him to me," Rodgers said angrily. "It's the least I can do for a good man."

Amaru grinned hideously through his agony. "Fools, crazy fools," he sneered. "You'll never leave the Pueblo de los Muertos alive."

"Pueblo de los Muertos means city of the dead," Shannon translated.

Pitt knelt beside Amaru. "You act pretty sure of yourself for a man in your position."

"The last laugh will be mine." Amaru's face contorted in a sudden spasm of pain. "You have angered the *Solpemachaco* and blundered into the path of powerful men. Their wrath will be terrible."

"Not exactly a sweet-tempered group you're associated with. What do you call them again?"

Amaru went silent. He was becoming weak from shock and the loss of blood. Slowly, with much difficulty, he lifted a hand and pointed a finger at Pitt. "You are cursed. Your bones will rest with the Chachapoyas forever." Then, his eyes went unfocused, closed, and he fainted.

Pitt stared at Shannon. "Who are the Chachapoyas?"

"Known as the Cloud People," Shannon explained. "They were a pre-Inca culture that flourished high in the Andes from A.D. 800 to 1480, when they were conquered by the Incas. It was the Chachapoyas who built this elaborate necropolis for the dead."

Pitt rose to his feet, removed the guard's felt hat from his head and dropped it on Amaru's chest. He turned and walked into the main chamber of the temple and spent the next few minutes examining the incredible cache of Chachapoyan artifacts. He was admiring a large clay mummy case when Rodgers rushed up, looking disturbed.

"Where did you say you left Doc Miller?" Rodgers asked, half out of breath.

"On the landing above the exterior steps."

"You'd better show me."

Pitt followed Rodgers outside the arched entrance. He stopped and stared down at a bloodstain on the stone landing, then looked up questioningly. "Who moved the body?"

"If you don't know," said an equally mystified Rodgers, "I certainly don't."

"Did you look around the base of the temple? Maybe he fell—"

"I sent four of the archaeology students down to search. They found no sign of the Doc."

"Could any of the students have moved him?"

"I checked. They're all as bewildered as we are."

"Dead bodies do not get up and walk off," said Pitt flatly.

Rodgers looked around the outside of the temple, then gave a shrug. "It looks as if this one did."

7

THE AIR CONDITIONER WHIRRED AND CIRCULATED COOL DRY air inside the long motor home that served as the archaeology project's headquarters in Chachapoya. Juan Chaco sat up in full wakefulness almost instantly when a voice came over the radio speaker mounted on a wall behind the driver's compartment.

"Saint John calling Saint Peter." The voice came sharp and distinct. "Saint John calling Saint Peter. Are you there?"

Chaco moved quickly across the interior of the plush motor home and pressed the transmit button on the radio. "I am here and listening."

"Turn on the recorder. I don't have time to repeat myself or explain the situation in detail."

Chaco acknowledged and switched on a cassette recorder. "Ready to receive."

"Amaru and his followers were overpowered and taken prisoner. They are now being held under guard by the archaeologists. Amaru was shot and may be badly wounded."

Chaco's face suddenly turned grim. "How is this possible?"

"One of the men from NUMA, who responded to your

distress call, somehow escaped from the sinkhole and pursued Amaru and his captives to the valley temple where he managed to subdue our overpaid cutthroats one by one."

"Then our plan to frighten the archaeologists from our collection grounds has failed."

"Miserably," replied the caller. "Once Dr. Kelsey saw the artifacts awaiting shipment, she guessed the setup."

"What of Miller?"

"They suspect nothing."

"At least something went right," said Chaco.

"If you send in a force before they leave the valley," explained the familiar voice, "we can still salvage the operation."

"It was not our intention to harm our Peruvian students," said Chaco. "The repercussions from my countrymen would spell the end to any further business between us."

"Too late, my friend. Now that they realize their ordeal was caused by a looting syndicate instead of Shining Path terrorists, they can't be allowed to reveal what they've seen. We have no choice but to eliminate them."

"None of this would have occurred if you had prevented Dr. Kelsey and Miles Rodgers from diving in the sacred well."

"Short of committing murder in front of the students, there was no stopping them."

"Sending out the rescue call was a mistake."

"Not if we wished to avoid serious inquiry by your government officials. Their drownings would have appeared suspicious if the correct rescue measures hadn't been taken. We cannot afford to expose the *Solpemachaco* to public scrutiny. Besides, how could we know that NUMA would respond from out of nowhere?"

"True, an event that was inconceivable at the time."

As Chaco spoke, his empty eyes gazed at a small stone statue of a winged jaguar that was dug up in the valley of the dead. Finally he said quietly, "I'll arrange for our hired mercenaries from the Peruvian army to drop in the Pueblo de los Muertos by helicopter within two hours."

"Do you have confidence in the commanding officer to do the job?"

Chaco smiled to himself. "If I can't trust my own brother, who can I trust?"

Pitt stood gazing down at the pool of crimson on the landing above the near-vertical stairway leading to the floor of the valley.

"He was dead," Rodgers said incredulously. "I was standing as close to him as I am to you when Amaru put a bullet through his heart. Blood was everywhere. You saw him lying here. There can be no doubt in your mind Doc was a corpse."

"Are you sure it was Doc Miller?" Pitt asked.

"Of course it was Doc," Rodgers said emphatically. "Who else do you think it was?"

"How long have you known him?"

"By reputation, at least fifteen years. Personally, I only met him five days ago." Rodgers stared at Pitt as if he were a madman. "Look, you're fishing in empty waters. Doc is one of the world's leading anthropologists. His face has graced a hundred articles in dozens of magazines from the *Smithsonian* to the *National Geographic.* He was easily recognizable."

"Just fishing," Pitt said in a patient explaining tone. "Nothing like a wild plot to stir the mind—"

He broke off as Shannon and Giordino sprinted into view around the circular base of the temple. Even at this height above the ground he could see they appeared agitated. He waited until Giordino was halfway up the stairs before he shouted.

"Don't tell me, somebody beat you to the radio and smashed it."

Giordino paused, leaning against the sheer stairway. "Wrong," he shouted back. "It was gone. Snatched by person or persons unknown."

Pitt turned to Rodgers. "What about your communications at the sinkhole site?"

The photographer shook his head. "One of Amaru's men shot our radio to junk the same as yours."

"Don't tell me," Shannon said resignedly, "we have to trudge thirty kilometers back through the forest primeval to the project site at the sinkhole, and then another ninety kilometers to Chachapoya?"

"Maybe Chaco will become worried when he realizes all contact is lost with the project and send in a search party to investigate," Rodgers said hopefully.

"Even if they traced us to the City of the Dead," Pitt said slowly, "they'd arrive too late. All they'd find would be dead bodies scattered around the ruins."

Everyone glanced at him in puzzled curiosity.

"Amaru claimed we have upset the applecart of powerful men," Pitt continued by way of explanation, "and that they would never allow us to leave this valley alive for fear that we would expose their artifact theft operation. He referred to them as the *Solpemachaco*, whatever that translates into."

"*Solpemachaco*," Shannon echoed. "A combination Medusa/dragon myth from the local ancients. Folklore passed down through the centuries describes *Solpemachaco* as an evil serpent with seven heads who lives in a cave. One myth claims he lives here in the Pueblo de los Muertos."

Giordino yawned indifferently. "Sounds like a bad screenplay starring another monster from the bowels of the earth."

"More likely a clever play on words," said Pitt. "A metaphor as a code name for an international looting organization with a vast reach into the underground antiquities market."

"The serpent's seven heads could represent the masterminds behind the organization," suggested Shannon.

"Or seven different bases of operation," added Rodgers.

"Now that we've cleared up that mystery," Giordino said wryly, "why don't we clear out of here and head for the sinkhole?"

"Because they'd be waiting when we got there," said Pitt.

"You really believe they'll send men to kill us?" Shannon said, her expression more angry than fearful.

Pitt nodded. "I'd bet my pension on it. Whoever made off with the radio most certainly tattled on us. I judge his pals will soar into the valley like maddened hornets in . . ." he paused to glance at his watch before continuing, ". . . about an hour and a half. After that, they'll shoot down anyone who vaguely resembles an archaeologist."

"And there are the lives of those kids to consider," said Shannon, suddenly looking a little pale.

"I suggest we round up everyone and evacuate the temple," Pitt said briskly.

"Then what?" demanded Rodgers.

"First, we look around for Amaru's landing site."

Giordino rolled his eyes. "I know that look. He's hatching another scheme."

"Nothing too contrived," Pitt said patiently. "I figure that after the bushwhackers land and begin chasing around the ruins searching for us, we'll borrow their helicopter and fly off to the nearest luxury hotel and a refreshing bath."

Everyone stared at Pitt as if he'd just stepped out of a Martian space capsule. Giordino was the first to break the stunned silence.

"See," he said with a wide grin. "I told you so."

8

Pɪᴛᴛ'ꜱ ᴇꜱᴛɪᴍᴀᴛᴇ ᴏꜰ ᴀɴ ʜᴏᴜʀ ᴀɴᴅ ᴀ ʜᴀʟꜰ ᴡᴀꜱ ꜱʜʏ ʙʏ ᴏɴʟʏ ten minutes. The stillness of the valley was broken by the throb of rotor blades whipping the air as two Peruvian military helicopters flew over the crest of a saddle between mountain peaks and descended in a clearing amid the ruins less than 100 meters (328 feet) from the front of the conical temple structure. The troops spilled out rapidly through the rear clamshell doors under the beating rotor blades and lined up at rigid attention as though they were standing for inspection.

These were no ordinary soldiers dedicated to preserving the peace of their nation. They were mercenary misfits who hired themselves out to the highest bidder. At the direction of the officer in charge, a captain attired in full dress uniform, the two platoons of thirty men each were formed into one closely packed battle line led by two lieutenants. Satisfied the line was straight, the captain raised a swagger stick above his head and motioned for the officers under his command to launch the assault on the temple. Then he climbed a low wall to direct the one-sided battle from what he thought was a safe viewpoint.

The captain shouted encouragement to his men, urging them to bravely charge up the steps of the temple. His voice echoed because of the hard acoustics of the ruins. But he broke off and uttered a strange *awking* sound that became a fit of gagging pain. For a brief instant he stiffened, his face twisted in incomprehension, then he folded forward and pitched off the wall, landing with a loud crack on the back of his head.

A short, dumpy lieutenant in baggy combat fatigues rushed over and knelt beside the fallen captain, looked up at the funeral palace in dazed understanding, opened his mouth to shout an order, then crumpled over the body beneath him, the sharp crack of a Type 56-1 rifle the last thing he heard before death swept over him.

From the landing on the upper level of the temple, flat on his stomach behind a small barricade of stones, Pitt stared down at the line of confused troops through the sights of the rifle and fired another four rounds into their ranks, picking off the only remaining officer.

Cautiously, he pulled the assault rifle back from the tight peephole between the stones and surveyed the ground below. The Peruvian mercenaries had fanned out behind the stone ruins. A few scattered shots were fired upward at the temple, chipping the stone carvings before ricocheting and whining off into the cliff of tombs behind. The sergeants had taken command and were concentrating on a tactic to eliminate this unexpected resistance.

Pitt ducked back behind the stone barricade as a torrent of automatic weapons fire peppered the outside columns, sending chips of stone flying in all directions. This came as no surprise. Pitt could easily predict that they were gambling their entire force on a frontal assault up the stairway. What he hadn't foreseen was that they were going to reduce a lot of the palace of the dead on top of the temple to rubble before charging up the stairway.

Pitt let loose a long burst from the Chinese automatic rifle until the final shell spit across the stone floor. He rolled to one side and was in the act of inserting another long, curved ammo stick in the gun's magazine when he heard a *whoosh,* and a forty-millimeter rocket sailed up and burst against one side of the temple 8 meters (26 feet) behind Pitt.

There was a loud ringing in Pitt's ears, the reverberating roar of the detonation, the pounding of his own heart. He was momentarily blinded and his nose and throat were immediately filled with dust. He frantically rubbed his eyes clear and gazed down at the surrounding ruins. He was just in time to see the black smoke cloud and bright flash produced by the rocket's booster. He ducked with his hands over his head as another rocket slammed into the ancient stone and exploded with a deafening roar. The vicious blow pelted Pitt with flying rubble and the concussion knocked the breath out of him.

For a moment he lay motionless, almost lifeless. Then he struggled painfully to his hands and knees, coughing dust, seized the rifle, and crawled back into the interior of the palace. He took a last look at the mountain of precious artifacts and paid a final call on Amaru.

The grave looter had regained consciousness and glared at Pitt, his hands clutching his right knee, now clotted with dried blood, the murderous face masked in hate. There was a strange coldness about him now, an utter indifference to the pain. He radiated evil.

"Your friends have a destructive nature," said Pitt, as another rocket struck the temple.

"You are trapped," Amaru rasped in a low tone.

"Thanks to your staged murder of Dr. Miller's imposter. He made off with your radio and called in reinforcements."

"You will suffer as you have made me suffer."

"Sorry, I have other plans."

Amaru tried to rise up on an elbow and say something, but Pitt was gone.

He rushed to the rear opening again. A mattress and pair of knives he had scrounged from living quarters inside the cliff tomb discovered by Giordino and Shannon sat beside the window. He laid the mattress over the lower sill, then lifted his legs outside and sat on it. He cast aside the rifle, gripped the knives in outstretched hands, and glanced apprehensively at the ground 20 meters (65 feet) below. He dug the heels of his sneakers into the steep slope and jammed the knife blades into the stone blocks for brakes. Without a backward glance, he launched himself over the side, and slid down the wall, using the mattress as a toboggan/sled.

Giordino, with Shannon and the students trailing behind him and Rodgers bringing up the rear, cautiously climbed a stairway from an underground tomb where they had been hiding when the helicopters landed. Giordino paused, raised his head slightly over a fallen stone wall, and scanned the landscape. The helicopters were sitting only 50 meters (164 feet) away, engines idling, the two-man flight crews calmly sitting in their cockpits watching the assault on the temple.

He selected the one in the rear as a prime candidate for escape. It was only a few meters from a narrow ravine they could move in without being seen, and more important, it was out of easy view of the crew seated in the forward craft. "Pass the word," he ordered over the sounds of battle, "we're going to hijack the second chopper in line."

Pitt shot uncontrollably down the side of the temple, like a plummeting boulder on a path that took him between the stone animal heads protruding from the convex sloping walls with only centimeters to spare. His hands gripped the knife handles like vises, and he pushed with all the strength in his sinewy arms as the braking blades began to throw out sparks of protest from the friction of steel against hard stone. The rear edges of the rubber heels on his sneakers were being ground smooth by the rough surface of the wall. And yet he accelerated with dismaying speed. His two greatest fears were falling forward and tumbling head-first like a cannonball into the ground or striking with such force that he broke a leg. Either calamity and he was finished, dead meat for the Peruvians who wouldn't treat him kindly for killing their officers.

Still fighting grimly but hopelessly to arrest his velocity, Pitt flexed his legs a split second before he struck the ground with appalling force. He let loose of the knives on impact as his feet drove into the ooze of rain-soaked soil. Using his momentum, he rolled over on one shoulder and tumbled twice as required in a hard parachute landing. He lay in the mud for a few moments, thankful he hadn't landed on a rock, before rising experimentally to his feet and checking for damage.

One ankle slightly sprained, but still in working condition, a few abrasions on his hands, and an aching shoulder appeared to be the only damage. The damp earth had saved him from serious injury. The faithful mattress was in shreds. He took a deep breath, happy at still being intact. Having no time to waste, Pitt broke into a run, keeping as much of the ruins as possible between him and the troops massing for an assault up the temple stairs.

Giordino could only hope that Pitt had survived the rockets and somehow made it safely down the wall of the temple without being spotted and shot. He crouched and ran into a blind position behind the trailing helicopter as a squad of troops began charging up the precipitous temple steps. The reserve squad remained below while pouring a covering storm of rifle fire at the now shattered palace of the dead.

Every one of the Peruvians had his attention focused on the attack. No one saw Giordino, clutching an automatic rifle, steal around the tail boom of the helicopter and enter through the rear clamshell doors. He hurried inside and dropped flat, his eyes taking in the empty troop carrier and cargo compartment and the two pilots in the cockpit with their backs turned to him, intently watching the one-sided battle.

With practiced stealth Giordino moved with incredible quickness for a man built like a compact bulldozer. The pilots did not hear him or feel his presence as he came up behind their seats. Giordino reversed the rifle and clubbed the copilot on the back of the neck. The pilot heard the thud and twisted around in his seat. Before he could blink an eye, Giordino had delivered a sharp blow to the head.

Quickly he dragged the unconscious pilots to the doorway and dumped them on the ground. He frantically waved to Shannon, Rodgers, and the students, who were hiding in the ravine. "Hurry!" he shouted.

The archaeologists broke from cover and dashed through the open door into the helicopter in seconds. Giordino had already returned to the cockpit and was hurriedly scanning the instruments and the console between the pilots' seats to familiarize himself with the controls.

"Are we all here?" he asked Shannon as she slipped into the copilot's seat beside him.

"All but Pitt."

He did not reply, but glanced out the window. The troops on the stairway, becoming more courageous at encountering no defensive fire, surged onto the landing and inside the fallen palace of the dead. Only seconds were left before the attackers realized they'd been had.

Giordino turned his attention back to the controls. The helicopter was an old Russian-built Mi-8 assault transport, designated a Hip-C by NATO during the Cold War years. A rather ancient, ugly craft, thought Giordino, with twin 1500-horsepower engines that could carry four crew and thirty passengers. Since the engines were already turning, Giordino placed his right hand on the throttles.

"You heard me?" said Shannon nervously. "Your friend isn't with us."

"I heard." With a total absence of emotion, Giordino increased power.

Pitt crouched behind a stone building and peered around a corner, hearing the growing whine of the turboshaft engines and seeing the five-bladed main rotor slowly increase its revolutions. Though only 30 meters (98 feet) of open ground, completely devoid of any brush or cover, separated Pitt from the helicopter, it seemed more like a mile and a half.

There was no longer any need for caution. He had to make a run for it. He leaned down and gave his bad ankle a fast massage to knead out a growing tenseness. He plunged forward like a sprinter and raced into the open.

The rotors were beating the ground into dust when Giordino lifted the old Hip-C into a hover. In the main compartment, the students and Rodgers saw Pitt launch his dash toward the gaping clamshell doors. They all began shouting encouragement as he pounded over the soft ground. Their shouts turned urgent as a sergeant happened to glance away from the battle scene and saw Pitt chasing after the rising helicopter.

The sergeant's shouts—they were almost screams—carried over the last echoes of the firing from atop the temple. "They're escaping! Shoot them!"

Pitt ignored the bullet that cut a crease in his right

thigh. He had other priorities than feeling pain. And then he was under the long tail boom and in the shadow of the clamshell doors, and Rodgers and the Peruvian young people were on their stomachs, leaning out, reaching out to him in the opening between the doors. The helicopter shuddered as it was buffeted by its own downdraft and lurched backward. Pitt extended his arms and jumped.

Up front, Giordino bent the helicopter into a hard turn, putting the rotor blades dangerously close to a grove of trees. A bullet shattered his side window and sprayed a shower of silvery fragments across the cockpit, cutting a small gash across his nose. The helicopter took several more hits before he yanked it over the grove and below the far side, out of the line of fire from the Peruvian assault force.

"Anyone hit back there?" he shouted over his shoulder into the main cabin.

"Just little old me."

Giordino and Shannon twisted in their seats in unison at recognizing the voice. Pitt. A rather exhausted and mud-encrusted Pitt, it was true, a Pitt with one leg seeping blood through a hastily tied bandanna. But a Pitt as indefatigable as ever leaned through the cabin door with a smirk on his face.

A vast wave of relief swept over Giordino, and he flashed a smile.

Pitt leaned over Giordino's shoulder and examined the instrument panel, his eyes coming to rest on the fuel gauges. He reached over and tapped the instrument glass. Both needles quivered just below the three-quarter mark. "How far do you figure she'll take us?"

"Fuel range should be in the neighborhood of three hundred and fifty kilometers. If a bullet didn't bite a hole in one of the tanks, I'd guess she'll carry us about two hundred and eighty."

"Must be a chart of the area around somewhere and a pair of dividers."

Shannon found a navigation kit in a pocket beside her seat and passed it to Pitt. He removed a chart and unfolded it. Pitt laid out a course to the Peruvian coast.

"I estimate roughly three hundred kilometers to the *Deep Fathom.*"

"What's *Deep Fathom?*" asked Shannon.

"Our research ship."

"Surely you don't intend to land at sea when one of Peru's largest cities is much closer?"

"She means the international airport at Trujillo," explained Giordino.

"The *Solpemachaco* has too many friends to suit me," said Pitt. "Friends who have enough clout to order in a regiment of mercenaries at a moment's notice. We'll be safer on board an American ship outside their offshore limit until we can arrange for our U.S. Embassy staff to make a full report to honest officials in the Peruvian government."

"Forgetting a little something, aren't you?" said Shannon wearily. "If my math is correct, our fuel tanks will run dry twenty kilometers short of your ship. I hope you aren't proposing we swim the rest of the way."

"We solve that insignificant problem," said Pitt calmly, "by calling up the ship and arranging for it to run full speed on a converging course."

"Every klick helps," said Giordino, "but we'll still be cutting it a mite fine."

"Survival is guaranteed," Pitt said confidently. "This aircraft carries life vests for everyone on board plus two life rafts. I know—I checked when I walked through the main cabin." He paused, turned, and looked back. Rodgers was checking to see all the students had their shoulder harnesses on properly.

"Our pursuers will be on to us the instant you make contact with your vessel," Shannon persisted bleakly.

"They'll know exactly where to intercept and shoot us down."

"Not," Pitt replied loftily, "if I play my cards right."

Setting the office chair to almost a full reclining position, communications technician Jim Stucky settled in comfortably and began reading a paperback mystery novel by Wick Downing. He had finally gotten used to the thump that reverberated throughout the hull of the NUMA oceanographic ship, *Deep Fathom,* every time the sonar unit bounced a signal off the seafloor of the Peru Basin. He was in the middle of the first chapter when Pitt's voice crackled over the speaker.

"NUMA calling *Deep Fathom.* You awake, Stucky?"

Stucky jerked erect and pressed the transmit button. "This is *Deep Fathom.* I read you, NUMA. Please stand by." While Pitt waited, Stucky alerted his skipper over the ship's speaker system.

Captain Frank Stewart hurried from the bridge into the communications cabin. "Did I hear you correctly? You're in contact with Pitt and Giordino?"

Stucky nodded. "Pitt is standing by."

Stewart picked up the microphone. "Dirk, this is Frank Stewart."

"Good to hear your voice again, Frank."

"What have you guys been up to? Admiral Sandecker has been erupting like a volcano the past twenty-four hours, demanding to know your status."

"Believe me, Frank, it hasn't been a good day."

"What is your present position?"

"Somewhere over the Andes in an antique Peruvian military chopper."

"What happened to our NUMA helicopter?" Stewart demanded.

"The Red Baron shot it down," said Pitt hastily. "That's not important. Listen to me carefully. We took bullet strikes in our fuel tanks. We can't stay in the air for more than a half hour. Please meet and pick us up in the town square of Chiclayo. You'll find it on your charts of the Peruvian mainland. Use our NUMA backup copter."

Stewart looked down at Stucky. Both men exchanged puzzled glances. Stewart pressed the transmit button again. "Please repeat. I don't read you clearly."

"We are required to land in Chiclayo due to loss of fuel. Rendezvous with us in the survey helicopter and transport us back to the ship. Besides Giordino and me, there are twelve passengers."

Stewart looked dazed. "What is going on? He and Giordino flew off the ship with our only bird. And now they're flying a military aircraft that's been shot up with twelve people on board. What's this baloney about a backup chopper?"

"Stand by," Stewart transmitted to Pitt. Then he reached out and picked up the ship's phone and buzzed the bridge. "Find a map of Peru in the chart room and bring it to communications right away."

"You think Pitt has fallen off his pogo stick?" asked Stucky.

"Not in a thousand years," answered Stewart. "Those guys are in trouble and Pitt's laying a red herring to mislead eavesdroppers." A crewman brought the map, and Stewart stretched it flat on a desk. "Their rescue mission took them on a course almost due east of here. Chiclayo is a good seventy-five kilometers southwest of his flight path."

"Now that we've established his con job," said Stucky, "what's Pitt's game plan?"

"We'll soon find out." Stewart picked up the microphone and transmitted. "NUMA, are you still with us?"

"Still here, pal," came Pitt's imperturbable voice.

"I will fly the spare copter to Chiclayo and pick up you and your passengers myself. Do you copy?"

"Much appreciated, skipper. Always happy to see you never do things *halfway*. And put on some speed will you?" said Pitt. "I need a bath real bad. See you soon."

Stucky stared at Stewart and laughed. "Since when did you learn to fly a helicopter?"

Stewart laughed back. "Only in my dreams."

"Do you mind telling me what I missed?" Stucky asked.

"Not at all. Pitt and Giordino don't have enough fuel to reach the ship, so we're going to put on all speed and meet them approximately halfway between here and the shore, hopefully before they're forced to ditch in water infested with sharks."

9

GIORDINO GLANCED WARILY AT THE FUEL GAUGES. THE needles were edging uncomfortably close to the red. His eyes returned to the green foliage rushing past below. The forest was thick and the clearings were scattered with large boulders. It was a decidedly unfriendly place to force-land a helicopter.

Pitt had limped back into the cargo compartment and begun passing out the life vests. Shannon followed, firmly took the vests out of his hands, and handed them to Rodgers.

"No, you don't," she said firmly, pushing Pitt into a canvas seat mounted along the bulkhead of the fuselage. She nodded at the loosely knotted, blood-soaked bandanna around his leg. "You sit down and stay put."

She found a first-aid kit in a metal locker and knelt in front of him. Without the slightest sign of nervous stress, she cut off Pitt's pant leg, cleaned the wound, and competently sewed the eight stitches to close the wound before wrapping a bandage around it.

"Nice job," said Pitt admiringly. "You missed your calling as an angel of mercy."

"You were lucky." She snapped the lid on the first-aid kit. "The bullet merely sliced the skin."

"Why do I feel as though you've acted on a soap opera?"

Shannon smiled. "I was raised on a farm with five brothers who were always discovering new ways to injure themselves."

"What turned you to archaeology?"

"There was an old Indian burial mound in one corner of our wheat field. I used to dig around it for arrowheads. For a book report in high school, I found a text on the excavation of the Hopewell Indian culture burial mounds in southern Ohio. Inspired, I began digging into the site on our farm. After finding several pieces of pottery and four skeletons, I was hooked. Hardly a professional dig, mind you. I learned how to excavate properly in college and became fascinated with cultural development in the central Andes, and made up my mind to specialize in that area."

Pitt looked at her silently for a moment. "When did you first meet Doc Miller?"

"Only briefly about six years ago when I was working on my doctorate. I attended a lecture he gave on the Inca highway network that ran from the Colombian–Ecuador border almost five thousand kilometers to central Chile. It was his work that inspired me to focus my studies on Andean culture. I've been coming down here ever since."

"Then you didn't really know him very well?" Pitt questioned.

Shannon shook her head. "Like most archaeologists, we concentrated on our own pet projects. We corresponded occasionally and exchanged data. About six months ago, I invited him to come along on this expedition to supervise the Peruvian university student volunteers. He was between projects and accepted. Then he kindly offered to fly down from the States five weeks early to begin preparations, arranging permits from the

Peruvians, setting up the logistics for equipment and supplies, that sort of thing. Juan Chaco and he worked closely together."

"When you arrived, did you notice anything different about him?"

She thought a moment. "Since Phoenix, he had grown a beard and lost about fifteen pounds, but now that I think of it, he rarely removed his sunglasses."

"Any change in his voice?"

She shrugged. "A little deeper perhaps. I thought he had a cold."

"Did you notice whether he wore a ring? One with a large amber setting?"

Her eyes narrowed. "A sixty-million-year-old piece of yellow amber with the fossil of a primitive ant in the center? Doc was proud of that ring. I remember him wearing it during the Inca road survey, but it wasn't on his hand at the sacred well. When I asked him why it was missing, he said the ring became loose on his finger after his weight loss and he left it home to be resized. How do you know about Doc's ring?"

Pitt had been wearing the amber ring he had taken from the corpse at the bottom of the sacred well with the setting unseen under his finger. He slipped it off and handed it to Shannon without speaking.

She held it up to the light from a round window, staring in amazement at the tiny ancient insect imbedded in the amber. "Where . . . ?" her voice trailed off.

"Whoever posed as Doc murdered him and took his place. You accepted the imposter because there was no reason not to. The possibility of foul play never entered your mind. The killer's only mistake was forgetting to remove the ring when he threw Doc's body into the sinkhole."

"You're saying Doc was murdered before I left the States?" she stated in bewilderment.

"Only a day or two after he arrived at the campsite,"

Pitt explained. "Judging from the condition of the body, he must have been under water for more than a month."

"Strange that Miles and I missed seeing him."

"Not so strange. You descended directly in front of the passage to the adjoining cavern and were sucked in almost immediately. I reached the bottom on the opposite side and was able to swim a search grid, looking for what I thought would be two fresh bodies before the surge caught me. Instead, I found Doc's remains and the bones of a sixteenth-century Spanish soldier."

"So Doc really was murdered," she said as a look of horror dawned on her face. "Juan Chaco *must* have known, because he was the liaison for our project and was working with Doc before we arrived. Is it possible he was involved?"

Pitt nodded. "Up to his eyeballs. If you were smuggling ancient treasures, where could you find a better informant and front man than an internationally respected archaeological expert and government official?"

"Then who was the imposter?"

"Another agent of the *Solpemachaco*. A canny operator who staged a masterful performance of his death, with Amaru's help. Perhaps he's one of the men at the top of the organization who doesn't mind getting his hands dirty. We may never know."

"If he murdered Doc, he deserves to be hanged," Shannon said, her hazel eyes glinting with anger.

"At least we'll be able to nail Juan Chaco to the door of a Peruvian courthouse—" Pitt suddenly tensed and swung toward the cockpit as Giordino threw the helicopter in a steeply banked circle. "What's up?"

"A gut feeling," Giordino answered. "I decided to run a three-sixty to check our tail. Good thing I'm sensitive to vibes. We've got company." He nodded out of the windshield to his left at a helicopter crossing a low ridge of mountains to the east.

"They must have guessed our course and overhauled us after you reduced speed to conserve fuel," Pitt surmised.

A burst of flame and a puff of smoke erupted from the open forward passenger door of the pursuing aircraft, and a rocket soared through the sky, passing so close to the nose of the helicopter Pitt and Giordino felt they could have reached out the side windows and touched it.

Giordino slammed the collective pitch into an abrupt ascent and shoved the throttles to their stops in an attempt to throw off the launcher team's aim.

Pitt took a radio headset and clamped it over his ears. Then he clutched both sides of the open cockpit door with his hands to stay on his feet during a sharp turn. He plugged the lead from the headset into a socket mounted on the bulkhead and hailed Giordino. "Put on your headset so we can coordinate our defense."

Giordino didn't answer as he mashed down on the left pedal and skidded the craft around in a flat turn. As if he were juggling, he balanced his movements with the controls while slipping the headset over his ears.

Grabbing whatever handhold was within reach, Pitt staggered to the side passenger door, undogged the latches, and slid the door back until it was wide open. Shannon, her face showing more concern than fear, crawled across the floor with a cargo rope and wrapped one end around Pitt's waist as he was reaching for the automatic rifle Giordino had used to knock out the Peruvian pilots. Then she tied the opposite end to a longitudinal strut.

"Now you won't fall out," she exclaimed.

Pitt smiled. "I don't deserve you." Then he was lying flat on his stomach aiming the rifle out the door. Pitt didn't aim at the pilots in the cockpit, he sighted at the engine hump below the rotor and squeezed the trigger. The gun spat twice and went silent.

"What's wrong?" inquired Giordino.

"This gun had only two rounds in it," Pitt snapped.

"When I took it off one of Amaru's gunmen, I didn't stop to count the shells."

Furious with frustration, Pitt jerked out the clip and saw it was empty. "Did any of you bring a gun on board?" he shouted to Rodgers and the petrified students.

Rodgers, tightly strapped in a seat with legs braced against a bulkhead to avoid being bounced around by Giordino's violent tactics, spread his hands. "We left them behind when we made a break for the ship."

At that instant a rocket burst through a port window, flamed across the width of the fuselage, and exited through the opposite side of the helicopter without bursting or injuring anyone. Designed to detonate after striking armored vehicles or fortified bunkers, the rocket failed to explode after striking thin aluminum and plastic. If one hits the turbines, Pitt thought uneasily, it's all over. He stared wildly about the cabin, saw that they had all released their shoulder harnesses and lay huddled on the floor under the seats as if the canvas webbing and small tubular supports could stop a forty-millimeter tank-killing rocket. The wildly swaying aircraft threw him against the door frame. His eyes fell on one of the life rafts. He broke into a wild grin. "Al, you hear me?"

"I'm a little busy to take calls," Giordino answered tensely.

"Lay this antique on her port side and fly above them."

"Whatever you're concocting, make it quick before they put a rocket up our nose or we run out of fuel."

"Back by popular demand," Pitt said. "Mandrake Pitt and his death-defying magic act." He unsnapped the buckles on the tie-down straps holding one of the life rafts to the floor. The fluorescent orange raft was labeled Twenty-Man Flotation Unit, in English, and weighed over 45 kilograms (100 pounds). Leaning out the door secured by the rope Shannon had tied around his waist, both legs and feet spread and set, he hoisted the uninflated life raft onto his shoulder and waited.

Giordino was tiring. Helicopters require constant hands-on concentration just to stay in the air. The general rule of thumb is that most pilots fly solo for an hour. After that, they turn control over to their backup or copilot. Giordino had been behind the controls for an hour and a half, was denied sleep for the past thirty-six hours, and now the strain of throwing the aircraft all over the sky was rapidly draining what strength he had in reserve. For almost six minutes, an eternity in a dogfight, he had prevented his adversary from gaining a brief advantage for a clear shot from the men manning the rocket launcher.

The other craft passed directly across Giordino's vulnerable glass-enclosed cockpit. For a brief instant in time he could clearly see the Peruvian pilot. The face under the combat flight helmet flashed a set of white teeth and waved. "He's laughing at me," Giordino blurted in fury.

"What did you say?" came Pitt.

"Those baboons think this is funny," Giordino said savagely. He knew what he had to do. He had noticed an almost indiscernible quirk to the enemy pilot's flying technique. When he bent left there was no hesitation, but he was a fraction of a second slow in banking right. Giordino feinted left and abruptly threw the nose skyward and curled right. The other pilot caught the feint and promptly went left but reacted too slowly to Giordino's wild ascending turn and twist in the opposite direction. Before he could counter, Giordino had hurled his machine around and over the attacker.

Pitt's opportunity came in just the blink of an eye, but his timing was right on the money. Lifting the life raft above his head with both hands as easily as if it were a sofa pillow, he thrust it out the open door as the

Peruvian chopper whipped beneath him. The orange bundle dropped with the impetus of a bowling ball and smashed through one of the gyrating rotor blades 2 meters (about 6 feet) from the tip. The blade shattered into metallic slivers that spiraled outward from the centrifugal force. Now unbalanced, the remaining four blades whirled in ever-increasing vibration until they broke away from the rotor hub in a rain of small pieces.

The big helicopter seemed to hang poised for a moment before it yawed in circles and angled nose-first toward the ground at 190 kilometers (118 miles) an hour. Pitt hung out the door and watched as the Peruvian craft bored through the trees and crashed into a low hill only a few meters below the summit. The big injured bird came to rest on its right side, a crumpled lump of twisted metal. And then it was lost in a huge fireball that erupted and wrapped it in flames and black smoke.

"This has to be the first time in history an aircraft was knocked out of the sky by a life raft," said Giordino.

"Improvisation." Pitt laughed softly, bowing to Shannon, Rodgers, and the students who were all applauding with rejuvenated spirits. "Improvisation." Then he added, "Fine piece of flying, Al. None of us would be breathing but for you."

"Ain't it the truth, ain't it the truth," said Giordino, turning the nose of the craft toward the west and reducing the throttle settings to conserve fuel.

Pitt gazed over Giordino's shoulder at the gauges. Both showed flickering red warning lights. He could also see the drawn look of fatigue on his friend's face. "Take a break and let me spell you at the controls."

"I got us this far. I'll take us what little distance we have left before the tanks run dry."

Pitt did not waste his breath in debate. He never ceased to marvel at his childhood friend's intrepid calm, his glacial fortitude; he could have searched the world and never found another friend like the tough burly Italian. "Okay, you take her in. I'll sit this one out and pray for a tailwind."

Pitt returned to the cargo cabin and approached Rodgers. "We've got to dump as much weight as possible, except for survival equipment like the life vests and the remaining raft. Everything else goes, excess clothing, tools, hardware, seats, anything that isn't welded or bolted down."

Everyone pitched in and passed whatever objects they could find to Pitt, who heaved them out the passenger door. When the cabin was bare the chopper was lighter by almost 136 kilograms (300 pounds).

Pitt limped back to the cockpit, slid into the copilot's seat, and picked up the radio microphone. He brushed aside all caution as he pressed the transmit button.

"NUMA calling *Deep Fathom*. Talk to me, Stucky."

"You guys landed in Chiclayo yet?" Stucky's familiar voice came over the speaker.

"We were sidetracked and decided to head home," said Pitt. "We do not have a visual on you. Do you have us on radar?"

"Affirmative," answered Stucky. "Change your heading to two-seven-two magnetic. That will put us on a converging course."

"Altering course to two-seven-two," Giordino acknowledged.

"How far to rendezvous?" Pitt asked Stucky.

"The skipper makes it about sixty kilometers."

"You'd better prepare for a water rescue. All predictions point to a wet landing," Pitt said.

"I'll pass the word to the skipper. Alert me when you ditch."

Pitt looked down at the deep cobalt blue of the water only 10 meters (33 feet) beneath the belly of the chopper. The sea looked reasonably smooth. He called Shannon to the cockpit. She appeared in the doorway, looked down at him, and smiled faintly. "Is your ship in sight?"

"Just over the horizon. But not close enough to reach with the fuel that's left. Tell everybody to prepare for a water landing. Have Rodgers move the life raft close to the passenger door and be ready to heave it in the water as soon as we ditch. And impress upon him the importance of pulling the inflation cord *after* the raft is safely through the door. I for one do not want to get my feet wet."

Giordino pointed dead ahead. "The *Deep Fathom*."

Pitt nodded as he squinted at the dark tiny speck on the horizon. He spoke into the radio mike. "We have you on visual, Stucky."

"Come to the party," answered Stucky. "We'll open the bar early just for you."

"I don't imagine the admiral will take kindly to that suggestion," answered Pitt.

Their employer, chief director of the National Underwater and Marine Agency, Admiral James Sandecker, had a regulation etched in stone banning all alcoholic spirits from NUMA vessels.

"We just lost an engine," announced Giordino conversationally.

Pitt's eyes darted to the instruments. Across the board, the needles of the gauges monitoring the port turbine were flickering back to their stops. He turned and looked up at Shannon. "Warn everyone that we'll impact the water on the starboard side of the aircraft."

Shannon looked confused. "Why not land vertically?"

"If we go in bottom first, the rotor blades settle, strike the water, and shatter on a level with the fuselage. The whirling fragments can easily penetrate the cabin's skin, especially the cockpit, resulting in the loss of our intrepid pilot's head. Coming down on the side throws the shattered blades out and away from us."

Shannon nodded. "Understood."

"Immediately after impact," Pitt continued, "get the students out the door before this thing sinks. Now get to your seat and buckle up." Then he slapped Giordino on the shoulder. "Take her in while you still have power," he said as he snapped on his safety harness.

Giordino needed no coaxing. Before he lost his remaining engine, he pulled back on the collective pitch and pulled back the throttle on his one operating engine. As the helicopter lost its forward motion from a height of 3 meters above the sea, he leaned it gently onto the starboard side. The rotor blades smacked the water and snapped off in a cloud of debris and spray as the craft settled in the restless waves. The impact came with the jolt of a speeding car hitting a sharp dip in the road. Giordino shut down the one engine and was pleasantly surprised to find the old Mi-8, Hip-C floating in the sea as if she belonged there.

"End of the line!" Pitt boomed. "Everyone out!"

Rodgers slid open the passenger door and dropped the collapsible twenty-person life raft into the water. He was extra careful not to pull the inflation cord too soon and was relieved to hear the hiss of compressed air and see the raft puff out safely beyond the door. In a few moments it was bobbing alongside the helicopter, its mooring line tightly clutched in Rodgers's hand.

"Out you go," Rodgers yelled, herding the young Peruvian archaeology students through the door and into the raft.

Pitt released his safety harness and hurried into the rear cabin. Shannon and Rodgers had the evacuation running smoothly. All but three of the students had climbed into the raft. A quick examination of the aircraft made it clear she couldn't stay afloat for long. Already the floor of the fuselage was beginning to slant toward the rear, and the waves were sloshing over the sill of the open passenger door.

"We haven't much time," he said, helping Shannon into the raft. Rodgers went next and then he turned to Giordino. "Your turn, Al."

Giordino would have none of it. "Tradition of the sea. All walking wounded go first."

Before Pitt could protest, Giordino shoved him out the door, and then followed as the water swept over his ankles. Breaking out the raft's paddles, they pushed clear of the helicopter as its long tail boom dipped into the waves. Then a large swell surged through the open passenger door and the helicopter slipped backward into the uncaring sea.

No one spoke. They all seemed saddened to see the helicopter go. It was as if they all suffered a personal loss. Pitt and Giordino were at home on the water. The others, suddenly finding themselves floating on a vast sea, felt an awful sense of emptiness coupled with the dread of helplessness. The latter feeling was particularly enhanced when a shark's fin abruptly broke the water and ominously began circling the raft.

"All your fault," Giordino said to Pitt in mock exasperation. "He's homed in on the scent of blood from your leg wound."

Pitt peered into the transparent water, studying the sleek shape as it passed under the raft, recognizing the horizontal stabilizerlike head with the eyes mounted like aircraft wing lights on the tips. "A hammerhead. No more than two and a half meters long. I shall ignore him."

Shannon gave a shudder and moved closer to Pitt and clutched his arm. "What if he decides to take a bite out of the raft and we sink?"

Pitt shrugged. "Sharks seldom find life rafts appetizing."

"He invited his pals for dinner," said Giordino, pointing to two more fins cutting the water.

Pitt could see the beginnings of panic on the faces of

the young students. He nestled into a comfortable position on the bottom of the raft, elevated his feet on the upper float, and closed his eyes. "Nothing like a restful nap under a warm sun on a calm sea. Wake me when the ship arrives."

Shannon stared at him in disbelief. "He must be mad."

Giordino quickly sized up Pitt's scheme and settled in. "That makes two of us."

No one knew quite how to react. Every pair of eyes in the raft swiveled from the seemingly dozing men from NUMA to the circling sharks and back again. The panic slowly subsided to uneasy apprehension while the minutes crawled by as if they were each an hour long.

Other sharks joined the predinner party, but all hearts began filling with newfound hope as the *Deep Fathom* hove into view, her bows carving the water in a spray of foam.

10

JUAN CHACO'S WORLD HAD CRACKED AND CRUMBLED TO dust around him. The disaster in the Valley of Viracocha was far worse than anything he could have imagined. His brother had been the first to be killed, the artifact smuggling operation was in shambles, and once the American archaeologist, Shannon Kelsey, and the university students told their story to the news media and government security officials, he would be thrown out of the Department of Archaeology in disgrace. Far worse, there was every possibility he would be arrested, tried for selling his nation's historical heritage, and sentenced to a very long jail term.

He was a man wracked with anxiety as he stood beside the motor home in Chachapoya and watched the tilt-rotor aircraft come to a near halt in the air as the twin outboard engines on the end of the wings swiveled from forward flight to vertical. The black, unmarked craft hovered for a few moments before the pilot gently settled the extended landing wheels on the ground.

A heavily bearded man in dirty rumpled shorts and a khaki shirt with an immense bloodstain in its center exited the nine-passenger cabin and stepped to the ground. He looked neither right nor left, the expression on his face set and grim. Without a word of greeting, he walked past Chaco and entered the motor home. Like a chastised collie, Chaco followed him inside.

Cyrus Sarason, the impersonator of Dr. Steven Miller, sat heavily behind Chaco's desk and stared icily. "You've heard?"

Chaco nodded without questioning the bloodstain on Sarason's shirt. He knew the blood represented a fake gunshot wound. "I received a full report from one of my brother's fellow officers."

"Then you know Dr. Kelsey and the university students slipped through our fingers and were rescued by an American oceanographic research ship."

"Yes, I am aware of our failure."

"I'm sorry about your brother," Sarason said without emotion.

"I can't believe he's gone," muttered Chaco, strangely unmoved. "His death doesn't seem possible. The elimination of the archaeologists should have been a simple affair."

"To say your people bungled the job is an understatement," said Sarason. "I warned you those two divers from NUMA were dangerous."

"My brother did not expect organized resistance by an army."

"An army of one man," Sarason said acidly. "I observed the action from a tomb. A lone sniper atop the temple killed the officers and held off two squads of your intrepid mercenaries, while his companion overpowered the pilots and commandeered their helicopter. Your brother paid dearly for his overconfidence and stupidity."

"How could a pair of divers and a juvenile group of archaeologists scourge a highly trained security force?" Chaco asked in bewilderment.

"If we knew the answer to that question, we might learn how they knocked the pursuing helicopter out of the air."

Chaco stared at him. "They can still be stopped."

"Forget it. I'm not about to compound the disaster by destroying a U.S. government ship and all on board. The damage is already done. According to my sources in Lima, full exposure, including Miller's murder, was communicated to President Fujimori's office by Dr. Kelsey soon after she boarded the ship. By this evening, the story will be broadcast all over the country. The Chachapoyan end of our operation is a washout."

"We can still bring the artifacts out of the valley." The recent demise of Chaco's brother had not fully pushed aside his greed.

Sarason nodded. "I'm ahead of you. A team is on its way to remove whatever pieces survived the rocket attack launched by those idiots under your brother's command. It's a miracle we still have something to show for our efforts."

"I believe there is a good possibility a clue to the Drake *quipu* may still be found in the City of the Dead."

"The Drake *quipu*." Sarason repeated the words with a faraway look in his eyes. Then he shrugged. "Our organization is already working on another angle for the treasure."

"What of Amaru? Is he still alive?"

"Unfortunately, yes. He'll live the rest of his days as a cripple."

"Too bad. He was a loyal follower."

Sarason sneered. "Loyal to whoever paid him best. Tupac Amaru is a sociopathic killer of the highest order. When I ordered him to abduct Miller and hold him prisoner until we concluded the operation, he put a bullet in the good doctor's heart and threw him in the sinkhole. The man has the mind of a rabid dog."

"He may still prove useful," said Chaco slowly.

"Useful, how?"

"If I know his mind, he'll swear vengeance on those responsible for his newly acquired handicap. It might be wise to unleash him on Dr. Kelsey and the diver called Pitt to prevent them from being used by international customs investigators as informants."

"We'd be skating on thin ice if we turned a crazy man like him loose. But I'll keep your suggestion in mind."

Chaco went on. "What plans do the *Solpemachaco* have for me? I am finished here. Now that my countrymen will know I have betrayed their trust with regard to our historical treasures, I could spend the rest of my life in one of our filthy prisons."

"A foregone conclusion." Sarason shrugged. "My sources also revealed that the local police have been ordered to pick you up. They should arrive within the hour."

Chaco looked at Sarason for a long moment, then said slowly: "I am a scholar and a scientist, not a hardened criminal. There is no telling how much I might reveal during lengthy interrogation, perhaps even torture."

Sarason suppressed a smile at the veiled threat. "You are a valuable asset we cannot afford to lose. Your expertise and knowledge of ancient Andean cultures is second to none. Arrangements are being made for you to take over our collection facilities in Panama."

Chaco suddenly looked wolfish. "I'm flattered. Of course I accept. I will need help getting out of the country."

"Not to worry," said Sarason. "You'll accompany me." He nodded out a window at the ominous black aircraft sitting outside the motor home, the big three-bladed rotors slowly beating the air at idle. "In that aircraft we can be in Bogota, Colombia, within four hours."

Chaco couldn't believe his luck. One minute he was a step away from disgrace and prison for defrauding his government, the next he was on his way to becoming an extremely wealthy man. The memory of his sibling was rapidly fading; they were only half-brothers and had

never been close anyway. While Sarason patiently
waited, Chaco quickly gathered some personal items and
stuffed them in a suitcase. Then the two men walked out
to the aircraft together.

Juan Chaco never lived to see Bogota, Colombia.
Farmers tilling a field of sweet potatoes near an isolated
village in Ecuador paused to look up in the sky at the
strange droning sound of the tilt-rotor as it passed
overhead 500 meters (1600 feet) above the ground.
Suddenly, in what seemed a horror fantasy, they caught
sight of the body of a man dropping away from the
aircraft. He frantically kicked his legs and clawed madly
at the air as if he could somehow slow his plunging
descent.

Chaco struck the ground in the middle of a small
corral occupied by a scrawny cow, missing the startled
animal by only 2 meters. The farmers reverently lifted
the broken remains of the mysterious man who had
dropped from the sky and buried him in a small graveyard beside the ruins of an old church, unlamented and
unknown, but embellished in myth for generations yet to
come.

11

THE TOP OF SHANNON'S HEAD WAS WRAPPED TURBAN-STYLE with a towel, her hair still wet after a hot bath in the captain's cabin. Her skin glowed all over and smelled of lavender soap after washing the sweat and grime out of her pores and the jungle mud from under her nails. One of the shorter crewmen, who was close to her size, lent her a pair of coveralls. As soon as Shannon was dressed she promptly threw the swimsuit and the dirty blouse in a trash container. They held memories she'd just as soon forget.

She was just tying her long hair in a braid when Pitt knocked on the door. They stood there for a moment staring at each other before breaking into laughter.

"I hardly recognized you," she said, taking in a clean and shaven Pitt wearing a brightly flowered Hawaiian aloha shirt and light tan slacks.

"We don't exactly look like the same two people," he said with an engaging smile. "How about a tour of the ship before dinner?"

"I'd like that."

The *Deep Fathom* was a state-of-the-art scientific work boat, and she looked it. Her official designation was Super-Seismic Vessel. She was primarily designed for deep ocean geophysical research, but she could also undertake a myriad of other subsea activities, from mining excavation to deep water salvage and manned and unmanned submersible launch and recovery.

The ship's hull was painted in NUMA's traditional turquoise with a white superstructure and azure blue cranes. From bow to stern she stretched the length of a football field, berthing up to thirty-five scientists and twenty crew. Although she didn't look it from the outside, her interior living quarters were as plush as most luxurious passenger liners. Her dining room was fitted out like a fine restaurant and the galley was run by a first-rate chef.

Pitt led Shannon up to the navigation bridge. "Our brain center," he pointed out, sweeping one hand around a vast room filled with digital arrays, computers, and video monitors mounted on a long console that ran the full width of the bridge beneath a massive expanse of windows. "Most everything on the ship is controlled from here, except the operation of deep water equipment. That takes place in compartments containing electronics designed for specialized deep sea projects."

"You never fully explained what you're doing in the waters off Peru."

"We're probing the seas in search of new medicine," he answered. "Marine creatures and the microorganisms that dwell in the depths have been an untapped source, and might well be the hope of curing every affliction, including the common cold, cancer, or AIDS. The test results on a chemical isolated from kelp look especially encouraging in combating a drug-resistant strain of tuberculosis."

"Are there many scientists working on these miracle cures?" Shannon asked.

Pitt shook his head. "Around the world, maybe fifty or sixty. Marine medical research is still in its infancy."

"How long before we see the drugs on the market?"

"Doctors won't be prescribing many of these medications for another ten years."

Shannon walked over to an array of monitors that filled an entire panel of one bulkhead. "This looks impressive."

"Our secondary mission is to map the seafloor wherever the ship sails."

"What are the monitors showing?"

"You're looking at the bottom of the sea in a myriad of shapes and images," Pitt explained. "Our long-range, low-resolution side-scan sonar system can record a swath in three-dimensional color up to fifty kilometers wide."

Shannon stared at the incredible display of ravines and mountains thousands of meters below the ship. "I never thought I'd be able to observe the land beneath the sea this clearly. It's like staring out the window of an airliner over the Rocky Mountains."

"With computer enhancement it becomes even sharper."

They left the bridge, and he showed her through the ship's laboratory where a team of chemists and marine biologists were fussing over a dozen glass tanks teeming with a hundred different denizens from the deep, studying data from computer monitors, and examining microorganisms under microscopes.

"After retrieval from the bottom," said Pitt, "this is where the first step in the quest for new drugs begins."

"What is your part in all of this?" Shannon asked.

"Al Giordino and I operate the robotic vehicles that probe the seafloor for promising organism sites. When we think we've located a prime location, we go down in a submersible to collect the specimens."

She sighed. "Your field is far more exotic than mine."

Pitt shook his head. "I disagree. Searching into the origins of our ancestors can be pretty exotic in its own right. If we feel no attraction for the past, why do millions of us pay homage to ancient Egypt, Rome, and Athens every year? Why do we wander over the battle-fields of Gettysburg and Waterloo or stand on the cliffs and look down on the beaches of Normandy? Because we have to look back into history to see ourselves."

They had strolled out on deck and were leaning over the railing, watching the white foam thrown from the *Deep Fathom*'s bow slide past the hull and merge with the froth from the wake, when skipper Frank Stewart appeared.

"It's official," he said in his soft Alabama drawl, "we've been ordered to transport the Peruvian young people and Dr. Kelsey to Lima's port city of Callao."

"You were in communication with Admiral San-decker?" inquired Pitt.

Stewart shook his head. "His director of operations, Rudi Gunn."

"After we set everyone on shore, I assume we sail back on-site and continue with the project?"

"The crew and I do. You and Al have been ordered to return to the sacred well and retrieve Dr. Miller's body."

Pitt's eyes narrowed. "Sandecker's right-hand man flies over sixty-five hundred kilometers from Washington to oversee a body recovery? What gives?"

"More than meets the eye, obviously," said Stewart. He turned and looked at Shannon. "Gunn also relayed a message to you from a David Gaskill. He said you'd recall the name."

She seemed to stare at the deck in thought for a moment. "Yes, I remember, he's an undercover agent with the U.S. Customs Service who specializes in the illicit smuggling of antiquities."

Stewart continued, "Gaskill said to tell you he thinks he's traced the Golden Body Suit of Tiapollo to a private collector in Chicago."

Shannon gripped the handrail until her knuckles turned ivory.

"Good news?" asked Pitt.

"The Golden Body Suit of Tiapollo," she murmured reverently, "was lost to the world in a daring robbery at the Museo Nacional de Antropologia in Seville in 1922. There isn't an archaeologist alive who wouldn't sign away his or her pension to study it."

"What exactly makes it so special?" asked Stewart.

"It is considered the most prized artifact to ever come out of South America because of its historic significance," Shannon lectured, as if entranced. "The gold casing covered the mummy of a great Chachapoyan general known as Naymlap, from the toes to the top of the head. The Spanish conquerors discovered Naymlap's tomb in 1547 in a city called Tiapollo high in the mountains. The event was recorded in two early documents but today Tiapollo's precise location is unknown. I've only seen old black-and-white photos of the suit, but you could tell that the intricately hammered metalwork was breathtaking. The iconography, the traditional images, and the designs on the exterior were lavishly sophisticated and formed a pictorial record of a legendary event."

"Picture writing, as in Egyptian hieroglyphics?" asked Pitt.

"Very similar."

"What we might call an illustrated comic strip," added Giordino as he stepped out on deck.

Shannon laughed. "Only without the panels. The panels were never fully deciphered. The obscure references seem to indicate a long journey by boat to a place somewhere beyond the empire of the Aztecs."

"For what purpose?" asked Stewart.

"To hide a vast royal treasure that belonged to Huascar, an Inca king who was captured in battle and murdered by his brother Atahualpa, who was in turn executed by the Spanish conqueror Francisco Pizarro. Huascar possessed a sacred gold chain that was two hundred and fourteen meters long. One report given to the Spaniards by Incas claimed that two hundred men could scarcely lift it."

"Roughly figuring that each man hoisted sixty percent of his weight," mused Giordino, "you're talking over nine thousand kilograms or twenty thousand pounds of gold."

"On today's gold market that works out to well over a hundred million dollars," Pitt added, a faraway look in his eye.

Shannon nodded. "That's just the price of the gold. As an artifact it is priceless."

"The Spanish never got their hands on it?" Pitt asked Shannon.

"No, along with a vast hoard of other royal wealth, the chain disappeared. You've probably all heard the story of how Huascar's brother Atahualpa tried to buy his freedom from Pizarro and his conquistadors by offering to fill a room that measured seven meters in length by five meters wide with gold."

"Has to be a world's record for ransom," mused Stewart.

"According to the legend," Shannon continued, "the supply was coming up short, so he went after his brother's treasures. Huascar's agents warned him of the situation, and he conspired to have his kingdom's treasures carried off secretly before Atahualpa and Pizarro could get their hands on them. Guarded by loyal Chachapoyan warriors, commanded by General Naymlap, untold tons of gold and silver objects, along with the chain, were secretly transported by a huge human train to the coast, where they were loaded on board a fleet of reed and balsa rafts that sailed toward an unknown destination far to the north."

"Is there any factual basis to the story?" Pitt asked.

"Between the years 1546 and 1568, a Jesuit historian and translator, Bishop Juan de Avila, recorded many mythical accounts of early Peruvian cultures. He was told four different stories about a great treasure belonging to the Inca kingdom that their ancestors helped carry across the sea to an island far beyond the land of the Aztecs, where it was buried. Supposedly it is guarded by a winged jaguar until the day the Incas return and retake their kingdom in Peru."

"There must be a hundred coastal islands between here and California," said Stewart.

Shannon followed Pitt's gaze down to the restless sea. "There is, or I should say was, another source of the legend."

"All right," said Pitt, "let's hear it."

"When the Bishop was questioning the Cloud People, as the Chachapoyans were called, one of the tales centered on a jade box containing a detailed chronicle of the voyage."

"An animal skin painted with symbolic pictographs?"

"No, a *quipu,*" Shannon replied softly.

Stewart tilted his head quizzically. "A what?"

"Quipu, an Inca system for working out mathematical problems and for record keeping. Quite ingenious, really. It was a kind of ancient computer using colored strands of string or hemp with knots placed at different intervals. The various color-coded strands signified different things—blue for religion, red for the king, gray for places and cities, green for people, and so forth. A yellow thread could indicate gold while a white one referred to silver. The placement of knots signified numbers, such as the passage of time. In the hands of a *quipu-mayoc,* a secretary or clerk, the possibilities of creating everything from records of events to warehouse inventories were endless."

Pitt said, "And this was used to give an account of the voyage, including time, distances, and location?"

"That was the idea," Shannon agreed.

"Any clues as to whatever became of the jade box?"

"One story claims the Spaniards found the box with its *quipu* and not knowing its value, sent it to Spain. But during shipment aboard a treasure galleon bound for Panama, the box, along with a cargo of precious artifacts and a great treasure of gold and silver, was captured by the English sea hawk, Sir Francis Drake."

"What a tale," Pitt muttered quietly. His eyes seemed to turn dreamlike as his mind visualized something beyond the horizon. "But the best part is yet to come."

Shannon and Stewart both stared at him. Pitt's gaze turned skyward as a sea gull circled the ship and then winged toward land. There was a look of utter certainty in his eyes as he faced them again, a crooked smile curving his lips, the wavy strands of his ebony hair restless in the breeze.

"Why do you say that?" Shannon asked hesitantly.

"Because I'm going to find the jade box."

"You're putting us on." Stewart laughed.

"Not in the least." The distant expression on Pitt's craggy face had changed to staunch resolve.

"And I know just who to call to help me find it."

12

St. Julien Perlmutter weighed in at close to 181 kilograms (400 pounds). Besides eating, his other burning passion was ships and shipwrecks. He had accumulated what was acknowledged by archival experts as the world's most complete collection of literature and records on historic ships. Maritime museums around the world counted the days until overindulgence did him in, so they could pounce like vultures and absorb the collection into their own libraries.

There was a reason Perlmutter always entertained in restaurants instead of at his spacious carriage house in Georgetown outside the nation's capital. A gigantic mass of books was stacked on the floor, on sagging shelves, and in every nook and cranny of his bedroom, the living and dining rooms, and even in the kitchen cabinets. Archival experts would have required a full year to sort out and catalogue the thousands of books stuffed in the carriage house. But not Perlmutter. He knew precisely where any particular volume was stashed and could pick it out within seconds.

He was dressed in his standard uniform of the day, purple pajamas under a red and gold paisley robe, standing in front of a mirror salvaged from a stateroom on the *Lusitania,* trimming a magnificent gray beard, when his private line gave off a ring like a ship's bell.

"St. Julien Perlmutter here. State your business in a brief manner."

"Hello, you old derelict."

"Dirk!" he boomed, recognizing the voice, his blue eyes twinkling from a round crimson face. "Where are you calling from?"

"A ship off the coast of Peru."

"I'm afraid to ask what you're doing down there."

"A long story."

"Aren't they all?"

"I need a favor."

Perlmutter sighed. "What ship is it this time?"

"The *Golden Hind.*"

"Francis Drake's *Golden Hind?*"

"The same. Drake captured a Spanish galleon—"

"The *Nuestra Señora de la Concepción,*" Perlmutter interrupted. "Captained by Juan de Anton, bound for Panama City from Callao de Lima with a cargo of bullion and precious Inca artifacts. As I recall, it was in March of 1578."

There was a moment of silence at the other end of the line. "Why is it when I talk to you, Julien, you always make me feel as if you took away my bicycle?"

"I thought you'd like a bit of knowledge to cheer you up." Perlmutter laughed. "What precisely do you wish to know?"

"When Drake seized the *Concepción,* how did he handle the cargo?"

"The event was quite well recorded. He loaded the gold and silver bullion, including a hoard of precious gems and pearls, on board the *Golden Hind*. The amount was enormous. His ship was dangerously overloaded, so he dumped several tons of the silver into the water by Cano Island off the coast of Ecuador before continuing on his voyage around the world."

"What about the Inca treasures?"

"They were left in the cargo holds of the *Concepción*. Drake then put a prize crew on board to sail her back through the Magellan Strait and across the Atlantic to England."

"Did the galleon reach port?"

"No," answered Perlmutter thoughtfully. "It was presumed lost with all hands."

"I'm sorry to hear that," said Pitt, disappointment in his voice. "I had hopes it might have somehow survived."

"Come to think of it," recalled Perlmutter, "a myth did arise concerning the *Concepción's* disappearance."

"What was the gist of it?"

"A fanciful story, little more than rumor, said the galleon was caught in a tidal wave that carried it far inland. Never verified or documented, of course."

"Do you have a source for the rumor?"

"Further research will be needed to verify details, but if my memory serves me correctly, the tale came from a mad Englishman the Portuguese reported finding in a village along the Amazon River. Sorry, that's about all I can give you on the spur of the moment."

"I'd be grateful if you dug a little deeper," said Pitt. "If anyone can track down a sea mystery, you can."

"I have an utter lack of willpower when it comes to delving into one of your enigmas, especially after we found old Abe Lincoln on a Confederate ironclad in the middle of the Sahara Desert together."

"I leave it to you, Julien."

"Ironclads in a desert, Noah's Ark on a mountain, Spanish galleons in a jungle. Why don't ships stay on the sea where they belong?"

"That's why you and I are incurable lost shipwreck hunters," said Pitt cheerfully.

"What's your interest in this one?" Perlmutter asked warily.

"A jade box containing a knotted cord that gives directions to an immense Inca treasure."

Perlmutter mulled over Pitt's brief answer for several seconds before he finally said, "Well, I guess that's as good a reason as any."

Hiram Yaeger was chief of NUMA's communications and information network. Admiral Sandecker had pirated him away from a Silicon Valley computer corporation to build a vast data library, containing every book, article, and thesis, scientific or historical, fact or theory, ever known to be written about the sea.

He was sitting at his own private terminal in a small side office of the computer data complex that took up the entire tenth floor of the NUMA building when his phone buzzed. Without taking his eyes from a monitor that showed how ocean currents affected the climate around Australia, he picked up the receiver, then smiled when he heard the familiar voice on the other end of the line.

"Good to hear from you, Mr. Special Projects Director. The office topic of the day says you're enjoying a fun-filled holiday in sunny South America."

"You heard wrong, pal."

"Are you calling from the *Deep Fathom?*"

"Yes, Al and I are back on board after a little excursion into the jungle."

"What can I do for you?"

"Delve into your data bank and see if you can find any record of a tidal wave that struck the shoreline between Lima, Peru, and Panama City sometime in March of 1578."

Yaeger sighed. "Why don't you also ask me to find the temperature and humidity on the day of creation?"

"Give it your best try."

"How soon do you need it?"

"Unless the admiral has you on a priority project, drop everything else and go."

"All right," said Yaeger, eager for the challenge. "I'll see what I can come up with."

"Thanks, Hiram. I owe you."

"About a hundred times over."

"And don't mention this to Sandecker," said Pitt.

"I thought it sounded like another one of your schemes. Mind telling me what this is all about?"

"I'm looking for a lost Spanish galleon in a jungle."

"But of course, what else?" Yaeger said with routine resignation. He had learned long before never to anticipate Pitt.

"I'm hoping you can find me a ballpark to search."

"As a matter of fact, I can already narrow your field of search by a wide margin."

"What do you know that I don't?"

Yaeger smiled to himself. "The lowlands between the west flank of the Andes and the coast of Peru have an average temperature of eighteen degrees Celsius or sixty-five degrees Fahrenheit and an annual rainfall that would hardly fill a thimble, making it one of the world's coldest and driest low altitude deserts. No jungle for a ship to get lost in there."

"So what's your hot spot?" asked Pitt.

"Ecuador. The coastal region is tropical all the way to Panama."

"A precision display of deductive reasoning. You're okay, Hiram."

"I'll have something for you in twenty-four hours."

"I'll be in touch."

As soon as he put down the phone, Yaeger began assembling his thoughts. He never failed to find the novelty of a shipwreck search stimulating. The areas he planned to investigate were neatly filed in the computer of his mind. During his years with NUMA, he had discovered that Dirk Pitt didn't walk through life like other men. Simply working with Pitt and supplying data information had been one long, intrigue-filled, vicarious adventure, and Yaeger took pride in the fact that he had never fumbled the ball that was passed to him.

13

As Pitt was making plans to search for a land-locked Spanish galleon, Adolphus Rummel, a noted collector of South American antiquities, stepped out of the elevator into his plush penthouse apartment twenty floors above Lake Shore Drive in Chicago.

Like many of his extremely wealthy peers who amassed priceless collections of antiquities from the black market with no questions asked, Rummel was unmarried and reclusive. No one was ever allowed to view his pre-Columbian artifacts. Only his accountant and attorney were aware of their existence, but they had no idea of how extensive his inventory was.

In the nineteen fifties German-born Rummel smuggled a cache of Nazi ceremonial objects across the Mexican border. Selling his hoard to collectors at premium prices, Rummel took the profits and launched an auto junkyard that he built into a scrap metal empire, netting him nearly 250 million dollars over forty years.

After a business trip to Peru in 1974, he developed an interest in ancient South American art and began buying from dealers, honest or criminal. Source did not matter to him. Rummel gave no thought to whether his acquired pieces were legally excavated or stolen from a museum.

They were for his satisfaction and enjoyment, and his alone.

He walked past the Italian marble walls of his foyer and approached a large mirror with a thick gilded frame covered with naked cherubs entwined around a continuous grapevine. Twisting the head of a cherub in one corner, Rummel sprang the catch that unlatched the mirror, revealing a concealed doorway. Behind the mirror a stairway led down into eight spacious rooms lined with shelves and filled with tables supporting at least thirty glass cases packed with more than two thousand ancient pre-Columbian artifacts.

Reverently, as if walking down the aisle of a church toward the altar, he moved about the gallery, cherishing the beauty and craftsmanship of his private hoard. It was a ritual he performed every evening before going to bed, almost as if he were a father looking in on his sleeping children.

Rummel's pilgrimage finally ended at the side of a large glass case that was the centerpiece of the gallery. It held the crowning treasure of his collection. Gleaming under halogen spotlights, the Golden Body Suit of Tiapollo lay in splendor, arms and legs outstretched, the mask sparkling with emeralds in the eye sockets. The magnificent brilliance of the artistry never failed to move Rummel.

Rummel did not hesitate to pay one million two hundred thousand dollars in cash when he was approached by a group of men who were members of a clandestine underground syndicate that specialized in the theft of precious art objects.

Having had his nightly gratification, Rummel turned off the lights, returned upstairs to the foyer, closed the mirror, and retired to his bedroom to read before falling asleep.

* * *

In another apartment directly level and across the street from Rummel's building, United States Customs Agent David Gaskill sat and peered through a pair of high-powered binoculars mounted on a tripod as the artifacts collector prepared for bed.

Another agent might have been bored after nearly a week of stakeout, but not Gaskill. An eighteen-year veteran of the Customs Service, Gaskill looked more like a football coach than a special government agent. An African American, his skin was more doeskin brown than dark coffee, and his eyes were a mixture of mahogany and green. A huge mountain of a man, he was once an all-star linebacker for the University of Southern California.

Gaskill had been fascinated by pre-Columbian art ever since a field trip to the Yucatan Peninsula during school. When stationed in Washington, D.C., he was working on a case involving the smuggling of carved Mayan stone panels when he received a tip that was passed along to him by Chicago police from a cleaning woman. She had accidentally discovered photographs protruding from a drawer in Rummel's penthouse of what she believed to be a man's body covered in gold. Thinking that someone might have been murdered, she stole a photo and turned it over to the police. A detective who had worked on art fraud cases recognized the golden object as an antiquity and called Gaskill.

Rummel's name had always been high on the Customs Service's list of people who collected ancient art without concern about where it came from, but there was never any evidence of illegal dealings, nor did Gaskill have a clue where Rummel kept his hoard. The special agent, who possessed the expertise of an antiquities scholar, immediately recognized the photo supplied by the cleaning lady as the long-lost Golden Body Suit of Tiapollo.

He set up an immediate round-the-clock surveillance of Rummel's penthouse and had the old man tailed from the time he left the building until he returned. But six days of tight scrutiny had turned up no indication of where Rummel's collection was hidden. The suspect never varied his routine. After leaving for his office at the lower end of Michigan Avenue, where he'd spend four hours, sifting through his investments, it was lunch at a run-down cafe where he always ordered bean soup and a salad. The rest of the afternoon was spent prowling antique stores and art galleries. Then dinner at a quiet German restaurant, after which he would take in a movie or a play. He usually arrived home at eleven-thirty. The routine never varied.

"Doesn't he ever get tired of his regimented existence?" muttered Special Agent Winfried Pottle.

Gaskill pulled back from the binoculars and made a dour face at his second-in-command of the surveillance team. Unlike Gaskill in his Levi's and USC football jacket, Pottle was a slim man with sharp features and soft red hair, who dressed in three-piece suits complete with pocket watch and chain.

"I shudder to think how you'd behave if you had his money," Gaskill said.

"If I had invested a king's ransom in stolen Indian art, I doubt if I could do as good a job of hiding it."

"Rummel has to conceal it somewhere," said Gaskill with a slight trace of discouragement. Makes no sense for a man to build a world-class collection of ancient artifacts and then never go near it."

"Did you ever consider the possibility that our sources might be wrong or highly exaggerated?" asked Pottle gloomily.

Gaskill slowly shook his head. "Rummel's got it stashed somewhere. I'm convinced."

Pottle stared across at Rummel's apartment as the lights blinked out. "If you're right, and if I were Rummel, I'd never let it out of my sight."

"Sure you would—" Gaskill stopped abruptly as

Pottle's comment triggered a thought. "Your tiny mind just made a good point."

"It did?" muttered a confused Pottle.

"What rooms do not have windows in the penthouse? The ones we can't observe?"

Pottle looked down at the carpet in thought for a moment. "According to the floor plan, two bathrooms, a pantry, the short hall between the master and guest bedrooms, and the closets."

"We're missing something."

"Missing what? Rummel seldom remembers to draw his curtains. We can watch ninety percent of his movements once he steps off the elevator. No way he could store a ton of art treasures in a couple of bathtubs and a closet."

"True, but where does he spend the thirty or forty minutes from the time he exits the lobby and steps into the elevator until he sets foot in his living room? Certainly not in the foyer."

"Maybe he sits on the john."

Gaskill smiled faintly, then stood and walked over to a coffee table and spread out a set of blueprints of Rummel's penthouse obtained from the building's developer. He studied them for what had to be the fiftieth time. "The artifacts *have* to be in the building."

"We've checked every apartment from the main floor to the roof," said Pottle. "They're all leased by live-in tenants."

"What about the one directly below Rummel?" asked Gaskill.

Pottle thumbed through a sheaf of computer papers. "Sidney Kammer and wife, Candy. He's one of those high-level corporate attorneys who saves his clients from paying a bushel of taxes."

Gaskill looked at Pottle. "When was the last time Kammer and his wife made an appearance?"

Pottle scanned the log they maintained of residents

who entered and left the building during the surveillance. "No sign of them. They're no-shows."

"I bet if we checked it out, the Kammers live in a house somewhere in a plush suburb and never set foot in their apartment."

"They could be on vacation."

The voice of agent Beverly Swain broke over Gaskill's portable radio. "I have a large moving van backing into the basement of the building."

"Are you manning the front security desk or checking out the basement?" asked Gaskill.

"Still in the lobby, walking my post in a military manner," Swain answered. A blond California beach girl before joining Customs, she was the best undercover agent Gaskill had on his team and the only one inside Rummel's building.

"Run tape on the front entrance," ordered Gaskill. "Then trot down to the basement and question the movers. Find out if they're moving someone in or out of the building, what apartment, and why they're working at this hour."

"On my way," Swain answered.

Now that Rummel's penthouse was dark, Gaskill took a few minutes away from the binoculars to knock off half a dozen glazed donuts and down a thermos bottle of cold milk. He was sadly contemplating the empty donut box when Swain reported in.

"The movers are unloading furniture for an apartment on the nineteenth floor. They're ticked off at working so late but are being well paid for overtime. They can't say why the client is in such a rush, only that it must be one of those last-minute corporate transfers."

"Any possibility they're smuggling artifacts into Rummel's place?"

"They opened the door of the van for me. It's packed with art deco–style furniture."

"Okay, monitor their movements every few minutes."

Pottle scribbled on a notepad and hung up a wall phone in the kitchen. When he returned to Gaskill's position at the window, he had a cagey grin on his face. "I bow to your intuition. Sidney Kammer's home address is in Lake Forest."

"I'll bet you Kammer's biggest client turns out to be Adolphus Rummel," Gaskill ventured.

"And guess who Kammer leases his apartment to."

"Got to be Adolphus Rummel."

Pottle looked pleased with himself. "I think we can safely shout *Eureka.*"

Gaskill stared across the street through an open curtain into Rummel's living room, suddenly knowing his secret. His dark eyes deepened as he spoke. "A hidden stairway leading from the foyer," he said, carefully choosing his words as if describing a screenplay he was about to write. "Rummel walks off the elevator, opens a hidden door to a stairway and descends to the apartment below his penthouse, where he spends forty-five minutes gloating over his private store of treasures. Then he returns upstairs and sleeps the sleep of a satisfied man."

Pottle had to reach up to pound Gaskill on the shoulder. "Congratulations, Dave. Nothing left now but to obtain a search warrant and conduct a raid on Rummel's penthouse."

Gaskill shook his head. "A warrant, yes. A raid by an army of agents, no. Rummel has powerful friends in Chicago. We can't afford a big commotion that could result in a media barrage of criticism or a nasty lawsuit. Particularly if I've made a bad call. A quiet little search by you and me and Bev Swain will accomplish whatever it takes to ferret out Rummel's artifact collection."

Pottle slipped on a trench coat and headed for the door. "Judge Aldrich is a light sleeper. I'll roust him out of bed and be back with the paperwork before the sun comes up."

"Make it sooner." Gaskill smiled wryly. "I'm itching with anticipation."

After Pottle left, Gaskill called up Swain. "Give me a status report on the movers."

In the lobby of Rummel's apartment building, Bev Swain sat behind the security desk and stared up at an array of four monitors. She watched as the furniture haulers moved out of camera range. Pressing the buttons on a remote switch, she went from camera to camera, mounted at strategic areas inside the building. She found the movers coming out of the freight elevator on the nineteenth floor.

"So far they've brought up a couch, two upholstered chairs with end tables, and what looks like boxed crates of household goods, dishes, kitchen and bathroom accessories, clothing. You know, stuff like that."

"Do they return anything to the truck?"

"Only empty boxes."

"We think we've figured where Rummel stashes his artifacts. Pottle's gone for a warrant. We'll go in as soon as he returns."

"That's good news," Swain said with a sigh. "I've almost forgotten what the world looks like outside this lobby."

Gaskill laughed. "It hasn't improved. Sit tight for a few more hours."

As he stood next to Pottle and Swain in the elevator rising to Rummel's penthouse, Gaskill skimmed the wording of the warrant for the third time. The judge had allowed a search of Rummel's penthouse, but not Kammer's apartment on the floor below, because he failed to see just cause. A minor inconvenience. Instead of going directly into what Gaskill was certain were the rooms that held the artifacts, they would have to find a hidden access and come down from the top.

Swain had punched in the security code that allowed
the elevator to rise beyond the residents' apartments and
open directly into Rummel's penthouse. The doors
parted and they stepped onto the marble floor of the
foyer. Pottle found the button to a speaker box on a
credenza and pressed it. A loud buzzer was heard
throughout the penthouse.

After a short pause, a voice fogged with sleep answered. "Who's there?"

"Mr. Rummel," said Pottle into the speaker. "Will
you please come to the elevator?"

"You'd better leave. I'm calling security."

"Don't bother. We're federal agents. Please comply
and we'll explain our presence."

Rummel appeared in pajamas, slippers, and an old-
fashioned chenille robe.

Gaskill cleared his throat. "My name is David Gaskill
I'm a special agent with the United States Customs
Service. I have an authorized federal court warrant to
search the premises."

Rummel indifferently slipped on a pair of rimless
glasses and began reading the warrant as if it were the
morning newspaper. "Look through my rooms all you
want. I have nothing to hide."

Gaskill knew it was nothing but an act. "We're only
interested in your foyer."

He had briefed Swain and Pottle on what to search for
and they immediately set to work. Every crack and seam
was closely examined. But it was the mirror that intrigued Swain. Gazing into the reflective backing, she
found it free of even the tiniest imperfection. The glass
was beveled around the edges with etchings of flowers in
the corners. Her best guess was that it was eighteenth
century.

Next she studied the intricately sculptured frame
crowded with cherubs overlaid in gold. Keenly observant
she noticed the tiny seam on the neck of one cherub

The gilt around the edges looked worn from friction. Swain gently grasped the head and tried to turn it clockwise. It remained stationary. She tried the opposite direction, and the head rotated until it was facing backward. There was a noticeable *click,* and one side of the mirror came ajar and stopped a few centimeters from the wall.

She peered through the crack down the hidden stairwell and said, "Good call, boss."

Rummel paled as Gaskill silently swung the mirror wide open. He smiled broadly as he was swept by a wave of satisfaction. This was what Gaskill liked best about his job, the game of wits culminating in ultimate triumph over his antagonist.

"Will you please lead the way, Mr. Rummel?"

"The apartment below belongs to my attorney, Sidney Kammer," said Rummel, a shrewd gleam forming in his eyes. "Your warrant only authorizes you to search my penthouse."

Gaskill groped about in his coat pocket for a moment before extracting a small box containing a bass plug, a fishing lure he had purchased the day before. He extended his hand and dropped the box down the stairs. "Forgive my clumsiness. I hope Mr. Kammer doesn't mind if I retrieve my property."

"That's trespassing!" Rummel blurted.

There was no reply. Followed by Pottle, the burly Customs agent was already descending the stairway, pausing only to retrieve his bass plug box. What he saw upon reaching the floor below took his breath away.

Magnificent pre-Columbian artworks filled room after room of the apartment. Glass-enclosed Incan textiles hung from the ceilings. One entire room was devoted solely to ceremonial masks. Another held religious altars and burial urns. Others were filled with ornate headdresses, elaborately painted ceramics, and exotic sculptures.

All doors in the apartment had been removed fo
easier access, the kitchen and bathrooms stripped o
their sinks, cupboards and accessories to provide mor
space for the immense collection. Gaskill and Pottle
stood overwhelmed by the spectacular array of antiquities. The quantity went far beyond what they expected

After the initial amazement faded, Gaskill rushed
from room to room, searching for the pièce de résistance
of the collection. What he found was a shattered, empty
glass case in the center of a room. Disillusionment
flooded over him.

"Mr. Rummel!" he shouted. "Come here!"

Escorted by Swain, a thoroughly defeated and dis
traught Rummel shuffled slowly into the exhibition
room. He froze in sudden horror as though one of the
Inca battle lances on the wall had pierced his stomach

"It's gone!" he gasped. "The Golden Body Suit o
Tiapollo is gone."

Gaskill's face went tight and cold. The floor around
the empty display case was flanked by a pile of furniture
consisting of a couch, end tables, and two chairs. He
looked from Pottle to Swain. "The movers," he rasped i
a tone barely audible. "They've stolen the suit from righ
under our noses."

"They left the building over an hour ago," said Swain
tonelessly.

Pottle looked dazed. "Too late to mount a search
They've already stashed the suit by now." Then he
added, "If it isn't on an airplane flying out of the
country."

Gaskill sank into one of the chairs. "To have come so
close," he murmured vacantly. "I just hope the sui
won't be lost for another eighty-three years."

PART II

IN SEARCH OF THE *CONCEPCIÓN*

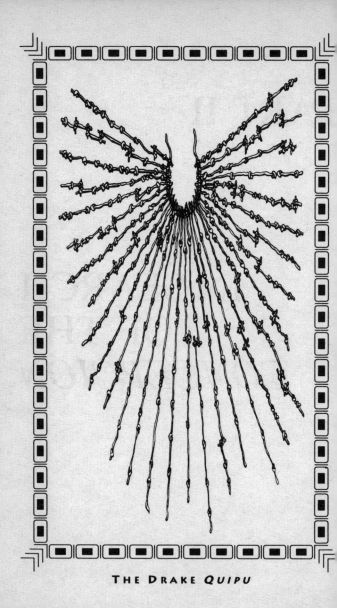

THE DRAKE *QUIPU*

14

PERU'S PRINCIPAL SEAPORT, CALLAO, WAS FOUNDED BY FRAN-cisco Pizarro in 1537 and quickly became the main shipping port for the gold and silver plundered from the Inca empire. Now joined with Lima as one sprawling metropolitan area, the combined cities host a population of nearly 6.5 million.

Situated on the west bank of the Andes along the lowlands, Callao and Lima have an annual rainfall of only 41 millimeters (1.5 inches), making the surrounding land area one of the earth's chilliest and driest deserts in the lower latitudes.

After rounding the northern tip of San Lorenzo, the large offshore island that protects Callao's natural maritime shelter, Captain Stewart ordered slow speed as a launch came alongside the *Deep Fathom* and the harbor pilot jumped onto a boarding ladder and climbed on board. Once the pilot steered the ship safely inside the main channel, Captain Stewart took command of the bridge again and adroitly eased the big research ship to a stop beside the dock of the main passenger terminal.

Everyone lining the ship's rail was surprised to see over a thousand people jamming the dock. Along with an armed military security force and a large contingent of police, TV news cameras and press photographers quickly began jockeying for position as the gangway was lowered. Beyond the news media stood a group of smiling government officials, and behind them the happily waving parents of the archaeology students.

"Still no Dixieland band playing 'Waiting for the Robert E. Lee,'" Pitt said, feigning a disappointed tone.

Unnoticed by the crowd, a small man wearing glasses and carrying a briefcase expertly squeezed through the milling throng and slipped around the cordon of security guards. He bounded up the still-lowering gangway before anyone could stop him and leaped onto the deck with the elated expression of a running back who has just crossed a goal line. He approached Pitt and Giordino and grinned.

"Why is it prudence and discretion are beyond your talents?"

"We try not to fly in the face of public opinion," Pitt said before smiling broadly and embracing the little man. "Good to see you, Rudi."

"Seems we can't get away from you," said Giordino warmly.

Rudi Gunn, the deputy director of NUMA, shook Stewart's hand and was introduced to Shannon and Rodgers. "Will you excuse me if I borrow these two rogues before the welcoming ceremonies?" he asked graciously.

Without waiting for an answer, he stepped through a hatch and walked down an alleyway with ease. Gunn had helped design the *Deep Fathom* and was very familiar with the ship's deck layout. He stopped before the doorway to the conference room, opened it and entered. He went directly to the head of a long table and fished through his briefcase for a yellow legal pad filled with notations as Pitt and Giordino settled into a pair of leather chairs.

Pitt was the first to speak. "Why the frenzy to send Al and me back to that rotten sinkhole to retrieve a body?"

"The request came from U.S. Customs. They made an urgent appeal to Admiral Sandecker to borrow his best men," Gunn said.

"What can NUMA do for Customs that's so special?" asked Pitt.

Gunn spread a sheaf of papers on the table. "The issue is complex but involves the plunder of ancient art."

"Isn't that a little out of our line? Our business is underwater exploration and research."

"Destruction for the purpose of looting underwater archaeological sites *is* our business," Gunn stated earnestly.

"Where does recovering Dr. Miller's body enter the picture?"

"Only the first step of our cooperation with Customs. The murder of a world-renowned anthropologist is the bedrock of their case. They suspect the killer is a high-level member of an international looting syndicate, and they need proof for an indictment. They also hope to use the killer as a key to unlock the door leading to the masterminds of the entire theft and smuggling operation. As for the sacred well, Customs and Peruvian authorities believe a vast cache of artifacts was raised from the bottom and has already been shipped to black-market receiving stations around the world. Miller discovered the theft and was terminated to shut him up. They want us, you and Al in particular, along with Shannon Kelsey and Miles Rodgers, to search the floor of the well for evidence."

"And our plan to explore for the lost galleon?"

"Complete the job on the well, and I'll authorize a small budget out of NUMA to fund your search. That's all I can promise."

Pitt took a deep breath and relaxed in his chair.

"Might as well do something useful while Yaeger and Perlmutter conduct their research. They should have some solid leads by the time we stumble out of the jungle."

In the few days since Pitt had seen Doc Miller's body it had changed for the worse. Tiny pieces were missing from the exposed skin areas. Pitt was at a loss to explain this until he glimpsed a strange brightly speckled fish with luminous scales dart in and begin nibbling one of Doc's eyes. He brushed away the carnivorous fish, the size of a small trout, and wondered how it came to be stranded in a deep pool in the middle of a jungle.

He gave a hand signal to Giordino who removed a rubberized body bag from a pack that was strapped to his chest above his weight belt. They wasted no time in examining the body but moved as fast as their hands would let them, pulling the body bag over the corpse while trying not to stir up a cloud of silt.

"We have the body contained and are on our way up."

"Acknowledged," Gunn replied from above. "We will lower a sling with a stretcher."

Pitt grabbed Giordino's arm through the silt cloud, signaling for a mutual ascent. They began raising the remains of Doc Miller to the sunlight. After reaching the surface, they gently eased the body onto the stretcher and secured it with buckled straps. Then Pitt advised Gunn.

"Ready for lift."

As Pitt watched the stretcher rise toward the rim of the sinkhole, he sadly wished he had known the genuine Steve Miller instead of the imposter. The esteemed anthropologist had been murdered without knowing why.

There was nothing more to be done. Their part of the body retrieval operation was finished. Pitt and Giordino could only float and wait for the winch to lower the cable again. Giordino looked over at Pitt expectantly and removed the breathing regulator from his mouth.

We still have plenty of air, he wrote on a communications board. *Why not poke around while we're waiting for the next elevator?*

To Pitt the suggestion struck a harmonious chord. Unable to remove his head mask and speak, he replied on his own communications board: *Stay close to me and grab hold if struck by surge.* Then he gestured downward. Giordino nodded and faithfully swam alongside as they jackknifed and kicked once more toward the floor of the sinkhole.

The puzzle in Pitt's mind was the lack of artifacts in the silt. After probing the sinkhole's floor for half an hour, they found no sign of ancient artifacts. Nothing except the armor on the intact skeleton he had discovered on his first dive, and the dive gear Pitt had cast off before his climb out of the well. Two minutes was all it took to relocate the site. The bony hand was still raised, one finger pointing in the direction where Miller had lain.

Pitt slowly drifted around the armor-encased Spaniard, examining every detail, occasionally glancing up and around the dim reaches of the sinkhole, alert to any disturbance in the silt that signaled the approach of the mysterious surge. He felt his every movement was followed from deep within the empty eye sockets of the skull. The sunlight from above filtered through the slime and painted the bones a ghostly shade of green.

Pitt was beginning to sense that the skeleton did not belong here. He rubbed a finger lightly over the breastplate. A thin smudge of rust came away, revealing smooth, unpitted, uncorroded metal beneath. The leather straps that held the armor against the chest were incredibly well preserved. And so were the fasteners that joined the straps. They had the appearance of metal buckles on old shoes that had sat inside a trunk in an attic for one or two generations.

He swam a few meters away from the skeleton and pulled a bone out of the silt, a tibia by the shape of it. He returned and held it against the Spaniard's protruding forearm and hand. The bone from the silt was much rougher and pitted as well as more deeply stained from the minerals in the water. The bony structure of the skeleton was smooth in comparison. Next he studied the teeth, which were in remarkably good condition. Pitt found caps on two molars, not gold but silver. Pitt was no expert on sixteenth-century dentistry, but he knew that Europeans didn't even begin to fill cavities and cap teeth until the late eighteenth century.

"Rudi?"

"I'm listening," answered Gunn.

"Please send down a line. I want to lift something."

"A line with a small weight attached to the end is on the way."

"Try to drop it where you see our bubbles."

"Will do." There was a pause, and then Gunn's voice came back over Pitt's earphones with a slight edge to it. "Your archaeologist lady is raising hell. She says you can't touch anything down there."

"Either drop the line or throw her over the edge," Pitt snapped obstinately.

"Stand by."

Moments later a small steel hook attached to a nylon line materialized through the green void and landed in the silt two meters away. Giordino effortlessly swam over, snagged the line with one hand, and returned. Then Pitt very carefully wrapped the loose end of the line around a strap holding the breastplate to the skeleton and cinched it with the hook. He stared at Giordino and made the thumbs-up gesture. Giordino nodded and was mildly surprised when Pitt released the line, allowing it to slacken and leaving the skeleton where it lay.

They took turns being lifted out of the sinkhole. As the crane raised him by his safety line, Pitt looked down and vowed he would never again enter that odious slough. At the rim, Gunn was there to help swing him onto firm ground and remove his full face mask.

He was struggling out of his dive suit when Shannon stormed up to him. "I warned you not to disturb any artifacts," she said firmly.

Pitt looked at her for a long moment, his green eyes strangely soft and understanding. "There is nothing left to touch," he said finally. "Somebody beat you to it. Any artifacts that were in your sacred pool a month ago are gone. Only the bones of animals and sacrificial victims are left scattered on the bottom."

Her face turned incredulous and the hazel eyes flew very wide. "Are you certain?"

"Would you like proof?"

"We have our own equipment. I'll dive into the pool and see for myself."

"Not necessary," he advised.

She turned and called to Miles Rodgers. "Let's get suited up."

"You begin probing around in the silt and you will surely die," Pitt said, with all the emotion of a professor lecturing to a physics class.

Maybe Shannon wasn't listening to Pitt, but Rodgers was. "I think we had better listen to what Dirk is saying."

"I don't wish to sound nasty, but he lacks the necessary credentials to make a case."

"What if he's right?" Rodgers asked innocently.

"I've waited a long time to explore and survey the bottom of the pool. You and I came within minutes of losing our lives trying to unlock its secrets. I can't believe there isn't a time capsule of valuable antiquities down there."

Pitt took the line leading down into the water and held it loosely in his hand. "Here is the verification. Pull on this line and I guarantee you'll change your mind."

"You attached the other end?" she challenged him. "To what?"

"A set of bones masquerading as a Spanish conquistador."

Uncertainty crept into her expression. "You're not making sense."

"Perhaps a little demonstration is in order." Pitt gently pulled in the line until it became taut. Then he gave it a hard jerk.

For a moment nothing happened. Then a rumbling came from the bottom of the well, swelling in volume, sending tremors through the limestone walls. The violence of the explosion was electrifying. The underwater blast came like the eruption of a huge depth charge as a seething column of white froth and green slime burst out of the sinkhole, splattering everyone and everything standing within 20 meters (66 feet) of the edge. The thunder of the explosion rolled over the jungle as the spray fell back into the sinkhole, leaving a heavy mist that swirled into the sky and temporarily blocked out the sun.

Everyone around the edge of the sacred well stood like statues suddenly frozen in shock. Only Pitt looked as though he'd witnessed an everyday event.

Fading incomprehension and the tentative beginnings of understanding appeared in Shannon's eyes. "How did you know . . ."

"That there was a booby trap?" Pitt finished. "No great deduction. Whoever buried a good forty-five kilograms of high explosive under the skeleton made two major mistakes. One, why clean out every antiquity but the most obvious? And two, the bones couldn't have been more than fifty years old and the armor hasn't rusted enough to have been underwater for four centuries."

"Who would have done such a thing?" asked Rodgers dazedly.

"The same man who murdered Doc Miller," answered Pitt.

"The imposter?"

"More likely Amaru. The man who took Miller's place didn't want to risk exposure and investigation by Peruvian authorities, not before they cleaned out the City of the Dead. The *Solpemachaco* had robbed the sacrificial well of its artifacts long before you arrived. That's why the imposter sent out a call for help when you and Shannon vanished in the sinkhole. It was all part of the plot to make your deaths look like an accident."

Shannon's eyes took on a saddened and disillusioned look. "Then all antiquities from the sacred well are gone."

"I'm sorry all your hopes and efforts have come to grief," Pitt said sincerely.

Rudi Gunn walked back from the helicopter that was transporting Miller's body to the morgue in Lima. "Sorry to interrupt," he said to Pitt. "Our job is finished here. I suggest we pack up the helicopter and lift off."

Pitt nodded and turned to Giordino. "On to the *quipu*, shall we?"

15

In a remote, barren part of the Southwest desert, a few kilometers east of Douglas, Arizona, and only 75 meters (246 feet) from the border between Mexico and the United States, the hacienda *La princesa* loomed like a Moorish castle at an oasis. The owner, Joseph Zolar, made no mystery of the fact that he acquired the hacienda as a retreat for entertaining celebrities, high government officials, and wealthy business leaders on a lavish scale.

An antiquarian and fanatical art collector, Zolar had amassed a vast accumulation of art objects and antiques, both good and bad. But every piece was certified by experts and government agents as having been legally sold from the country of origin and imported with the proper papers. He paid his taxes, his business dealings were aboveboard, and he never allowed his guests to bring drugs into his home. No scandal had ever stained Joseph Zolar.

He stood on a roof terrace amid a forest of potted plants and watched as a private jet touched down on the estate runway that stretched across the desert floor. The jet was painted a golden tan with a bright purple stripe running along its fuselage. Yellow letters on the stripe read *Zolar International*. He watched as a man casually dressed in a flowered sport shirt and khaki shorts left the aircraft and settled in the seat of a waiting golf cart.

Zolar waited at the top of the stairs as his guest climbed toward the terrace. They greeted each other warmly and embraced. "Good to see you in one piece, Cyrus."

Sarason grinned. "You don't know how close you came to losing a brother."

"Come along, I've held lunch for you." Zolar led Sarason through the maze of potted plants to a lavishly set table beneath a palapa roof of palm fronds.

Sarason noticed a table with what looked like four weathered tree limbs about one meter in length lying across its surface. Intrigued, he walked over and studied them more closely. He recognized them as sun-bleached roots of cottonwood trees that had grown naturally into grotesque human-shaped figures, complete with torsos, arms and legs, and rounded heads. Faces were crudely carved in the heads and painted with childlike features. "New acquisitions?" he asked.

"Very rare religious ceremonial idols belonging to an obscure tribe of Indians," answered Zolar.

"How did you come by them?"

"A pair of illegal artifact hunters found them in an ancient stone dwelling they discovered under the overhang of a cliff."

"Are they authentic?"

"Yes, indeed." Zolar took one of the idols and stood it on its feet. "To the Montolos, who live in the Sonoran Desert near the Colorado River, the idols represent the gods of the sun, moon, earth, and life-giving water. They were carved centuries ago and used in special ceremonies to mark the transition of boys and girls into young adulthood. The rite is full of mysticism and staged every two years. These idols are the very core of the Montolo religion."

"What do you estimate they're worth?"

"Possibly two hundred thousand dollars to the right collector."

"That much?"

Zolar nodded. "Providing the buyer doesn't know about the curse that stalks those who possess them."

Sarason laughed. "There is always a curse."

Zolar shrugged. "Who can say? I do have it on good authority that the two thieves have suffered a run of bad luck. One was killed in an auto accident and the other has contracted some sort of incurable disease."

"And you believe that hokum?"

"I only believe in the finer things of life," said Zolar, taking his brother by the arm. "Come along. Lunch awaits."

After the food was served, Zolar nodded at Sarason. "So, brother, tell me about Peru."

It always amused Sarason that their father had insisted on his sons and daughters adopting and legalizing different surnames. As the oldest, only Zolar bore the family name. The far-flung international trade empire that the senior Zolar had amassed before he died was divided equally between his five sons and two daughters. Each had become a corporate executive officer of either an art and antique gallery, an auction house, or an import/export firm.

The family's seemingly separate operations were in reality one entity, a jointly owned conglomerate secretly known as the *Solpemachaco*. Unknown and unregistered with any international government financial agencies or stock markets, its managing director was Joseph Zolar in his role as family elder.

"Nothing short of a miracle that I was able to save most of the artifacts and successfully smuggle them out of the country after the blunders committed by our ignorant rabble. Not to mention the intrusion by members of our own government."

"U.S. Customs or drug agents?" asked Zolar.

"Neither. Two engineers from the National Underwater and Marine Agency. They showed up out of nowhere when Juan Chaco sent out a distress call after Dr. Kelsey and her photographer became trapped in the sacred well."

"How did they cause problems?"

Sarason related the entire story from the murder of the true Dr. Miller by Amaru to the escape of Pitt and the others from the Valley of the Viracocha to the death of Juan Chaco. He finished by giving a rough tally of the artifacts he had salvaged from the valley, and how he arranged to have the cache transported to Callao, then smuggled out of Peru in a secret cargo compartment inside an oil tanker owned by a subsidiary of Zolar International.

Zolar stared into the desert without seeing it. "The *Aztec Star*. She is scheduled to reach San Francisco in four days."

"That puts her in brother Charles's sphere of activity."

"Yes, Charles has arranged for your shipment to be transported to our distribution center in Galveston where he will see to the restoration of the artifacts."

After a pause, Zolar added, "But there is still Tupac Amaru. What is his situation?"

"He should have died," replied Sarason. "Yet when I returned to the temple after the attack of our gun-happy mercenaries, I found him buried under a pile of rubble and still breathing. As soon as the artifacts were cleared out and loaded aboard three additional military helicopters, whose flight crews I was forced to buy off at a premium, I paid the local *huaqueros* to carry him to their village for care. He should be back on his feet in a few days."

"You might have been wise to remove Amaru too."

"Not to worry. Oddly, it was Chaco who gave me the idea of keeping Amaru on the payroll. The man may well prove to be a valuable asset."

"You mean as a hired killer."

"I prefer to think of him as someone who eliminates obstacles. Let's face it, brother. I can't continue eliminating our enemies by myself without risk of eventual discovery and capture. The family should consider itself fortunate that I am not the only one who has the capacity to kill if necessary. Amaru makes an ideal executioner. He enjoys it."

"Just be sure you keep him on a strong leash when he's out of his cage."

"Not to worry," said Sarason firmly. Then he changed the subject. "Any buyers in mind for our Chachapoyan merchandise?"

"A drug dealer by the name of Pedro Vincente," replied Zolar. "He hungers after anything that's pre-Columbian. He also pays a cash premium since it's a way for him to launder his drug profits."

"And you take the cash and use it to finance our underground art and artifact operations."

"An equitable arrangement for all concerned."

"How soon before you make the sale?"

"I'll set up a meeting with Vincente right after Sister Marta has your shipment cleaned up and ready for display. You should have your share of the profits within ten days."

Sarason nodded. "I think you see through me, Joseph. I'm seriously considering retiring from the family business while I'm still healthy."

Zolar looked at him with a shifty grin. "You do and you'll be throwing away two hundred million dollars."

"What are you talking about?"

"Your share of the treasure."

Sarason paused with a forkful of pork in front of his mouth. "What treasure?"

"You're the last of the family to learn what ultimate prize is within our grasp."

"I don't follow you."

"The object that will lead us to Huascar's treasure."
Zolar looked at him slyly for a moment, then smiled.
"We have the Golden Body Suit of Tiapollo."

The fork dropped to the plate as Sarason stared in
total incredulity. "You found Naymlap's mummy encased in his suit of gold? It is actually in your hands?"

"Our hands, little brother. One evening, while searching through our father's old business records, I came
upon a ledger itemizing his clandestine transactions. It
was he who masterminded the mummy's theft from the
museum in Spain."

"The old fox, he never said a word."

"He considered it the highlight of his plundering
career, but too hot a subject to reveal to his own family."

"How did you track it down?"

"Father recorded the sale to a wealthy Sicilian mafi-
oso. I sent our brother Charles to investigate, not expecting him to learn anything from a trail over seventy years
old. Charles found the late mobster's villa and met with
the son, who said his father had kept the mummy and its
suit hidden away until he died in 1984 at the ripe old age
of ninety-seven. The son then sold the mummy on the
black market through his relatives in New York. The
buyer was a rich junk dealer in Chicago by the name of
Rummel."

"How much did it cost to buy the suit from the junk
dealer?"

"Not a cent. We stole it. As luck would have it, our
brother Samuel in New York had sold Rummel most of
his collection of illegal pre-Columbian antiquities and
knew the location of the concealed gallery that held the
suit. He and Charles worked together on the theft."

"I still can't believe it's in our hands."

"A near thing too. Charles and Sam barely smuggled it
from Rummel's penthouse before Customs agents
stormed the place."

"Do you think they were tipped off?"

Zolar shook his head. "Not by anyone on our end. Our brothers got away clean."

"Where did they take it?" asked Sarason.

Zolar smiled, but not with his eyes. "Nowhere. The mummy is still in the building. They rented an apartment six floors below Rummel and hid it there until we can safely move it to Galveston for a proper examination. Both Rummel and the Customs agents think it was already smuggled out of the building by a moving van."

"A nice touch. But what happens now? The images engraved in the gold body casing have to be deciphered. Not a simple exercise."

"I've hired the finest authorities on Inca art to decode and interpret the glyphs. A husband and wife team. He's an anthropologist and she's an archaeologist who excels as a decoding analyst with computers."

"I should have known you'd cover every base," said Sarason, stirring his coffee. "But we'd better hope their version of the text is correct, or we'll be spending a lot of time and money chasing up and down Mexico after ghosts."

"Time is on our side," Zolar assured him confidentially. "Who but us could possibly have a clue to the treasure's burial site?"

16

After a fruitless excursion to the archives of the Library of Congress, where he had hoped to find documentary evidence leading to the *Concepción*'s ultimate fate, Julien Perlmutter sat in the vast reading room. He closed a copy of the diary kept by Francis Drake and later presented to Queen Elizabeth, describing his epic voyage. The diary, lost for centuries, had only recently been discovered in the dusty basement of the royal archives in England.

He leaned his great bulk back in the chair and sighed. The diary added little to what he already knew. Drake had sent the *Concepción* back to England under the command of the *Golden Hind*'s sailing master, Thomas Cuttill. The galleon was never seen again and was presumed lost at sea with all hands.

Beyond that, the only mention of the fate of the *Concepción* was unverified. It came from a book Perlmutter could recall reading on the Amazon River, published in 1939 by journalist/explorer Nicholas Bender, who followed the routes of the early explorers in search of El Dorado. Perlmutter called up the book from the library staff and reexamined it. In the Note section there was a short reference to a 1594 Portuguese survey expedition that had come upon an Englishman living

141

with a tribe of local inhabitants beside the river. The Englishman claimed that he had served under the English sea dog, Francis Drake, who placed him in command of a Spanish treasure galleon that was swept into a jungle by an immense tidal wave.

Perlmutter made a note of the publisher. Then he signed the Drake diary and Bender's book back to the library staff and caught a taxi home.

Perlmutter sat in the backseat of the cab and stared out the window at the passing automobiles and buildings without seeing them. Did Nicholas Bender quote a genuine source, or did he embellish a myth as so many nonfiction authors were prone to do?

The question was still goading his mind when he walked into the clutter that was his office. A ship's clock on the mantel read three thirty-five in the afternoon. Still plenty of time to make calls before most businesses closed. He settled into a handsome leather swivel chair behind his desk and punched in the number for New York City information. The operator gave him the number of Bender's publishing house almost before he finished asking for it.

"Falkner and Massey," answered a female voice.

"I'd like to talk to the editor of Nicholas Bender, please."

"Nicholas Bender?"

"He's one of your authors."

"I'm sorry, sir, I don't know the name."

"Mr. Bender wrote nonfiction adventure books a long time ago. Perhaps someone who has been on your staff for a number of years might recall him?"

"I'll direct you to Mr. Adams, our senior editor. He's been with the company longer than anyone I know."

"Thank you."

There was a good thirty-second pause, and then a man answered. "Frank Adams here."

"Mr. Adams, my name is St. Julien Perlmutter."

"A pleasure, Mr. Perlmutter. I've heard of you. You're down in Washington, I believe."

"Yes, I live in the capital."

"Keep us in mind should you decide to publish a book on maritime history."

"I've yet to finish any book I started." Perlmutter laughed. "We'll both grow old waiting for a completed manuscript from me."

"At seventy-four, I'm already old," said Adams congenially.

"The very reason I rang you," said Perlmutter. "Do you recall a Nicholas Bender?"

"I do indeed. He was somewhat of a soldier of fortune in his youth. We've published quite a few of the books he wrote describing his travels in the days before globe-trotting was discovered by the middle class."

"I'm trying to trace the source of a reference he made in a book called *On the Trail of El Dorado.*"

"That's ancient history. We must have published that book back in the early forties."

"Nineteen thirty-nine to be exact."

"How can I help you?"

"I was hoping Bender might have donated his notes and manuscripts to a university archive. I'd like to study them."

"I really don't know what he did with his material," said Adams. "I'll have to ask him."

"He's still alive?" Perlmutter asked in surprise.

"Oh dear me, yes. I had dinner with him not more than three months ago."

"He must be in his nineties."

"Nicholas is eighty-four. I believe he was just twenty-five when he wrote *On the Trail of El Dorado.*"

"May I have a number where I can reach him?"

"I doubt whether he'll take any calls from strangers.

Since his wife died, Nicholas has become somewhat of a recluse."

"I don't mean to sound heartless," said Perlmutter. "But it is most urgent that I speak to him."

"Since you're a respected authority on maritime lore and a renowned gourmand, I'm sure he wouldn't mind talking to you. But first, let me pave the way just to play safe. What is your number should he wish to call you direct?"

Perlmutter gave Adams the phone number for the line he used only for close friends. "Thank you, Mr. Adams. If I ever do write a manuscript on shipwrecks, you'll be the first editor to read it."

He hung up, ambled into his kitchen, opened the refrigerator, expertly shucked a dozen Gulf oysters, poured a few drops of Tabasco and sherry vinegar into the open shells, and downed them. His timing was perfect. He had no sooner polished off the oysters when the phone rang.

"Julien Perlmutter here."

"Hello," replied a deep voice. "This is Nicholas Bender. Frank Adams said you wished to speak to me."

"Yes, sir, thank you. I didn't expect you to call me so soon."

"Always delighted to talk to someone who has read my books," said Bender cheerfully. "Not many of you left."

"The book I found of interest was *On the Trail of El Dorado.*"

"Yes, yes, I nearly died ten times during that trek."

"You made a reference to a Portuguese survey mission that found a crewman of Sir Francis Drake living among the natives along the Amazon River."

"Thomas Cuttill," Bender replied without the slightest hesitation. "I recall including the event in my book, yes."

"I wonder if you could refer me to the source of your

nformation," said Perlmutter, his hopes rising with Bender's quick recollection.

"The source is, Mr. Perlmutter, is the journal of Thomas Cuttill. I have it in my possession."

"Are you serious?" Perlmutter blurted.

"Indeed," Bender answered triumphantly. "Cuttill ave it to the leader of the Portuguese survey party with he request that it be sent to London. The Portuguese, owever, turned it over to the viceroy at Macapa. He ncluded it with dispatches he forwarded to Lisbon, where it passed through any number of hands before nding up in an antique bookstore, where I bought it for he equivalent of thirty-six dollars. That was a lot of money back in 1937, at least to a lad of twenty-three who was wandering the globe on a shoestring."

"The journal must be worth considerably more than thirty-six dollars today."

"I'm sure of it. A dealer once offered me ten thousand or it."

"You turned him down?"

"I've never sold mementos of my journeys so someone else could profit."

"May I fly up to Vermont and read the journal?" asked Perlmutter cautiously.

"I'm afraid not."

Perlmutter paused as he wondered how to persuade Bender to allow him to examine Cuttill's journal.

"But I'll tell you what I'll do, Mr. Perlmutter. I'll send you the book as a gift."

"My goodness, sir, you don't have to—"

"No, no, I insist. Frank Adams told me about your magnificent library on ships. I'd rather someone like you, who can appreciate the journal, possess it rather han a collector who simply puts it on a shelf to impress his friends."

"That's very kind of you," said Perlmutter sincerely. "I'm truly grateful for your kind generosity."

"Take it and enjoy," Bender said graciously. "I assum⟩
you'd like to study the journal as soon as possible."

"I don't want to inconvenience you."

"Not at all. I'll send it Federal Express so you'll have ⟩
in your hands first thing tomorrow."

"Thank you, Mr. Bender. Thank you very much. I'⟩
treat the journal with every bit of the respect it de⟩
serves."

"Good. I hope you find what you're looking for."

At twenty minutes after ten o'clock the next mornin⟩
Perlmutter threw open the door before the Feder⟩
Express driver could punch the doorbell button. "Yo⟩
must be expecting this, Mr. Perlmutter," said the youn⟩
black-haired man, wearing glasses and a friendly smile

"Like a child waiting for Santa." Perlmutter laughe⟨
signing for the reinforced envelope.

He hurried into his study, pulling the tab and openin⟩
the envelope as he walked. He sat at his desk, slipped o⟩
his glasses, and held the journal of Thomas Cuttill in hi⟩
hands as if it were the Holy Grail. The cover was the ski⟩
of some unidentifiable animal and the pages were yel⟩
lowed parchment in a state of excellent preservation
The ink was brown, probably a concoction Cuttill ha⟨
managed to brew from the root of some tree. There wer⟩
no more than twenty pages. The entries were written i⟩
the quaint Elizabethan prose of the day. The handwrit
ing seemed labored, with any number of misspelling⟩
indicating a man who was reasonably well educated fo⟩
the times. The first entry was dated March 1578, but wa⟩
written much later:

Mine strange historie of the passte sexteen yeares,
by Thomas Cuttill, formerly of Devonshire.

It was the account of a shipwrecked sailor, cast awa⟩
after barely surviving the sea's violent fury, only to en⟩

ure incredible hardships in a savage land in his unsuc-
essful attempt to return home. Cuttill's persistence,
is will to survive, and his ingenuity in overcoming ter-
ible obstacles made a profound impression on Perl-
nutter. Cuttill was a man he would like to have known.

After Perlmutter finished reading the journal, he
eaned back in his swivel chair, removed his glasses and
ubbed his eyes. Any doubts he might have had in the
ack of his mind about the authenticity of the journal
ad quickly evaporated. Perlmutter felt certain the ex-
eriences and hardships suffered by Francis Drake's
ailing master truly occurred, and that the account was
onestly set down by someone who lived what he wrote.

Perlmutter resettled his glasses on his imposing red
ose and turned to the final entry of the narrative:

> *Me mind is as set as a stout ship before a narth
> winde. I shalle not retarn to mye homelande. I feare
> Captaan Drake was maddened for me not bringen
> the achant tresures and the jaade boxe withe the
> notted stringe to England soos it cud be preezentid
> to guude Queen Bess. I left it withe the wraaked
> ship. I shalle be baryed heer among the peapol who
> have becume my famly. Writen bye the hande of
> Thomas Cuttill, sailing mastere of the* Golden
> Hinde *this unknown day in the yeare 1594*

Perlmutter gently closed the fragile journal, lifted his
ulk from the chair and began to pace around the room,
ands clasped behind his back.

A crewman of Francis Drake *had* truly lived and died
somewhere along the Amazon River. A Spanish galleon
was thrown into a coastal jungle by an immense tidal
wave. And a jade box containing a knotted cord *did* exist
at one time. Could it still lie amid the rotting timbers of
the galleon, buried deep in a rain forest? A four-

hundred-year-old mystery had suddenly surfaced from the shadows of time and revealed an enticing clue Perlmutter was pleased with his successful investigative effort, but he well knew that confirmation of the myth was merely the first enticing step in a hunt for treasure

The next trick, and the most perplexing one, was to narrow the theater of search to as small a stage as possible.

Hiram Yaeger was hooked into a vast high-speed computing network with the capacity to transfer enormous amounts of digital data between libraries, newspaper morgues, research laboratories, universities, and historic archives anywhere in the world. By tapping into the gigabit network, Yaeger began retrieving and assembling enough data to enable him to lay out a search grid with a 60 percent probability factor of containing the four-century-old landlocked galleon.

He was so deeply involved with the search for the *Nuestra Señora de la Concepción* that he did not notice nor hear Admiral James Sandecker step into his office and sit down in a chair behind him. "Making any progress?" he asked Yaeger.

"Sorry, Admiral." Yaeger spoke without turning around. "I didn't see you come in. I was in the midst of collecting data on the water currents off Ecuador."

"Don't lie to me, Hiram," Sandecker said, with the look of a ferret on a hunt. "I know what you're up to."

"Sir?"

"You're searching for a stretch of coastline where a tidal wave struck in 1578."

"A tidal wave?"

"Yes, you know, a big wall of water that barreled in from the sea and carried a Spanish galleon over a beach and into a jungle." The admiral puffed out a cloud of noxious smoke and went on. "I wasn't aware that I had authorized a treasure hunt on NUMA's time and budget."

Yaeger paused and swiveled around in his chair. "You know?"

"The word is *knew*. Right from the beginning. Now what have you dug up?"

Yaeger smiled wanly and answered. "Thanks to global positioning satellites, we can look at details of Central and South America that were never mapped before. Maps showing tropical rain forests that grow along the coastline were studied first. I quickly dismissed Peru because its coastal regions are deserts with little or no vegetation. That still left over a thousand kilometers of forested shore along northern Ecuador and almost all of Colombia. Again, I was able to eliminate about forty percent of the coastline with geology too steep or unfavorable for a wave with enough mass and momentum to carry a five-hundred-and-seventy-ton ship any distance overland. Then I knocked off another twenty percent for open grassland areas without thick trees or other foliage that could hide the remains of a ship."

"That still leaves Pitt with a search area four hundred kilometers in length. You'll have to whittle the grid down to no more than twenty kilometers if you want to give Pitt a fighting chance of finding the wreck."

"Bear with me, Admiral," said Yaeger patiently.

Sandecker stared at the screen for a long moment, then said slowly, "Can your electronic contraption do a simulation of the tidal wave sweeping the galleon onto shore?"

"Okay, let's see what I can do with digital imagery."

Yaeger typed a series of commands on his keyboard and sat back, staring at the monitor for several seconds, examining the image he produced on the screen. Then he used a special function control to fine-tune the graphics until he could generate a realistic and dramatic simulation of a tidal wave crossing an imaginary shoreline. "There you have it," he announced. "Virtual reality configuration."

"Now generate a ship," ordered Sandecker.

Yaeger was not an expert on the construction of sixteenth-century galleons, but he produced a respectable image of one rolling slowly on the waves that was equal to a projector displaying moving graphics at sixty frames per second. The galleon appeared so realistic any unsuspecting soul who walked into the room would have thought they were watching a movie.

"How does it look, Admiral?"

"Hard to believe a machine can create something so lifelike," said Sandecker, visibly impressed.

The two men watched, fascinated, as the monitor displayed a sea so blue and distinct it was like looking through a window at the real thing. Then slowly, the water began convulsing into a wave that rolled away from the land, stranding the galleon on the seabed, as dry as if it were a toy boat on the blanket of a boy's bed. Then the computer visualized the wave rushing back toward shore, rising higher and higher, then cresting and engulfing the ship under a rolling mass of froth, sand, and water, hurling it toward land at an incredible speed, until finally the ship stopped and settled as the wave smoothed out and died.

"Five kilometers," murmured Yaeger. "She looks to be approximately five kilometers from the coast."

"No wonder she was lost and forgotten," said Sandecker. "I suggest you contact Pitt and make arrangements to fax your computer's grid coordinates."

Yaeger gave Sandecker a suspicious look. "Are you authorizing the search, Admiral?"

Sandecker feigned a look of surprise as he rose and walked toward the door. Just before exiting, he turned and grinned impishly. "I can't very well authorize what could turn out to be a wild goose chase, now can I?"

"You think that's what we're looking at, a wild goose chase?"

Sandecker shrugged. "You've done your magic. If the ship truly rests in a jungle and not on the bottom of the sea, then the burden falls on Pitt and Giordino to go in and find her."

17

After a short layover at the Lima airport to pick up the EG&G magnetometer that was flown in from the *Deep Fathom* by a U.S. Embassy helicopter, Pitt, Giordino, and Gunn boarded a commercial flight to Quito, the capital of Ecuador. It was after two o'clock in the morning when they landed in the middle of a thunderstorm. As soon as they stepped through the gate they were met by a representative of the state oil company, who was acting on behalf of the managing director Gunn had negotiated with for a helicopter. He quickly herded them into a limousine that drove to the opposite side of the field, followed by a small van carrying their luggage and electronic equipment. The two-vehicle convoy stopped in front of a fully serviced McDonnell Douglas Explorer helicopter.

"They owed us bigger than I thought," said Pitt, ignoring the downpour and staring blissfully at the big, red, twin-engined helicopter with no tail rotor.

"Is it a good aircraft?" asked Gunn naively.

"Only the finest rotorcraft in the sky today," replied Pitt. "Stable, reliable, and smooth as oil on water. Costs about two point seven-five million. We couldn't have asked for a better machine to conduct a search and survey project from the air."

"How far to the Bay of Caraquez?"

"About two hundred and ten kilometers. We can make it in less than an hour with this machine."

Giordino nodded toward the helicopter. "I recommend we throw our baggage and electronic gear on board and get a few hours sleep before dawn."

"That's the best idea I've heard all day," Pitt agreed heartily.

Once their equipment was stowed, Giordino and Gunn reclined the backrests of two passenger seats and fell asleep within minutes. Pitt sat in the pilot's seat under a small lamp and studied the data accumulated by Perlmutter and Yaeger. He was too excited to be tired, certainly not on the eve of a shipwreck search. Most men turn from Jekyll to Hyde whenever the thought of a treasure hunt floods their brain. But Pitt's stimulant was not greed but the challenge of entering the unknown to pursue a trail laid down by adventurous men like him, who lived and died in another era, men who left a mystery for later generations to unravel.

Pitt turned his attention to the *Nuestra Señora de la Concepción*. Perlmutter had included illustrations and cutaway plans of a typical Spanish treasure galleon that sailed the seas during the sixteenth and seventeenth centuries. Pitt's primary interest was in the amount of iron that was on board for the magnetometer to detect. Perlmutter was certain the two cannon she reportedly carried were bronze and would not register on an instrument that measures the intensity of the magnetic field produced by an iron mass.

It was an exercise in the dark. Pitt was hardly an authority on sixteenth-century sailing ships. He could only rely on Perlmutter's best guess as to the total iron mass on board the *Concepción*. The best estimate ran between one and three tons. Enough, Pitt fervently hoped, for the magnetometer to detect the galleon's anomaly from 50 to 75 meters in the air.

Anything less, and they'd stand about as much chance of locating the galleon as they would of finding a floating bottle with a message in the middle of the South Pacific.

It was about five in the morning, with a light blue sky turning orange over the mountains to the east, as Pitt swung the McDonnell Douglas Explorer helicopter over the waters of the Bay of Caraquez. Fishing boats were leaving the bay and heading out to sea for the day's catch. The crewmen paused as they readied their nets, looked up at the low-flying aircraft and waved. Pitt waved back as the shadow of the Explorer flickered over the little fishing fleet and darted toward the coastline. The dark, radiant blue of deep water soon altered to a turquoise green streaked by long lines of breaking surf that materialized as the seafloor rose to meet the sandy beach.

"We're approaching the lower half of our grid," Pitt said over his shoulder to Gunn, who was hunched over the proton magnetometer.

"You can run your first lane," declared Gunn. "All systems are up and tuned."

"How far from the coast are we going to start mowing the lawn?" Giordino asked, referring to the seventy-five-meter-wide grid lanes they planned to cover.

"We'll begin at the three-kilometer mark and run parallel to the shore," answered Pitt, "running lanes north and south as we work inland."

"Length of lanes?" inquired Gunn, peering at the stylus marking the graph paper and the numbers blinking on his digital readout window.

"Two kilometers at a speed of twenty knots."

"We can run much faster," said Gunn. "The mag system has a very fast cycle rate. It can easily read an anomaly at a hundred knots."

"We'll take it nice and slow," Pitt said firmly. "If we

don't fly directly over the target, any magnetic field we hope to find won't make much of an impression on your gamma readings."

The sun was up now and the sky was clear of all but a few small, wispy clouds. Pitt took a final look at the instruments and then nodded. "Okay, guys, let's find ourselves a shipwreck."

Back and forth over the thick jungle they flew, the air-conditioning system keeping the hot, humid atmosphere outside the aircraft's aluminum skin. The day wore on and by noon they had achieved nothing. The magnetometer failed to register so much as a tick. To someone who had never searched for an unseen object, it might have seemed discouraging, but Pitt, Giordino, and Gunn took it in stride. They had all known shipwreck or lost aircraft hunts that had lasted as long as six weeks without the slightest sign of success.

"How much have we covered?" asked Gunn for the first time since the search began.

"Two kilometers into the grid," Pitt answered. "We're only now coming into Yaeger's prime target area."

"Three hours of fuel left," said Giordino, tapping the two fuel gauges. He showed no sign of fatigue or boredom; if anything he seemed to be enjoying himself.

Two hours and fifteen minutes later they had traveled the twenty-eight lanes it took to cover kilometers five and six. They definitely had a problem now as they were beyond Yaeger's estimated target site. None of them believed a tidal wave could carry a 570-ton ship more than 5 kilometers (3 miles) over land from the sea. Certainly not a wave with a crest less than 30 meters (98 feet) high. Their confidence ebbed as they worked farther out of the prime search area. They were beginning to feel they had not been dealt a lucky hand and steeled themselves for a long and arduous search.

"Mark it!" Gunn burst abruptly.

Pitt responded by copying the navigation coordinates. "Do you have a target?"

"I recorded a slight bump on my instruments. Nothing big, but definitely an anomaly."

"Shall we turn back?" asked Giordino.

Pitt shook his head. "Let's finish the lane and see if we pick up a stronger reading on the next heading."

No one spoke as they completed the lane, made a complete 180-degree turn and headed back on a reverse course 75 meters (246 feet) farther to the east. Pitt and Giordino could not resist stealing a glance downward at the rain forest, hoping to spot a sign of the wreck, but knowing it was next to impossible to see through the thick foliage. It was a wilderness truly terrible in its monotonous beauty.

"Coming opposite the mark," Pitt alerted them. "Now passing."

The sensor, trailing on an arc behind the helicopter, lagged slightly before crossing the site of Gunn's anomaly reading. "Here she comes!" he said excitedly. "Looking good. The numbers are climbing. Come on, give with the big gamma readings."

Pitt and Giordino leaned out their windows and stared down, but saw only a dense canopy of tall trees rising in tiered galleries. It required no imagination to see the rain forest was a forbidding and dangerous place. It looked quiet and deadly. They could only guess at what perils lurked in the menacing shadows.

"We have a hard target," said Gunn. "Not a solid mass, but scattered readings, the kind of display I would expect from bits and pieces of iron dispersed around a wrecked ship."

Pitt wore a big smile as he reached over and lightly punched Giordino on the shoulder. "Never a doubt."

Giordino grinned back. "That was some wave to have carried the ship seven kilometers inland."

"She must have crested close to fifty meters," Pitt calculated.

"I think we passed over her from bow to stern," said Gunn. "This must be the place."

"This must be the place," Giordino repeated happily.

Pitt hovered as Gunn gave bearing commands while they probed for the highest readings from the magnetometer which would show the Explorer was directly over the wreck site. "Bring her twenty meters to starboard. Now thirty meters astern. Too far. Ten meters ahead. Hold it. That's it. We can drop a rock on her."

Ten minutes later Pitt was secure in a safety harness connected to a cable leading to a winch mounted on the roof of the helicopter's cabin. While Giordino hovered the craft just above the top of the trees, Gunn operated the controls to the winch.

"We should be back in two hours," Gunn yelled back over the sound of the rotors and the engine exhaust. He pushed the descent button and Pitt dropped below the skids of the helicopter and soon disappeared into the dense vegetation as if he had jumped into a green ocean.

As he hung supported by his safety harness, machete gripped in his right hand, a portable radio in his left, Pitt felt almost as if he were once again dropping into the green slime of the sacrificial well. He could not tell for certain how high he was above the ground, but he estimated the distance from the roof of the forest to its floor to be at least 50 meters (164 feet).

Seen from the air, the rain forest looked like a chaotic mass of struggling plant growth. The trunks of the taller trees were crowded with dense layers of shorter growth, each seeking its share of sunlight. The twigs and leaves nearest the sun danced under the downdraft provided by the helicopter's rotor, giving them the appearance of a restless, undulating ocean.

Pitt held an arm over his eyes as he slowly descended through the first tier of the green canopy, narrowly brushing past the limbs of a high mahogany tree that was sprouting clusters of small white flowers. He used his feet to spring without difficulty out of the way of the thicker branches. As he frantically pushed aside a branch that was rising between his legs, he frightened a pair of spider monkeys that leapt chattering around to the other side of the tree.

"You say something?" asked Gunn over the radio.

"I flushed a pair of monkeys during their siesta," Pitt replied.

"Do you want me to slow you down?"

"No, this is fine. I've passed through the first layer of trees. Now it looks like I'm coming down through what I'd guess is laurel."

"Yell if you want me to move you around," said Giordino over the cockpit radio.

"Maintain your position," Pitt directed. "Shifting around might snag the descent cable and leave me hanging up here till I'm an old man."

Pitt entered a thicker maze of branches and quickly managed to cut a tunnel with his machete without having to order Gunn to reduce his rate of descent. He was invading a world seldom seen, a world filled with beauty and danger.

"Stop the winch," he said as he felt firm ground beneath his feet. "I'm down."

"Any sign of the galleon?" Gunn asked anxiously.

Pitt did not immediately answer. He tucked the machete under his arm and turned a complete circle, unclipping the safety harness as he surveyed his surroundings. It was like being at the bottom of a leafy ocean. There was scarcely any light, and what little was available had the same eerie quality a diver would experience at 60 meters (196 feet) beneath the surface of the sea. The dense vegetation blotted out most of the color spectrum from the little sunlight that reached him, leaving only green and blue mixed with gray.

He was pleasantly surprised to find the rain forest was not impassable at ground level. Except for a soft carpet of decomposing leaves and twigs, the floor beneath the canopy of trees was comparatively free of growth, with none of the heaps of moldering vegetation he had expected. Now that he was standing in the sunless depths he could easily understand why plant life that grew close to the ground was scarce.

"I see nothing that resembles the hull of a ship," he said. "No ribs, no beams, no keel."

"A bust," said Gunn, the disillusionment coming through in his voice. "The mag must have read a natural iron deposit."

"No," Pitt replied, striving to keep his voice calm, "I can't say that."

"What are you telling us?"

"Only that the fungi, insects, and bacteria that call this place home have made a meal out of every organic component of the ship. Not too surprising when you figure that they had four hundred years to devour it down to the keel."

Gunn was silent, not quite comprehending. Then it struck him like a lightning bolt.

"We found it," he yelped. "You're actually standing on the wreck of the galleon."

"Dead center."

"You say all sign of the hull is gone?" Giordino cut in.

"All that remains is covered by moss and humus, but I think I can make out some ceramic pots, a few scattered cannon shot, one anchor, and a small pile of ballast stones. The site reads like an old campsite with trees growing through the middle of it."

"Shall we hang around?" asked Giordino.

"No, get your tails to Manta and refuel. I'll poke around for the jade box until you get back."

"Can we drop you anything?"

"I shouldn't need anything but the machete."

"You still have the smoke canisters?" Giordino asked

"Two of them clipped to my belt."

"Set one off soon as you hear us return."

"Never fear," Pitt said blithely. "I'm not about to try walking out of here."

"See you in two hours," said Gunn, his spirits brimming.

"Try to be on time."

In a different circumstance, at a different time, Pitt might have experienced a fit of depression as the sound of the McDonnell Douglas Explorer died away, leaving behind the heavy atmosphere of the rain forest. But he was energized at knowing that somewhere within a short distance of where he was standing, buried in the ancient pile of debris, was the key to a vast treasure. He did not throw himself into a frenzy of wild digging. Instead, he slowly walked through the scattered remains of the *Concepción* and studied her final position and configuration. He could almost trace the original outline by the shape of the broken mounds of debris.

The shaft and one fluke of an anchor that protruded from the humus beneath the more recently fallen leaves indicated the location of the bow. He did not think that sailing master Thomas Cuttill would store the jade box in the cargo hold. The fact that Drake intended it as a gift to the queen suggested that he kept it near him, probably in the great cabin in the stern occupied by the captain of the ship. Using the plans as a guide, he carefully measured off his steps until he estimated he was in the area of the hold where the valuable cargo would have been stored.

Pitt went to work clearing what he thought was a heavy layer of compost. It proved to be only 10 centimeters (4 inches) thick. He had only to brush away the decomposing leaves with his hands to reveal several beautifully carved stone heads and full figures of various sizes. He guessed they were religious animal gods. A sigh of relief escaped his lips at discovering that the wreck of the galleon was untouched.

Pitt eagerly dug deeper, ignoring torn fingernails and the slime that smeared his hands. He found a cache of jade, elegantly ornate and painstakingly carved. There were so many pieces he soon lost count. They were mingled with mosaics made of mother-of-pearl and turquoise.

Pitt paused and wiped the sweat from his face with his forearm. He glanced at his watch. Over an hour had passed since he dropped through the trees. He left the mass of jumbled antiquities and continued moving toward what had once been the captain's cabin on the stern of the galleon.

He was swinging the blade of the machete back and forth to sweep the dead vegetation away from a debris mound when the blade suddenly clanged on a solid metal object. Kicking the leaves to the side he found that he had stumbled on one of the ship's two cannons. The bronze barrel had long since been coated by a thick green patina and the muzzle was filled with compost accumulated through the centuries.

Pitt could no longer tell where his perspiration left off and the humid moisture from the forest began. It was like working in a steam bath, with the added annoyance of tiny gnatlike insects that swarmed around his unprotected head and face. Fallen vines wrapped around his ankles, and twice he slipped on the wet plant growth and fell. A layer of clay soil and decayed leaves adhered to his body, giving him the look of some swamp creature from a haunted bog. The steamy atmosphere was slowly sapping his strength, and he fought back an overwhelming urge to lie down on a soft pile of leaves and take a nap, an urge that abruptly vanished at the repulsive sight of a bushmaster slithering across a nearby heap of ballast stones. The largest poisonous snake in the Americas, 3 meters (10 feet) long, pink and tan with dark diamond-shaped blotches, the notorious pit viper was extremely lethal. Pitt gave it a wide berth and kept a wary eye for its relatives.

He knew he was in the right area when he uncovered the big pintles and gudgeons, now badly rusted, that once held and pivoted the rudder. His foot accidentally kicked something buried in the ground, an unidentifiable circular band of ornate iron. When he bent down for a closer inspection he saw shards of glass. He checked Perlmutter's illustrations and recognized the object as the stern running light. The rudder fittings and the lamp told him that he was standing over what had been the captain's cabin. Now his search for the jade box began in earnest.

In forty minutes of searching on his hands and knees he found an inkwell, two goblets, and the remains of several oil lamps. Without stopping to rest, he carefully brushed away a small heap of leaves and found himself looking into a green eye that stared back through the dank humus. He wiped his wet hands on his pants, took a bandanna from his pocket, and lightly cleaned the features around the eye. A human face became visible, one that had been artistically carved with great care from a solid piece of jade. Pitt held his breath.

Keeping his enthusiasm in check, he painstakingly dug four small trenches around the unblinking face, deep enough to see that it was the lid to a box about the size of a twelve-volt car battery. When the box was totally uncovered, he lifted it from the moist soil where it had rested since 1578 and set it between his legs.

Pitt sat in wondrous awe for the better part of ten minutes, afraid to pry off the lid and find nothing but damp rot inside. With great trepidation he took a small Swiss army knife from one pocket, swung out the thinnest blade and began to jimmy the lid. The box was so tightly sealed he had to constantly shift the knife blade around the box, prying each side a fraction of a millimeter before moving on to the next. Twice he paused to wipe away the sweat that trickled into his eyes. Finally, the lid popped free. Then, irreverently, he clenched the face by the nose, lifted the lid and peeked inside.

The interior of the box was lined with cedar and contained what looked to him to be a folded mass of multicolored knotted string. Several of the strands had faded but they were intact and their colors could still be distinguished. Pitt couldn't believe the remarkable state of preservation, until he closely studied the antiquity and realized it was made, not from cotton or wool, but twisted coils of tinted metal.

"That's it!" he shouted, startling a tree full of macaws, who winged into the depths of the rain forest amid a chorus of shrieking chatter. "The Drake *quipu.*"

He was still sitting there amid the ghosts of the English and Spanish seamen, oblivious to a swarm of biting insects, the stabbing pain from his gashed arm, and the clammy dampness, when the returning helicopter came within earshot from somewhere in the shrouded sky.

18

A SMALL VAN, MARKED WITH THE NAME OF A WELL-KNOWN express package company, drove up a ramp and stopped at the shipping and receiving door of a sizable one-story concrete building. The structure covered one city block of a huge warehouse complex near Galveston, Texas. There was no company sign on the roof or walls. The only evidence that it was occupied came from a small brass plaque beside the door that read Logan Storage Company. It was just after six o'clock in the evening. Too late for employees to be working on the job but still early enough not to arouse the suspicion of the patrolling security guards.

Without exiting the van, the driver punched in a code on a remote control box that deactivated the security alarm and raised the big door. As it rose to the ceiling, it revealed the interior of a vast storehouse filled to the roof support girders with seemingly endless racks packed with furniture and ordinary household goods. There was no hint of life anywhere on the spacious concrete floor. Now assured that all employees had left for home, the driver moved the van inside and waited for the door to close. Then he drove onto a platform scale large enough to hold an eighteen-wheel truck and trailer.

He stepped from the vehicle and walked over to a

small instrument panel on a pedestal and pressed a code into a switch labeled Engage Weigh-in. The platform vibrated and then began to sink beneath the floor, revealing itself to be a huge freight elevator. After it settled onto the basement floor, the driver eased the van into a large tunnel while behind him the elevator automatically returned to the upper storage floor.

The tunnel stretched for nearly a full kilometer before ending deep beneath the main floor of another huge warehouse. Here in a vast subterranean complex the Zolar family conducted their criminal operations, while operating as a legitimate business on the main floor.

The driver exited the tunnel and entered an enormous sprawling secret sub-basement whose interior floor space was even larger than the main surface level 20 meters (66 feet) above. About two-thirds of the area was devoted to the accumulation, storage, and eventual sale of stolen and smuggled artworks. The remaining third was set aside for the Zolar family's thriving artifact forgery and fabrication program. This subterranean level was known only to the immediate members of the Zolar family, a few loyal copartners in the operation, and the original construction crew, who were brought in from Russia and then returned when the subterranean rooms were completed, so no outsiders could reveal the facility's existence.

The driver slipped from behind the steering wheel, walked around to the rear of the van and pulled a long metal cylinder from inside that was attached to a cart whose wheels automatically unfolded once it was pulled free, like an ambulance gurney. When all four wheels were extended, he rolled the cart and cylinder across the huge basement toward a closed room.

As he pushed, the van driver stared at his reflection in the polished metal of the cylinder. He was of average height with a well-rounded stomach. His medium brown hair was clipped short in a military crew cut, and his cheeks and chin were closely shaven. A police detective, good at providing accurate descriptions, would have described Charles Zolar, legal name Charles Oxley, as a con man who did not look like a con man.

His brothers, Joseph Zolar and Cyrus Sarason, opened the door and stepped from the room to affectionately embrace him.

"Congratulations," said Sarason, "a remarkable triumph of subterfuge."

Zolar nodded. "Our father couldn't have planned a smoother theft. You've done the family proud."

"Praise indeed," Oxley said, smiling. "You don't know how happy I am to finally deliver the mummy to a safe place. He peered behind his brothers into the reaches of the vast storage room. "Are the glyph experts here?"

Sarason nodded. "A professor of anthropology from Harvard, who has made pre-Columbian ideographic symbols his life's work, and his wife, who handles the computer end of their decoding program. Henry and Micki Moore. They've been wearing blindfolds and listening to cassette players ever since our agents picked them up in a limo at their condo in Boston. After they were airborne in a chartered jet, the pilot was instructed to circle around for two hours before flying to Galveston. They were brought here from the airport in a soundproof delivery truck. It's safe to say they haven't seen or heard a thing."

"So for all they know, they're in a research laboratory somewhere in California or Oregon?"

"That's the impression laid on them during the flight," replied Sarason.

"They must have asked questions?"

"At first," answered Zolar. "But when our agents informed them they would receive two hundred and fifty thousand dollars in cash for decoding an artifact, the

Moores promised their full cooperation. They also promised to keep their lips sealed."

"And you trust them?" Oxley asked dubiously.

Sarason smiled malevolently. "Of course not."

Oxley didn't have to read minds to know that Henry and Micki Moore would soon be names on a tombstone.

While Zolar guided the Moores to the room, Oxley and Sarason carefully removed the golden mummy from the container and laid it on a table covered with several layers of velvet padding. The room had been furnished with a small kitchen, beds, and a bathroom. A large desk was set with note and sketch pads and several magnifying glasses with varied degrees of magnification. There was also a computer terminal with a laser printer loaded with the proper software. An array of overhead spotlights was positioned to accent the images engraved on the golden body suit.

When the Moores entered the room, their headsets and blindfolds were removed.

"I trust you were not too uncomfortable," said Zolar courteously.

The Moores blinked under the bright lights and rubbed their eyes. Henry Moore looked and acted the role of an Ivy League professor. Micki Moore was a good fifteen years younger than her husband. Like him, she had a slender figure, almost as thin as the seventies era fashion model she had once been. Her skin was on the dark side and the high, rounded cheekbones suggested American Indian genes somewhere in her ancestry. Her gray eyes focused and then darted from one masked brother to another before coming to rest on the Golden Body Suit of Tiapollo.

"A truly magnificent piece of work," she said softly. "You never fully described what it was you wanted my husband and me to decipher."

"We apologize for the melodramatic precautions," Zolar said sincerely. "But as you can see, this Inca artifact is priceless, and until it is fully examined by experts such as you, we do not wish word of its existence to reach certain people who might attempt to steal it."

Henry Moore ignored the brothers and rushed to the table. He took a pair of reading glasses from a case in his breast pocket, slid them over his nose and peered closely at the glyphs on one arm of the suit. "Remarkable detail," he said admiringly. "Except for textiles and a few pieces of pottery, this is the most extensive display of iconography I've ever seen produced on any object from the Late Horizon era."

"Do you see any problem in deciphering the images?" asked Zolar.

"It will be a labor of love," said Moore, without taking his eyes from the golden suit. "But Rome wasn't built in a day. It will be a slow process."

Sarason was impatient. "We need answers as soon as possible."

"You can't rush me," Moore said indignantly. "Not if you want an accurate version of what the images tell us."

Sarason moved close to the anthropologist. "You and your wife just do your job, no mistakes."

Zolar quickly stepped in to defuse what was rapidly developing into a nasty confrontation. "Please excuse my associate, Dr. Moore. I apologize for his rude behavior, but I think you understand that we're all a little excited about finding the golden suit."

"How did you come by it?" asked Moore.

"I can't say, but I will promise you that it is going back to Spain as soon as it has been fully studied by experts such as you and your wife."

A canny smile curled Moore's lips. "Very scrupulous of you, whatever your name is, to send it back to its rightful owners. But not before my wife and I decode the instructions leading to Huascar's treasure."

Oxley muttered something unintelligible under his breath as Sarason stepped toward Moore. But Zolar stretched out an arm and held him back. "You see through our masquerade."

"I do."

"Shall I assume you wish to make a counterproposal, Dr. Moore?"

Moore glanced at his wife. Then he turned to Zolar. "If our expertise leads you to the treasure, I don't think a twenty percent share is out of line."

Zolar nodded. "Considering the potential for incredible riches, I do believe Dr. Moore is being quite generous."

"I agree," said Oxley. "All things considered, the good professor's offer is not exorbitant." He held out his hand. "You and Mrs. Moore have a deal. If we find the treasure, your share is twenty percent."

Moore shook hands. He turned to his wife and smiled as if blissfully unaware of their death sentence. "Well, my dear, shall we get to work?"

PART III

THE DEMON
OF DEATH

TREASURE CHAMBER

CERRO EL CAPIROTE

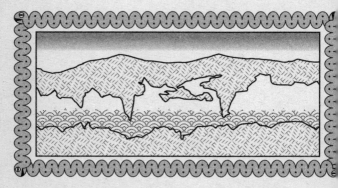

CROSS-SECTION OF UNDERGROUND RIVER

October 22, 2005
Washington, D.C.

19

CONGRESSWOMAN LOREN SMITH WAS WAITING AT THE CURB outside the terminal, her windblown cinnamon hair glistening under the morning sun, when Pitt walked out of the baggage area of Dulles airport. She lifted the sunglasses that hid her violet eyes, rose from behind the wheel, sat on top of the car seat, and waved.

Pitt set his bag and a large metal case containing the jade box on the sidewalk. "You stole one of my cars."

"That's the thanks I get for playing hooky from a committee hearing to meet you at the airport?"

Pitt stared down at the bright, fire engine red, 1953 Allard J2X that had won eight of the nine sports car races it had entered forty-five years earlier. There was not enough room for the two of them and his baggage in the small seating area, and the car had no trunk. "Where am I supposed to put my bags?"

She reached down on the passenger's seat and handed him a pair of bungee cords. "I came prepared. You can tie down your baggage on the trunk rack."

Pitt shook his head in wonderment. Loren was as bright and perceptive as they come. A five-term congresswoman from the state of Colorado, she was respected by her colleagues for her grasp of difficult issues and her

173

uncanny gift for coming up with solid solutions. Vivacious and outgoing in the halls of Congress, Loren was a private woman. Her only social interest outside her work was her friendship with Pitt.

"Where's Al and Rudi?" she asked, a look of concern in her eyes at seeing his unshaven face, haggard from exhaustion.

"On the next flight. They had a little business to clear up and return some equipment we borrowed."

After cinching his bags on a chrome rack mounted on the rear deck of the Allard, he opened the tiny passenger door, slid his long legs under the low dashboard and stretched them out to the firewall.

Loren slipped the Allard through the traffic with the ease of quicksilver running downhill through a maze. She soon pulled up in front of the old metal aircraft hangar, on the far end of Washington's international airport, that Pitt called home.

The structure had been built during the late nineteen thirties as a maintenance facility for early commercial airliners. In 1980, it was condemned and scheduled for demolition, but Pitt took pity on the deserted and forlorn structure and purchased it. Then he talked the local heritage preservation committee into having it placed on the National Register of Historic Landmarks. Afterward, except for remodeling the former upstairs offices into an apartment, he restored the hangar to its original condition.

Pitt never felt the urge to invest his savings and a substantial inheritance from his grandfather into stocks, bonds, and real estate. Instead, he chose antique and classic automobiles, and souvenirs large and small collected during his global adventures as special projects director for NUMA.

The ground floor of the old hangar was filled with nearly thirty old cars, from a 1932 Stutz towncar and French Avions Voisin sedan to a huge 1951 Daimler convertible, the youngest car in the collection. An early Ford Trimotor aircraft sat in one corner, its corrugated aluminum wing sheltering a World War II Messerschmitt ME 262 jet fighter. Along the far wall, an early Pullman railroad car, with Manhattan Limited lettered on the sides, rested on a short length of steel track. But perhaps the strangest item was an old Victorian claw-footed bathtub with an outboard motor clamped to the back. The bathtub, like the other collectibles inside the hangar, had its own unique story.

Loren stopped beside a small receiver mounted on a post. Pitt whistled the first few bars of "Yankee Doodle" and sound recognition software electronically shut down the security system and opened a big drive-through door. Loren eased the Allard inside and turned off the ignition.

"Come upstairs," she ordered. "I've planned a gourmet brunch in honor of your homecoming."

Pitt undid the cords to his baggage and followed Loren upstairs. True to her word, she had laid out a lavish setting on the formal table in his dining room. Pitt was starved and his anticipation was heightened by the appetizing aromas drifting from the kitchen.

Between mouthfuls, as he ravenously attacked Loren's Mexican brunch, Pitt began with his arrival at the sacrificial well and told her what happened up to his discovery of the jade box and the *quipu* in the Ecuadorian rain forest. He rounded out his narrative with the myths, the precious few facts, and finished with broad speculation.

Loren listened without interrupting until Pitt finished, then said, "Northern Mexico, you think?"

"Only a guess until the *quipu* is deciphered."

"How is that possible if, as you say, the knowledge about the knots died with the last Inca?"

"I'm banking on Hiram Yaeger's computer to come up with the key."

"A wild shot in the dark at best," she said.

"Our only prospect, but a good one." Pitt rose, pulled open the dining room curtains and gazed at an airliner that was lifting off the end of a runway, then sat down again. "Time is our real problem. The thieves who stole the Golden Body Suit of Tiapollo before Customs agents could seize it have a head start."

"Just be careful," Loren said. "I have a feeling your competitors are not nice people."

Early the next morning, a half hour ahead of the morning traffic rush, Pitt drove to the NUMA headquarters building. Not about to risk damage to the Allard by the crazy drivers of the nation's capital, he drove an aging but pristine 1984 Jeep Grand Wagoneer that he had modified by installing a Rodeck 500-horsepower V-8 engine taken from a hot rod wrecked at a national drag race meet. The driver of a Ferrari or Lamborghini who might have stopped beside him at a red light would never suspect that Pitt could blow their doors off from zero to a hundred miles an hour before their superior gear ratios and wind dynamics gave them the edge.

He slipped the Jeep into his parking space beneath the tall, green-glassed tower that housed NUMA's offices and took the elevator up to Yaeger's computer floor, the carrying handle of the metal case containing the jade box gripped tightly in his right hand. When he stepped into a private conference room he found Admiral Sandecker, Giordino, and Gunn already waiting for him. He set the case on the floor and shook hands.

"I apologize for being late."

"You're not late." Admiral James Sandecker spoke. "We're all early. In suspense and full of anticipation about the map, or whatever you call it."

"Quipu," explained Pitt patiently. "An Inca recording device."

A knock came on the door and a bald-headed, cadaverous man with a great scraggly Wyatt Earp moustache stepped into the room. He was wearing a crisp, white lab coat. Sandecker acknowledged him with a slight nod and turned to the others.

"I believe you all know Dr. Bill Straight," he said.

Pitt extended his hand. "Of course. Bill heads up the marine artifact preservation department. We've worked on several projects together."

"My staff is still buried under the two truckloads of antiquities from the Byzantine cargo vessel you and Al found imbedded in the ice on Greenland a few years ago."

"All I remember about that project," said Giordino, "is that I didn't thaw out for three months."

"Why don't you show us what you've got?" said Sandecker, unable to suppress his impatience.

Pitt opened the case, gently removed the jade box, and placed it on the conference table. Giordino and Gunn had already seen it during the flight from the rain forest to Quito, and they stood back while Sandecker, Yaeger, and Straight moved in for a close look.

"Masterfully carved," said Sandecker, admiring the intricate features of the face on the lid.

"A most distinctive design," observed Straight. "The serene expression, the soft look of the eyes definitely have an Asian quality about them. Almost a direct association with statuary art from the Cahola dynasty of southern India."

"Let's open it and get to that thing inside," ordered Sandecker.

Straight nodded at Pitt. "I'll let you do the honors."

Without a word, Pitt inserted a thin metal shaft under the lid of the box and carefully pried it open.

There it was. The *quipu*, lying as it had in the cedar-lined box for centuries. They stared curiously at it for almost a minute, wondering if its riddle could be solved.

Straight flexed his gloved fingers like a piano player

about to assault Franz Liszt's Hungarian Rhapsody Number Two. Then he took a deep breath and slowly reached into the box. He slipped a curved probe very carefully under several cables of the *quipu* and gently raised them a fraction of a centimeter. "Score one for our side," he sighed thankfully. "After lying in the box for centuries, the coils have not fused together or stuck to the wood. They pull free quite effortlessly."

"They appear to have survived the ravages of time extremely well," observed Pitt.

After examining the *quipu* from every angle, Straight then slipped two large tweezers under it from opposite sides. He hesitated as if bolstering his confidence, then began raising the *quipu* from its resting place. No one spoke, all held their breath until Straight laid the multicolored cables on a sheet of glass. Setting aside the tweezers in favor of the dental picks, he meticulously unfolded the cables one by one until they were all spread flat like a fan.

"There it is, gentlemen," he sighed with relief. "Now we have to soak the strands in a very mild cleaning solution to remove stains and corrosion. This process will then be followed by a chemical preservation procedure in our lab."

"How long before you can return it to Yaeger for study?" asked Sandecker

Straight shrugged. "Six months, maybe a year."

"You've got two hours," said Sandecker without batting an eye.

Four hours later Yaeger made his first breakthrough in deciphering the *quipu*'s message. "Incredible how something so simple can be so complex," he said, gazing at the vividly colored simulation of the cables that fanned out across a large monitor.

"Sort of like an abacus," said Giordino.

"Far more complicated." Pitt was leaning over Yaeger's shoulder, studying the image on the monitor. "The abacus is basically a mathematical device. The *quipu,* on the other hand, is a much more subtle instrument. Each color, coil thickness, placement and type of knot, and the tufted ends, all have significance. Fortunately, the Inca numerical system used a base of ten just like ours."

"Go to the head of the class." Yaeger nodded. "This one, besides numerically recording quantities and distances, also recorded a historical event. I'm still groping around in the dark, but, for example . . ." He paused to type in a series of instructions on his keyboard. Three of the *quipu's* coils appeared to detach themselves from the main collar and were enlarged across the screen. "My analysis proves pretty conclusively that the brown, blue, and yellow coils indicate the passage of time over distance. The numerous smaller orange knots that are evenly spaced on all three coils symbolize the sun or the length of a day."

"What brought you to that conclusion?"

"The key was the occasional interspacing of large white knots."

"Between the orange ones?"

"Right. The computer and I discovered that they coincide perfectly with phases of the moon. As soon as I can calculate astronomical moon cycles during the fifteen hundreds, I can zero in on approximate dates."

"Good thinking," said Pitt with mounting optimism. "You're onto something."

"The next step is to determine what each cable was designed to illustrate. As it turns out, the Incas were also masters of simplicity. According to the computer's analysis, the green coil represents land and the blue one the sea. The yellow remains inconclusive."

"So how do you read it?" asked Giordino.

Yaeger punched two keys and sat back. "Twenty-four days of travel over land. Eighty-six by sea. Twelve days in the yellow, whatever that stands for."

"The time spent at their destination," Pitt ventured.

Yaeger nodded in agreement. "That figures. The yellow coil might denote a barren land."

"Or a desert," said Giordino.

"Or a desert," Pitt repeated. "A good bet if we're looking at the coast of northern Mexico."

High on the funnel-shaped peak of a solitary mountain that rises like a graveyard monument in the middle of a sandy desert there is an immense stone demon.

It has stood there, legs tensed as if ready to spring, since prehistoric times, its claws dug into the massive basalt rock from which it was carved. From its pedestal on the summit, the beast's snakelike eyes command a panoramic vista of sand dunes, rocky hills and mountains, and the shimmering Colorado River that divides into streams across its silted delta before merging with the Sea of Cortez.

Weighing several tons and standing as high as a bull elephant, the winged jaguar with the serpent's head is one of only four known sculptures produced by unknown cultures before the appearance of the Spanish missionaries in the early fifteen hundreds. The other three are static crouching lions in a national park in New Mexico that were far more primitive in their workmanship.

It was said that the ancient people feared the awesome stone beast, believing it to be a guardian of the underworld, but present-day elders of the Cahuilla, Quechan, and Montolo tribes that live in the area cannot recall any significant religious traditions or detailed rituals that pertain to the sculpture. No oral history had been passed down, so they simply created their own myth on the ashes of a forgotten past. They invented a supernatural monster that all dead people must pass on their journey to the great beyond. If they led bad lives, the stone beast came to life. It snatched them in its mouth, chewed them

with its fangs, and spat them out as maimed and dis-
figured ghosts doomed to walk the earth forever as
malignant spirits. Only those good of heart and mind
were allowed to proceed unmolested into the afterworld.

Billy Yuma had no fear of the stone demon as he sat in
his pickup truck under the shadow of the mountain and
gazed up at the forbidding sculpture far above him. He
was hopeful his parents and his friends who had died
had been allowed to freely pass the guardian of the dead.
They were good people who had harmed no one. But it
was his brother, the black sheep of the family, that Billy
feared had become an evil ghost.

Like most Native Americans of the desert, Billy lived
in the constant presence of the hideously deformed
spirits who wandered aimlessly and did malicious
things. Ever since the tribe's most sacred and secret
religious objects were found missing from their hiding
place in an isolated ruin belonging to their ancestors,
whole villages had suffered ill fortune. Poor crops,
contagious sickness among the children, unseasonably
hot and dry weather. But by far the worst calamity was
the sudden increase of ghost sickness. People who had
never before seen or heard an evil spirit began describing
haunted visitations. Ghosts of early Montolos suddenly
appeared during their dreams, often materializing in
broad daylight. Almost everyone, including young children, claimed to have seen supernatural phantoms.

The theft of the wooden idols that represented the sun,
moon, earth, and water shattered the Montolos' religious
society. The anguish of not having their presence during
the initiation ceremony for entering adulthood devastated the tribe's young sons and daughters. Without the
carved deities the centuries-old rituals could not be
performed, leaving the young ones in adolescent limbo.
Without the sacred religious objects, all worship ceased.

Billy Yuma was desperate. The medicine man had
given him instructions while reading the embers of a

dying fire. To send his brother's ghost back to the underworld and save his family from further disaster, Billy had to find the lost idols and return them to their sacred hiding place in the ancient ruins of his ancestors. In a desperate attempt to end the hauntings and avoid more ill fortune he decided to fight evil with evil. He resolved to climb the mountain, confront the demon, and pray for its help in returning the precious idols.

About a third of the way up the south wall his heart hammered against his ribs and his lungs ached from the grueling effort. He could have stopped to rest and catch his breath, but he pushed on, determined to reach the peak without pause.

A shadow and a cold breeze suddenly passed over him. He shuddered from the unexpected chill. Was it a spirit? Where did they come from, he wondered. Could it be his brother was trying to make him fall to the rocks far below? Maybe the great stone beast knew he was approaching and was issuing a warning. Beset with foreboding, Billy kept on climbing, teeth clenched, staring only at the vertical rock before his eyes.

At last, just as his muscles were tightening and he was losing all feeling in his legs, the rock wall gave way to an easy incline, and he crawled onto the open surface of the peak. He rose to his feet as the final light of day faded. Though it was carved from the rock of the mountain, Billy swore that it glowed. He was tired and sore, but strangely he felt no fear of the time-worn effigy, despite the tales about how the restless spirits who were denied entry into the afterworld walked the haunted mountain.

He saw no sign of fearsome creatures lurking in the dark. Except for the jaguar with the serpent's head, the mountain was empty. Billy spoke out.

"I have come."

There was no answer. The only sounds came from the wind and the beat from the wings of a hawk. No eerie cries from the tormented souls of the underworld.

"I have climbed the enchanted mountain to pray to you," he said.

Still no sign or reply, but a chill went up his spine as he felt a presence. He heard voices speaking in a strange tongue. None of the words were familiar. Then he saw shadowy figures take shape.

The people were visible but transparent. They appeared to be moving about the mesa, taking no notice of Billy, walking around and through him as if it were he who did not exist. Their clothes were unfamiliar, not the brief cotton loincloths or rabbit-skin cloaks of his ancestors. These people were dressed as gods. Golden helmets adorned with brilliantly colored birds' feathers covered most of the phantoms' heads, while those who went bareheaded wore their hair in strange distinctive fashions. Their bodies were clothed with textiles Billy had never seen.

After a long minute the strange people seemed to dissolve and their voices ceased. Billy stood as still and silent as the rock beneath his feet. Who were these strange people who paraded before his eyes? Was this an open door to the spirit world, he wondered.

He moved closer to the stone monster, reached out a trembling hand and touched its flank. The ancient rock felt disturbingly hotter than it should have been from the day's heat. Then, incredibly, an eye seemed to pop open on the serpent's face, an eye with an unearthly light behind it.

Terror stirred through Billy's mind, but he was determined not to flinch. Later, he would be accused of an overactive imagination. But he swore a thousand times before his own death many years later that he had seen the demon stare at him from a sparkling eye. He summoned up his courage, dropped to his knees and spread out his hands. Then he began to pray. He prayed to the stone effigy through most of the night before falling into a trancelike sleep.

In the morning, as the sun rose and painted the clouds with a burst of gold, Billy Yuma awoke and looked around. He found himself lying across the front seat of his Ford pickup truck on the floor of the desert, far below the silent beast of the mountain that stared sightlessly across the dry waste.

20

JOSEPH ZOLAR STOOD AT THE HEAD OF THE GOLDEN SUIT,
watching Henry and Micki Moore huddle over the
computer and laser printer. After four days of round-the-
clock study, they had reduced the images from symbols
to descriptive words and concise phrases.

There was a fascination about the way they snatched
up the sheets as they rolled out onto the printer's tray,
excitedly analyzing their conclusions as a wall clock
ticked off the remaining minutes of their lives.

"Brunhilda has gone as far as she can go," said Yaeger,
referring to his beloved computer terminal. "Together,
we've painstakingly pieced together about ninety percent
of the stringed codes. After applying the most sophisticated and advanced information and data analysis techniques known to man, the best I can offer is a rough
account of the story."

Yaeger lowered the conference room lights. He
switched on a slide projector that threw an early Spanish
map of the coast of North and South America on the
wall screen. He picked up a metal pointer that telescoped
like an automobile radio aerial and casually aimed it in
the general direction of the map.

"Without a long-winded history lesson, I'll just say

185

that after Huascar, the legitimate heir to the Inca throne, was defeated and overthrown by his half-brother, Atahualpa, in 1533, he ordered his kingdom's treasury and other royal riches to be hidden high in the Andes.

"After Huascar was killed, it was Naymlap, Huascar's trusted adviser, who organized the movement of the treasury down from the mountains to the seashore, where he had assembled a fleet of fifty-five ships. Then, according to the *quipu,* after a journey of twenty-four days, it took another eighteen days just to load the immense treasure on board."

Yaeger tapped the pointer on a line that traced the voyage of Naymlap's treasure fleet. "From point of departure, north to their destination, the voyage took eighty-six days. No short cruise for primitive ships."

"And their final landfall?" Pitt prodded.

"On an island as you and I already discussed," Yaeger added. "It took the crews of the ships twelve days to stash the treasure in a cave, a large one according to the dimensions recorded on the *quipu.* An opening, which I translated as being a tunnel, runs from the highest point of the island down to the treasure cave."

Yaeger threw on an enlarged slide of the sea between Baja California and the mainland of Mexico on the screen. He tapped his pointer on the upper reaches of the Sea of Cortez, also known as the Gulf of California. "A factor that narrows the search zone considerably."

Pitt leaned forward, studying the chart on the screen. "The central islands of Angel de la Guarda and Tiburon stretch between forty and sixty kilometers. They each have several prominent pinnaclelike peaks. You'll have to cut it even closer, Hiram."

"I admit to a knowledge gap," Yaeger conceded. "The computer and I decoded ninety percent of the *quipu's* coils and knots. The other ten percent defies clear meaning. Two coils threw us off the mark. One made a vague reference to what Brunhilda interpreted as some kind of god or demon carved from stone. The second made no geological sense. Something about a river running through the treasure cave."

Gunn tapped his ballpoint pen on the table. "I've never heard of a river running under an island."

"To sum up," said Pitt, "we're searching for a steep outcropping of rock or pinnacle on an island in the Sea of Cortez with a stone carving of a demon on top of it."

"A generalization," Yaeger said, sitting down at the table. "But that pretty well summarizes what I could glean out of the *quipu.*"

"And if we find Huascar's treasure?" asked Pitt.

"Then we'll all be impoverished heroes."

Yaeger missed the point. "Impoverished?"

"What the admiral is implying," said Pitt, "is that the finders will not be the keepers."

Sandecker nodded. "Cry a river, gentlemen, but if you are successful in finding the hoard, every troy ounce of it will probably be turned over to the government of Peru."

Pitt and Giordino exchanged knowing grins, each reading the other's mind, but it was Giordino who spoke first.

"I'm beginning to think there is a lesson somewhere in all this."

Sandecker looked at him uneasily. "What lesson is that?"

"The treasure would probably be better off if we left it where it is."

Gaskill lay stretched out in bed, a cold cup of coffee and a dish with a half-eaten bologna sandwich beside him on the bedstand. The blanket warming his huge bulk was strewn with typewritten pages. He raised the cup and sipped the coffee before reading the next page of a book-length manuscript. The title was *The Thief Who Was Never Caught.* It was a nonfiction account of the search for the Specter, written by a retired Scotland Yard inspector by the name of Nathan Pembroke. A great pity, Gaskill thought, that no editor thought it worth publishing. He could think of at least ten famous art thefts that might have been solved if *The Thief Who Was Never Caught* had been printed and distributed.

Gaskill finished the last page an hour before dawn. He lay back on his pillow staring at the ceiling, fitting the pieces into neat little slots, until the sun's rays crept above the windowsill of his bedroom in the town of Cicero just outside Chicago. Suddenly, he felt as if a logjam had broken free and was rushing into open water.

Gaskill smiled like a man who held a winning lottery ticket as he reached for the phone. He dialed a number from memory and fluffed the pillows so he could sit up while waiting for an answer.

A very sleepy voice croaked, "Francis Ragsdale here."

"Sorry to wake you," said Gaskill, "but I have good news that couldn't wait."

"All right," Ragsdale mumbled through a yawn. "Let's hear it."

"I can tell you the name of the Specter."

"Who?"

"Our favorite art thief."

Ragsdale came fully awake. "The Specter? You made an I.D.?"

"Not me. A retired inspector from Scotland Yard who spent a lifetime writing an entire book on the Specter. Some of it's conjecture, but he's compiled some pretty convincing evidence."

"What does he have?"

Gaskill cleared his throat for effect. "The greatest art thief in history was named Zolar."

Pedro Vincente set down his beautifully restored DC-3 transport onto the runway of the airport at Harlingen, Texas. Two uniformed Customs agents were waiting when Vincente opened the passenger door and stepped to the ground.

"Mr. Vincente?" one of the agents asked politely. "Pedro Vincente?"

"Yes, I'm Vincente."

"We appreciate your alerting us of your arrival into the United States."

"Always happy to cooperate with your government," Vincente said.

The agent slipped the paper onto his clipboard and examined the entries. "Your departure point was Nicoya, Costa Rica?"

"That is correct."

"And your destination is Wichita, Kansas?"

"Yes."

"May I see your passport, please."

The routine never varied. Though Vincente often drew the same two agents, they always acted as if he were a tourist on his first visit to the States. The agent eyeballed the photo inside, comparing the straight, slicked-back black hair, partridge brown eyes, smooth olive complexion, and sharp nose. The height and weight showed a short man on the thin side whose age was forty-four.

The agent finished his appraisal of the passport and smiled officially. "Would you mind waiting in our office, Mr. Vincente, while we search your aircraft? I believe you're familiar with the procedure."

"Of course." He held up a pair of Spanish magazines. "I always come prepared to spend some time."

He was halfway to the office when he suddenly turned and shouted to the agent, "May I borrow your phone to call the fuel truck? I don't have enough in my tanks to make Wichita."

"Sure, just check with the agent behind the desk."

An hour later, Vincente was winging across Texas on his way to Wichita. Beside him in the copilot's seat were four briefcases stuffed with over six million dollars, smuggled on board just prior to takeoff by one of the two men who drove the refueling truck.

Like the Zolars and their criminal empire, Vincente directed his smuggling operation from a distance. Day-to-day activities were left to his lieutenants, none of whom had a clue to his real identity.

It was late afternoon when Vincente touched down on the narrow strip in the middle of a corn field. A golden-tan jet aircraft with a purple stripe running along its side was parked at one end. A large blue tent with an awning extending from the front had been erected beside the jet. A man in a white linen suit was seated under the awning beside a table set with a picnic lunch. Vincente waved from the cockpit, quickly ran through his postflight checklist, and exited the DC-3. He carried three of the briefcases, leaving one behind.

The man sitting at the table rose from his chair, came forward and embraced Vincente. "Pedro, always a delight to see you."

"Joseph, old friend, you don't know how much I look forward to our little encounters."

"Believe me when I say I'd rather deal with an honorable man like you than all my other clients put together."

Vincente followed Joseph Zolar under the awning and sat down as a young Latin American girl offered hors d'oeuvres. "Have you brought choice merchandise for me?"

Zolar nodded. "I have personally selected for your consideration the rarest of rare artifacts from the Incas of Peru. I've also brought extremely valuable religious objects from American Southwest Indians. I guarantee objects that have just arrived from the Andes will lift your matchless collection of pre-Columbian art above that of any museum in the world."

"I'm anxious to see them."

"My staff has them displayed inside the tent for your pleasure," said Zolar.

Zolar swept back the tent flap with a dramatic flourish. "Feast your eyes on the greatest collection of Chachapoyan art ever assembled."

The extensive array of precious handcrafted splendor stunned Vincente. He had never seen so many pre-Columbian antiquities so rich in rarity and beauty displayed in one place.

"This is unbelievable!" he gasped. "You have truly outdone yourself."

"No dealer anywhere has ever had his hands on such masterworks."

Vincente went from piece to piece, touching and examining each with a critical eye. Just to feel the embroidered textiles and gold ornaments with their gemstones took Vincente's breath away. It seemed utterly incongruous that such a hoard of wealth was sitting in a corn field in Kansas. At last he finally murmured in awe, "So this is Chachapoyan art."

"Every piece original and fully authenticated."

"I'll give you four million dollars for the lot."

"I appreciate the richness of your initial offer. But you know me well enough to understand I never haggle. There is one price, and one price only."

"Which is?"

"Six million."

Vincente cleared several artifacts, making an open space on one table. He opened the briefcases side by side, one at a time. All were filled with closely packed stacks of high denomination bills. "I only brought five million."

Zolar was not fooled for an instant. "A great pity I have to pass. I can't think of anyone I'd rather have sold the collection to."

Without a word, Vincente exited the tent and returned in a few minutes with the fourth briefcase. He set it beside the others and opened it. "Six million, five hundred thousand. You said you have some rare religious objects from the American Southwest. Are they included too?"

"For the extra five hundred thousand you can have them," answered Zolar. "You'll find the Indian religious idols under the glass case in the corner."

Vincente walked over and removed the glass dust cover. He stared at the strangely shaped gnarled figures. These were no ordinary ceremonial idols. Although they looked as if they had been carved and painted by a young child, he was aware of their significance from long experience of collecting objects from the American Southwest.

"Hopi?" he asked.

"No, Montolo. Very old. Very important in their ceremonial rituals."

Vincente reached down and began to pick one up for a closer look. His heart skipped the next three beats and he felt an icy shroud fall over him. The fingers of his hand did not feel as if they came in contact with the hardened root of a long-dead cottonwood tree. The idol felt more like soft flesh. Vincente could have sworn he heard it utter an audible moan.

"Did you hear that?" he asked, thrusting the idol back in the case as if it had burned his hand.

Zolar peered at him questioningly. "I didn't hear anything."

Vincente looked like a man having a nightmare. "Please, my friend, let us finish our business, and then you must leave. I do not want these idols on my property."

"Does that mean you don't wish to buy them?" Zolar asked, surprised.

"No, no. Spirits are alive in those idols. I can feel their presence."

"Superstitious nonsense."

Vincente grasped Zolar by the shoulders, his eyes pleading. "Destroy them," he begged. "Destroy them or they will surely destroy you."

21

UNDER AN INDIAN SUMMER SUN, TWO HUNDRED PRIME examples of automotive builders' art sat on the green grass of East Potomac Park and glittered like spangles under a theatrical spotlight.

The cars were classified by year, body style, and country of origin. Trophies were awarded to the best of their class and plaques to the runners-up. "Best of show" was the most coveted award. A few of the wealthier owners spent hundreds of thousands of dollars restoring their pride and joy to a level of perfection far beyond the car's original condition on the day it rolled out of the factory.

Unlike the more conservatively dressed owners of other cars, Pitt sat in an old-fashioned canvas lawn chair wearing a flowered Hawaiian aloha shirt, white shorts, and sandals. Behind him stood a gleaming, dark blue 1936 Pierce Arrow berline (sedan body with a divider window) that was hitched to a 1936 Pierce Arrow Travelodge house trailer painted a matching color.

In between answering questions from passersby about the car and trailer, he had his nose buried in a thick boater's guide to the Sea of Cortez.

Giordino, wearing baggy khaki shorts that dropped to

just above his knees and a T-shirt, approached the Pierce Arrow through the crowd. He was accompanied by Loren, who was carrying a picnic basket while Giordino balanced an ice chest on one shoulder.

Pitt pointed toward the open door of the sixty-two-year-old house trailer. "Why don't we step into my mobile palace and get out of the sun?"

Giordino hoisted the ice chest, carried it inside, and set it on a kitchen counter. Loren followed and began spreading the contents of the picnic basket across the table of a booth.

Giordino nodded at the open Sea of Cortez boating book. "Find any likely prospects?"

"Out of nearly a hundred islands in and around the Gulf that rise at least fifty meters above the sea, I've narrowed it down to two probables and four possibles. The rest don't fit the geological pattern."

"Can I see where you're going to search?" asked Loren, as she laid out a variety of cold cuts, cheeses, smoked fish, a loaf of sourdough bread, coleslaw, and down-home potato salad.

Pitt walked to a closet, pulled out a long roll of paper and spread it on the kitchen counter. "An enhanced picture of the Gulf. I've circled the islands that come closest to matching Yaeger's translation of the *quipu.*"

Loren and Giordino examined the photo, taken from a geophysical orbiting satellite, that revealed the upper reaches of the Sea of Cortez in astonishing detail. Pitt handed Loren a large magnifying glass.

Loren hovered over the islands Pitt had circled. Then she looked up at him. "I assume you intend to make an aerial survey of the most promising sites?"

"The next step in the process of elimination."

"By plane?"

"Helicopter."

"Looks to me like a pretty large area to cover by helicopter," said Loren. "What do you use for a base?"

"An old ferryboat."

"A ferry?" Loren said, surprised.

"Actually a car/passenger ferry that originally plied San Francisco Bay until 1957. She was later sold and used until 1962 by the Mexicans from Guaymas across the Gulf to Santa Rosalia. Then she was taken out of service. Rudi Gunn chartered her for a song."

"According to Rudi she's still used as a work boat," said Pitt, "and has a top deck large enough to accommodate a helicopter. He assures me that she'll make a good platform to launch reconnaissance flights."

"When search operations cease with daylight," Giordino continued to explain, "the ferry will cruise overnight to the next range of islands on Dirk's survey list. This approach will save us a considerable amount of flight time."

Loren handed Pitt a plate and silverware. "Sounds like you've got everything pretty well under control. What happens when you find what looks like a promising treasure site?"

"We'll worry about putting together an excavation operation after we study the geology of the island," Pitt answered.

"What about permits? You can't go running around digging for treasure in Mexico without permission from government authorities."

Pitt laid a hefty portion of mortadella on a slice of sourdough bread. "Admiral Sandecker thought it best to wait. We don't want to advertise our objective. If word got out that we had a line on the biggest bonanza in history, a thousand treasure hunters would descend on us like locusts."

Loren was silent while she ladled a spoonful of potato salad onto her plate, then asked, "Why don't you have someone on your team as insurance in the event local Mexican officials become suspicious and start asking questions?"

Pitt looked at her. "You mean a public relations expert?"

"No, a bona fide, card-carrying member of the United States Congress."

Pitt stared into Loren's violet eyes. "You?"

"Why not? The Speaker of the House has called for a recess next week. My aides can cover for me. I'd love to get out of Washington for a few days and see a piece of Mexico."

"Frankly," said Giordino, "I think it's a stellar concept." He gave Loren a smile. "Dirk is always more congenial when you're around."

"Can you put us closer to the dominant peak?" Sarason asked his brother Charles Oxley, who was at the controls of a small amphibious flying boat. "The crest of the lower one is too sharp for our requirements."

"Do you see something?"

Sarason peered through binoculars out a side window of the aircraft. "The island has definite possibilities, but it would help if I knew what sort of landmark to look for."

Moore snatched the binoculars from Sarason without asking and peered at the broken terrain running across the ridge of the island. After a few moments, he handed them back and relaxed in his seat with an iced shaker of martinis. "Not the one we're looking for," he proclaimed regally.

Sarason turned the page of the same boater's guide that was being used by Pitt. "Next search point is Isla Carmen. Size, one hundred and fifty square kilometers. Length, thirty kilometers. Has several peaks rising over three hundred meters."

"That's a pass," announced Moore. "Far too large."

"After that we have Isla Cholla, a small flat-topped rock with a light tower and a few fishing huts," Sarason said.

"Skip that one too," said Moore.

"Okay, next up is Isla San Ildefonso, six miles offshore east of San Sebastian."

"Size?"

"About two and a half square kilometers. No beaches."

"There has to be a beach," said Moore, taking another slug from his martini shaker. "The Incas could not have landed and unloaded their rafts without a beach."

"After San Ildefonso we come to Bahia Coyote," said Sarason. "There we'll have a choice of six islands that are little more than huge rocks rising from the sea."

Oxley eased the Baffin amphibian into a slow climb until he reached 700 meters (about 2300 feet). Then he set a course due north. Twenty-five minutes later the bay and the long peninsula that shield it from the Gulf came into view. Oxley descended and began circling the small rocky islands scattered around the entrance to the bay.

"Isla Guapa and Isla Bargo are possibilities," observed Sarason. "They both rise sharply from the water and have small but open summits."

Moore squirmed sideways in his seat and peered down. "They don't look promising to me—" He stopped talking and grabbed Sarason's binoculars again. "That island down there."

"Which one?" queried Sarason irritably. "There are six of them."

"The one that looks like a floating duck looking backward."

"Isla Bargo. Fits the profile. Steep walls on three sides, rounded crest. There is also a small beach in the crook of the neck."

"That's it," Moore said excitedly. "That must be it."

Sarason snatched back the glasses and studied the island. "There, on the crown. It looks like something carved in the rock."

"Don't pay any attention to that," said Moore, wiping a trickle of sweat from his forehead. "It doesn't mean a thing."

Sarason was no fool. Could it be a signpost cut by the Incas to mark the passageway to the treasure, he wondered in silence.

"I'll land and taxi to that little beach," said Oxley. "From the air, at least, it looks like a relatively easy climb to the summit."

Sarason nodded. "Take her down."

Oxley made two passes over the water off the island's beach, making certain there were no underwater reefs or rocks that could tear out the bottom of the aircraft. He came into the wind and settled the plane on the blue sea, striking the light swells and riding them like a speedboat across a choppy lake. The propellers flashed in the sun as they whipped sheets of spray over the wing.

The plane quickly slowed from the drag of the water as Oxley eased back on the throttles, keeping just enough power to move the plane toward the beach. Forty-six meters (151 feet) from shore, he extended the wheels into the water. The tires soon touched and gripped the sandy shelf that sloped toward the island. Two minutes later the plane rose from a low surf and rolled onto the beach like a dripping duck.

Two fishermen wandered over from a small driftwood shack and gawked at the aircraft as Oxley turned off the ignition switches and the propellers swung to a stop. The passenger door opened and Sarason stepped down to the white sand beach, followed by Moore and finally Oxley, who locked and secured the door and cargo hatch. As an added security measure, Sarason generously paid the fishermen to guard the plane. Then they set off on a scarcely defined footpath leading to the top of the island.

At first the trail was an easy hike but then it angled more steeply the closer they came to the summit. Moore stopped, gasping for air, sweat flowing freely. He looked on the verge of collapse when Oxley grabbed his hand and heaved him onto the flat top of the summit.

"Didn't anybody ever tell you booze and rock climbing don't mix?"

Moore ignored him. Then suddenly, the exhaustion washed away and he stiffened. His eyes squinted in drunken concentration. He brushed Oxley aside and stumbled toward a rock the size of a small automobile that was crudely carved in the shape of some animal.

"A dog," he gasped between labored breaths, "it's only a stupid dog."

"Wrong," said Sarason. "A coyote. The namesake of the bay. Superstitious fishermen carved it as a symbol to protect their crews and boats when they go to sea."

"Why should an old rock carving interest you?" asked Oxley.

"As an anthropologist, primitive sculptures can be a great source of knowledge."

Sarason was watching Moore, and for once his eyes were no longer filled with distaste. There was no question in his mind that the professor had given away the key to the treasure's location.

"You realize, of course, that we no longer require your services, don't you, Henry?"

Moore shook his head and spoke with an icy composure that seemed unnatural under the circumstances. "You'll never do it without me."

"A pathetic bluff," Sarason sneered. "Now that we know we're searching for an island with a sculpture, an ancient one I presume, what more can you possibly contribute to the search?"

Moore's drunkenness had seemingly melted away, and he abruptly appeared as sober as a judge. "A rock sculpture is only the first of several benchmarks the Incas erected. They all have to be interpreted."

Sarason smiled. It was a cold and evil smile. "You wouldn't lie to me now, would you, Henry? You wouldn't deceive my brother and me into thinking Isla Bargo isn't the treasure site so you can return later on your own and dig it up? I sincerely hope that little plot isn't running through your mind."

Moore glared at him, simple dislike showing where there should have been fear. "Blow off the top of the island," he said with a shrug, "and see what it gets you. Level it to the waterline. You won't find an ounce of Huascar's treasure, not in a thousand years. Not without someone who knows the secrets of the markers."

"He may be right," Oxley said quietly. "And if he's lying, we can return and excavate on our own. Either way, we win."

Leniency and patience, they were the watchwords for now, Sarason decided. He patted Moore on the back. "Forgive my frustration. Let's get back to the plane and call it a day. I think we could all use a cool bath and a good supper."

"I knew you'd see the light," said Moore. "I'll show you the way. All you boys have to do is keep the faith."

When they arrived back at the aircraft, Sarason entered first. On a hunch, he picked up Moore's discarded martini shaker and shook a few drops onto his tongue. Water, not gin.

Sarason silently cursed himself. He had not picked up on how dangerous Moore was. Why would Moore act the role of a drunk if not to lull everyone into thinking he was harmless? He slowly began to comprehend that Henry Moore was not entirely what he seemed. There was more to the famous and respected anthropologist than met the eye, much more.

As a man who could kill without the slightest remorse, Sarason should have recognized another killer when he saw one.

Micki Moore stepped out of the blue-tiled swimming pool below the hacienda and stretched out on a lounge chair. The hacienda was built around the pool and a large garden filled with a variety of tropical plants. All major rooms had balconies with dramatic views of the sea and the town of Guaymas. She was more than happy to relax around the pool or in her skylit bedroom with its own patio and Jacuzzi while the men flew up and down the Gulf in search of the treasure. She picked up her watch from a small table. Five o'clock. The conniving brothers and her husband would be returning soon. She sighed with pleasure at the thought of another fabulous dinner of local dishes and settled back for a brief nap. Just before she drifted off, she thought she heard a car drive up the road from town and stop at the front gate of the hacienda.

When she awoke a short time later, her skin felt cool and she sensed that the sun had passed behind a cloud. But then she opened her eyes, and was startled to see a man standing over her, his shadow thrown across the upper half of her body.

The eyes that stared at her looked like stagnant black pools. There was no life to them. Even his face seemed incapable of expression. The stranger appeared emaciated, as if he had been sick for a long time. Micki shivered as though an icy breeze suddenly swept over her. She thought it odd that he took no notice of her exposed body, but gazed directly into her eyes. She felt as if he were looking inside her.

"Who are you?" she asked. "Do you work for Mr. Zolar?"

He did not reply for several seconds. When he spoke, it was with an odd voice with no inflection. "My name is Tupac Amaru."

And then he turned and limped away.

22

FIFTY KILOMETERS (31 MILES) AFTER PASSING THROUGH Yuma, Arizona, across the Colorado River into California, Pitt swung the big Pierce Arrow left off Interstate Highway 8 and onto the narrow state road that led to the border towns of Calexico and Mexicali. Drivers and passengers in cars that passed, or those coming from the opposite direction, stared and gawked at the old classic auto and the trailer it pulled.

"How much farther to the border?" Loren asked.

"Another forty-two kilometers will put us into Mexico," he answered. "Then a hundred and sixty-five klicks to San Felipe. We should arrive at the dock, where Al and Rudi have tied up the ferry, by dinnertime."

"How about we stop at that truck stop up ahead?" She straightened and pointed through the flat, narrow windshield of the Pierce.

Pitt gazed over the ornate radiator cap, a crouched archer poised to fire an arrow. He saw a sign by the side of the road, dried and bleached by the desert sun, and on the verge of collapsing into the sand at any moment. The lettering was so old and faded he could hardly read the words.

Food a mother would love.
Only 2 more minutes to the Box Car Café.

"And besides," Loren threw in, "you need gas."

Pitt glanced at the fuel gauge. The needle stood steady at a quarter tank. "I guess it won't hurt to fill up before we cross the border."

The roadside restaurant and gas station came into view. All Pitt saw as they drove closer was a dilapidated pair of old railroad freight cars joined together, with two gas pumps out front and a neon EAT sign barely flickering in the shadow of the Box Car Café.

Pitt turned the outsize steering wheel and the Pierce rolled off the blacktop up to the gas pumps. The big V-12 engine was so whisper-quiet it was hard to tell it had stopped when he turned off the ignition. He opened the door that swung outward from the front, put a foot on the high running board and stepped down.

A metal sign liberally peppered with bullet holes said Self Service, so Pitt inserted the nozzle of the gas pump inside the Pierce Arrow's tank filler and squeezed the handle. When he had the engine rebuilt, the machine shop modified the valves to burn unleaded gas without problems.

The rails beneath the rusting wheel-trucks of the Box Car Café were buried in the sand. The weathered wooden walls had once been painted a reddish tan, and the lettering above the long row of crudely installed windows read Southern Pacific Lines. Thanks to the dry air, the body shells of the antique box cars had survived the ravages of constant exposure and appeared in relatively good condition.

Pitt owned a piece of railroad history, a Pullman car. It was part of the collection housed inside his hangar in Washington. The once-luxurious rail car had been pulled by the famed Manhattan Limited out of New York in the years prior to World War I. He judged these freight cars to have been built sometime around 1915.

He and Loren climbed a makeshift stairway and entered a door cut into the end of one car. The interior was time-worn but neat and clean. There were no tables, only a long counter with stools that stretched the length of the two attached cars. The open kitchen was situated on the opposite side of the counter and looked as if it was constructed from used lumber that had lain in the sun for several decades. Pictures on the walls showed early engines, smoke spouting from their stacks, pulling passenger and freight trains across the desert sands. The list of records on a Wurlitzer jukebox was a mix of favorite pop music from the forties and fifties and the sounds of steam locomotives. Two plays for twenty-five cents.

A tall man, in his early sixties, with gray hair and white beard, was wiping the oak countertop. He looked up and smiled, his blue-green eyes filled with warmth and congeniality. "Greetings, folks. Welcome to the Box Car Café. What can I get you?" He was wearing cowboy boots, denim pants, and a plaid shirt that was badly faded from too many washings.

"Your mesquite chiliburger," said Loren. "And coleslaw."

"I'm not real hungry," said Pitt. "I'll just have the coleslaw. Do you own this place?"

"Bought it from the original owner when I gave up prospecting." He turned to his stove.

"The box cars are interesting relics of railroad history. Were they moved here, or did the railroad run through at one time?"

"We're actually sitting on the siding of the old main line," answered the diner's owner. "The tracks used to run from Yuma to El Centro. The line was abandoned in 1947 for lack of business. The rise of truck lines did it in. These cars were bought by an old fella who used to be an engineer for the Southern Pacific. He and his wife made a restaurant and gas station out of them. With the main interstate going north of here and all, we don't see too much traffic anymore."

The owner/cook looked as if he might have been a fixture of the desert even before the rails were laid. He had the worn look of a man who had seen more than he should and heard a thousand stories that remained in his head. There was also an unmistakable aura of style about him, a sophistication that said he didn't belong in a godforsaken roadside tavern on a remote and seldom-traveled road through the desert.

For a fleeting instant, Pitt thought the old cook looked vaguely familiar. On reflection, though, Pitt figured the man only resembled someone he couldn't quite place. "I'll bet you can recite some pretty interesting tales about the dunes around here," he said, making idle conversation.

"A lot of bones lie in them, remains of pioneers and miners who tried to cross four hundred kilometers of desert from Yuma to Boriego Springs in the middle of summer."

"Once they passed the Colorado River, there was no water?" asked Loren.

"Not a drop, not until Boriego. That was long before the valley was irrigated. Only after them old boys died from the sun did they learn their bodies lay not five meters from water. The trauma was so great they've all come back as ghosts to haunt the desert."

Loren looked perplexed. "I think I missed something."

"There's no water on the surface," the old fellow explained. "But underground there's whole rivers of it, some as wide and deep as the Colorado."

Pitt was curious. "I've never heard of large bodies of water running under the desert."

"There's two for sure. One, a really big sucker, runs from upper Nevada south into the Mojave Desert and then west, where it empties into the Pacific below Los Angeles. The other flows west under the Imperial Valley of California before curling south and spilling into the Sea of Cortez."

"What proof do you have these rivers actually exist?" asked Loren. "Has anyone seen them?"

"The underground stream that flows into the Pacific," answered the cook, as he prepared Loren's chiliburger, "was supposedly found by an engineer searching for oil. He alleged his geophysical instruments detected the river and tracked it across the Mojave and under the town of Laguna Beach into the ocean. So far nobody has proved or disproved his claim. The river traveling to the Sea of Cortez comes from an old story about a prospector who discovered a cave that led down into a deep cavern with a river running through it."

Pitt tensed as Yaeger's translation of the *quipu* suddenly flashed through his mind.

The diner's owner talked without turning from his stove. "From the mouth of the cave, through a chain of caverns, he descended two kilometers deep into the earth until he encountered an underground river rushing through a vast canyon. It was there he claims he found rich deposits of placer gold."

The old cook turned and waved a spatula in the air. "People at the assay office stated that the sand he carried back from the underground canyon assayed at three thousand dollars per ton. A mighty good recovery rate when you remember that gold was only twenty dollars and sixty-five cents an ounce back then."

"Did he ever return to the canyon and the river?" asked Pitt.

"He tried, but a whole army of scavengers followed him back to the mountain, hungering for a piece of the River of Gold, as it became known. He got mad and dynamited a narrow part of the passage about a hundred meters inside the entrance. Brought down half the mountain. Neither he nor those who followed him were ever able to dig through the rubble or find another cave leading inside. He disappeared right after he blew the cave and was not seen again. There was talk that he found another way inside and died there. A few people believe in a great river that flows through a canyon deep beneath the sands, but most think it's only another tall tale of the desert."

Between bites of the chiliburger Loren asked, "You seem convinced that Hunt's river flows into the Sea of Cortez. How do you know it doesn't enter the Pacific off California?"

"Because of Hunt's backpack and canteen. He lost them in the cave and they were found six months later, having drifted up on a beach in the Gulf."

"Don't you think that's highly improbable? The pack and canteen could have belonged to anyone. Why would anyone believe they were his?" Loren questioned the cook as if she was sitting on a congressional investigation committee.

"I guess because his name was stenciled on them."

Pitt stabbed a fork at his coleslaw, but he was no longer hungry. His mind was shifting gears. "Do you happen to know approximately where his gear was found?"

"I haven't made a detailed study of the phenomena," answered the diner's owner, staring thoughtfully at the heavily scarred wooden floor. "But as I recollect, it was in the waters off Punta el Macharro."

"What part of the Gulf would that be?"

"On the western shore. Macharro Point, as we call it in English, is two or three kilometers above San Felipe."

Loren looked at Pitt. "Our destination."

Pitt made a wry smile. "Remind me to keep a sharp eye for dead bodies."

"You folks heading for San Felipe to do a little fishing?"

Pitt nodded. "I guess you might call it a fishing expedition."

"The scenery ain't much to look at once you drop below Mexicali. The desert seems desolate and barren to most folks, but it has countless paradoxes. There are more ghosts, skeletons, and myths per kilometer than any jungle or mountains on earth. Keep that in mind and you'll see them as sure as the Irish see leprechauns."

"We'll keep that in mind," Loren said, smiling, "when we cross over the prospector's underground River of Gold."

"Oh, you'll cross it all right," said the cook. "The sad fact is you won't know it."

After Pitt paid for the gas and the meal, he went outside and checked the Pierce Arrow's oil and water. The old cook accompanied Loren onto the dining car's observation platform.

Loren held out her hand. "It's been fun listening to your stories, Mr. . . . ."

"Cussler, Clive Cussler. Mighty nice to have met you, ma'am."

Loren was driving when they reached San Felipe. Pitt had stretched out in the backseat and was snoring away, but she did not bother to wake him. She guided the dusty, bug-splattered Pierce Arrow around the town's traffic circle, making a wide turn so she didn't run one side of the trailer over the curb, and turned south toward the town's breakwater-enclosed harbor.

Five kilometers south of town she turned left on a road leading toward the waters of the Gulf and stopped the Pierce alongside an antiquated ferryboat that looked like a ghost from a scrap yard. The impression was heightened by the low tide that had left the ferry's hull tipped on an angle with its keel sunk into the harbor bottom's silt.

"Rise and shine," she said, reaching over the seat and shaking Pitt.

Gunn and Giordino spotted them and waved. They walked across a gangplank to the dock as Pitt and Loren climbed from the car and stood gazing at the boat.

"What do you think of our work platform?" asked Giordino, gesturing grandly at the ferryboat. "Built in 1923. She was one of the last walking beam steamboats to be built."

Pitt lifted his sunglasses and studied the antique vessel.

The name painted across the center of the superstructure that housed the paddlewheels identified her as the *Alhambra*.

"Where did you steal that derelict?" he asked. "From a maritime museum?"

"To know her is to love her," said Giordino without feeling.

"She was the only vessel I could find quickly that could land a helicopter," Gunn explained. "Besides, I kept Sandecker happy by obtaining her on the cheap."

Though he made a show of disapproval, Pitt already felt great affection toward the old ferry. It was love at first sight. Antique automobiles, aircraft, or boats, anything mechanical that came from the past, fascinated him. Born too late, he often complained, born eighty years too late.

"And the crew?"

"An engineer with one assistant and two deckhands." Gunn paused and gave a wide boyish smile. "I get to man the helm while you and Al cavort around the Gulf in your flying machine."

"Speaking of the helicopter, where have you hidden it?"

"Inside the auto deck," replied Gunn. "Makes it convenient to service it without worrying about the weather. We push it out onto the loading deck for flight operations."

Pitt looked at Giordino. "What sort of time frame are we looking at?"

"Should be able to cover the area in three days."

"Excuse me," interrupted Loren. "May I ask two questions?"

The men paused and stared at her. Pitt bowed. "You have the floor, Congresswoman."

"The first is where do you plan to park the Pierce Arrow? It doesn't look safe enough around here to leave a hundred-thousand-dollar classic car sitting unattended on a fishing dock."

Gunn looked surprised that she should ask. "Didn' Dirk tell you? The Pierce and the trailer come on board the ferry. There's acres of room inside."

Pitt laughed. "You don't even have to unpack."

"And your other question?" inquired Gunn.

"I'm starved," she announced regally. "When do we eat?"

With the Pierce Arrow and its travel trailer safely tied down on the cavernous auto deck, Gunn at the wheel in the pilothouse, and Loren stretched on a lounge chair the ferry moved out of the breakwater harbor and made a wide turn to the south. The old boat presented an impressive sight as black smoke rose from her stack and her paddlewheels pounded the water.

While Giordino made a preflight inspection of the helicopter and topped off the fuel tank, Pitt was briefed on the latest developments by Sandecker in Washington over the Motorola Iridium satellite phone in the forward pilothouse. Not until an hour later, as the ferry steamed off Point Estrella, did Pitt switch off the phone and descend to the improvised flight pad on the open forward deck of the ferry. As soon as Pitt was strapped in the copilot's seat, Giordino lifted the turquoise NUMA craft off the ferry and set a parallel course along the coastline.

"What did the old boy have to say?" asked Giordino as he leveled the chopper off at 800 meters (2600 feet).

"The latest news is that we've been blindsided. Customs and the FBI dropped in out of the blue and informed him that a gang of art thieves is also on the trail of Huascar's treasure. He warned us to keep a sharp eye out for them."

"We have competition?"

"A family that oversees a worldwide empire dealing in stolen and forged works of art."

"What do they call themselves?" asked Giordino.

"Zolar International."

"How close do the Feds think Zolar is to the treasure?"

"They think he has better directions than we do."

"I'm willing to bet my Thanksgiving turkey we find the site first."

"Either way, you'd lose."

Giordino turned and looked at him. "Care to let your old buddy in on the rationale?"

"If we hit the jackpot ahead of them, we're supposed to fade into the landscape and let them scoop up the loot."

"Give it up?" Giordino was incredulous.

"Those are the orders," said Pitt, resentment written in his eyes.

"But why?" demanded Giordino.

"So Customs and the FBI can trail and trap them into an indictment and eventual conviction for some pretty heavy crimes."

Pitt motioned toward the rising sun. "Come around on an approximate heading of one-one-zero degrees."

Giordino took note of the eastern heading. "You want to check out the other side of the Gulf on the first run?"

"Only four islands have the geological features similar

to what we're looking for. But you know I like launching the search on the outer perimeters of our grid and then working back toward the more promising targets."

Giordino grinned. "Any sane man would begin in the center."

"Didn't you know?" Pitt came back. "The village idiot has all the fun."

23

T HAD BEEN A LONG FOUR DAYS OF SEARCHING. OXLEY WAS
discouraged, Sarason oddly complacent, while Moore
was baffled. They had flown over every island in the Sea
of Cortez that had the correct geological formations.
Several displayed features on their peaks that suggested
man-made rock carvings. But low altitude reconnais-
ance and strenuous climbs up steep palisades to verify
the rock structures up close revealed configurations that
appeared as sculpted beasts only in their imaginations.

Moore was plainly baffled. The rock carving had to
exist on an island in an inland sea. The pictographs on
the golden mummy suit were distinct, and there was no
mistaking the directions in his translation. For a man so
sure of himself, the failure was maddening.

Moore was also puzzled by Sarason's sudden change
in attitude. He no longer displayed animosity or anger,
Moore mused. Those strange almost colorless eyes always seemed to be in a constant state of observation,
never losing their intensity. Moore knew whenever he
gazed into them that he was facing a man who was no
stranger to death.

But there was a small measure of satisfaction. Sarason
was not clairvoyant. He could not have known, nor did

any man alive know except the President of the United States, that Professor Henry Moore, respected anthropologist, and his equally respected archaeologist wife, Micki, were experts in carrying out assassinations of foreign terrorist leaders. With their academic credentials they easily traveled in and out of foreign countries as consultants on archaeological projects. Interestingly, the CIA was in total ignorance of their actions. Their assignments came directly from an obscure agency calling itself the Foreign Activities Council that operated out of a small basement room under the White House.

Moore shifted restlessly in his seat and studied a chart of the Gulf. Finally he said, "Something is very, very wrong."

Oxley looked at his watch. "Five o'clock. I prefer to land in daylight. We might as well call it a day."

Sarason's expressionless gaze rested on the empty horizon ahead. Untypically, he acted relaxed and quiet. He offered no comment.

"It's got to be here," Moore said, examining the islands he had crossed out on his chart as if he had flunked a test.

"I have an unpleasant feeling we might have flown right by it," said Oxley.

Now that he saw Moore in a different light, Sarason viewed him with the respect one adversary has for another. He also realized that despite his slim frame, the professor was strong and quick. Struggling up the rocky walls of promising islands, gasping from aggravated exhaustion and playing drunk, was nothing more than an act. On two occasions, Moore leaped over a fissure with the agility of a mountain goat. On another, with seemingly little effort, he cast aside a boulder blocking his path that easily equaled his weight.

Sarason said, "Perhaps the Inca sculpture we're looking for was destroyed."

In the rear seat of the seaplane Moore shook his head.
"No, I'd have recognized the pieces."

"Suppose it was moved? It wouldn't be the first time
an ancient sculpture was relocated to a museum for
display."

"If Mexican archaeologists had taken a massive rock
carving and set it up for exhibit," said Moore doggedly,
"I'd have known about it."

"Then how do you explain that it is not where it is
supposed to be?"

"I can't," Moore admitted. "As soon as we land back
at the hacienda, I'll review my notes. There must be a
seemingly insignificant clue that I missed in my translation of the golden suit."

"I trust you will find it before tomorrow morning,"
Sarason said dryly.

Oxley fought the urge to doze off. He had been at the
controls since nine o'clock in the morning and his neck
was stiff with weariness. He held the control column
between his knees and poured himself a cup of coffee
from a thermos. He took a swallow and made a face. It
was not only cold but tasted as strong as battery acid.
Suddenly, his eye caught a flash of green from under a
cloud. He pointed out the window to the right of the
Baffin flying boat.

"Don't see many helicopters in this part of the Gulf,"
he said casually.

Sarason took the binoculars and peered at the turquoise helicopter. This was a different model from the
one that had landed at the sacrificial well. That one had a
shorter fuselage and landing skids. This one had retract-
able landing gear. But there was no mistaking the color
scheme and markings. He told himself it was ridiculous
to think the men in the approaching helicopter could
possibly be the same ones who appeared out of nowhere
in the Andes.

He trained the binoculars on the helicopter's cockpit. In another few seconds he would be able to discern the faces inside. For some strange, inexplicable reason his calm began to crack and he felt his nerves tighten.

"What do you think?" asked Giordino. "Could they be the ones?"

"They could be." Pitt stared through a pair of naval glasses at the amphibian seaplane flying on a diagonal course below the helicopter. "After watching the pilot circle Estanque Island for fifteen minutes as if he were looking for something on the peak, I think it's safe to say we've met up with our competition."

"What do you see?" asked Giordino, minding his flying.

"Some guy staring back at me through binoculars," replied Pitt with a grin.

"Maybe we should call them up and invite them over for a jar of Grey Poupon mustard."

The passenger in the seaplane dropped his glasses for a moment to massage his eyes before resuming his inspection. Pitt pressed his elbows against his body to steady his view. When he lowered the binoculars, he was no longer smiling.

"An old friend from Peru," he said in cold surprise.

Giordino turned and looked at Pitt curiously. "Old friend?"

"Dr. Steve Miller's imposter come back to haunt us."

Pitt's smile returned, and it was hideously diabolic. Then he waved.

If Pitt was surprised at the unexpected confrontation, Sarason was stunned. "You!" he gasped.

"What did you say?" asked Oxley.

His senses reeling at seeing the man who had caused him so much grief, uncertain if this was a trick of his mind, Sarason refocused the binoculars and examined

the man that was grinning fiendishly and waving slowly.
A slight shift of the binoculars and all color drained from
his face as he recognized Giordino as the pilot.

"The men in that helicopter," he said, his voice thick,
"are the same two who wreaked havoc on our operation
in Peru."

Oxley looked unconvinced. "Think of the odds, brother. Are you certain?"

"It's them, there can be no others. Their faces are
burned in my memory. They cost our family millions of
dollars in artifacts that were later seized by Peruvian
government archaeologists."

Moore was listening intently. "Why are they here?"

"The same purpose we are. Someone must have leaked
information on our project." He turned and glared at
Moore. "Perhaps the good professor has friends at
NUMA?"

"Think what you're saying," snapped Moore. "It is
absolutely impossible for them to know where to search.
My wife and I were the only ones ever to decode the
images on the golden mummy suit. Either this has to be a
coincidence or you're hallucinating."

Sarason did not hear Moore. The thought of Amaru
triggered something inside Sarason. He slowly regained
control, the initial shock replaced by malevolence. He
could not wait to unleash the mad dog from the Andes.

"This time," he murmured nastily, "they will be the
ones who pay."

Joseph Zolar had finally arrived in his jet and was
waiting in the dining room of the hacienda with Micki
Moore when the searchers entered wearily and sat down.
"I guess I don't have to ask if you've found anything. The
look on your faces reflects defeat."

"We'll find it," said Oxley through a yawn. "The
demon has to be out there somewhere."

"I hate to bring more grim tidings," Sarason said to

Zolar, "but we met up with my friends who messed things up in Peru."

Zolar looked at him, puzzled. "Not those two from NUMA?"

"The same. As incredible as it sounds, I believe they're after Huascar's gold too."

"I'm forced to agree," said Oxley. "Why else did they pop up in the same area?"

"Impossible for them to know something we don't," said Zolar.

"Perhaps they've been following you," said Micki.

Zolar smiled. "I think Mrs. Moore has given us the answer."

"Me?" wondered Micki. "All I suggested was—"

"They might have been following us."

"So?"

Zolar looked at her slyly. "We'll begin by requesting our mercenary friends in local law enforcement to begin earning their money by launching an investigation to find our competitor's base of operations. Once found, we'll follow *them*."

24

DARKNESS WAS ONLY A HALF HOUR AWAY WHEN GIORDINO
set the helicopter down neatly within the white circle
painted on the loading deck of the *Alhambra*. The
deckhands, who simply went by the names of Jesus and
Gato, stood by to push the craft inside the cavernous
auto deck and tie it down.

Loren and Gunn were standing outside the sweep of
the rotor blades. When Giordino cut the ignition switch,
they stepped forward. They were not alone. A man and a
woman moved out of the shadow of the ferry's huge
superstructure and joined them.

Pitt stepped from the helicopter's passenger door and
knitted his thick, black eyebrows in surprise. "I didn't
expect to see you two again, certainly not here."

Dr. Shannon Kelsey smiled, her manner coolly digni-
fied, while Miles Rodgers pumped Pitt's hand in a
genuine show of friendliness. "Hope you don't mind us
popping in like this," said Rodgers.

Giordino exited the helicopter and stared at the new-
comers with interest. "Hail, hail, the gang's all here," he
said in greeting. "Is this a reunion or an old mummy
hunters' convention?"

"Yes, what brings you to our humble ferry in the Sea
of Cortez?" asked Pitt.

"Government agents requested Miles and me to drop everything in Peru and fly here to assist your search," answered Shannon.

Pitt looked at Gunn. "Government agents?"

"They were Customs agents," Miles enlightened Pitt.

"They came to us because of my expertise in Andean culture and artifacts, Miles's reputation as a photographer, and mostly because of our recent involvement with you and NUMA," explained Shannon.

"And you volunteered," Pitt surmised.

Rodgers replied. "When the Customs agents informed us the gang of smugglers we met in the Andes are connected with the family of underground art dealers who are also searching for the treasure, we started packing."

"The Zolars?"

Rodgers nodded. "The possibility we might be of help in trapping Doc Miller's murderer quickly overcame any reluctance to become involved."

"Wait a minute," said Giordino. "The Zolars are involved with Amaru and the *Solpemachaco?*"

Rodgers nodded again. "You weren't told? No one informed you that the *Solpemachaco* and the Zolar family are one and the same?"

"I guess someone forgot," Giordino said caustically. He and Pitt looked at each other as understanding dawned. Each read the other's mind and they silently agreed not to mention their unexpected run-in with Doc Miller's imposter.

"Were you briefed on the instructions we deciphered on the *quipu?*" Pitt asked Shannon, changing the subject.

Shannon nodded. "I was given a full translation."

"By whom?"

"The courier who hand-delivered it was an FBI agent."

Pitt stared at Gunn and then Giordino with deceptive

alm. "The plot thickens. I'm surprised Washington didn't issue press kits about the search to the news media and sell the movie rights to Hollywood."

"If word leaks out," said Giordino, "every treasure hunter between here and the polar icecaps will swarm into the Gulf."

Fatigue began to tighten its grip on Pitt. "I hate to say it," he said slowly, staring at Shannon, "but it looks as if you and Miles made a wasted trip."

Shannon looked at him in surprise. "You haven't found the treasure site?"

"Did someone tell you we had?"

"We were led to believe you had pinned down the location," said Shannon.

"Wishful thinking," said Pitt. "We haven't seen a trace of a stone carving."

"Are you familiar with the symbol marker described by the *quipu?*" Gunn asked Shannon.

"Yes," she replied without hesitation. "The *Demonio del Muertos.*"

Pitt sighed. "The demon of the dead. You told us. I go to the back of the class for not making the connection."

"I remember," said Gunn. "A large grotesque rock sculpture with fangs and described as a Chachapoyan god of the underworld."

"Part jaguar, part condor, part snake, he sank his fangs into whoever disturbed the dead," Pitt added.

"The body and wings have the scales of a lizard," Shannon finished the description.

"Now that you know exactly what you're looking for," Loren said with renewed enthusiasm, "the search should go easier."

"So we know the I.D. of the beast that guards the hoard," said Giordino, bringing the conversation back to earth. "So what? Dirk and I have examined every island that falls within the pattern and we've come up empty. We've exhausted our search area, and what we might have missed our competitors have likely checked off their list too."

"Al's right," Pitt admitted. "We have no place left to search."

"You're sure you've seen no trace of the demon?" asked Rodgers.

Giordino shook his head. "Not so much as a scale or a fang."

Shannon scowled in defeat. "Then the myth is simply that . . . a myth."

"The treasure that never was," murmured Gunn. He collapsed dejectedly on an old wooden passenger's bench. "It's over," he said slowly. "I'll call the admiral and tell him we're closing down the project."

"Our rivals in the seaplane should be cutting bait and flying off into the sunset too," said Giordino.

"To regroup and try again," said Pitt. "They're not the type to fly away from a billion dollars in treasure."

Gunn looked up at him, surprised. "You've seen them?"

"We waved in passing," answered Pitt without going into detail.

"A great disappointment not to catch Doc's killer," Rodgers said sadly. "I also had high hopes of being the first to photograph the treasures and Huascar's golden chain."

Pitt suddenly returned to life, shrugging off the exhaustion and becoming his old cheerful self again. "I can't speak for the rest of you pitiful purveyors of doom, but I'm going to take a bath, grill a steak, get a good night's sleep, and go out in the morning and find that ugly critter guarding the treasure."

They all stared at him as if he had suffered a mental breakdown, all that is except Giordino. He didn't need a third eye to know Pitt was scenting a trail. "Why the about-face?"

"Do you remember when a NUMA search team found that hundred-and-fifty-year-old steamship that belonged to the Republic of Texas navy?"

"Back in 1987, wasn't it? The ship was the *Zavala.*"

"The same. And do you recall *where* it was found?"

"Under a parking lot in Galveston."

"Get the picture?"

"I certainly don't," snapped Shannon. "What are you driving at?"

"Whose turn is it to cook dinner?" Pitt inquired.

Gunn raised a hand. "My night in the galley. Why ask?"

"Because, after we've all enjoyed a good meal, I'll lay out Dirk's master plan."

"Which island have you selected?" Shannon asked cynically. "Bali Ha'i or Atlantis?"

"There is no island," Pitt answered mysteriously. "No island at all. The treasure that never was, but is, sits on dry land."

An hour and a half later, with Giordino standing at the helm, the old ferry reversed course as her paddlewheels drove her northward back toward San Felipe. While Gunn, assisted by Rodgers, prepared dinner in the ferry's galley, Pitt sat on a folding chair down in the engine room, chatting with the chief engineer as he soaked up the sounds, smells, and motion of the *Alhambra's* monstrous engines.

Gordo Padilla smoked the stub of a cigar while wiping a clean cloth over a pair of brass steam gauges. He wore scuffed cowboy boots, a T-shirt covered with bright illustrations of tropical birds, and a pair of pants cut off at the knees. His sleek, well-oiled hair was as thick as marsh grass, and the brown eyes in his round face wandered over the engines as he and Pitt chatted.

"Rosa, my wife," he said, "she thinks I love these engines more than her."

225

"Women have never understood the affection a man can have for a machine," Pitt agreed.

Just then, Jesus dropped down the ladder from the car deck and said something in Spanish to Padilla. He listened, nodded, and looked at Pitt. "Jesus says the lights of a plane have been circling the ferry for the past half hour."

Pitt stared for a moment at the giant crank that turned the paddlewheels. Then he smiled and said briefly, "A good sign."

"A sign of what?" Padilla asked curiously.

"The guys on the other side," he said in a cheery voice. "They've failed and now they hope to follow us to the mother lode. That gives an advantage to our team."

After a hearty dinner on one of the thirty tables in the yawning, unobstructed passengers' section of the ferry, the table was cleared and Pitt spread out a nautical chart and two geological land survey maps. Pitt spoke to them distinctly and precisely, laying out his thoughts so clearly they might have been their own.

"The landscape is not the same. There have been great changes in the past almost five hundred years." He paused and pieced together the three maps, depicting an uninterrupted view of the desert terrain from the upper shore of the Gulf north to the Coachella Valley of California.

"Thousands of years ago the Sea of Cortez used to stretch over the present-day Colorado Desert and Imperial Valley above the Salton Sea. Through the centuries, the Colorado River flooded and carried enormous amounts of silt into the sea. This buildup of silt left behind a large body of water that was later known as Lake Cahuilla, named, I believe, after the Indians who lived on its banks. As you travel around the foothills that rim the basin, you can still see the ancient waterline and find seashells scattered throughout the desert."

"Where did the Salton Sea come from?" asked Shannon.

"In an attempt to irrigate the desert, a canal was built to carry water from the Colorado River. In 1905, after unseasonally heavy rains and much silting, the river burst the banks of the canal and water poured into the lowest part of the desert's basin. A desperate dam operation stopped the flow, but not before enough water had flowed through to form the Salton Sea, with a surface eighty meters below sea level."

Pitt leaned over the maps and drew a circular line through the desert with a red felt-tip pen. "This is approximately where the Gulf extended in the late fourteen hundreds, before the river's silt buildup worked south."

"Less than a kilometer from the present border between the United States and Mexico," observed Rodgers.

"An area now mostly covered by wetlands and mud-flats known as the Laguna Salada."

"How does this swamp fit into the picture?" asked Gunn.

Pitt's face glowed with excitement. "The island where the Incas and the Chachapoyas buried Huascar's golden chain is no longer an island."

As if responding to a drill sergeant's command, everyone leaned over the charts and studied the markings Pitt had made indicating the ancient shoreline. Shannon pointed to a small snake Pitt had drawn that coiled around a high rock outcropping halfway between the marsh and the foothills of the Las Tinajas Mountains.

"What does the snake signify?"

"A kind of 'X marks the spot,'" answered Pitt.

Gunn closely examined the geological survey map. "You've designated a small mountain that, according to the contour elevations, tops out at slightly less than five hundred meters."

"What is it called?" Loren wondered.

"Cerro el Capirote," Pitt answered. "Capirote in English means a tall, pointed ceremonial hat, or what we used to call a dunce cap."

The mood on the passenger deck of the ferry was definitely on the upswing. New hope had been injected into a project that had come within a hair of being written off as a failure. Pitt's unshakable confidence had infected everyone. It was as if all doubt had been thrown overboard. Suddenly, they all took finding the demon perched on the peak of Cerro el Capirote for granted.

If they had the slightest hint that Pitt had reservations, the excitement would have died a quick death. He felt secure in his conclusions, but he was too pragmatic not to harbor a few small doubts.

And then there was the dark side of the coin. He and Giordino had not mentioned that they had identified Doc Miller's killer as one of the other searchers. They both quietly realized that the Zolars or the *Solpemachaco,* whatever devious name they went under in this part of the world, were not aware that the treasure was in Pitt's sights.

Pitt began to picture Tupac Amaru in his mind, the cold, lifeless eyes, and he knew the hunt was about to become ugly and downright dirty.

25

THEY SAILED THE *ALHAMBRA* NORTH OF PUNTA SAN FELIPE and heaved to when her paddlewheels churned up a wake of red silt. A few kilometers ahead, the mouth of the Colorado River, wide and shallow, gaped on the horizon.

Pitt adjusted his safety harness. Shannon was strapped in the copilot's seat and Giordino and Rodgers sat in the rear passenger section of the cabin. He waved goodbye to Gunn and Loren, who were standing on the deck of the ferryboat.

His hands danced over the cyclic and collective pitch sticks as the rotors turned, gathering speed until the whole fuselage shuddered. And then the *Alhambra* was falling away, and he slipped the helicopter sideways across the water like a leaf blown by the wind. Once safely free of the ferry, he gently slipped the cyclic forward and the aircraft began a diagonal climb on a northerly course. At 500 meters (1640 feet) Pitt adjusted the controls and straightened out in level flight.

He flew above the drab waters of the upper Gulf for ten minutes before crossing into the marshlands of the Laguna Salada. A vast section of the flats was flooded from recent rains.

The giant slough was soon left behind as Pitt banked the helicopter across the sand dunes that marched from the mountains to the edge of the Laguna Salada. Now the landscape took on the characteristics of a faded brown moon. Beautiful to the eye but deadly to the body that struggled to survive its horror during the blazing heat of summer.

"There's a blacktop road," announced Shannon, motioning downward.

"Highway Five," said Pitt. "It runs from San Felipe to Mexicali."

"Is this part of the Colorado Desert?" asked Rodgers.

"The desert north of the border is called that because of the Colorado River. In fact this is all part of the Sonoran Desert."

"People actually live down there?" Shannon asked in surprise.

"Mostly Indians," replied Pitt. "The Sonoran Desert is perhaps the most beautiful of all the world's deserts."

Giordino leaned out a side window for a better view and peered into the distance through the trusty binoculars. He patted Pitt on the shoulder. "Your hot spot is coming up off to port."

Pitt nodded, made a slight course change and peered at a solitary mountain rising from the desert floor directly ahead. Cerro el Capirote was aptly named. Though not exactly conical in shape, there was a slight resemblance to a dunce cap with the tip flattened.

"I think I can make out an animal-like sculpture on the summit," observed Giordino.

"I'll descend and hover over it," Pitt acknowledged.

He cut his airspeed, dropped, and swung around the top of the mountain. He approached and circled cautiously, on the watch for sudden downdrafts. Then he hovered the helicopter almost nose-to-nose with the grotesque stone effigy. Mouth agape, it seemed to stare back with the truculent expression of a hungry junkyard dog.

"Step right up, folks," hawked Pitt as if he were a

carnival barker, "and view the astounding demon of the underworld who shuffles cards with his nose and deals 'em with his toes."

"It exists," cried Shannon, flushed with excitement, as they all were. "It truly exists."

"You've got to land," demanded Rodgers. "We must get a closer look."

"Too many high rocks around the sculpture," said Pitt. "I have to find a flat spot to set down."

"There's a small clearing free of boulders about forty meters beyond the demon," Giordino said, pointing through the windscreen over Pitt's shoulder.

Pitt nodded and banked around the towering rock carving so he could make his approach into the wind blowing across the mountain from the west. He reduced speed, eased back the cyclic stick. The turquoise helicopter hovered a moment, flared out, and then settled onto the only open space on the stone summit of Cerro el Capirote.

Giordino was first out, carrying tie-down lines that he attached to the helicopter and wrapped around rock outcroppings. When he completed the operation, he moved in front of the cockpit and drew his hand across his throat. Pitt shut off the engine and the rotor blades wound down.

Rodgers jumped down and offered a hand to Shannon. She hit the ground and took off at a run over the uneven terrain toward the stone effigy. Pitt stepped from the helicopter last, but did not follow the others. He casually raised the binoculars and scanned the sky in the direction of the faint sound of an aircraft engine. The seaplane was only a silver speck against a dome of blue. The pilot had maintained an altitude of 2000 meters (6500 feet) in an attempt to remain unseen. But Pitt was not fooled. His intuition told him he was being tailed the instant he lifted off from the *Alhambra*. Spotting the enemy only confirmed his suspicions.

Before he joined the others already gathered around the stone beast, he took a moment and stepped to the edge of the craggy wall and stared down. Satisfaction swelled within him. He had made a good call. The ancients had indeed selected an imposing spot to hide their treasure.

When he finally approached the huge stone beast, Shannon was making detailed measurements of the jaguar body while Rodgers busied himself shooting roll after roll of photos. Giordino appeared intent on searching around the pedestal for a trace of the entrance to the passageway leading down into the mountain.

"The ancients must have had a strange sense of humor to create a god whose looks could sour milk," Pitt said.

"The legend is vague but it contends that a condor laid an egg that was eaten and vomited by a jaguar. A snake was hatched from the egg and slithered into the sea where it grew fish scales. The rest of the mythological account says that because the beast was so ugly and shunned by the other gods who thrived in the sun, it lived underground where it eventually became the guardian of the dead."

"The original ugly duckling fairy tale."

"He's hideous," Shannon said solemnly, "and yet I can't help feeling a deep sadness for him. I don't know if I can explain it properly, but the stone seems to have a life of its own—"

Pitt interrupted her by abruptly raising a hand for silence. "You hear something, a strange sound like someone crying?"

She cocked an ear and listened, then shook her head. "I only hear the shutter and automatic winding mechanism on Miles's camera."

The eerie sound Pitt thought he heard was gone. He grinned. "Probably the wind."

Pitt left Shannon and Miles to their work and walked over to Giordino, who was tapping the rock around the beast's pedestal with a miner's pick. "See any hint of a passage?" Pitt asked.

"Not unless the ancients discovered a method for fusing rock," answered Giordino. "This big gargoyle is carved from an immense slab of solid granite that forms the core of the mountain. I can't find a telltale crack anywhere around the statue's base. If there's a passage, it has to be somewhere else on the mountain."

Pitt tilted his head, listening. "There it is again."

"You mean that banshee wail?"

"You heard it?" Pitt asked in surprise.

"I figured it was just wind whistling through the rocks."

"There isn't any wind."

A curious look crossed Giordino's face as he wetted one index finger with his tongue and tested the air. "You're right. Nary a stir."

"It's not a steady sound," said Pitt. "I only notice it at intervals."

"I picked up on that too. It comes like a puff of breath for about ten seconds and then fades for nearly a minute."

Pitt nodded happily. "Could it be we're describing a vent to a cavern?"

"Let's see if we can find it," Giordino suggested eagerly.

Like clockwork, the strange wail came and went. Pitt waited until he heard three sequences. Then he motioned for Giordino to move along the north side of the peak. No reply was necessary, no words passed between them. They had been close friends since they were children and had maintained close contact during their years together in the Air Force. When Pitt joined NUMA at Admiral Sandecker's request twelve years ago, Giordino went with him. Over time they learned to respond to each other without needless talk.

Giordino moved down a steep slope for about 20 meters (65 feet) before stopping. He paused and listened while awaiting Pitt's next gesture. The dismal wail came stronger to him than it did to Pitt. But he knew that the sound reverberated off the boulders and was distorted. He didn't hesitate when Pitt motioned him away from where it sounded loudest and pointed to a spot where the side of the peak suddenly dropped off in a narrow chute 10 meters (33 feet) deep.

While Giordino was lying on his stomach surveying a way down to the bottom of the chute, Pitt came over, crouched beside him, and held out a hand, palm down.

The wail came again and Pitt nodded, his lips parting in a tight smile. "I can feel a draft. Something deep inside the mountain is causing air to be expelled from a vent."

"I'll get the rope and flashlight from the chopper," said Giordino, rising to his feet and trotting toward the aircraft. In two minutes he was back with Shannon and Miles.

Her eyes fairly sparkled with anticipation. "Al says you found a way inside the mountain."

Pitt nodded. "We'll know shortly."

Giordino tied one end of a nylon line around a large rock. "Who gets the honor?"

"I'll toss you for it," said Pitt.

"Heads."

Pitt flipped a quarter and watched as it clinked and spun to a stop on a small, flat surface between two massive boulders. "Tails, you lose."

Giordino shrugged without complaint, knotted a loop and passed it over and then under Pitt's shoulders. "Never mind bedazzling me with mountain climbing tricks. I'll let you down, and I'll pull you up."

Pitt accepted the fact his friend's strength was greater than his own. Giordino's body may have been short but his shoulders were broad, and his muscled arms were a match for a professional wrestler.

"Mind you don't get rope burn," Pitt cautioned him.

"Mind you don't break a leg, or I'll leave you for the gargoyle," said Giordino, handing Pitt the flashlight. Then he slowly paid out the line, lowering Pitt between the walls of the narrow chute.

When Pitt's feet touched the bottom, he looked up. "Okay, I'm down."

"What do you see?"

"A small cleft in the rock wall just large enough to crawl through. I'm going in."

"Don't remove the rope. There could be a sharp drop just inside the entrance."

Pitt lay on his stomach and wormed through the narrow fissure. It was a tight squeeze for 3 meters (10 feet) before the entryway widened enough so he could stand. He switched on the flashlight and swung its beam along the walls. The light showed he was at the head of a passageway that appeared to lead down into the bowels of the mountain. The floor was smooth with steps hewn into the rock every few paces.

Dank air rushed past him like the steamy breath of a giant. He moved his fingertips over the rock walls. They came away wet with moisture. Driven by curiosity, Pitt moved along the passageway until the nylon became taut and he was stopped from venturing further. He aimed the light ahead into the darkness. The cold hand of fear gripped him around the neck as a pair of eyes flashed back at him.

There, upon a pedestal of black rock, seemingly sculpted by the same hand as the demon on the mountain peak above, glaring toward the entrance to the passage, was another, smaller *Demonio del Muertos*. This one was inlaid with turquoise stone and had white, polished quartz for teeth and red gemstones for eyes.

Pitt thought seriously of casting off the rope and exploring further. But he felt it wouldn't be fair to the others. They should all be in on the discovery of the treasure chamber together. Reluctantly, he returned to the crack in the wall and squirmed back into daylight.

When Giordino helped him over the edge of the chute, Shannon and Rodgers were waiting in hushed expectation.

"What did you see?" Shannon blurted, unable to contain her excitement. "Tell us what you found!"

Pitt stared at her without expression for a moment, then broke into an elated grin. "The entrance to the treasure is guarded by another demon, but otherwise the way looks clear."

Everyone shouted in elation. Shannon and Rodgers hugged and kissed. Giordino slapped Pitt on the back so hard it jarred his molars. Intense curiosity seized them as they peered over the edge of the chute at the small opening leading inside the mountain.

"How wide is the opening?" asked Rodgers.

"Dr. Kelsey might make it through on her hands and knees, but we boys will have to snake our way in."

Shannon eagerly slipped down the rope as smoothly as if she did it twice a day and crawled into the narrow aperture in the rock. Rodgers went next, followed by Giordino, with Pitt bringing up the rear.

Giordino turned to Pitt. "If I get caught in a cave-in, you will dig me out."

"Not before I dial nine-one-one."

Shannon and Rodgers had already moved out of sight down the stone steps and were examining the second *Demonio del Muertos* when Pitt and Giordino caught up to them.

They finished their brief examination of the remarkable relic of antiquity and continued along the passageway. The damp air that came up from below drew the sweat through their pores. Despite the humidity they had to be careful they didn't step too heavily or their footsteps raised clouds of choking dust.

"They must have taken years to carve this tunnel," said Rodgers.

Pitt reached up and ran his fingers lightly over the limestone roof. "I doubt they excavated it from scratch. They probably hollowed out an existing fissure. Whoever they were, they weren't short."

"How can you tell?"

"The roof. We don't have to stoop. It's a good foot above our heads."

Rodgers gestured at a large plate set on an angle in a wall niche. "This is the third one of these things I've seen since we entered. What do you suppose their purpose was?"

Shannon rubbed away the centuries-old coating of dust and saw her reflection on a shining surface. "Highly polished silver reflectors," she explained. "The same system used by the ancient Egyptians for lighting interior galleries. The sun striking a reflector at the entrance bounced from reflector to reflector throughout the chambers and illuminated them without the smoke and soot given off by oil lamps."

"I wonder if they knew they were paving the way for environmentally friendly technology?" murmured Pitt randomly.

The echoing sound of their footsteps spread ahead and behind them like ripples on a pond. It was an eerie, claustrophobic sensation, knowing they were entering the dead heart of the mountain. The stagnant air became so thick and heavy with moisture it dampened the dust on their clothing. Fifty meters (164 feet) later they entered a small cavern with a long gallery.

The chamber was nothing less than a catacomb, honeycombed with crypts hewn into the walls. The mummies of twenty men, wrapped tightly in beautifully embroidered woolen mantles, lay head to toe. They were the remains of the guards who faithfully guarded the treasure, even after death, waiting for the return of their countrymen from an empire that no longer existed.

"These people were huge," said Pitt. "They must have stood two hundred and eight centimeters or six foot ten inches tall."

"A pity they aren't around to play in the NBA," muttered Giordino.

Shannon closely examined the design on the mantles. "Legends claim the Chachapoyas were as tall as trees."

Pitt scanned the chamber. "One missing."

Rodgers looked at him. "Who?"

"The last man, the one who tended to the burial of the guardians who went before."

Beyond the gallery of death they came to a larger chamber that Shannon quickly identified as the living quarters of the guardians before they died. A wide, circular stone table with a surrounding bench rose out of the floor that formed their base. The table had evidently been used to eat on. The bones of a large bird still rested on a silver platter that sat on the smoothly polished stone surface along with ceramic drinking vessels. Beds had been chiseled into the walls, some still with woolen covers neatly folded in the middle. Rodgers caught sight of something bright lying on the floor. He picked it up and held it under the light of the Coleman.

"What is it?" asked Shannon.

"A massive gold ring, plain, with no engravings."

"An encouraging sign," said Pitt. "We must be getting close to the main vault."

Shannon hurried off ahead of the men through another portal at the far end of the guardians' living quarters that led into a cramped tunnel with an arched ceiling, similar to an ancient cistern wide enough for only one person to pass through at a time. This passageway seemed to wind down through the mountain for an eternity.

"How far do you think we've come?" asked Giordino.

"My feet feel like ten kilometers," Shannon answered, suddenly weary.

Pitt had paced the distance they'd traveled down the stone steps since leaving the crypts. "The peak of Cerro el Capirote is only five hundred meters above sea level. I'd guess we've reached the desert floor and dropped twenty or thirty meters below it."

They descended along the tunnel another ten minutes when Shannon suddenly stopped and held up a hand. "Listen!" she commanded. "I hear something."

After a few moments, Giordino said, "Sounds like someone left a tap on."

"A rushing stream or a river," Pitt said softly, recalling the old café owner's words.

As they moved closer, the sound of the moving water increased and reverberated within the confined space. The air had cooled considerably and smelled pure and less stifling. They rushed forward, anxiously hoping each bend in the passage was the last. And then the walls abruptly spread into the darkness and they rushed headlong into what seemed like a vast cathedral that revealed the mountain as hollow.

Shannon screamed a full-fledged shriek that echoed through the chamber as if intensified by huge rock concert amplifiers.

Giordino, not one to scare easily, looked as if he'd seen a ghost.

Rodgers stood petrified, his outstretched arm frozen like an iron support, holding the Coleman lantern they had brought. "What is it?" he finally gasped, hypnotized by the ghostly apparition that rose in front of them and glistened under the bright light.

Pitt's heart pumped a good five liters of adrenaline through his system, but he remained calm and surveyed the towering figure that looked like a monstrosity out of a science fiction horror movie.

The huge specter was a ghastly sight. Standing straight
the apparition towered above them, its grisly features
displaying grinning teeth, its eye sockets wide open. Pitt
judged the horror to be a good head taller than him.
High above one shoulder, a bony hand held an ornate
battle club with a notched edge. Then Pitt determined
what it was.

The last guardian of Huascar's treasure had been
frozen for all time into a stalagmite.

"How did he get like that?" Rodgers asked in awe.

Pitt pointed to the roof of the cavern. "Ground water
dripping from the limestone ceiling released carbon
dioxide that splattered on the guardian and eventually
covered him with a thick coating of calcite crystals. In
time, he was encased like a scorpion inside a gift shop
acrylic resin paperweight."

"But how in the world could he die and remain in an
upright position?" queried Shannon, coming out of her
initial fright.

Pitt ran his hand lightly over the crystallized mantle.
"We'll never know unless we chisel him out of his
transparent tomb. It seems incredible, but knowing he
was dying he must have constructed a support to prop
him in a standing position with his arm raised, and then
he took his life, probably by poison."

"These guys took their jobs seriously," muttered Giordino.

As if drawn by some mysterious force, Shannon
moved within a few centimeters of the hideous wonder
and stared up into the distorted face beneath the crystals. "The height, the blond hair. He was Chachapoya,
one of the Cloud People."

"He's a long way from home," said Pitt. He held up
his wrist and checked the time. "Two and a half hours to
go before the Coleman runs out of gas. We'd better keep
moving."

Though it didn't seem possible, the immense grotto

spread into the distance until their light beams barely revealed the great arched ceiling, far larger than any conceived or built by man. The babbling brook sound they had heard farther back in the passageway they now saw was the rush of water around the rockbound banks of a long, low island that protruded from the middle of the river.

But it was not the discovery of an extraordinary unknown river flowing far beneath the floor of the desert that captivated and enthralled them. It was a dazzling sight no ordinary imagination could ever conceive. There, stacked neatly on the level top of the island, rose a mountain of golden artifacts.

The effect of two flashlights and the Coleman lantern on the golden hoard left the explorers speechless.

Here was Huascar's golden chain coiled in a great spiral 10 meters in height. Here also was the great gold disk from the Temple of the Sun, beautifully crafted and set with hundreds of precious stones. There were golden plants, water lilies and corn, and solid gold sculptures of kings and gods, women, llamas, and dozens upon dozens of ceremonial objects, beautifully formed and inlaid with huge emeralds. Here also, stacked as if inside a moving van, were tons of golden statues, furniture, tables, chairs, and beds, all handsomely engraved. The centerpiece was a huge throne made from solid gold inlaid with silver flowers.

Nor was this all. Arranged row after row, standing like phantoms, their mummies encased in golden shells, were twelve generations of Inca royalty. Beside each one lay his armor and headdresses and exquisitely woven clothing.

"In my wildest dreams," Shannon murmured softly, "I never envisioned a collection this vast."

Giordino and Rodgers were both paralyzed with astonishment. No words came from either one of them. They could only gape.

241

"Any chance we can get over to the island so I can study the artifacts?" asked Shannon.

"I'll need to get closeups," added Rodgers.

"Not unless you can walk across thirty meters of rushing water," said Giordino.

Pitt scanned the cavern by sweeping his light along the barren floor. "Looks like the Chachapoyas and the Incas took their bridge with them. You'll have to do your study and shoot your pictures of the treasure from here."

"I'll use my telephoto and pray my flash carries that far," said Rodgers hopefully.

"What do you suppose all this is worth?" asked Giordino.

"You'd have to weigh it," said Pitt, "figure in the current market price of gold, and then triple your total for the value as rare artifacts."

"I'm certain the treasure is worth double what the experts estimated," said Shannon.

Giordino looked at her. "That would be as high as three hundred million dollars?"

Shannon nodded. "Maybe even more."

"It isn't worth a good baseball card," remarked Pitt, "until it's brought to the surface. Not an easy job to barge the larger pieces, including the chain, off an island surrounded by a rushing flow of water, and then haul them up a narrow passageway to the top of the mountain. From there, you'll need a heavy transport helicopter just to carry the golden chain."

"You're talking a major operation," said Rodgers.

Pitt held his light on the great coiled chain. "Nobody said it was going to be easy. Besides, bringing out the treasure isn't our problem."

Shannon gave him a questioning stare. "Oh, no? Then who do you expect to do it?"

Pitt stared back. "Have you forgotten? We're supposed to stand aside and hand it over to our old pals from the *Solpemachaco.*"

The thought had slipped her mind after gazing enthralled at the wealth of golden artifacts. "An outrage," Shannon said furiously. "The archaeological discovery of the century, and I can't direct the recovery program."

"Why don't you lodge a complaint?" said Pitt.

She glared at him, puzzled. "What are you talking about?"

"Let the competition know how you feel."

"How?"

"Leave them a message."

"You're crazy."

"That observation has been cropping up quite a bit lately," said Giordino.

Pitt took the rope slung over Giordino's shoulder and made a loop. Then he twirled the rope like a lariat and threw the loop across the water, smiling triumphantly as it settled over the head of a small golden monkey on a pedestal.

"Ah, ha!" he uttered proudly. "Will Rogers had nothing on me."

26

WHEN PITT HOVERED THE HELICOPTER ABOVE THE *ALHAM-bra*, no one stood on the deck to greet the craft and its passengers. The ferry looked deserted. The auto deck was empty, as was the wheelhouse. To all appearances, she looked like a ship that had been abandoned by her crew.

The sea was calm and there was no pitch or roll. Pitt lowered the helicopter onto the wood deck and shut down the engines as soon as the tires touched down. He sat there as the sound of the turbine and rotor blades slowly died into a morbid silence. He waited a full minute but no one appeared. He opened the entry door and dropped to the deck. Then he stood there waiting for something to happen.

Finally, a man stepped from behind a stairwell and approached, coming to a halt about 5 meters from the chopper. Even without the phony white hair and beard, Pitt easily recognized the man who had impersonated Dr. Steven Miller in Peru. He was smiling as if he'd caught a record fish.

"A little off your beat, aren't you?" said Pitt, unruffled.

"You seem to be my never-ending nemesis, Mr. Pitt."

"A quality that thrills me no end. What name are you going under today?"

244

"Not that it's of use to you, but I am Cyrus Sarason."

"I can't say I'm pleased to see you again."

Sarason moved closer, peering over Pitt's shoulder at the interior of the helicopter. His face lost the gloating smile and twisted into tense concern. "You are alone? Where are the others?"

"What others?" Pitt asked innocently.

"Dr. Kelsey, Miles Rodgers, and your friend, Albert Giordino."

"Since you have the passenger list memorized, you tell me."

"Please, Mr. Pitt, you would do well not to toy with me," Sarason warned him.

"They were hungry, so I dropped them off at a seafood restaurant in San Felipe."

"You're lying."

Pitt didn't take his gaze off Sarason to scan the decks of the ferry. Guns were trained on him. That was a certainty he knew without question. He stood his ground and faced Miller's killer as if he didn't have a care in the world.

"So sue me," Pitt retorted, and laughed.

"You're hardly in a position to be contemptuous," Sarason said coldly. "Perhaps you don't realize the seriousness of your situation."

"I think I do," said Pitt, still smiling. "You want Huascar's treasure, and you'd murder half the good citizens of Mexico to get it."

"Fortunately, that won't be necessary. I do admit, however, two-thirds of a billion dollars makes an enticing incentive."

"Aren't you interested in knowing how and why we were conducting our search at the same time as yours?" asked Pitt.

It was Sarason's turn to laugh. "After a little persuasion, Mr. Gunn and Congresswoman Smith were most cooperative in telling me about Drake's *quipu*."

"Not very smart, torturing a United States legislato: and the deputy director of a national science agency."

"But effective, nonetheless."

"Where are my friends and the ferry's crew?"

"I wondered when you'd get around to that question.'

"Do you want to work out a deal?" Pitt didn't miss the predator's eyes staring unblinkingly in an attempt to intimidate. He stared back.

Sarason shook his head. "I see no reason why I should bargain. You have nothing to trade. You're obviously not a man I can trust. And I have all the chips. In short, Mr Pitt, you have lost the game before you draw your cards."

"Then you can afford to be a magnanimous winner and produce my friends."

Sarason made a thoughtful shrug, raised his hand, and made a beckoning gesture. "The least I can do before I hang some heavy weights on you and drop you over the side."

Four burly dark-skinned men, who looked like bouncers hired from local cantinas, prodded the captives from the passageway with automatic rifles, and lined them up on the deck behind Sarason.

Gordo Padilla came first, followed by Jesus, Gato, and the assistant engineer. The bruises and dried blood on their faces showed that they had been knocked around but were not hurt seriously. Gunn had not gotten off so lightly. He had to be half dragged from the passageway. He had been beaten, and Pitt could see the blotches of blood on his shirt and the crude rags wrapped around his hands. Then Loren was standing there, her face drawn and her lips and cheeks swollen and puffed up as though stung by bees. Yet she still held her head proudly and shook off the guards' hands as they roughly pushed her forward. Her expression was one of defiance until she saw Pitt standing there.

"Oh, no, Dirk!" she exclaimed. "They've got you too."

Gunn painfully raised his head and muttered through lips that were split and bleeding. "I tried to warn you, but . . ."

Sarason smiled, unfeeling. "I think what Mr. Gunn means to say is that he and your crew were overpowered by my men after they kindly allowed us to board your ferry from a chartered fishing boat after begging to borrow your radio."

Pitt's anger came within a millimeter of driving him to inflict pain on those who had brutalized his friends. He took a deep breath to regain control. He swore under his breath that the man standing in front of him would pay. Not now. But the time would surely come if he didn't try anything foolish.

He glanced casually toward the nearest railing, gauging its distance and height. Then he turned back to Sarason.

"I don't like big, tough men who beat up defenseless women," he said conversationally. "And for what purpose? The location of the treasure is no secret to you."

"Then it's true," Sarason said with a pleased expression. "You found the beast that guards the gold on the top of Cerro el Capirote."

"If you had dropped for a closer look instead of playing peekaboo in the clouds, you'd have seen the beast for yourself."

Pitt's last words brought a flicker of curiosity to the beady eyes.

"You were aware you were being followed?" asked Sarason.

"It goes without saying that you would have searched for our helicopter after our chance meeting in the air yesterday. My guess is you checked out landing fields on both sides of the Gulf last night and asked questions

until someone in San Felipe innocently pointed the wa
to our ferry."

"You're very astute."

"Not really. I made the mistake of overestimating you
I didn't think you'd act like a reckless amateur and begin
mutilating the competition. An act that was completel
unwarranted."

Puzzlement filled Sarason's eyes. "What goes on here
Pitt?"

"All part of the plan," answered Pitt almost jovially
"I purposely led you to the jackpot."

"A barefaced lie."

"You've been set up, pal. Get wise. Why do you think
let off Dr. Kelsey, Rodgers, and Giordino before
returned to the ferry? To keep them out of your dirty
hands, that's why."

Sarason said slowly, "You couldn't have known we
were going to capture your boat before you came
back."

"Not with any certainty. Let's say my intuition was
working overtime. That and the fact my radio calls to the
ferry went unanswered."

A shrewd hyenalike look slowly spread across Sara
son's face. "Nice try, Pitt. You'd make an excellent
writer of children's stories."

"You don't believe me?" Pitt asked, as if surprised.

"Not a word."

"What are you going to do with us?"

Sarason looked disgustingly cheerful. "You're more
naive than I gave you credit for. You know full well
what's going to happen to you."

Sarason looked at the setting sun. "It's getting late in
the day. I think we've chatted long enough." He turned
and spoke a name that sent a shiver through Pitt.
"Tupac. Come and say hello to the man who made you a
cripple."

Tupac Amaru stepped from behind one of the guards and stood in front of Pitt, his teeth set and grinning like a skull on a pirate's Jolly Roger flag. He had the joyful look of a butcher sizing up a slab of prime, specially aged beef.

"I told you I would make you suffer as you made me," Amaru said ominously.

Pitt studied the evil face with a strangely paralyzed intensity. He didn't need a football coach to diagram what was in store for him. He braced his body to begin the scheme he had formed in the back of his mind right after he had stepped out of the helicopter. He moved toward Loren, but stepped slightly sideways and inconspicuously began to hyperventilate.

"If you are the one who harmed Congresswoman Smith, you will die as surely as you stand there with that stupid look on your face."

Sarason laughed. "No, no. You, Mr. Pitt, are not going to kill anybody."

"Neither are you. Even in Mexico you'd hang if there was a witness to your executions."

"I'd be the first to admit it." Sarason surveyed Pitt inquiringly. "But what witness are you talking about?" He paused to sweep an arm around the empty sea. "As you can see, the nearest land is empty desert almost twenty kilometers away, and the only vessel in sight is our fishing boat standing off the starboard bow."

Pitt tilted his head up and stared at the wheelhouse. "What about the ferryboat's pilot?"

All the heads turned as one, all that is except Gunn's. He nodded unobserved at Pitt and then raised a hand, pointing at the empty pilothouse. "Hide, Pedro!" he cried loudly. "Run and hide."

Three seconds were all Pitt needed. Three seconds

to run four steps and leap over the railing into the
sea.

Two of the guards caught the sudden movement from
the edge of their vision, whirled and fired one quick
burst from their automatic rifles on reflex. But they fired
high, and they fired late. Pitt had struck the water and
vanished into the murky depths.

27

PITT HIT THE WATER STROKING AND KICKING WITH THE
fervor of someone possessed. An Olympic committee of
judges would have been impressed; he must have set a
new world record for the underwater dash. The water
was warm but the visibility below the surface was less
than a meter due to the murk caused by silt flowing in
from the Colorado River. The blast of the gunfire was
magnified by the density of the water and sounded like
an artillery barrage to Pitt's ears.

The bullets struck and penetrated the sea with the
unlikely sound of a zipper being closed. Pitt leveled out
when his hands scoured the bottom, causing an eruption
of fine silt. He recalled learning during his U.S. Air Force
days that a bullet's velocity was spent after traveling a
meter and a half (5 feet) through water. Beyond that
depth, it sank harmlessly to the seafloor.

When the light above the surface went dark, he knew
he had passed under the port side of the *Alhambra*'s hull.
His timing was lucky. It was approaching high tide and
the ferryboat was now riding two meters off the bottom.

He swam slowly and steadily, exhaling a small amount
of air from his lungs, angling on a course astern that he
hoped would bring him up on the starboard side near the

big paddlewheels. His oxygen intake was nearly exhausted, and he began to see a darkening fuzziness creeping around the borders of his vision, when the shadow of the ferry abruptly ended and he could see a bright surface again.

He broke into air 2 meters (6.5 feet) abaft of the sheltered interior of the starboard paddlewheel. There was no question of his risking exposure. It was that or drown. The question was whether Sarason's goons had predicted what his game plan would be and run over from the opposite side of the vessel. He could still hear sporadic gunfire striking the water on the port side, and his hopes rose. They weren't on to him, at least not yet.

Pitt sucked in hurried breaths of pure air while getting his bearings. And then he was diving under the temporary safety of the ferry's huge paddlewheels. He lifted his head above the water.

Pitt hung on to one of the floats and waited as a small school of nosy spotted sand bass circled around his legs. He was not completely out of the woods yet. There was an access door for crewmen to perform maintenance on the paddlewheel. He decided to remain in the water.

He could hear footsteps running on the auto deck above, accented by an occasional burst of gunfire. Pitt couldn't see anything, but he didn't need a lecture to know what Sarason's men were doing. They were roving around the open decks above, shooting at anything that vaguely resembled a body under the water. He could hear voices shouting, but the words came muffled. No large fish within a radius of 50 meters (164 feet) survived the bombardment.

The click of the lock on the access door came as he had expected. He slipped deeper into the water until only half his head was exposed but he was still hidden to anyone above by one of the huge floats.

He could not see the unshaven face that peered downward through the paddlewheel at the water, but this time he heard a voice loud and clear from behind the intruder at the door, a voice he had come to know too well. He could feel the hairs stiffen on the nape of his neck at hearing the words spoken by Amaru.

"See any sign of him?"

"Nothing down here but fish," grunted the searcher in the access door, catching sight of the spotted sand bass.

"He didn't surface away from the ship. If he's not dead, he must be hiding somewhere underneath the ship."

"I won't feel satisfied until I see the body," said Amaru in a businesslike tone.

"Back to the forward boarding ramp," Amaru ordered. "The fishing boat is returning."

Pitt could hear the diesel throb and feel the beat of the fishing boat's propellers through the water as it pulled alongside to take off Sarason and his mercenary scum.

Nearly an hour passed before he sensed the sounds of the fishing boat die in the distance. This was followed by the beating rotor of a helicopter lifting off the ferry, indisputably the NUMA helicopter. Another gift to the criminals, Pitt thought angrily.

Darkness had fallen and no lights reflected on the water. Pitt wondered why the men on the upper decks had taken so long to evacuate the vessel. His absolute conviction was that one or more would be left behind to take care of him in the event the dead came back to life. Amaru and Sarason could not kill the others unless they knew with cold certainty that Pitt was dead and could tell no tales to the authorities, especially the news media.

He turned and swam slowly toward the end of the ferryboat where he had left the helicopter. He took the risk of being seen by surfacing briefly alongside the hull beneath the deck overhang to take another breath. After nearly an hour and a half's immersion, he felt waterlogged. He did not feel overly fatigued, but he sensed his strength was reduced by a good 20 percent. He slipped under the hull again and made for the shallow rudders fitted on the end. They soon loomed out of the murky water. He reached out and gripped one and slowly raised his face out of the water.

No leering face stared back, no guns aimed between his eyes. He hung on to the rudder and floated, relaxing and building back his strength. He listened, but no sound came from the auto deck above.

Finally, he pulled himself up far enough to lift his eyes over the raised edge of the entry/exit ramp. The *Alhambra* was in complete darkness with neither interior nor exterior lights showing. Her decks appeared still and lifeless. As he suspected, the NUMA helicopter was gone. The tingling fear of the unknown traveled up his spine.

This wasn't one of his better days, Pitt thought. His friends were captured and held hostage. They might be dead. A thought he refused to dwell on. He'd lost another NUMA aircraft. Stolen by the very criminals he was supposed to entice into a trap. The ferryboat was sinking beneath him and he was dead certain one or more killers were lurking somewhere on board to exact a terrible revenge.

How long he hung on the rudder he couldn't be sure. Maybe five minutes, maybe fifteen. His eyes were accustomed to the dark, but all he could see inside the big auto deck was the dim reflection of the chrome bumpers and radiator grill of the Pierce Arrow. He hung there waiting to see a movement or hear the faint sound of stealth. The deck that stretched into the gaping cavern looked frightening. But he had to enter it if he wanted a weapon, he thought nervously, any weapon to protect himself from men who intended to turn him into sushi.

Unless Amaru's men had made a professional search of the old Travelodge, they wouldn't have found the Colt .45 automatic where Pitt kept it in the vegetable drawer of the refrigerator.

He gripped the deck overhang and heaved himself on board. It took Pitt all of five seconds to run across the deck, sweep the door of the trailer against its stops, and leap inside. In a clockwork motion, he tore open the door to the refrigerator and pulled open the vegetable drawer. The Colt automatic lay where he'd left it. For a brief instant relief washed over him like a waterfall as he gripped the trusty weapon in his hand.

His feeling of deliverance was short-lived. The Colt felt light in his hand, too light. He pulled back the slide and ejected the magazine. It and the firing chamber were empty. With mushrooming despair and desperation he checked the drawer beside the stove that held the kitchen knives. They were gone, along with all the silverware. The only weapon in the trailer was the seemingly useless Colt automatic.

Cat and mouse.

They were out there all right. Pitt now knew Amaru was going to take his time and toy with his prey before dismembering him and throwing the pieces over the side. Pitt treated himself to a few moments for strategy. He sat down in the dark on the trailer's bed and calmly began planning his next moves.

If any of the killers were haunting the auto deck, they could easily have shot, knifed, or bashed Pitt with a club during his dash to the trailer. For that matter, there was nothing stopping them from breaking in and ending it here. Amaru was a sly hombre, Pitt grudgingly admitted to himself. The South American had guessed Pitt was still alive and would head for any available weapon at the first opportunity. Searching the trailer and finding the gun was shrewd. Removing the bullets but leaving the gun in its place was downright sadistic. That was merely the first step in a game of torment and misery before the final deathblow. Amaru intended to make Pitt twist in the wind before he killed him.

First things first, Pitt decided. Ghouls were lurking in

the dark all right, ghouls who wanted to murder him. They thought he was as defenseless as a baby, and he was on a sinking ship with nowhere to go. And that was precisely what he wanted them to think.

If Amaru was in no rush, neither was he.

Pitt leisurely removed his wet clothes and soggy shoes and toweled himself dry. Next he donned a dark gray pair of pants, a black cotton sweatshirt, and a pair of sneakers. Then he made and calmly ate a peanut butter sandwich and drank two glasses of Crystal Light. Feeling rejuvenated, he pulled open a small drawer beneath the bed and checked the contents of a leather gun pouch. The spare magazine was gone, just as he knew it would be. But a small flashlight was there, and in one corner of the drawer he found a small plastic bottle with a label advertising its contents as vitamin supplement A, C, and beta carotene. He shook the bottle and grinned like a happy camper when it rattled.

He unscrewed the lid and poured eight .45-caliber bullets into his hand. Things are looking up, he thought. Amaru's cunning fell a notch below perfection. Just one more manifestation of Pitt's law, he thought: "Every villain has a plan with at least one flaw."

Pitt glanced at his watch. Nearly twenty minutes had passed since he entered the trailer. He rummaged through a clothing drawer until he found a dark blue ski mask and slipped it over his head. Next he found his Swiss army knife in the pocket of a pair of pants thrown over a chair.

He pulled a small ring in the floor and raised a trapdoor he'd built into the trailer for additional storage space. He lifted out the storage box, set it aside and squirmed through the narrow opening left in the floor. Lying on the deck beneath the trailer, he peered into the darkness and listened. Not a sound. His unseen hunters were patient men.

Coldly and deliberately, Pitt rolled from under the

trailer and moved like a phantom through a nearby open hatch down a companion ladder into the engine room.

The engine room looked deserted, but then he tensed. There was a soft mumbling sound like somebody trying to talk through a gag. Pitt swung the beam of the flashlight up into the giant A-frames that supported the walking beam. Someone was up there. Four of them were up there.

Gordo Padilla, his assistant engineer, Jesus and Gato, all hung upside down, tightly bound and gagged with duct tape, their eyes pleading. Pitt pried open the largest blade of the Swiss army knife and quickly cut them down, freeing their hands and allowing them to pull the tape from their mouths.

"Muchas gracias, amigo," Padilla gasped. "They were going to cut our throats like sheep."

"When did you see them last?" asked Pitt softly.

"No more than ten minutes ago. They could return at any second."

"You've got to get away from the boat."

Padillo's face lit up under the beam of the flashlight. "There is a small six-man raft tied to the railing near the galley."

"You'd better hope it still floats." He handed Padilla his knife. "Take this to cut away the raft."

"What about you? Aren't you coming with us?"

"Give me ten minutes to conduct a quick search of the ship for the others. If I've found no sign of them by then, you and your crew get free in the raft while I create a diversion."

Padilla embraced Pitt. "Luck be with you."

It was time to move on.

Before he traveled to the upper decks, Pitt dropped into the water that was rapidly filling the bilges and turned off the valves of the seacocks. He decided against climbing back up the companion ladder or using a stairway. He had the uneasy feeling that somehow Amaru was following his every move. He climbed up the engine to the top of the steam cylinder and then took a Jacob's ladder to the top of the A-frame before stepping off onto the top deck of the ferry just aft of its twin smokestacks.

Pitt felt no fear of Amaru. Pitt had won the first round in Peru because Amaru wrote him off as a dead man after dropping the safety line into the sacred pool. The South American killer was not infallible. He would err again because his mind was clouded with hate and revenge.

Pitt worked his way down after searching both pilothouses. He found no sign of Loren or Rudi in the vast passenger seating section, the galley, or the crew's quarters. The search went quickly.

Never knowing who or what he might encounter in the dark, or when, Pitt investigated most of the ship on his hands and knees, scurrying from nook to cranny like a crab, using whatever cover was available. The ship seemed as deserted as a cemetery, but by no stretch of his imagination did he believe for a moment the killers had abandoned the ship.

The rules had not changed. Loren and Rudi Gunn had been removed from the ferry alive because Sarason had a reasonably good hunch Pitt was still alive. The mistake was trusting the murder to a man fired with vengeance. Amaru was too sick with hate to take Pitt out cleanly. Loren and Rudi Gunn had a sword hanging over their heads, but it wouldn't fall until the word went out that Pitt was absolutely and convincingly terminated.

The ten minutes were up. There was nothing left for him but to cause a distraction so Padilla and his crew could paddle the raft into the darkness. Once he was certain they were away Pitt would try to swim to shore.

What saved him in the two seconds after he detected the soft sounds of bare feet padding across the deck was a lightning fall to his hands and knees. It was an obsolete football tackle that no longer worked with more sophisticated training techniques. The movement was pure reflex. If he had swung around, flicked on the flashlight and squeezed the trigger at the dark mass that burst out of the night, he would have lost both hands and his head under the blade of a machete that sliced the air like an aircraft propeller.

The man that tore out of the dark could not halt his forward momentum. His knees struck Pitt's crouching body and he flew forward out of control as if launched by a huge spring and crashed heavily onto the deck, the machete spinning over the side. Rolling to one side, Pitt beamed the light on his assailant and pulled the trigger of the Colt. The report was deafening, the bullet entering the killer's chest just under the armpit. A short gasp and the body on the deck shriveled and went still.

"A nice piece of work, gringo," Amaru's voice boomed through a loudspeaker. "Manuel was one of my best men."

Pitt did not waste his breath on a reply. His mind rapidly turned over the situation. It suddenly became clear to him that Amaru had followed his movements once he reached the open decks. The need for stealth was finished. They knew where he was, but he couldn't see them. The game was over. He could only hope Padilla and his men were going over the side unnoticed.

For effect, he fired three more shots in the general direction Amaru's voice came from.

"You missed." Amaru laughed. "Not even close."

Pitt stalled by firing one shot every few seconds until the gun was empty. He had run out of delaying tactics and could do no more. His situation was made even more desperate when Amaru, or one of his men, turned on the ferryboat's navigation and deck lights, leaving him as exposed as an actor on an empty stage under a spotlight. He pressed his back against a bulkhead and stared at the railing outside the galley. The raft was gone—the lines were cut and dangling. Padilla and the rest had slipped into the darkness before the lights came on.

"I'll make you a deal you don't deserve," said Amaru in a congenial tone. "Give up now and you can die quickly. Resist and your death will come very slowly. Do not waste our time making up your mind. We have other—"

Pitt wasn't in the mood to hear more. He was as certain as he could ever be that Amaru was trying to hold his attention while another of the murderers crept close enough to stick a knife somewhere it would hurt. He did not have the slightest intention of waiting to be made sport of by a gang of sadists. He sprinted across the deck and leaped over the side of the ferry for the second time that evening.

A gold-medal diver would have gracefully soared into the air and performed any number of jackknifes, twists, and somersaults before cleanly entering the water 15 meters (50 feet) below. He'd have also broken his neck and several vertebrae after crashing into the bottom silt only two meters below the surface. Pitt had no aspirations of ever trying out for the U.S. diving team. He went over the side feet first before doubling up and striking the water like a cannonball.

Amaru and his remaining two men ran to the edge of the top deck and looked down.

"Can you see him?" asked Amaru, peering into the dark water.

"No, Tupac, he must have gone under the hull."

"The water is turning dirty," exclaimed another voice. "He must have buried himself in the bottom mud."

"This time we're not taking any chances. Juan, the case of concussion grenades we brought from Guaymas. We'll crush him to pulp. Throw them about five meters from the hull, especially in the water around the paddle-wheels."

Pitt made a crater in the seafloor. He didn't impact ard enough to cause any physical damage, but enough ɔ stir up a huge cloud of silt. He uncoiled and swam way from the *Alhambra,* unseen from above.

He was afraid that once he cleared the cover of murk e might still be seen by the killers. This was not to be. Ie swam underwater as far as he could until his lungs egan to burn. When he came to the surface, he broke it ghtly, trusting in the ski mask to keep his head invisible n the black water. A hundred meters (328 feet) and he vas beyond the reach of the lights illuminating the ferry. Ie could barely distinguish the dark figures moving bout on the upper deck. He wondered why they weren't hooting into the water. Then he heard a dull thud, saw he white water rise in a towering splash and felt a surge f pressure that squeezed the air out of him.

Underwater explosives! They were trying to kill him vith the concussion from underwater explosives. Four nore detonations followed in quick succession. Fortu- ately, they came from the area amidships, near the addlewheels. By swimming away from one end of the oat, Pitt had distanced himself from the main force of he detonations.

He doubled over with his knees in front of his chest to bsorb the worst of the impact. Thirty meters closer and e would have been pounded into unconsciousness. ixty meters (200 feet) and he would have been crushed o putty. Pitt increased the gap between himself and the erry until the eruptions came.

He looked up at a clear sky and checked the north star or his approximate bearings. At 14 kilometers (8.7 niles) away, the desolate west coast of the Gulf was the losest land. He tore off the ski mask and rolled over. ʾace toward the carpet of stars across the sky, he began a omfortable backstroke toward the west.

Pitt was in no condition to try out for the swimming

team either. After two hours, his arms felt as if they wer
lifting twenty-pound weights with each stroke. After si:
hours, his muscles protested with aches he didn't believ
possible. And then finally, and most thankfully, fatigu
began to dull the pain. He used the old Boy Scout trick o
removing his pants, tying the ankles into knots an
swinging them over his head to catch the air, making :
reasonably efficient float for rest stops that became mor
numerous as the night wore on.

There was never any question of stopping and lettin;
himself drift in the hope of being spotted by a fishin;
boat in daylight. The vision of Loren and Rudi in th
hands of Sarason was more than an ample stimulus t
drive him on.

The stars in the eastern sky were beginning to fade an
blink out when his feet hit bottom, and he staggered ou
of the water onto a sandy beach where he collapsed an
immediately fell asleep.

28

RAGSDALE, WEARING AN ARMORED BODY SUIT BENEATH A PAIR
of workman's coveralls, casually walked up to the side
door of a small warehouse with a For Lease sign in the
front window. He laid the empty toolbox he carried on
the ground, took a key from his pocket, and opened the
door.

Inside, a combined team of twenty FBI and eight
Customs agents had assembled and were making last-
minute preparations for the raid on the Zolar International building directly across the street. Advance teams
had alerted local law enforcement to the operation and
scouted the entire industrial complex for unusual activity.

Most of the men and the four women wore assault
suits and carried automatic weapons, while several professional experts in the art and antiquities field wore
street clothes. The latter were burdened with suitcases
crammed with catalogues and photographs of known
missing art objects targeted for seizure.

The plan called for the agents to split off into specific
assignments once they entered the building. The first
team was to secure the building and round up the
employees, the second was to search out any stolen

cache, while the third was to investigate the administration offices for any paper trail that led to theft operations or illegal purchases. Working separately, a commercial business team specializing in art handling was standing by to crate, remove and store the seized goods. The U.S. Attorney's Office, working on the case for both the FBI and Customs, had insisted the raid be carried out in a faultless manner and that confiscated objects be treated with a velvet touch.

Agent Gaskill was standing at an operations board in the center of the command post. He turned at Ragsdale's approach and smiled. "Still quiet?"

The FBI agent sat down in a canvas chair. "All clear except for the gardener trimming the hedge around the building. The rest of the grounds are as quiet as a churchyard."

"Pretty clever of the Zolars to use a gardener as a security guard," said Gaskill. "If he hadn't mowed the lawn four times this week, we might have ignored him."

"That and the fact our surveillance identified his Walkman headset as a radio transmitter," added Ragsdale.

"A good sign. If they have nothing to hide, why the wily tactics?"

"Don't get your hopes up. The Zolar warehouse operations may look suspicious, but when the FBI walked in with a search warrant two years ago, we didn't find so much as a stolen ballpoint pen."

"Same with Customs when we talked agents at Internal Revenue into conducting a series of tax audits. Zolar and his family surfaced as pure as the driven snow."

Ragsdale nodded a "thank you" as one of his agents handed him a cup of coffee. "All we've got going for us this time around is the element of surprise. Our last raid failed after a local cop, who was on Zolar's payroll, tipped him off."

"We should be thankful we're not walking into a high-security armed fortress."

"Anything from your undercover informant?" asked Gaskill.

Ragsdale shook his head. "He's beginning to think we've put him in the wrong operation. He hasn't turned up the slightest hint of unlawful activities."

"No one in or out of the building except bona fide employees. No illegal goods received or shipped in the past four days. Do you get the feeling we're waiting for it to snow in Galveston?"

"It seems that way."

Gaskill stared at him. "Do you want to rethink this thing and call off the raid?"

Ragsdale stared back. "The Zolars aren't perfect. There has to be a flaw in their system somewhere, and I'm staking my career that it's across the street in that building."

Gaskill laughed. "I'm with you, buddy, right on down to forced early retirement."

Ragsdale held up a thumb. "Then the show goes on in eight minutes as planned."

Two agents driving a pickup truck borrowed from the Galveston Sanitation Department pulled up at the curb opposite the gardener who was cultivating a flower bed beside the Zolar building. The man in the passenger seat rolled down the window and called out, "Excuse me."

The gardener turned and stared questioningly at the truck.

The agent made a friendly smile. "Can you tell me if your driveway gutters backed up during the last rain?"

Curious, the gardener stepped out of the flower bed

and approached the truck. "I don't recall seeing any backup," he replied.

The agent held a city street map out the window. "Do you know if any of the surrounding streets had drainage problems?"

As the gardener leaned down to study the map, the agent's arm suddenly lashed out and tore the transmitter from the gardener's head and jerked the cable leading from the microphone and headphones from its socket in the battery pack. "Federal agents," snapped the agent. "Stand still and don't wink an eye."

The agent behind the wheel then spoke into a portable radio. "Go ahead, it's all clear."

The federal agents did not smash into the Zolar International building with the lightning speed of a drug bust, nor did they launch a massive assault like the disaster that occurred years before in the compound in Waco, Texas. This was no high-security, armed fortress. One team quietly surrounded the building's exits while the main group calmly entered through the main entrance.

The office help and corporate administrators showed no sign of fear or anxiety. They appeared confused and puzzled. The agents politely but firmly herded them out onto the main floor of the warehouse where they were joined by the workers in the storage and shipping section and the artisans from the artifact preservation department. Two buses were driven through the shipping doors and loaded with the Zolar International personnel, who were then taken to FBI headquarters in nearby Houston for questioning. The entire roundup operation took less than four minutes.

The paperwork team, made up mostly of FBI agents trained in accounting methods and led by Ragsdale, went to work immediately, searching through desks, examining files, and scrutinizing every recorded transaction. Gaskill, along with his Customs people and professional art experts, began cataloguing and photographing the thousands of art and antique objects stored throughout the building. The work was tedious and time-consuming and produced no concrete evidence of stolen goods.

Shortly after one o'clock in the afternoon, Gaskill and Ragsdale sat down in Joseph Zolar's luxurious office to compare notes amid incredibly costly art objects. The FBI's chief agent did not look happy.

"This is beginning to have the look of a big embarrassment followed by a storm of nasty publicity and a gigantic lawsuit," Ragsdale said dejectedly.

"No sign of criminal activity in the records?" asked Gaskill.

"Nothing that stands out. We'll need a good month for an audit to know for certain if we have a case."

Gaskill sighed. "I hate to say it, but it appears the Zolars are a lot smarter than the best combined investigative teams the United States government can field."

A few moments later, the two Customs agents who had worked with Gaskill on the Rummel raid in Chicago, Beverly Swain and Winfried Pottle, stepped into the office. Their manner was official and businesslike, but there was no hiding the slight upward curl of their lips. Ragsdale and Gaskill had been so absorbed in their private conversation that they hadn't noticed the two younger Customs agents had not entered through the office door, but from the adjoining, private bathroom.

"Got a minute, boss?" Beverly Swain asked Gaskill.

"What is it?"

"I think our instruments have detected some sort of shaft leading under the building," answered Winfried Pottle.

"What did you say?" Gaskill demanded quickly.

Ragsdale looked up. "Instruments?"

"The ground-penetrating sonic/radar detector we borrowed from the Colorado School of Mines," explained Pottle. "Its recording unit shows a narrow space beneath the warehouse floor leading into the earth."

A faint ray of hope suddenly passed between Ragsdale and Gaskill. They both came to their feet. "How did you know where to look?" asked Ragsdale.

Pottle and Swain could not contain their smiles of triumph. Swain nodded at Pottle who answered, "We figured that any passageway leading to a secret chamber had to start or end at Zolar's private office, a connective tunnel he could enter at his convenience without being observed."

"His personal bathroom," Gaskill guessed wonderingly.

"A handy location," Swain confirmed.

Ragsdale took a deep breath. "Show us."

Pottle and Swain led them into a large bathroom with a marble floor and an antique sink, commode, and fixtures, with teak decking from an old yacht covering the walls. They motioned to a modern sunken tub with a Jacuzzi that seemed oddly out of place with the more ancient decor.

"The shaft drops under the bathtub," said Swain, pointing.

"Are you sure about this?" asked Ragsdale skeptically. "The shower stall strikes me as a more practical setup for an elevator."

"Our first thought too," answered Pottle, "but our instrument showed solid concrete and ground beneath the shower floor."

Pottle lifted a long tubular probe that was attached by an electrical cable to a compact computer with a paper printout. He switched on the unit and waved the end of the probe around the bottom of the tub. Lights on the computer blinked for a few seconds and then a sheet of paper rolled through a slot on the top. When the recording paper stopped flowing, Pottle tore it off and held it up for everyone to see.

In the center of an otherwise blank sheet of paper, a black column extended from end to end.

"No doubt about it," announced Pottle, "a shaft with the same dimensions as the bathtub that falls underground."

"And you're sure your electronic marvel is accurate?" said Ragsdale.

"The same type of unit found previously unknown passages and chambers in the Pyramids of Giza last year."

Gaskill said nothing as he stepped into the tub. He fiddled with the nozzle, but it simply adjusted for spray and direction. Then he sat down on a seat large enough to hold four people. He turned the gold-plated hot and cold faucets, but no water flowed through the spout.

He looked up with a big smile. "I think we're making progress."

Next he wiggled the lever that raised and lowered the plug. Nothing happened.

"Try twisting the spout," suggested Swain.

Gaskill took the gold-plated spout in one of his massive hands and gave it a slight turn. To his surprise it moved and the tub began to slowly sink beneath the bathroom floor. A reverse turn of the spout and the tub returned to its former position. He knew, he *knew,* this simple little water spout and this stupid bathtub were the keys that could topple the entire Zolar organization and shut them down for good. He grinned at the others and said gleefully, "Going down?"

The unusual elevator descended for nearly thirty seconds before coming to a stop in another bathroom. Pottle judged the drop to be about 20 meters (65 feet). They stepped from the bathroom into an office that was almost an exact copy of the one above. The lights were on but no one was present. With Ragsdale in the lead, the little group of agents cracked open the door of the office and peered out onto the floor of an immense storehouse of stolen art and antiquities. They were all stunned by the size of the chamber and the enormous inventory of the objects. Gaskill made a wild guess of at least ten thousand pieces as Ragsdale slipped into the storeroom and made a fast recon. He was back in five minutes.

"Four men working with a forklift," he reported, "lowering a bronze sculpture of a Roman legionnaire into a wooden crate about halfway down the fourth aisle. Across on the other side, in a closed-off area, I counted six men and women working in what looked to be the artifact forgery section. A tunnel leads through the south wall, I'd guess to a nearby building that acts as a front for the shipping and receiving of the stolen property."

"It must also be used for the covert employees to enter and exit," suggested Pottle.

"We've hit the jackpot. I can recognize four works of stolen art from here," murmured Gaskill.

"We'd better stay put," said Ragsdale softly, "until we can shuttle reinforcements from above."

"I volunteer to operate the ferry service," said Swain with a grin. "What woman can pass up the opportunity to sit in a fancy bathtub that moves from floor to floor?"

As soon as she left, Pottle stood guard at the door to the storage area while Gaskill and Ragsdale searched Zolar's underground office. The desk produced little of value so they turned their attention to searching for a storeroom. They quickly found what they were looking for behind a tall sideboard bookcase that swiveled out from the wall on small castors. Pushed aside, it revealed a long, narrow chamber lined with antique wooden cabinets, standing floor to ceiling. Each cabinet held file folders in alphabetical order containing acquisition and sales records of the Zolar family operations as far back as 1929.

"It's here," muttered Gaskill in wonder. "It's all here." He began pulling files from a cabinet.

"Incredible," Ragsdale agreed, studying files from another cabinet that stood in the middle of the storeroom. "For sixty-nine years they kept a record of every piece of art they stole, smuggled, and forged, including financial and personal data on the buyers."

Gaskill groaned. "Take a look at this one."

Ragsdale took the offered file and scanned the first two pages. When he looked up his face was marked with disbelief. "If this is true, Michelangelo's statue of King Solomon in the Eisenstein Museum of Renaissance Art in Boston is a fake."

"And a good one, judging by the number of experts who authenticated it."

"But the former curator knew."

"Of course," said Gaskill. "The Zolars made him an offer he couldn't refuse. According to this report, ten extremely rare Etruscan sculptures excavated illegally in northern Italy, and smuggled into the United States, were exchanged along with the forged King Solomon for the genuine article. Since the fake was too good to be caught, the curator became a big hero with the trustees and patrons by claiming he had enhanced the museum's collection by persuading an anonymous moneybags to donate the objects."

"I wonder how many other cases of museum fraud we'll find," mused Ragsdale.

"I suspect this may only be the tip of the iceberg. These files represent thousands upon thousands of illegal deals to buyers who turned a blind eye in the direction the objects came from."

Ragsdale smiled. "I'd like to be a mouse hiding in the wall when the U.S. Attorney's Office finds out we've laid about ten years' worth of legal work on them."

"You don't know federal prosecutors," said Gaskill. "When they get a load of all the wealthy businessmen, politicians, sports and entertainment celebrities who willfully purchased hot art, they'll think they've died and gone to heaven."

"Maybe we'd better rethink all the exposure," cautioned Ragsdale.

"What've you got cooking?"

"We know that Joseph Zolar and his brothers, Charles Oxley and Cyrus Sarason, are in Mexico where we can't arrest and take them into custody without a lot of legal hassle. Right?"

"I follow."

"So we throw a blanket on this part of the raid," explained Ragsdale. "From all indications, the employees on the legitimate side of the operation have no idea what's going on in the basement. Let them go back to work tomorrow as if the raid turned up nothing. Business as usual. Otherwise, if they get wind that we've shut down their operation and federal prosecutors are building an airtight case, they'll go undercover in some country where we can't grab them."

Gaskill rubbed his chin thoughtfully. "Won't be easy keeping them in the dark. Like all businessmen on the road, they probably keep in daily communication with their operations."

"We'll use every underhanded trick in the book and fake it." Ragsdale laughed. "Set up operators to claim construction work severed the fiber optic lines. Send out phony memos over their fax lines. Keep the workers we've taken into custody on ice. With luck we can blindside the Zolars for forty-eight hours while we figure a scam to entice them over the border."

Gaskill looked at Ragsdale. "You like to play long shots, don't you, my man?"

"I'll bet a year's salary on a three-legged horse if there is the tiniest chance of putting these scum away for good."

"I like your odds." Gaskill grinned. "Let's shoot the works."

29

MANY OF BILLY YUMA'S VILLAGE CLAN OF ONE HUNDRED seventy-six people survived by raising squash, corn, and beans; others cut juniper and manzanita to sell for fence posts and firewood. A new source of income was the revival of interest in their ancient art of making pottery. Several of the Montolo women still created elegant pottery that had recently come into demand by collectors, hungry for Indian art.

After hiring out as a cowboy to a large ranchero for fifteen years, Yuma finally saved enough money to start a small spread of his own. He and his wife, Polly, managed a good living compared to most of the native people of northern Baja, she firing her pots, and he raising livestock.

After his midday meal, as he did every day, Yuma saddled his horse, a buckskin mare, and rode out to inspect his herd for sickness or injury. The harsh and inhospitable landscape with its bounty of jagged rocks, cactus, and steep-sided arroyos could easily maim an unwary steer.

He was searching for a stray calf when he saw the stranger approaching on the narrow trail leading to his village.

The man who walked through the desert seemed out of place. Unlike hikers or hunters, this man wore only the clothes on his back—no canteen, no backpack; he didn't even wear a hat to shade his head from the afternoon sun. There was a tired, worn-to-the-bones look about him, and yet he walked in purposeful, rapid strides as if he was in a hurry to get somewhere. Curious, Billy temporarily suspended his hunt for the calf and rode through a creek bed toward the trail.

Pitt had hiked 14 kilometers across the desert after coming out of an exhausted sleep. The sun was already pouring down on the desert when he awoke, but the temperature was a bearable 30 degrees Celsius (86 degrees Fahrenheit). The sweat dried quickly on his body, and he felt the first longing for water. He licked his lips and tasted salt from his swim through the sea.

After a quick dive in the water to refresh himself, he cut west across the desert toward Mexico Highway 5, twenty, maybe thirty kilometers away. Once he reached the pavement, he could flag a ride into Mexicali, and then make his way across the border into Calexico. That was the plan, unless the local Baja telephone company had thoughtfully and conveniently installed a pay phone in the shade of a handy mesquite tree.

He gazed out over the Sea of Cortez and took one final look at the *Alhambra* in the distance. The old ferryboat looked to have settled in the water up to her deck overhang and was resting in the silt at a slight list. Otherwise she seemed sound.

She also looked deserted. There were no search boats or helicopters in sight, launched by an anxious Giordino and U.S. Customs agents north of the border. Not that it mattered. Any search team flying a reconnaissance over the boat, he figured, wouldn't expect to look for anyone on land. He elected to walk out.

He maintained a steady 7-kilometer-an-hour pace across the isolated environment. Two hours into his journey, he came to a dusty footpath and followed it. Thirty minutes later he spotted a man sitting astride a horse beside the trail. Pitt walked up to the man and held up a hand in greeting. The rider gazed back through eyes worn and tired from the sun.

Pitt studied the stranger, who wore a straw cowboy hat with a large brim turned up on the sides, a long-sleeved cotton shirt, worn denim pants, and scuffed cowboy boots. The black hair under the hat showed no tendency toward gray. He was small and lean and could have been anywhere between fifty and seventy. His skin was burnt bronze with a washboard of wrinkles. The hands that held the reins were leathery and creased with many years of labor. This was a hardy soul, Pitt observed, who survived in an intolerant land with incredible tenacity.

"Good afternoon," Pitt said pleasantly.

Like most of his people Billy was bilingual, speaking native Montolan among his friends and family and Spanish to outsiders. But he knew a fair amount of English, picked up from his frequent trips over the border to sell his cattle and purchase supplies. "You know you trespass on private Indian land?" he replied stoically.

"No, sorry. I was cast ashore on the Gulf. I'm trying to reach the highway and a telephone."

"You lose your boat?"

"Yes," Pitt acknowledged. "You could say that."

"We have a telephone at our meeting house. Glad to take you there."

"I'd be most grateful."

Billy reached down a hand. "My village is not far. You can ride on back of my horse."

Pitt hesitated. He definitely preferred mechanical means of transportation. To his way of thinking four wheels were better than four hooves any day. But he wasn't about to look one with a gift in the mouth. He took Billy's hand and was amazed at the strength displayed by the wiry little man as he hoisted Pitt's 82 kilograms (181 pounds) up behind him without the slightest grunt of exertion.

"By the way, my name is Dirk Pitt."

"Billy Yuma," said the horseman without offering his hand.

They rode in silence for half an hour before cresting a butte overgrown with yucca. They dropped into a small valley with a shallow stream running through it and passed the ruins of a Spanish mission, destroyed by religion-resistant Indians three centuries ago. Crumbling adobe walls and a small graveyard were all that remained. The graves of the old Spaniards near the top of a knoll were long since grown over and forgotten. Lower down were the more recent burials of the townspeople. One tombstone in particular caught Pitt's eye. He slipped to the ground over the rump of the horse and walked over to it.

The carved letters on the weathered stone were distinct and quite readable.

Patty Lou Cutting
2/11/24—2/3/34
The sun be warm and kind to you.
The darkest night some star shines through.
The dullest morn a radiance brew.
And where dusk comes, God's hand to you.

"Who was she?" asked Pitt.

Billy Yuma shook his head. "The old ones do not know. They say the grave was made by strangers in the night."

Pitt stood and looked over the sweeping vista of the

Sonoran Desert. A light breeze gently caressed the back of his neck. A red-tailed hawk circled the sky, surveying its domain. The land of mountains and sand, jackrabbits, coyotes, and canyons could intimidate as well as inspire. This is the place to die and be buried, he thought. Finally, he turned from Patty Lou's last resting place and waved Yuma on. "I'll walk the rest of the way."

Yuma nodded silently and rode ahead, the hooves of the buckskin kicking up little clouds of dust.

Pitt followed down the hill to a modest farming and ranching community. They traveled along the streambed where three young girls were washing clothes under the shade of a cottonwood tree.

The heart of the Montolo community consisted of several houses and buildings. Some were built from mesquite branches that were coated with mud, one or two from wood, but most were constructed of cement blocks. The only apparent influence of modern living was weathered poles supporting electrical and phone lines, a few battered pickup trucks, and one satellite dish.

Yuma reined in his horse in front of a small building that was open on three sides. "Our meeting house," he said. "There's a phone inside. You have to pay."

Pitt smiled, investigated his still soggy wallet, and produced an AT&T card. "No problem."

Yuma nodded and led him into a small office equipped with a wooden table and four folding chairs. The telephone sat on a very thin phone book that was lying on the tile floor.

The operator finally answered after seventeen rings. *"Sí, por favor?"*

"I wish to make a credit card call."

"Yes, sir, your card number and the number you're calling," the operator replied in fluent English.

"At least my day hasn't been all bad," Pitt sighed at hearing an understanding voice.

The Mexican operator connected him to an American operator. She transferred him to information to obtain the number for the Customs offices in Calexico and then put his call through. A male voice answered.

"Customs Service, how can I help you?"

"I'm trying to reach Albert Giordino of the National Underwater and Marine Agency."

"One moment, I'll transfer you. He's in Agent Starger's office."

Two clicks and a voice that seemed to come from a basement said, "Starger here."

"This is Dirk Pitt. Is Al Giordino handy?"

"One moment. Giordino is standing right here. I'll put him on an extension."

"Al," said Pitt, "are you there?"

"Good to hear your voice, pal. I take it something went wrong."

"In a nutshell, our friends from Peru have Loren and Rudi. I helped the crew escape on a life raft. I managed to swim to shore. I'm calling from an Indian village in the desert north of San Felipe and about thirty kilometers west of where the *Alhambra* lies half-sunk in the muck."

"I'll dispatch one of our helicopters," said Starger. "I'll need the name of the village for the pilot."

Pitt turned to Billy Yuma. "What do you call your community?"

Yuma nodded. "Canyon Ometepec."

Pitt repeated the name, gave a more in-depth report on the events of the last eighteen hours and hung up. "My friends are coming after me," he said to Yuma.

"By car?"

"Helicopter."

"You an important man?"

Pitt laughed. "No more than the mayor of your village."

"No mayor. Our elders meet and talk on tribal business."

Two men walked past, leading a burro that was buried under a load of manzanita limbs. The men and Yuma merely exchanged brief stares. There were no salutations, no smiles.

"You look tired and thirsty," said Yuma to Pitt. "Come to my house. My wife will make you something to eat while you wait for your friends."

It was the best offer Pitt had all day and he gratefully accepted.

Billy Yuma's wife, Polly, was a large woman. Her face was round and wrinkled with enormous dark brown eyes. She hustled around a wood stove that sat under a ramada next to their cement brick house. The Indians of the Southwest deserts preferred the shade and openness of a ramada for their kitchen and dining areas to the confining and draftless interior of their houses. Pitt noticed that the ramada's roof was constructed from the skeletal ribs of the saguaro cactus tree and was supported by mesquite poles surrounded by a wall of standing barbed ocotillo stems.

After he drank five cups of water from a big olla, or pot, whose porous walls let it sweat and keep its contents cool, Polly fed him shredded pork and refried beans with fried cholla buds that reminded him of okra. The tortillas were made from mesquite beans she had pounded into a sweet-tasting flour.

Pitt couldn't recall eating a more delightful meal.

Polly seldom spoke, and when she did utter a few words they were addressed to Billy in Spanish. Pitt thought he detected a hint of humor in her big brown eyes, but she acted serious and remote.

"I do not see a happy community," said Pitt, making conversation.

Yuma shook his head sadly. "Sorrow fell over my people and the people of our other tribal villages when our most sacred religious idols were stolen. Without them our sons and daughters cannot go through the initiation of adulthood. Since their disappearance, we have suffered much misfortune."

"Not the Zolars," Pitt breathed.

"What, señor?"

"An international family of thieves who have stolen half the ancient artifacts ever discovered."

"Mexican police told us our idols were stolen by American pothunters who search sacred Indian grounds for our heritage to sell for profit."

"Very possible," said Pitt. "What do your sacred idols look like?"

Yuma stretched out his hand and held it about a meter above the floor. "They stand about this high and their faces were carved many centuries ago by my ancestors from the roots of cottonwood trees."

"The chances are better than good that your idols were bought from the pothunters by the Zolars for peanuts, and then resold to a wealthy collector for a fat price."

"These people are called Zolars?"

"Their family name. They operate under a shadowy organization called *Solpemachaco.*"

"I do not know the word," said Yuma. "What does it mean?"

"A mythical Inca serpent with several heads that takes up housekeeping in a cave."

"Never heard of him."

"I think he may be related to another legendary monster the Peruvians called the *Demonio del Muertos,* who guards their underworld."

Yuma gazed thoughtfully at his work-worn hands. "We too have a legendary demon of the underworld who keeps the dead from escaping and the living from entering. He also passes judgment on our dead, allowing the good to pass and devouring the bad."

"A Judgment Day demon," said Pitt.

Yuma nodded solemnly. "He lives on a mountain not far from here."

"Cerro el Capirote," Pitt said softly.

"How could a stranger know that?" Yuma asked, looking deeply into Pitt's green eyes.

"I've been to the peak. I have seen the winged jaguar with the serpent's head, and I guarantee you he wasn't put there to secure the underworld or judge the dead."

"You seem to know much about this land."

"No, actually very little. But I'd be most interested in hearing any other legends about the demon."

"There is one other," Yuma conceded. "Enrique Juarez, our oldest tribal elder, is one of the few remaining Montolos who remember the old stories and ancient ways. He tells of golden gods who came from the south on great birds with white wings that moved over the surface of the water. They rested on an island in the old sea for a long time. When the gods finally sailed away, they left behind the stone demon. A few of our brave and curious ancestors went across the water to the island and never returned. The old people were frightened and believed the mountain was sacred and all intruders would be devoured by the demon." Yuma paused and gazed into the desert. "The story has been told and retold from the days of my ancestors. Our younger children, who are schooled in modern ways, think of it simply as an old people's fairy tale."

"A fairy tale mixed with historical fact," Pitt assured Yuma. "Believe me when I tell you a vast hoard of gold lies inside Cerro el Capirote. Put there not by golden gods from the south, but Incas from Peru, who played on your ancestors' reverence of the supernatural by carving the stone monster to instill fear and keep them off the island. As added insurance, they left a few guards behind to kill the curious until the Spanish were driven from their homeland, and they could come back and reclaim the treasure for their new king. It goes without saying, history took a different turn. The Spaniards were there to stay and no one ever returned."

Billy Yuma was not a man given to extreme emotion. His wrinkled face remained fixed. Only his dark eyes widened. "A great treasure lies under Cerro el Capirote?"

Pitt nodded. "Very soon men with evil intentions are coming to force their way inside the mountain to steal the Inca riches."

"They cannot do that," Yuma protested. "Cerro el Capirote is magic. It is on our land, Montolo land. The dead who did not pass judgment live outside its walls."

"That won't stop these men, believe me," said Pitt seriously.

"My people will make a protest to our local police authorities."

"If the Zolars run true to form, they've already bribed your law enforcement officials."

· "These evil men you speak of. They are the same ones who sold our sacred idols?"

"As I suggested, it's very possible."

Billy Yuma studied him for a moment. "Then we do not have to trouble ourselves with their trespass onto our sacred ground."

Pitt did not understand. "May I ask why?"

Reality slowly faded from Billy's face and he seemed to enter a dreamlike state. "Because those who have taken the idols of the sun, moon, earth, and water are cursed and will suffer a terrible death."

"You really believe that, don't you?"

"I do," Yuma answered somberly. "In my dreams I see the thieves drowning."

"Drowning?"

"Yes, in the water that will make the desert into the garden it was for my ancestors."

Pitt considered making a contrary reply. He was not one to deposit his money in the bank of dreams. But the intractable gaze in Yuma's eyes, the case-hardened tone of his voice, moved something inside Pitt.

He began to feel glad that he wasn't related to the Zolars.

30

Amaru stepped down into the main *sala* of the hacienda. "Please excuse me for keeping you waiting, gentlemen."

"Quite all right," said Zolar. "Now that the fools from NUMA have led us directly to Huascar's gold, we made good use of your tardiness by discussing methods of bringing it to the surface."

Amaru nodded and looked around the room. There were four men there besides himself. Seated on sofas around the fireplace were Zolar, Oxley, Sarason, and Moore. Their faces were expressionless, but there was no concealing the feeling of triumph in the air.

"Any word of Dr. Kelsey, the photographer Rodgers, and Albert Giordino?" Sarason inquired.

"My contacts over the border believe Pitt told you the truth on the ferry when he said he dropped them off at the U.S. Customs compound in Calexico," answered Amaru.

"He must have smelled a trap," said Moore.

"That was obvious when he returned to the ferryboat alone," Sarason said sharply to Amaru. "You had him in your hands and you let him escape."

"Not forgetting the crew," added Oxley.

"I promise you, Pitt did not escape. He was killed when my men and I threw concussion grenades into the water around him. As to the ferryboat's crew, the Mexican police officials you've paid to cooperate will ensure their silence for as long as necessary."

"Still not good," said Oxley. "With Pitt, Gunn, and Congresswoman Smith missing, every federal agent between San Diego and Denver will come nosing around."

Zolar shook his head. "They have no legal authority down here. And our friends in the local government would never permit their entry."

Sarason looked angrily at Amaru. "You say Pitt's dead. Then where is the body?"

Amaru stared back nastily. "Pitt is feeding the fishes. There is no way he could have survived the underwater detonations."

"The man has survived far worse," Sarason said. "I won't be satisfied until I see the remains."

"You also botched the scuttling of the ferryboat," Oxley said to Amaru. "You should have sailed her into deep water before opening the seacocks."

"Or better yet, set her on fire, along with Congresswoman Smith and the deputy director of NUMA," said Zolar, lighting a cigar.

"Police Comandante Cortina will conduct an investigation and announce that the ferryboat along with Congresswoman Smith and Rudi Gunn was lost in an unfortunate accident," said Sarason.

Zolar glared at him. "That won't solve the problem of interference from American law enforcement officials. Their Justice Department will demand more than a local investigation if Pitt survives to expose the blundering actions of your friend here."

"Forget Pitt," Amaru said flatly. "Nobody had a stronger reason for seeing him dead than me."

Oxley glanced from Amaru to Zolar. "We can't gamble on speculation. No way Cortina can hold off a joint investigation by the Mexican and American governments for more than a few days."

Sarason shrugged. "Time enough to remove the treasure and be gone."

"Even if Pitt walks out of the sea to tell the truth," said Henry Moore, "it's your word against his. He can't prove your connection with the torture and disappearance of Smith and Gunn. Who would believe a family of respected art dealers was involved with such things? You might arrange for Cortina to accuse Pitt of committing these crimes so he could grab the treasure for himself."

"I approve of the professor's concept," said Zolar. "Our influential friends in the police and military can easily be persuaded to arrest Pitt if he shows his face in Mexico."

"So far so good," said Sarason. "But what about our prisoners? Do we eliminate them now or later?"

"Why not throw them in the river that runs through the treasure cavern?" suggested Amaru. "Eventually, what's left of their bodies will probably turn up in the Gulf. By the time the fish get through with them, about all a coroner will be able to determine is that they died from drowning."

Zolar looked around the room at his brothers and then to Moore who looked oddly uneasy. After a moment he turned to Amaru. "A brilliant scenario. Simple, but brilliant nonetheless. Any objections?"

There were none.

"I'll contact Comandante Cortina and brief him on his assignment," Sarason volunteered.

Zolar waved his cigar and flashed his teeth in a broad smile. "Then it's settled. While Cyrus and Cortina lay a smoke screen for American investigators, the rest of us will pack up and move from the hacienda to Cerro el Capirote and begin retrieving the gold at first light tomorrow."

* * *

The next morning, a small army of soldiers set up a command post and sealed off the desert for two miles around the base of Cerro el Capirote. No one was allowed in or out. The mountain's peak had become a staging area with all treasure recovery operations conducted from the air. Pitt's stolen NUMA helicopter, repainted with Zolar International colors, lifted into a clear sky and dipped on a course back to the hacienda. A few minutes later, a heavy Mexican army transport helicopter hovered and settled down. A detachment of military engineers in desert combat fatigues jumped to the ground, opened the rear cargo door and began unloading a small forklift, coils of cable, and a large winch.

Officials of the state of Sonora who were on the Zolars' payroll had approved all the necessary licenses and permits within twenty-four hours, a process that would normally have taken months and perhaps years. The Zolars had promised to fund new schools, roads, and a hospital. Their cash had greased the palms of the local bureaucracy and eliminated the usual rivers of red tape. Full cooperation was given by an unwitting Mexican government misled by corrupt bureaucrats. Joseph Zolar's request for a contingent of engineers from a military base on the Baja Peninsula was quickly approved. Under the terms of a swiftly drawn up contract with the Ministry of the Treasury, the Zolars were entitled to 25 percent of the treasure. The rest was to be deposited with the national court in Mexico City.

The only problem with the agreement was that the Zolars had no intention of keeping their end of the bargain. They weren't about to split the treasure with anyone.

Once the golden chain and the bulk of the treasure had been hauled to the top of the mountain, a covert operation was created to move the hoard under cover of darkness to a remote military airstrip near the great sand

dunes of the Altar Desert just south of the Arizona
border. There, it would be loaded aboard a commercial
jet transport, painted with the markings and colors of a
major airline company, and then flown to a secret
distribution facility owned by the Zolars in the small city
of Nador on the north coast of Morocco.

Everyone had been ferried from the hacienda to the
mountaintop as soon as it became daylight. No personal
effects were left behind. Only Zolar's jetliner remained,
parked on the hacienda's airstrip, ready for takeoff on a
moment's notice.

Oxley quickly discovered the small aperture leading
inside the mountain and wasted no time in directing a
military work crew to enlarge it. He stayed behind to
oversee the equipment staging while Zolar, Sarason, and
the Moores set off down the passageway followed by a
squad of engineers, who carried portable fluorescent
lights.

When they reached the second demon, Micki lovingly
touched its eyes, just as Shannon Kelsey had done before
her. She sighed. "A marvelous piece of work."

"Beautifully preserved," Henry Moore agreed.

"It will have to be destroyed," said Sarason indifferently.

"What are you talking about?" demanded Moore.

"We can't move it. The ugly beast fills up most of the
tunnel. There is no way we can drag Huascar's chain
over, around, or between its legs."

Micki's face went tense with shock. "You can't destroy
a masterwork of antiquity."

"We can and we will," Zolar said, backing his brother.
"I agree it's unfortunate. The sculpture has to go."

Moore's pained expression slowly turned hard, and he
looked at his wife and nodded. "Sacrifices must be
made."

Micki understood. If they were to seize enough of the
golden riches to keep them in luxury for the rest of their

lives, they would have to close their eyes to the demoli
tion of the demon.

They pushed on as Sarason lagged behind and ordered
the engineers to place a charge of explosives under the
demon. "Be careful," he warned them in Spanish. "Use
a small charge. We don't want to cause a cave-in."

Zolar was amazed at the Moores' vast energy and
enthusiasm after they encountered the crypt of the
treasure guardians. If left on their own, they would have
spent a week studying the mummies and the burial
ornaments before pushing on to the treasure chamber.

"Let's keep going," said Zolar impatiently. "You can
nose around the dead later."

Reluctantly, the Moores continued into the guardians
living quarters, lingering only a few minutes before
Sarason rejoined his brother and urged them onward.

The sudden sight of the guardian encased in calcite
crystals shocked and stunned all of them, as it had Pitt
and his group. Henry Moore peered intently through the
translucent sarcophagus.

"An ancient Chachapoya," he murmured as if standing before a crucifix. "Preserved as he died. This is an
unbelievable discovery."

"He must have been a noble warrior of very high
status," said Micki in awe.

"A logical conclusion, my dear. This man had to be
very powerful to bear the responsibility of guarding an
immense royal treasure."

"What do you think he's worth?" asked Sarason.

Moore turned and scowled at him. "You can't set a
price on such an extraordinary object. As a window to
the past, he is priceless."

"I know a collector who would give five million dollars
for him," said Zolar, as if he were appraising a Ming
vase.

A few minutes later, they stood in a shoulder-to-
shoulder line on the edge of the subterranean riverbank

nd stared mesmerized at the array of gold, highlighted
by the portable fluorescent lamps carried by the military
ngineers. All they saw was the treasure. The sight of a
iver flowing through the bowels of the earth seemed
nsignificant.

"Spectacular," whispered Zolar. "I can't believe I'm
ooking at so much gold."

"This easily exceeds the treasures of King Tut's
omb," said Moore.

"How magnificent," said Micki, clutching her hus-
and's arm. "This has to be the richest cache in all the
Americas."

Sarason's amazement quickly wore off. "Very clever,"
ne charged. "Storing the treasure on an island sur-
ounded by a strong current makes recovery doubly
omplicated."

"Yes, but we've got cables and winches," said Moore.
"Think of the difficulty they had in moving all that gold
over there with nothing but hemp rope and muscle."

Micki spied a golden monkey crouched on a pedestal.
"That's odd."

Zolar looked at her. "What's odd?"

She stepped closer to the monkey and its pedestal
which was lying on its side. "Why would this piece still
be on this bank of the river?"

"Yes, it does seem strange this object wasn't placed
with the others," said Moore. "It almost looks as if it was
hrown here."

Sarason pointed to gouges in the sand and calcium
crystals beside the riverbank. "I'd say it was dragged off
he island."

"It has writing scratched on it," said Moore.

"Can you decipher anything?" asked Zolar.

"Doesn't need deciphering. The markings are in English."

Sarason and Zolar stared at him. "No jokes, Professor," said Zolar.

"I'm dead serious. Somebody engraved a message int
the soft gold on the bottom of the pedestal, quite recentl
by the looks of it."

"What does it say?"

Moore motioned for an engineer to aim his lamp a
the monkey's pedestal, adjusted his glasses and bega
reading aloud.

Welcome members of the Solpemachaco
*to the underground thieves and plunderers
annual convention.
If you have any ambitions in life other than
the acquisition of stolen loot, you have
come to the right place.
Be our guests and take only the objects
you can use.*
   Your congenial sponsors,
Dr. Shannon Kelsey, Miles Rodgers, Al Giordino,
& Dirk Pitt.

There was a moment of sober realization, and ther
Zolar snarled at his brother. "What is going on here
What kind of foolish trick is this?"

Sarason's mouth was pinched in a bitter line. "Pit
admitted leading us to the demon," he answered reluc
tantly, "but he said nothing of entering the mountai
and laying eyes on the treasure."

"Generous with his information, wasn't he? Why
didn't you tell me this?"

Sarason shrugged. "He's dead. I didn't think it mat
tered."

Micki turned to her husband. "I know Dr. Kelsey.
met her at an archaeology conference in San Antonio
She has a splendid reputation as an expert on Andea
cultures."

Moore nodded. "Yes, I'm familiar with her work."
He stared at Sarason. "You led us to believe Congress

woman Smith and the men from NUMA were merely on
a treasure hunt. You said nothing of involvement by
professional archaeologists."

"Does it make any difference?"

"Something is going on beyond your control," warned
Moore. He looked as if he was enjoying the Zolars'
confusion. "If I were you, I'd get the gold out of here as
fast as possible."

His words were punctuated by a muffled explosion far
up into the passageway.

"We have nothing to fear so long as Pitt is dead,"
Sarason kept insisting. "What you see here was done
before Amaru put a stop to him." But he was damp with
cold sweat. Pitt's mocking words rang in his ears:
"You've been set up, pal."

PART IV

NIGHTMARE
PASSAGE

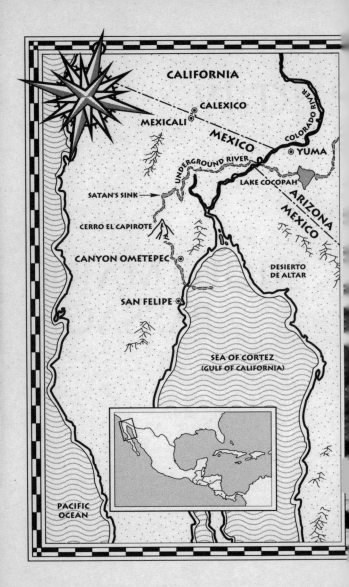

October 31, 2005
Satan's Sink, Baja, Mexico

31

TO ADMIRAL JAMES SANDECKER, PITT'S AUDACIOUS PLAN TO come in through the back door of Cerro el Capirote in a wild attempt to save Loren Smith and Rudi Gunn was nothing less than suicidal. He knew the reasons Pitt had for risking his life: rescuing two close friends from death, evening the score with a pair of murderers, and snatching a wondrous treasure from the hands of thieves. Those were grounds for justification of other men. Not Pitt. His motivation went much deeper. To challenge the unknown, laugh at the devil, and dare the odds. Those were his stimulants.

As for Giordino, Pitt's friend since childhood, Sandecker never doubted for an instant the rugged Italian would follow Pitt into a molten sea of lava.

Sandecker could have stopped them. But he hadn't built what was thought of by many as the finest, most productive, and budget efficient agency in the government without taking his fair share of risky gambles. His fondness for marching out of step with official Washington made him the object of respect as well as envy. The other directors of national bureaus would never consider hands-on control of a hazardous project in the field that might run the risk of censure from Congress and force

resignation by presidential order. Sandecker's only re
gret was that this was one adventure he couldn't lea
himself.

He paused after carrying a load of dive gear from th
old Chevy down the tubular bore and looked at Dr. Pete
Duncan—a U.S. Geological Survey hydrologist who ha
arrived by chartered jet only an hour after Sandecke
contacted him in San Diego—who sat beside the sink
hole, busily overlaying a transparency of a topographica
map onto a hydrographic survey of known undergroun
water systems.

The two charts were enlarged to the same scale
enabling Duncan to trace the approximate course of th
subterranean river. Around him, the others were settin
out the dive gear and float equipment. "As the cro
flies," Duncan said to no one specifically, "the distanc
between Satan's Sinkhole and Cerro el Capirote work
out to roughly thirty kilometers."

Sandecker turned to Pitt. "How long do you think i
will take you to get there?"

"Running with a current of nine knots," said Pitt, "w
should make the treasure cavern in three hours."

Duncan looked doubtful. "I've never seen a river tha
didn't meander. If I were you I'd add another two hour
to my estimated time of arrival."

"The *Wallowing Windbag* will make up the time,"
Giordino said confidently as he stripped off his clothes

"Only if you have clear sailing all the way. You're
entering the unknown. There is no second-guessing th
difficulties you might encounter. Submerged passage
extending ten kilometers or more, cascades that fall th
height of a ten-story building, or unnavigable rapid
through rocks. White-water rafters have a saying—i
there is a rock, you'll strike it. If there is an eddy, you'l
get caught in it."

"Anything else?" Giordino grinned, unshaken by
Duncan's dire forecast. "Like vampires or gluttonous

monsters with six jaws of barracuda teeth lurking in the dark to have us for lunch?"

"I'm only trying to prepare you for the unexpected," Duncan said. "The best theory I can offer that might give you a small sense of security is that I believe the main section of the river system flows through a fault in the earth. If I'm right, the channel will travel in an erratic path but with a reasonably level depth."

Pitt patted him on the shoulder. "We understand and we're grateful. But at this stage, all Al and I can do is hope for the best, expect the worst, and settle for anything in between."

"When you swam out of the sinkhole's feeder stream into the river," Sandecker asked Duncan, "was there an air pocket?"

"Yes, the rock ceiling rose a good ten meters above the surface of the river."

"How far did it extend?"

"We were hanging onto the fixed guideline for dear life against the current and only got a brief look. A quick sweep of my light failed to reveal the end of the gallery."

"With luck, they'll have an air passage the entire trip."

"A lot of luck," said Duncan skeptically, his eyes still drawn to the chart overlays. "As underground rivers go, this one is enormous. In sheer length, it must be the longest unexplored subterranean water course through a field of karst."

Giordino hesitated in strapping on a small console containing pressure gauges, a compass, and a depth meter to his arm. "What do you mean by karst?"

"Karst is the term for a limestone belt that is penetrated by a system of streams, passages, and caverns."

"It makes one wonder how many other unknown rivers are flowing under the earth," said Pitt.

"I'll be grateful for all the scientific data you can bring back from this one," acknowledged Duncan. "Finding a golden treasure under Cerro el Capirote may fire the imagination, but in reality it's incidental to the discovery of a water source that can turn millions of acres of desert into productive farm and ranch land."

"Perhaps the gold can fund the pumping systems and pipelines for such a project," said Pitt.

"Certainly a dream to consider," added Sandecker.

Giordino held up an underwater camera. "I'll bring back some pictures for you."

"Thank you," said Duncan gratefully. "I'd also appreciate another favor."

Pitt smiled. "Name it."

He handed Pitt a plastic packet in the shape of a basketball but half the size. "A dye tracer called Fluorescein Yellow with Optical Brightener. I'll buy you the best Mexican dinner in the Southwest if you'll throw it into the river when you reach the treasure chamber. That's all. As it floats along the river the container will automatically release the dye over regular intervals."

"You want to record where the river outlet emerges into the Gulf."

Duncan nodded. "That will give us an important hydrologic link."

He was also going to ask if Pitt and Giordino might take water samples, but thought better of it. He had already pushed them as far as he dared. If they were successful in navigating the river as far as the hollow interior of Cerro el Capirote, then he and his fellow scientists could mount subsequent scientific expeditions based on the data acquired by Pitt and Giordino.

Over the next ten minutes, Pitt and Giordino geared up and went over the plans for their journey. They had made countless dives together under a hundred different water and weather conditions, but none of this distance through the depths of the earth. Like doctors discussing a delicate brain operation, no detail was left to chance. Their survival depended on it.

Communication signals were agreed upon, buddy-

reathing strategies in case of air loss, the drill for
nflating and deflating the *Wallowing Windbag,* who was
n control of what equipment—all procedures were
leliberated and jointly approved.

"I see you're not wearing a pressurized dry suit,"
bserved Sandecker as Pitt pulled on his wet suit.

"The water temperature is a few degrees on the cool
ide, but warm enough so we don't have to worry about
ypothermia. A wet suit gives us more freedom of
movement than a dry suit that is pressurized by air
anks. This will prove a dire necessity if we find our-
elves struggling in the water to right the *Wallowing
Windbag* after it is flipped over by raging rapids."

Instead of the standard backpack, Pitt attached his air
anks to a harness around his hips for easier access
hrough narrow passages. He was also festooned with
reathing regulators, air lines leading to dual valve
manifolds, pressure gauges, and a small backup bottle
illed with pure oxygen for decompression. Then came
veight belts and buoyancy compensators.

"No mixed gas?" queried Sandecker.

"We'll breathe air," Pitt replied as he checked his
egulators.

"What about the danger of nitrogen narcosis?"

"Once we're clear of the bottom of the sinkhole and
he lower part of the feeder stream before it upslopes to
he river, we'll avoid any further deep diving like the
plague."

"Just see that you stay well above the threshold,"
Sandecker warned him, "and don't go below thirty
meters. And once you're afloat keep a sharp eye for
submerged boulders."

Those were the words the admiral spoke. What he
didn't say was, "If something goes wrong and you need
immediate help, you might as well be on the third ring of
Saturn." In other words, there could be no rescue or
evacuation.

Pitt and Giordino made a final predive check of eac
other's equipment by the side of the pool and tested thei
quick-release buckles and snaps to ensure their smoot
removal in an emergency. Instead of divers' hoods, the
strapped construction workers' hardhats to their head
with dual-sealed miners' lamps on the front. Then the
poised on the edge of the sinkhole and slipped into th
water.

Sandecker and Duncan hoisted a long, pressure-seale
aluminum canister and struggled to lower one end int
the sinkhole. The canister, measuring one meter in widt
by four in length, was articulated in the middle for easie
maneuvering through tight spaces. Heavy and cumber
some on land from the lead ballast required to give i
neutral buoyancy, it was easily moved by a diver under
water.

Giordino bit on his mouthpiece, adjusted his mask
and took hold of a handgrip on the forward end of th
canister. He threw a final wave as he and the caniste
slowly sank together below the water surface. Pitt looke
up from the water and shook hands with Duncan.

"Whatever you do," Duncan warned him, "mind yo
don't let the current sweep you past the treasure chamber. From that position to where the river emerges int
the Gulf has to be over a hundred kilometers."

"Don't worry, we won't spend any more time down
there than we have to."

"I wish there was another way into the mountain."

Pitt shook his head. "It can only be done with a dive
raft operation."

"Bring Loren and Rudi back," replied Sandecker,
fighting off a surge of emotion.

"You'll see them soon," Pitt promised.

And then he was gone.

32

The voice of his radio operator roused Captain Juan Diego from his reverie, and he turned from gazing out his command tent at the cone-shaped mountain. There was an indescribable ugliness about Cerro el Capirote and the bleak desert that surrounded it, he thought. This was a wasteland compared to the beauty of his native state of Durango.

"Yes, what is it, Sergeant?"

The radio operator had his back to him and Diego couldn't see the puzzled look on the soldier's face. "I called the security posts for their hourly status reports and received no response from Posts Four and Six."

Diego sighed. He didn't need unexpected predicaments. Colonel Campos had commanded him to set up a security perimeter around the mountain and he had followed orders. No reason was given, none was asked. Consumed with curiosity, Diego could only watch the helicopters arrive and depart and wonder what was going on up there.

"Contact Corporal Francisco at Post Five and have him send a man to check Four and Six." Diego sat down at his field desk and duly noted the lack of response in his daily report as a probable breakdown in communica-

tions equipment. The possibility there was a real prob
lem never entered his mind.

"I can't raise Francisco at Post Five either," the
radioman informed him.

Diego finally turned. "Are you certain your equipment
is working properly?"

"Yes, sir. The transmitter is sending and receiving
perfectly."

"Try Post One."

The radioman adjusted his headphones and signaled
the post. A few moments later, he turned and shrugged
"I'm sorry, Captain, Post One is silent too."

"I'll see to this myself," Diego said irritably. He
picked up a portable radio and headed from the tent
toward his command vehicle. Suddenly, he stopped in
his tracks and stared dumbly.

The army command vehicle was sitting with the left
front end jacked up, the wheel and the spare tire both
nowhere to be seen. "What is going on?" he muttered to
himself. Is this some sort of prank, he wondered, or
could Colonel Campos be testing him?

He spun around on his heel and started for the tent but
took only two steps. As if conjured up out of nothingness
by a spell, three men blocked his way. All held rifles
pointed at his chest. The first question that ran through
his mind was why were Indians, dressed as if they were
on a cattle drive, sabotaging his equipment?

"This is a military zone," he blurted. "You are not
permitted here."

"Do as you're told, soldier boy," said Billy Yuma,
"and none of your men will get hurt."

Diego suddenly guessed what had happened to his
security posts. And yet he was confused. There was no
way a few Indians could capture forty trained soldiers
without firing a shot. He addressed his words to Yuma,
whom he took to be the leader.

"Drop your weapons before my men arrive or you will be placed under military arrest."

"I'm sorry to inform you, soldier boy," Yuma said, taking delight in intimidating the officer in his neatly pressed field uniform and brightly shined combat boots, "but your entire force has been disarmed and is now under guard."

"Impossible!" snapped Diego haughtily. "No mob of sand rats can stand up against trained troops."

Yuma shrugged indifferently and turned to one of the men beside him. "Fix the radio inside the tent so it won't work."

"You're crazy. You can't destroy government property."

"You have trespassed on our land," said Yuma in a low voice. "You have no authority here."

"I order you to put those guns down," commanded Diego, reaching for his sidearm.

Yuma stepped forward, his weathered face expressionless, and rammed the muzzle of his old Winchester rifle deep into Captain Diego's stomach. "Do not resist us. If I pull the trigger, your body will silence the gunfire to those on the mountain."

The sudden, jolting pain convinced Diego these men were not playing games. They knew the desert and could move through the terrain like ghosts. His orders were to prevent possible encroachment by wandering hunters or prospectors. Nothing was mentioned about an armed force of local Indians who lay in ambush. Slowly, he handed over his automatic pistol to one of Yuma's men, who stuffed the barrel down the waist of his denim pants.

"Your radio too, please."

Diego reluctantly passed over the radio. "Why are you doing this?" he asked. "Don't you know you are breaking the law?"

"If you soldier boys are working with the men who are defiling our sacred mountain, it is you who are breaking the law, our law. Now, no more talk. You will come with us."

In silence, Captain Diego and his radioman were escorted half a kilometer (a third of a mile) to a large overhanging rock protruding from the mountain. There, out of sight of anyone on the peak, Diego found his entire company of men sitting nervously in a tight group while several Indians covered them with their own weapons.

They scrambled to their feet and came to attention, their faces reflecting relief at seeing their commanding officer. Two lieutenants and a sergeant came up and saluted.

"Is there no one who escaped?" asked Diego.

One of the lieutenants shook his head. "No, sir. They were on us before we could resist."

Diego looked around at the Indians guarding his men. Including Yuma, he counted only sixteen. "Is this all of you?" he asked unbelievingly.

Yuma nodded. "We did not need more."

"What are you going to do with us?"

"Nothing, soldier boy. My neighbors and I have been careful not to harm anyone. You and your men will enjoy a nice siesta for a few hours, and then you'll be free to leave our land."

"And if we attempt to escape?"

Yuma shrugged indifferently. "Then you will be shot. Something you should think about, since my people can hit a running rabbit at fifty meters."

Yuma had said all he had to say. He turned his back on Captain Diego and began climbing an almost unrecognizable trail between a fissure on the south wall of the mountain. No words were spoken between the Montolos. As if on silent command, ten men followed Billy Yuma while five remained behind to guard the prisoners.

The ascent went faster than the last time. He prof-
ited from his mistakes and ignored the wrong turns he
had taken that curved into blind chutes. He remembered the good handholds and avoided the ones that
were badly eroded. But it was still tough going on a
trail no self-respecting pack mule would be caught
dead on.

After he reached a flat ledge, he stopped to catch his
breath. His heart was beginning to pound, but his body
was tensed with the nervous energy of a racehorse ready
to burst from the gate. He pulled an old pocket watch
from his pants pocket and checked the time. He nodded
to himself in satisfaction and held the watch face for the
others to see. They were twenty minutes ahead of
schedule.

High above, on the mountain's summit, the helicopters hovered like bees around a hive. They were loaded
with as much of the treasure as they could lift before
struggling into the sky and setting a course for the
airstrip in the Altar Desert.

Colonel Campos's officers and men were working so
fast, and were so awed by the golden hoard, none thought
to check the security forces stationed around the base of
the mountain. The radio operator on the peak was too
busy coordinating the comings and goings of the helicopters to ask for a report from Captain Diego. No one took
the time to look over the edge at the deserted encamp-
ment below. Nor did they notice the small band of men
who were slowly climbing ever closer to the mountaintop.

Police Comandante Cortina was not a man who
missed much. As his police helicopter rose from Cerro el
Capirote for the return trip to his headquarters, he
stared down at the stone beast and caught something
that was missed by all the others. A pragmatic man, he
closed his eyes and put it off as a trick of sunlight and
shadows, or perhaps the angle of his view. But when he

refocused his eyes on the ancient sculpture, he could have sworn the vicious expression had altered. The menacing look was gone.

To Cortina, just before it slipped out of view of his window, the fang-filled jaws on the guardian of the dead were frozen in a smile.

THE WALLOWING WINDBAG

33

THE EIGHT AIR CHAMBERS OF THE *WALLOWING WINDBAG*
were filled and the hull fully inflated, deployed, and
ready to do battle with the river. Known as a water
rescue response vehicle, the ungainly Hovercraft could
ride on a cushion of air effortlessly over boiling rapids,
quicksand, thin ice, and polluted quagmires. Vehicles in
use by police and fire departments around the country
had saved countless victims from death by drowning.
Now this one was going on an endurance trial its
builders never conceived.

Three meters (10 feet) in length and 1.5 meters (5 feet)
wide, the compact craft mounted a four-cycle, 50-
horsepower engine that could propel her over a flat
surface at 64 kilometers an hour.

"Our engineers did a fine job of modifying the height
for us," said Giordino.

Before they cast off, they stowed and tied down ten
reserve air tanks, extra air bottles to reinflate the Hovercraft, a battery of lights including two aircraft landing
lights built into waterproof housings, spare batteries,
first-aid equipment, and three additional breathing regulators.

From a watertight container Pitt retrieved his battered, old .45 Colt automatic and two ammo clips. He

smiled as he also found a thermos of coffee and four
bologna sandwiches. Admiral Sandecker never forgot the
details that make for a successful operation. Pitt put the
thermos and sandwiches back in the container. There
was no time for a picnic. They had to push on if they
were to reach the treasure chamber before it was too late
to save Loren and Rudi. He inserted the gun and extra
ammo clips into a plastic bag and sealed the opening.
Then he unzipped the front of his wet suit and slipped
the bag inside next to his stomach and climbed aboard
the Hovercraft. "Gear stashed?"

"All buttoned down."

"Ready to shove off?"

"Start her up."

Pitt crouched in the stern just ahead of the engine fan.
He engaged the starter and the air-cooled engine sput-
tered to life. The small engine was well muffled and the
exhaust sounded only as a muted throb.

Giordino took his position in the bow of the craft and
turned on one of the landing lights, illuminating the
cavern as bright as daylight.

The Hovercraft moved off the shoreline, suspended on
its self-produced 20-centimeter (8 inch) cushion of air
into the mainstream of the river. Pitt held the vertical
grips of the control bar in each hand and easily steered
an arrow-straight course over the flowing current.

It seemed strange to be skimming over the water
surface without a sensation of contact. From the bow,
Giordino could look down into the remarkably transparent water that had turned from the cobalt blue of the
sinkhole to a deep aqua green and see startled albino
salamanders and small schools of blind cave fish darting
amid the spherical boulders that carpeted the river
bottom like fallen ornaments. He kept busy reporting the
river conditions ahead and snapping photos as Pitt
maneuvered and recorded data on his computer for
Peter Duncan.

Even with their rapid motion through the large corridors, their sweat and the extreme humidity combined to form a halolike mist around their heads. They ignored the phenomenon and the darkness behind them, never looking back as they continued deeper into the river-carved canyon.

For the first 8 kilometers (5 miles) it was clear sailing and they made good time. They skimmed over bottomless pools and past forbidding galleries that extended deep into the walls of the caverns. The ceilings in the string of river chambers varied from a high of 30 meters (98 feet) to barely enough room to squeeze the Hovercraft through. They bounced over several small, shallow cascades without difficulty and entered a narrow channel where it took all their concentration to avoid the ever-present rocks. Then they traveled through one enormous gallery that stretched almost 3 kilometers (slightly under 2 miles) and was filled with stunning crystals that glinted and sparkled beneath the aircraft light.

On two different occasions, the passage became flooded when the ceiling merged with the water surface. Then they went through the routine of deflating the *Wallowing Windbag* until it achieved neutral buoyancy, returned to breathing from their air tanks, and drifted with the current through the sunken passage, dragging the flattened Hovercraft and its equipment behind them until they emerged into an open cavern and reinflated it again. There were no complaints over the additional effort. Neither man expected a smooth cruise down a placid river.

After traveling through a second submerged passage and reinflating their boat, Pitt observed that the current's pace had quickened by two knots and the river gradient began dropping at a faster rate. Like leaves through a gutter drain, they rushed into the eternal land of gloom, never knowing what dangers lurked around the next bend.

The rapids increased frighteningly as the Hovercraft ↕s suddenly swept into a raging cataract. The emerald ⊔ter turned a boiling white as it cascaded through a ⊔ssage strewn with boulders. Now the *Wallowing Wind-g* was rearing up like a rodeo bronco as it surged ⊔tween the rocks and plunged sickeningly into the next ⊔ugh. Every time Pitt told himself the rapids couldn't ⊔ssibly get more violent, the next stretch of river ⊔mmed the Hovercraft into a seething frenzy that ⊔ried it completely on more than one occasion. But the ⊔thful little craft always shook off the froth and fought ⊔ck to the surface.

Pitt struggled to keep the boat on a straight course. If ⊔ey swung halfway around broadside to the tumult, all ⊔ances for survival would have been lost. Giordino ⊔abbed the emergency oars and put his back into ⊔eping the boat steady. They swept around a sharp ⊔rve in the river over massive rocks, some partly ⊔bmerged and kicking up great waves.

Their ordeals never ceased. They were caught in a ⊔irling eddy like a cork being sucked down a drain. Pitt ⊔aced his back against an air-filled support cell to stay ⊔right and pushed the throttle to its stop. The howl of ⊔e racing engine was lost in the roar of the rapids. All ⊔s will and concentration were focused on keeping the ⊔overcraft from twisting broadside from the force of the ⊔eeding current as Giordino assisted by pulling might-⊔ on the oars.

Lost when Giordino took up the oars, the landing ⊔ghts had fallen overboard into the froth. Now the only ⊔ght came from the lamps on their hardhats. It seemed a ⊔etime had passed before they finally broke clear of the ⊔hirlpool and were hurled back into the rapids.

Pitt eased back on the throttle and relaxed his hands ⊔n the grips of the control bar. There was no point in ⊔ghting the river now. The *Wallowing Windbag* would go ⊔here the surging water threw it.

Giordino peered into the black unknown ahead, ho
ing to see calmer water. What he saw was a fork in t
river that divided the mainstream into two differe
galleries. He shouted above the tumult, "We're comi
to a junction!"

"Can you tell which is the main conduit?" Pitt yell
back.

"The one on the left looks larger!"

"Okay, pull to port!"

The Hovercraft came terrifyingly close to bei
smashed against the great mass of rock that split t
river and only missed turning turtle by a hair as it w
overwhelmed by a giant backwash. The little vessel d
into the turbulence and lurched forward sickening
burying its bow under a wall of water. Somehow
regained a level keel before being thrown forward by t
relentless current.

For an instant Pitt thought he'd lost Giordino, b
then the burly little man rose out of the deep pool filli
the inside of the boat and shook his head to clear tl
dizziness brought on by being spun around like a ball
a roulette wheel. Incredibly, he cracked a smile an
pointed to his ears.

Pitt understood. The continuous roar of the rapi
seemed to be slackening. The Hovercraft responded
his control again, but sluggishly, because it was half-fu
of water. The excess weight was making it impossible t
maintain an air-cushion. He increased the throttle an
yelled to Giordino.

"Start bailing!"

The boat designers had thought of everything. Gio
dino inserted a lever into a small pump and bega
shoving it back and forth, causing a gush of water t
shoot through a pipe over the side.

Pitt leaned over and studied the depths under hi
headlamps. The channel seemed more constricted, an
although the rocks were no longer churning up the wate

e river seemed to be moving at a horrifying speed. ddenly, he noticed that Giordino had stopped bailing d was listening with an apocalyptic look on his face. nd then Pitt heard it too.

A deep rumble boomed from the black void down- er.

Giordino stared at him. "I think we just bought the rm!" he shouted.

A vision of going over Niagara Falls in a barrel came Pitt. This was no spout from above they were ap- oaching. The sound that reverberated through the vern was that of an enormous volume of water rushing er an immense cascade.

"Hit the inflator on your buoyancy compensator!" Pitt ared above the chaos.

The water was sweeping them along at a good twenty ots and appeared to be funneling into a concentrated rge. A million liters of water sucked them toward the seen precipice. They rounded the next bend and sailed to a maelstrom of mist. The thunderous rumble be- me deafening.

There was no fear, no sense of helplessness, no feeling f despair. All Pitt felt was a strange numbness as if all ower of intelligent thought had abruptly evaporated. It emed to him that he was entering a nightmare where othing had any shape or form. His final moment of arity came when the *Wallowing Windbag* hung sus- ended for a moment before soaring into the mist.

With no point of reference, there was no sensation of lling; rather, it seemed as if they were flying through a loud. Then his hold on the control bar was lost and he as hurled out of the Hovercraft. He thought he heard iordino shout something, but the voice was lost in the ar of the falls. The drop through the vortex seemed to ke forever. And then came the impact. He struck a eep pool at the base of the falls like a meteor. The air as driven from his lungs and he thought at first that he

was smashed to bloody pulp on rocks, but then he f
the comforting squeeze of water all around him.

Instinctively holding his breath, he fought to reach t
surface. Aided by his inflated buoyancy compensator,
quickly broke clear and was immediately swept away
the torrent. Rocks reached out for him like shroud
predators of the underworld. He was flung down a sp
of rapids, colliding, he'd have sworn, with every bould
that protruded from the river. The contact rasped ar
shredded his wet suit, stripping skin from his legs ar
outspread arms. He suffered a blow to his chest and th
his head struck something hard and ungiving. But for t
protection of the hardhat that absorbed 80 percent of t
blow, he'd have cracked his skull.

Incredibly, his buoyancy compensator stayed inflate
and he floated half-unconscious through a short spill
rapids. One of the lights on his helmet was smashed k
the impact and the other one seemed to cast an indistin
red beam. Gratefully, he felt loose stone beneath his fe
and saw he was being spun toward shallows leading to
small open space along the shoreline. He swam until h
knees scraped the coarse gravel, struggling to loosen th
grip of the murderous current. He extended his hands t
pull himself over the slippery stones onto the dry shelf.
groan of pain escaped his lips as one of his wrist
exploded in agony. At some point after going over th
falls, he had broken something there. His wrist was nc
all that was broken. He'd also cracked two or more rib
on his left side.

The rumbling thunder of the falls sounded far in th
distance. Slowly his mind came back on track and h
wondered how far he'd been swept by the torrent. Then
as more of the cobwebs cleared, he remembered Gio
dino. In desperation he shouted Al's name, his voic
echoing through the air chamber, hoping but never reall
expecting to hear a reply.

"Over here."

The answer didn't come much louder than a whisper, but Pitt heard it as if it came out of a loudspeaker. He rose unsteadily to his feet, trying to get a fix. "Say again."

"I'm only six meters upstream of you," said Giordino. "Can't you see me?"

A red haze seemed to block Pitt's field of vision. He rubbed his eyes and found he could focus them again. He also realized the red haze that had been clouding his sight came from blood that was spilling from a gash in his forehead. Now he could clearly discern Giordino lying on his back a short distance away, half out of the water.

He staggered over to his friend, clutching the left side of his chest in a vain attempt to contain the pain. He knelt stiffly beside Giordino. "Am I ever glad to see you. I thought you and the *Windbag* had sailed off without me."

"The remains of our trusty boat were swept downstream."

"Are you badly injured?" Pitt asked.

Giordino smiled gamely, held up his hands and wiggled his fingers. "At least I can still play Carnegie Hall."

"Play what? You can't even carry a tune." Then Pitt's eyes filled with concern. "Is it your back?"

Giordino weakly shook his head. "I stayed with the *Windbag* and my feet were caught in the lines holding the equipment when she struck bottom. Then she went one way, and I went the other. I think both legs are broken below the knees." He explained his injuries as calmly as if he were describing a pair of flat tires.

Pitt gently felt Giordino's calves as his friend clenched his fists. "Lucky you. Simple breaks, no compound fractures."

Giordino stared up at Pitt. "You look like you went through the spin cycle in a washing machine."

"A few scrapes and bruises," Pitt lied.

"Then why are you talking through clenched teeth?

Pitt didn't answer. He tried to call up a program of the computer on his arm, but it had been knocke against a rock and was broken. He unbuckled the stra and threw it in the river. "So much for Duncan's data

"I lost the camera too."

"Tough break. Nobody will be coming this way aga soon, certainly not over those falls."

"Any idea how far to the treasure cavern?" aske Giordino.

"A rough guess? Maybe two kilometers."

Giordino looked at him. "You'll have to go it alone

"You're talking crazy."

"I'll only be a burden." He was no longer smilin "Forget about me. Get to the treasure cavern."

"I can't leave you here."

"Busted bones or not, I can still float. I'll follow yo later."

"Take care when you get there," said Pitt grimly. "Yo may drift, but you can't escape the current. Mind yo stay close to shore out of the mainstream or you'll b swept beyond recovery."

"No big deal if I am. Our air tanks went with th *Wallowing Windbag*. If we meet a flooded gallery be tween here and the treasure chamber longer than we ca hold our breath, we'll drown anyway."

"You're supposed to look on the bright side."

Giordino removed a spare flashlight from a be around one thigh. "You'll need this. Your headlam looks like it lost a fight with a rock. Come to think of i your face is a mess too. You're bleeding all over th shredded remains of your nice clean wet suit."

"Another dip in the river will fix that," said Pitt attaching the flashlight around the forearm above hi broken left wrist where the computer used to be. H dropped his weight belt. "I won't be needing this an longer."

"Aren't you taking your air tank?"

"I don't want to be hindered any more than I have to."

"What if you come to a flooded chamber?"

"I'll have to free dive through as far as I can on my ¬ngs."

"One last favor," said Giordino, holding up the empty ¬arness straps that once supported his air tanks. "Wrap ¬y legs together to keep them from flopping around."

Pitt cinched the straps as tight as he dared, conscious ¬f his broken wrist and the need to be gentle. Except for ¬ sharp intake of breath, Giordino uttered no sound. ¬Rest up for at least an hour before you follow," Pitt ¬rdered.

"Just get a move on and do what you can to save Loren ¬nd Rudi. I'll be along as soon as I'm able."

"I'll keep a watch for you."

"Better find a big net."

Pitt gave Giordino's arm a farewell grip. Then he ¬vaded into the river until the current swept him off his ¬eet and carried him into the next cavern.

Giordino watched until Pitt's light vanished around ¬he next bend in the canyon and was lost in the darkness. ¬wo kilometers (1.2 miles), he mused. He hoped the final ¬g of the journey was in air-filled chambers.

34

YUMA HAD LAIN ON A LEDGE FOR NEARLY A FULL MINUTE catching his breath and waiting for his heart to slow When he lifted his head over the rim, he saw a strange looking little man with a bald head and huge glasses incongruously dressed in a business suit with shirt an tie, staring back at him. To Yuma, the man reminde him of the government officials who passed through th Montolo village once a year, promising aid in the form of fertilizer, feed and grain, and money, but went on their way and never delivered. After climbing over th rim of the slope he also spotted a group of men standing by a helicopter 30 meters (100 feet) away. They did no notice him. He had planned the climb to terminate behind the great stone demon out of sight of anyone. He had come this far without causing injury or death, and Yuma hated to start now.

"Walk back toward me," he ordered the man. "Stand next to the demon."

As he saw more men materializing behind Yuma, the man snapped. He turned and began to run, shouting "Intruders! Shoot them!"

Yuma's relatives and neighbors, guns at the ready, fanned out like ghosts in a cemetery as they encircled the

elicopter. Zolar swore loudly. "Where did these Indians
ome from?"

"No time to reason why," snapped Oxley. "We're
ulling out."

He jumped through the cargo hatch and pulled Zolar
n after him.

"The gold warriors!" Zolar protested. "They're not
oaded."

"Forget them."

"No!" Zolar resisted.

"You fool. Can't you see, those men are armed. The
army engineers can't help us." He turned and yelled to
the pilot of the helicopter. "Lift off! *Ándale, ándale!*"

Yuma and his tribal members were only 10 meters
from the helicopter now. So far no shots had been fired.
The sight of the sun glinting off the golden warriors
momentarily stunned the Montolos. The only pure gold
object any of them had ever seen was a small chalice on
the altar of the little mission church in the nearby village
of Ilano Colorado.

Dust began to swirl as the pilot applied the throttles
and the rotor blades of the helicopter furiously beat the
air. Zolar grimly hung on to a strap inside the cargo bay.
"Cyrus is still down in the cavern."

"He's with Amaru and his men. Not to worry. Their
automatic weapons are more than a match for a few
Indians carrying hunting rifles and shotguns. They'll
leave in the last helicopter still on the mountain."

Yuma's prearranged plan with Pitt was accomplished.
He and his people had secured the summit and forced
the evil ones from the sacred mountain of the dead.
Now, curiosity drew Yuma to the enlarged opening to
the interior passageway. He had a nagging ache to
explore the cavern and see with his own eyes the river
described by Pitt. The water he saw in his dreams. But

the older men were too frightened to enter the bowels o
the sacred mountain, and the gold created a problem
with the younger men. They wanted to drop everything
and carry it off before armed troops returned.

"This is our mountain," said one young man, the son
of Yuma's neighboring rancher. "The little golden people
belong to us."

"First we must see the river inside the mountain,"
countered Yuma.

"It is forbidden for the living to enter the land of the
dead," warned Yuma's older brother.

A nephew stared at Yuma doubtfully. "There is no
river that runs beneath the desert."

"I believe the man who told me."

"You cannot trust the gringo, no more than those with
Spanish blood in their veins."

Yuma shook his head and pointed to the gold. "This
proves he did not lie."

"The soldiers will come back and kill us if we do not
leave," protested another villager.

"The golden people are too heavy to carry down the
steep trail," the young man argued. "They must be
lowered by rope down the rock walls. That will take
time."

"Let us offer prayers to the demon and be on our way,"
said the brother.

The young man persisted. "Not until the golden
people are safely below."

Yuma reluctantly gave in. "So it is, my family, my
friends. I will keep my promise and enter the mountain
alone. Take the men of gold, but hurry. You do not have
much daylight left."

As he turned and walked through the enlarged opening
leading to the passageway, Yuma felt little fear.

Good had come from the climb to the top of the
mountain. The evil men were cast down. The demon was
at peace again. Now, with the blessing of the demon,

Billy Yuma felt confident he could safely enter the land of the dead. And maybe find a trail leading to the lost sacred idols of his people.

Loren sat huddled in the cramped rock cell, sinking into the quicksand of self-pity. She had no more fight left in her. The hours had merged until time lost all sense of meaning. She could not remember when she had last eaten. She tried to recall what it felt like to be warm and dry, but that memory seemed like an event that occurred ages ago.

She looked over at Rudi Gunn. He had hardly moved at all since they had been led to that damp little cave. She didn't have to be a doctor to see that he had slipped badly in that time. Tupac Amaru, in a storm of sadistic wrath, had broken several of Gunn's fingers by stomping them. Amaru had also injured Gunn severely by kicking him repeatedly in the stomach and head. If Rudi didn't receive medical attention very soon, he might die.

Loren's mind turned to Pitt. Every conceivable road to freedom was blocked unless he could ride to their rescue at the head of the U.S. Cavalry. Not a likely prospect.

She had no right to give up. But Pitt was dead, crushed by concussion grenades in the sea. If her countrymen could have sent a group of Special Forces over the border to save her, they would have done so by now.

She had watched through the cave opening as the golden treasure was hauled past her cell and through the guardians' chamber up to the peak of the hollow mountain. When all the gold was gone, she knew it would be time for her and Rudi to die.

They did not have to wait long. One of Amaru's foul-smelling henchmen walked up to their guard and gave him an order. The ugly slug turned and motioned them out of the cave. *"Salga, salga,"* he commanded them.

Loren shook Gunn awake and helped him rise to his feet. "They want to move us," she told him softly.

Gunn looked at her dazedly, and then incredibly, he forced a tight smile. "About time they upgraded us to a better room."

With Gunn shuffling alongside Loren, her arm around his waist, his over her shoulders, they were led to a flat area between the stalagmites near the shoreline of the river. Amaru was joking with four of his men who were grouped around him. Another man she recognized from the ferryboat as Cyrus Sarason. The Latin Americans appeared cool and relaxed, but Sarason was sweating heavily and his shirt beneath his armpits was stained.

In contrast, Amaru looked as if he were bursting at the seams with nervous energy. He came over and roughly cupped Loren's chin with one hand.

"Are you ready to entertain us?"

"Leave her be," said Sarason. "There is no need to prolong our stay here."

Little Rudi Gunn, grievously injured and barely able to stand, suddenly crouched, launched himself forward, and rammed his head into the belly of the man about to assault Loren. His charge had all the impact of a broomstick against the gate of a fortress. The big Peruvian barely grunted before delivering a passionless backhand that sent Gunn sprawling across the floor of the cavern.

"Throw the little man in the river," ordered Amaru.

"No!" Loren cried. "Don't kill him."

One of Amaru's men took Gunn by the ankle and began dragging him toward the water.

"You may be making a mistake," cautioned Sarason.

Amaru looked at him queerly. "Why?"

"This river probably enters the Gulf. Instead of providing a floating body for identification, perhaps it might be wiser if they disappear forever."

Amaru paused thoughtfully for a moment. Then he laughed. "An underground river that carries them into the Sea of Cortez. I like that. American investigators will never suspect that they were killed a hundred kilometers away from where they're found. The idea appeals to me." He made a motion to the man holding Gunn to continue. "Heave him as far as you can into the current."

"No, please," Loren begged. "Let him live and I'll do whatever you demand."

"You'll do that anyway," Amaru said impassively.

The guard hurled Gunn into the river with the ease of an athlete throwing the shotput. There was a splash, and Gunn vanished beneath the black water without a word.

Amaru turned back to Loren and nodded at Julio. "Let the show begin."

Loren screamed and moved like a cat. She sprang at the man who gripped her arm and rammed the long nails of her thumbs deeply into his eyes.

Amaru walked up to Loren and slapped her hard across the face. She staggered back but did not fall. "You will pay for that," he said with icy calm. "When you have served your purpose, you shall receive the same treatment before you die."

The fear in Loren's eyes had been replaced with raging anger. She kicked out at Amaru. He took the blows as if they were no more annoying than an attack by a mosquito. Infuriated, he punched her in the stomach.

Loren doubled up, choking in agony and at the same time gasping for breath. She sank to her knees and slowly fell on her side, still doubled up and clutching her stomach with her arms.

Then abruptly, her hands were free and she clawed her attacker across the face. He sat back stunned, parallel streaks of red blooming on both cheeks, and stared dumbly at the two men who had suddenly released her arms and hands. "You idiots, what are you doing?" he hissed.

The men who were facing the river fell backward in

open-mouthed shock. They crossed themselves as if warding off the devil. Their eyes were not on Loren. They were staring into the river beyond. Confused, Amaru turned and peered into the dark waters. What he saw was enough to turn a sane man mad. His mouth dropped open in shock at the sight of an eerie light moving under the water toward him. They all gaped as if hypnotized as the light surfaced and became part of a helmeted head.

Like some hideous wraith rising from the murky abyss of a watery hell, a human form slowly arose from the black depths of the river and moved toward the shore. The apparition, with black seaweedlike shreds hanging from its body, looked like something that belonged not to this world but to the deepest reaches of an alien planet. The effect was made even more shocking by the reappearance of the dead.

Clenched under the right arm, as a father might carry his child, was the inert body of Rudi Gunn.

Sarason's face looked like a white plaster death mask. Sweat poured down his forehead. For a man who did not excite easily, his eyes were near-crazed with shock. He stood silent, as the monstrosity left him too stunned to speak.

Amaru leaped to his feet and tried to speak, but only a whispered croak came out. His lips quivered as he rasped, "Go back, *diablo,* go back to *infierno.*"

The phantom gently lowered Gunn to the ground. He removed his helmet with one hand. Then he unzipped the front of his wet suit and reached inside. The green eyes could be seen now, cast on Loren's exposed position on the cold, hard rock. They glinted under the artificial lights with a terrible anger.

The men stared dumbly as the Colt thundered once, twice in the cavern. Julio moaned in a far corner unable to see, his hands still over his injured eyes.

Loren was beyond screaming. She stared at the man

from the river, recognizing him but convinced she was seeing a hallucination.

The shock of disbelief, then horror at the realization of who the apparition was, made Amaru's heart turn cold. "You!" he gasped in a strangled voice.

"You seem surprised to see me, Tupac," said Pitt easily. "Cyrus looks a little green around the gills too."

"You're dead. I killed you."

"Do a sloppy job, get sloppy results." Pitt cycled the Colt from man to man and spoke to Loren without looking at her. "Are you badly hurt?"

For a moment she was too stunned to answer. Then finally, she stammered, "Dirk . . . is it really you?"

"If there's another one, I hope they catch him before he signs my name to a lot of checks. I'm sorry I didn't get here sooner."

She nodded. "Thanks to you I'll survive to see these beasts pay."

"You won't have to wait long," Pitt said with a voice of stone. "Are you strong enough to make it up the passageway?"

"Yes, yes," Loren murmured as the reality of her salvation began to sink in. She rose unsteadily to her feet. She pointed down at Gunn. "Rudi is in a bad way."

Pitt's teeth were bared, murder glaring out of his opaline green eyes. "Cyrus here just volunteered to carry Rudi topside." Pitt casually waved the gun in the direction of Sarason.

Sarason knew he could expect a bullet, and fright was slowly replaced by self-preservation. His scheming mind began to focus on a plan to save himself. He sagged to the rock floor as if overcome with shock, his right hand resting on a knee only centimeters away from a .38-caliber derringer strapped to his leg just inside his boot. "How did you get here?" he asked, stalling.

Pitt was not taken in by the mundane question. "We came on an underground cruise ship."

"We?"

"The rest of the team should be surfacing at any moment," Pitt bluffed.

Amaru suddenly shouted at his men. "Rush him!"

They were hardened killers but they had no wish to die. They made no effort to reach for the automatic rifles they had laid aside. One look down the barrel of Pitt's .45 beneath the burning eyes was enough to deter anyone who did not cherish suicidal tendencies.

"You yellow dogs!" Amaru snarled.

"Still ordering others to do your dirty work, I see," said Pitt. "It appears I made a mistake not killing you in Peru."

"I vowed then you would suffer as you made me."

"Don't bet your *Solpemachaco* pension on it."

"You intend to murder us in cold blood, without the decency of a fair trial," protested Sarason as his hand crept past his knee toward the concealed derringer. Only then did he notice that Pitt's injuries went beyond the bloody gash across the forehead. There was a fatigued droop to the shoulders, an unsteadiness to his stance. The skewed left hand was pressed against his chest. Broken wrist and ribs, Sarason surmised. His hopes rose as he realized that Pitt was on the thin edge of collapse.

"You're hardly one to demand justice," said Pitt, biting scorn in his tone. "A pity our great American court system doesn't hand out the same punishment to killers they gave to their victims."

"And you are not one to judge my actions. If not for my brothers and me, thousands of artifacts would be rotting away in the basements of museums around the world. We preserved the antiquities and redistributed them to people who appreciate their value."

Pitt stopped his roving gaze and focused on Sarason. "You call that an excuse? You justify theft and murder on a grand scale so you and your criminal relatives can make fat profits. The magic words for you, pal, are charlatan and hypocrite."

"Shooting me won't put my family out of business."

"Haven't you heard?" Pitt grimly smiled. "Zolar International just went down the toilet. Federal agents raided your facilities in Galveston. They found enough loot to fill a hundred galleries."

Sarason tilted his head back and laughed. "Our headquarters in Galveston is a legitimate operation. All merchandise is lawfully bought and sold."

"I'm talking about the second facility," Pitt said casually.

A flicker of apprehension showed in Sarason's tan face. "There is only *one* building."

"No, there are two. The storage warehouse separated by a tunnel to transport illegal goods to the Zolar building with a subterranean basement housing smuggled antiquities, an art forgery operation, and a vast collection of stolen art."

Sarason looked as if he'd been struck across the face with a club. "How could you know any of this?"

"A pair of federal agents, one from Customs, the other from the FBI, described the raid to me in vivid terms. I should also mention that they'll be waiting with open arms when you attempt to smuggle Huascar's treasure into the United States."

Sarason's fingers were a centimeter away from the little twin-barreled gun. "Then the joke's on them," he said, resurrecting his blasé facade. "The gold isn't going to the United States."

"No matter," Pitt said with quiet reserve. "You won't be around to spend it."

Hidden by a knee crossed over one leg, Sarason's fingers met and cautiously began slipping the two-shot derringer from his boot. He reckoned that Pitt's injuries would slow any reaction time by a split second, but decided against attempting a snap, wildly aimed shot. If he missed with the first bullet, Sarason well knew that despite Pitt's painful injuries there wouldn't be a chance to fire the second. He hesitated as his mind engineered a diversion. He looked over at Amaru and the two men eyeing Pitt with anger. Julio was of no use to him.

"If we all attacked him at the same time," Sarason said as conversationally as if they were all seated around a dining table, "he might kill two or even three of us before the survivor killed him."

Pitt's expression turned cold and remote. "The question is, who will be the survivor?"

Amaru did not care who would live or die. His hatred for the man who crippled him triggered a rage fueled by the memory of pain and mental agony. Without a word, he launched himself at Pitt.

In a muscled flash of speed, Amaru closed like a snarling dog, reaching out for Pitt's gun hand. The shot took the Peruvian in the chest and through a lung, the report coming like a booming crack. The impact would have stopped the average man, but Amaru was a force beyond himself, driven like a maddened pit bull. He gave an audible grunt as the air was forced from his lungs, and then he crashed into Pitt, sending him reeling backward toward the river.

A groan burst from Pitt's lips as his cracked ribs protested the collision in a burst of pain. He desperately spun around, throwing off Amaru's encircling grip around his gun hand and hurling him aside. Through his pain, Pitt's hand instinctively held steady on the Colt. His next bullet dropped the grotesque one-eyed guard with a quick shot to the neck. He ignored the blind Julio and shot the remaining henchman in the center of his chest.

Pitt heard Loren's scream of warning as if it were far off in the distance. Too late he saw Sarason pointing the derringer at him. His body lagged behind his mind and moved a fraction slow.

He saw the fire from the muzzle and felt a terrible hammer blow in his left shoulder before he heard the blast. It flung him around, and he went down sprawling in the water with Amaru crawling after him like a wounded bear intent on shredding a disabled fox. The current caught him in its grasp and pulled him from shore. He grabbed desperately at the bottom stones to impede the surge.

Sarason slowly walked to the water's edge and stared at the struggle going on in the river. Amaru had clenched his arms around Pitt's waist and was trying to drag him under the surface. With a callous grin, Sarason took careful aim at Pitt's head. "A commendable effort, Mr. Pitt. You are a very durable man. Odd as it sounds, I will miss you."

But the *coup de grace* never came. Like black tentacles, a pair of arms circled around Sarason's legs and gripped his ankles. He looked down wildly at the unspeakable thing that was gripping him and began frantically beating at the head that rose between the arms.

Giordino had followed Pitt, drifting down the river. The current had not been as strong as he'd expected upstream from the treasure island and he had been able to painfully drag himself into the shallows unnoticed. He had cursed his helplessness at not being physically able to assist Pitt in fighting off Amaru, but when Sarason unknowingly stepped within reach, Giordino made his move and snagged him.

He ignored the brutal blows to his head. He looked up at Sarason and spoke in a voice that was thick and deep. "Greetings from Hades, butthead."

Sarason recovered quickly at the sight of Giordino and jerked one foot free to maintain his balance. Because Giordino made no attempt to rise to his feet, Sarason immediately perceived that his enemy was somehow badly injured from the hips down. He viciously kicked Giordino, hitting one thigh. He was rewarded by a sharp groan as Giordino's body jumped in a tormented spasm and he released Sarason's other ankle.

"From past experience," Sarason said, regaining his composure, "I should have known you'd be close by."

He stared briefly at the derringer, knowing he had only one bullet left, but aware there were four or five automatic weapons lying nearby. Then he glanced at Pitt and Amaru who were locked in a death struggle. No need to waste the bullet on Pitt. The river had taken the deadly enemies in its grip and was relentlessly sweeping them downstream. If Pitt somehow survived and staggered from the water, Sarason had an arsenal to deal with him.

Sarason made his choice. He stooped down and aimed the gun's twin barrels between Giordino's eyes.

Loren threw herself at Sarason's back, flinging her arms around him, trying to stop him. Sarason broke her grip as if it were string and shoved her aside without so much as a glance.

She fell heavily on one of the weapons that had been cast aside, lifted it and pulled the trigger. Nothing happened. She didn't know enough about guns to remove the safety. She gave a yelp as Sarason reached over and hit her on the head with the butt of the derringer.

Suddenly he spun around. Gunn, remarkably come to life, had tossed a river stone at Sarason that bounced off his hip with the feeble force of a weakly hit tennis ball.

Sarason shook his head in wonder at the fortitude and courage of people who resisted with such fervor. He almost felt sorry they would all have to die. He turned back to Giordino.

"It seems your reprieve was only temporary," he said with a sneer, as he held the gun at arm's length straight at Giordino's face.

In spite of the agony of his broken legs and the specter of death staring him in the face, Giordino looked up at Sarason and grinned venomously.

The shot came like a blast from a cannon inside the

vern, followed by the thump sound of lead bursting through living flesh. Giordino's expression went blank as Sarason's eyes gazed at him with a strange confused look. Then Sarason turned and mechanically took two steps onto shore, slowly pitched forward and struck the stone floor in a lifeless heap.

Giordino couldn't believe he was still alive. He looked up and gaped at a little man, dressed like a ranch hand and casually holding a Winchester rifle, who walked into the circle of light.

"Who are you?" asked Giordino.

"Billy Yuma. I came to help my friend."

Loren, a hand held against her bleeding head, stared at him. "Friend?"

"The man called Pitt."

At the mention of his name, Loren pushed herself to her feet and ran unsteadily to the river's edge. "I don't see him!" she cried fearfully.

Giordino suddenly felt his heart squeeze. He shouted Pitt's name but his voice only echoed in the cavern. "Oh, God, no," he muttered fearfully. "He's gone."

Gunn grimaced as he sat up and peered downriver into the ominous blackness. Like the others who had calmly faced death only minutes before, he was stricken to find that his old friend had been carried away to his death. "Maybe Dirk can swim back," he said hopefully.

Giordino shook his head. "He can't return. The current is too strong."

"Where does the river go?" demanded Loren with rising panic.

Giordino pounded his fist in futility and despair against the solid rock. "The Gulf. Dirk has been swept toward the Sea of Cortez a hundred kilometers away."

Loren sagged to the limestone floor of the cavern, her hands covering her face as she unashamedly wept. "He saved me only to die."

Billy Yuma knelt beside Loren and gently patted her

bare shoulder. "If no one else can, perhaps God w
help."

Giordino was heartsick. No longer feeling his ow
injuries, he stared into the darkness, his eyes unseein
"A hundred kilometers," he repeated slowly. "Even Go
can't keep a man alive with a broken wrist, cracked rib
and a bullet hole in the shoulder through a hundre
kilometers of raging water in total darkness."

After making everyone as comfortable as he coule
Yuma hurried back up to the summit where he told h
story. It shamed his relatives into entering the mountair
They fabricated stretchers out of material left by th
army engineers and tenderly carried Gunn and Giordin
from the river cavern up the passageway. An older ma
kindly offered a grateful Loren a blanket woven by hi
wife.

On Giordino's instructions, Gunn and his stretche
were strapped down in the narrow cargo compartment o
the stolen NUMA helicopter abandoned by the Zolars
Loren climbed into the copilot's seat as Giordino, hi
face contorted in torment, was lifted and maneuvered
behind the pilot's controls.

"We'll have to fly this eggbeater together," Giordino
told Loren as the pain in his legs subsided from shee:
agony to a throbbing ache. "You'll have to work the
pedals that control the tail rotors."

"I hope I can do it," Loren replied nervously.

"Use a gentle touch with your bare feet and we'll be
okay."

Over the helicopter's radio, they alerted Sandecker,
who was pacing Starger's office in the Customs Service
headquarters, that they were on their way. Giordino and
Loren expressed their gratitude to Billy Yuma, his family, and friends, and bid them a warm goodbye. Then
Giordino started the turbine engine and let it warm for a
minute while he scanned the instruments. With the

clic stick in neutral, he eased the collective pitch stick
full down and curled the throttle as he gently pushed
e stick forward. Then he turned to Loren.

"As soon as we begin to rise in the air, the torque effect
ill cause our tail to swing left and our nose to the right.
ightly press the left foot pedal to compensate."

Loren nodded gamely. "I'll do my best, but I wish I
idn't have to do this."

"We have no choice but to fly out. Rudi would be dead
efore he could be manhandled down the side of the
ountain."

The helicopter rose very slowly less than a meter off
ie ground. Giordino let it hang there while Loren
arned the feel of the tail rotor control pedals. At first
ie had a tendency to overcontrol, but she soon got the
ang of it and nodded.

"I think I'm ready."

"Then we're off," acknowledged Giordino.

Twenty minutes later, working in unison, they made a
erfect landing beside the Customs headquarters build-
ig in Calexico where Admiral Sandecker was standing
eside a waiting ambulance.

In that first moment when Amaru forced him beneath
ne water and he could feel the jaws of the current
urround his wrecked body, Pitt knew instantly that
here was no returning to the treasure cavern.

Even if both men had been uninjured, it would have
een no contest. Cutthroat killer that he was, Amaru was
o match for Pitt's experience underwater. Pitt took a
ieep breath before the river closed over his head,
vrapped his good right arm around his chest to protect
iis fractured ribs and relaxed amid the pain without
vasting his strength in fighting off his attacker.

Amazingly, he still kept his grip on the gun, although
o fire it underwater would probably have shattered

every bone in his hand. He felt Amaru's encircling ho
slide from his waist to his hips. The murderer was stron
as iron. He clawed at Pitt furiously, still trying for th
gun as they spun around in the current like toy dol
caught in a whirlpool.

Neither man could see the other as they swirled int
utter darkness. Without the slightest suggestion of ligh
Pitt felt as though he was submerged in ink.

Amaru's wrath was all that kept him alive in the ne:
forty-five seconds. It did not sink into his crazed min
that he was drowning twice—his bullet-punctured lun
was filling with blood while at the same time he wa
sucking in water. The last of his strength was fadin
when his thrashing feet made contact with a shoal tha
was built up from sand accumulating on the outer curv
of the river. He came up choking blood and water in
small open gallery and made a blind lunge for Pitt'
neck.

But Amaru had nothing left. All fight had ebbed away
Once out of the water he could feel the blood pumpin
from the wound in his chest.

Pitt found he was able, by a slight effort, to shov
Amaru back into the mainstream of the current. H
could not see the Peruvian drift away in the pitc
blackness, observe the face drained of color, the eye
glazed in hate and approaching death. But he heard th
malevolent voice slowly moving into the distance awa
from him.

"I said you would suffer," came the words slightl
above a hoarse murmur. "Now you will languish and di
in tormented solitude."

"Nothing like being swept up in a frenzy of poeti
grandeur," said Pitt icily. "Enjoy your trip to the Gulf.'

His reply was a cough and a gurgling sound and finall
silence.

The pain returned to Pitt with a vengeance. The fire
spread from his broken wrist to the bullet wound in hi

shoulder to his cracked ribs. He was not sure he had the strength left to fight it. Exhaustion slightly softened the agony. He felt more tired than he had ever felt in his life. He crawled onto a dry area of the shoal and slowly crumpled face forward into the soft sand and fell unconscious.

35

"I DON'T LIKE LEAVING WITHOUT CYRUS," SAID OXLEY AS HE scanned the desert sky to the southwest.

"Our brother has been in tougher scrapes before," said Zolar impassively. "A few Indians from a local village shouldn't present much of a threat to Amaru's hired killers."

"I expected him long before now."

"Not to worry. Cyrus will probably show up in Morocco with a girl on each arm."

They stood on the end of a narrow asphalt airstrip that had been grooved between the countless dunes of the Altar Desert so Mexican Air Force pilots could hold training exercises under primitive conditions. Behind them, with its tail section jutting over the edge of the sand-swept strip, a Boeing 747-400 jetliner, painted in the colors of a large national air carrier, sat poised for takeoff.

Zolar moved under the shade of the starboard wing and checked off the artifacts inventoried by Henry and Micki Moore as the Mexican army engineers loaded the final piece on board the aircraft. He nodded at the golden sculpture of a monkey that was being hoisted by a large forklift into the cargo hatch nearly 7 meters (23 feet) from the ground. "That's the last of it."

Oxley stared at the barrenness surrounding the airstrip. "You couldn't have picked a more isolated spot to trans-ship the treasure."

Zolar's pilot approached and gave an informal salute. 'My crew and I are ready when you are, gentlemen. We would like to take off before it's dark."

"Is the cargo fastened down securely?" asked Zolar.

The pilot nodded. "Not the neatest job I've seen. But considering we're not using cargo containers, it should hold until we land at Nador in Morocco, providing we don't hit extreme turbulence."

"Do you expect any?"

"No, sir. The weather pattern indicates calm skies all the way."

"Good. We can enjoy a smooth flight," said Zolar, pleased. "Remember, at no time are we to cross over the border into the United States."

"I've laid a course that takes us safely south of Laredo and Brownsville into the Gulf of Mexico below Key West before heading out over the Atlantic."

"How soon before we touch down in Morocco?" Oxley asked the pilot.

"Our flight plan calls for ten hours and fifty-five minutes. Loaded to the maximum, and then some, with several hundred extra pounds of cargo and a full fuel load, plus the detour south of Texas and Florida, we've added slightly over an hour to our flight time, which I hope to pick up with a tail wind."

Zolar looked at the last rays of the sun. "With time changes that should put us in Nador during early afternoon tomorrow."

The pilot nodded. "As soon as you are seated aboard, we will get in the air." He returned to the aircraft and climbed a boarding ladder propped against the forward entry door.

Zolar gestured toward the ladder. "Unless you've

taken a fancy to this sand pit, I see no reason to stand around here any longer."

Oxley bowed jovially. "After you." As they passed through the entry door, he paused and took one last look to the southwest. "I still don't feel right not waiting."

"If our positions were reversed, Cyrus wouldn't hesitate to depart. Too much is at stake to delay any longer. Our brother is a survivor. Stop worrying."

A few minutes later the turbines screamed and the big 747-400 rose above the rolling sand dunes, dipped its starboard wing and banked slightly south of east. Zolar and Oxley sat in a small passenger compartment on the upper deck just behind the cockpit.

"I wonder what happened to the Moores," mused Oxley, peering through a window at the Sea of Cortez as it receded in the distance. "The last I saw of them was in the cavern as the last of the treasure was being loaded on a sled."

"I know it sounds strange, but I had an uneasy feeling they wouldn't be easy to get rid of."

"I have to tell you. The same thing crossed Cyrus's mind too. In fact, he thought they were a pair of killers."

Oxley turned to him. "The wife too? You're joking."

"No, I do believe he was serious," Zolar said.

Oxley stared out the window of the plane. "I won't rest easy until the treasure is safely stored in Morocco and we learn that Cyrus has left Mexico."

Shortly after the aircraft had reached what the brothers believed was cruising altitude, they released their seat belts and stepped into the cargo bay where they began closely examining the incredible golden collection of antiquities. Hardly an hour had passed when Zolar stiffened and looked at his brother queerly.

"Does it feel to you like we're descending?"

Oxley was admiring a golden butterfly that was attached to a golden flower. "I don't feel anything."

Zolar was not satisfied. He leaned down and stared through a window at the ground less than 1000 meters below.

"We're too low!" he said sharply. "Something is wrong."

Oxley's eyes narrowed. He looked through an adjoining window. "You're right. The flaps are down. It looks like we're coming in for a landing. The pilot must have an emergency."

"Why didn't he alert us?"

At that moment they heard the landing gear drop. The ground was rising to meet them faster now. They flashed past houses and railroad tracks, and then the aircraft was over the end of the runway. The wheels thumped onto concrete and the engines howled in reverse thrust. The pilot stood on the brakes and soon eased off on the throttles as he turned the huge craft onto a taxiway.

A sign on the terminal read Welcome to El Paso.

Oxley stared speechless as Zolar blurted, "We've come down in the United States!"

He ran forward and began beating frantically on the cockpit door. There was no reply until the huge plane came to a halt outside an Air National Guard hangar at the opposite end of the field. Only then did the cockpit door slowly crack open.

"What are you doing? I'm ordering you to get back in the air immediately—" Zolar's words froze in his throat as he found himself staring down the muzzle of a gun pointed between his eyes.

The pilot was still seated in his seat, as were the copilot and flight engineer. Henry Moore stood in the doorway gripping a strange nine-millimeter automatic of his own design, while inside the cockpit Micki Moore was talking over the aircraft radio as she calmly aimed a Lilliputian .25-caliber automatic at the pilot's neck.

"Forgive the unscheduled stop, my former friends," said Moore in a commanding voice neither Zolar nor

Oxley had heard before, "but as you can see there's been a change of plan."

Zolar squinted down the gun barrel, and his face twisted from shock to menacing anger. "You idiot, you blind idiot, do you have any idea what you've done?"

"Why, yes," Moore answered matter-of-factly. "Micki and I have hijacked your aircraft and its cargo of golden artifacts. I believe you're aware of the old maxim: There is no honor among thieves."

"If you don't get this plane in the air quickly," Oxley pleaded, "Customs agents will be swarming all over it."

"Now that you mention it, Micki and I *did* entertain the idea of turning the artifacts over to the authorities."

"You can't know what you're saying."

"Oh, I most certainly do, Charley, old pal. As it turns out, federal agents are more interested in you and your brother than Huascar's treasure."

"Where did you come from?" Zolar demanded.

"We merely caught a ride in one of the helicopters transporting the gold. The army engineers were used to our presence and paid no attention as we climbed aboard the plane. We hid out in one of the restrooms until the pilot left to confer with you and Charles on the airstrip. Then we seized the cockpit."

"Why would federal agents take your word for anything?" asked Oxley.

"In a manner of speaking, Micki and I were once agents ourselves," Moore briefly explained. "After we took over the cockpit, Micki radioed some old friends in Washington who arranged your reception."

Zolar looked as if he were about to tear Moore's lungs out whether he got shot in the attempt or not. "You and your lying wife made a deal for a share of the antiquities. Am I right?" He waited for a reply, but when Moore remained silent he went on. "What percentage did they offer you? Ten, twenty, maybe as high as fifty percent?"

"We made no deals with the government," Moore said

slowly. "We knew you had no intention of honoring our agreement, and that you planned to kill us. We had planned to steal the treasure for ourselves, but as you can see, we had a change of heart."

"The way they act familiar with guns," said Oxley, "Cyrus was right. They *are* a pair of killers."

Moore nodded in agreement. "Your brother has an inner eye. It takes an assassin to know one."

A pounding came from outside the forward passenger door on the deck below. Moore gestured down the stairwell with his gun. "Go down and open it," he ordered Zolar and Oxley.

Sullenly, they did as they were told.

When the pressurized door was swung open, two men entered from a stairway that had been pushed up against the aircraft. Both wore business suits. One was a huge black man who looked as if he might have played professional football. The other was a nattily dressed white man. Zolar immediately sensed they were federal agents.

"Joseph Zolar and Charles Oxley, I am Agent David Gaskill with the Customs Service and this is Agent Francis Ragsdale of the FBI. You gentlemen are under arrest for smuggling illegal artifacts into the United States and for the theft of countless art objects from private and public museums, not excluding the unlawful forgery and sale of antiquities."

"What are you talking about?" Zolar demanded.

Gaskill ignored him and looked at Ragsdale with a big toothy smile. "Would you like to do the honors?"

Ragsdale nodded like a kid who had just been given a new disk player. "Yes, indeed, thank you."

As Gaskill cuffed Zolar and Oxley, Ragsdale read them their rights.

"You made good time," said Moore. "We were told you were in Calexico."

"We were on our way aboard a military jet fifteen

minutes after word came down from FBI headquarters in Washington," replied Ragsdale.

Oxley looked at Gaskill, a look for the first time empty of fear and shock, a sudden look of shrewdness. "You'll never find enough evidence to convict us in a hundred years."

Ragsdale tilted his head toward the golden cargo. "What do you call that?"

"We're merely passengers," said Zolar, regaining his composure. "We were invited along for the ride by Professor Moore and his wife."

"I see. And suppose you tell me where all the stolen art and antiquities in your facility in Galveston came from?"

Oxley sneered. "Our Galveston warehouse is perfectly legitimate. You've raided it before and never found a thing."

"If that's the case," said Ragsdale craftily, "how do you explain the tunnel leading from the Logan Storage Company to Zolar International's subterranean warehouse of stolen goods?"

The brothers stared at each other, their faces abruptly gray. "You're making this up," said Zolar fearfully.

"Am I? Would you like me to describe your tunnel in detail and provide a brief rundown on the stolen masterworks we found?"

"The tunnel—you couldn't have found the tunnel."

"As of thirty-six hours ago," said Gaskill, "Zolar International and your clandestine operation known as *Solpemachaco* are permanently out of business."

Ragsdale added, "A pity your dad, Mansfield Zolar, a.k.a. the Specter, isn't still alive or we could bust him too."

Zolar looked as if he were in the throes of cardiac arrest. Oxley appeared too paralyzed to move.

"By the time you two and the rest of your family,

artners, associates, and buyers get out of prison, you'll e as old as the artifacts you stole."

Federal agents began filling the aircraft. The FBI took harge of the air crew while the Customs people unbuck-ed the tie-down straps securing the golden artifacts. Ragsdale nodded to his team.

"Take them downtown to the U.S. Attorney's Office."

As soon as the shattered art thieves were led into two different cars, the agents turned to the Moores.

"I can't tell you how grateful we are for your coopera-ion," said Gaskill. "Nailing the Zolar family will put a uge dent in the art theft and artifact smuggling trade."

"We're not entirely benevolent," said Micki, happily elieved. "Henry feels certain the Peruvian government will post a reward."

Gaskill nodded. "I think you've got a sure bet."

"The prestige of being the first to catalogue and photograph the treasure will go a long way toward enhancing our scientific reputations," Henry Moore explained as he holstered his gun.

"Customs would also like a detailed report on the objects, if you don't mind?" asked Gaskill.

Moore nodded vigorously. "Micki and I will be happy to work with you. We've already inventoried the trea-sure. We'll have a report for you before it's formally returned to Peru."

"Where will you store it all until then?" asked Micki.

"In a government warehouse whose location we can't reveal," answered Gaskill.

"Is there any news on Congresswoman Smith and the man with NUMA?"

Gaskill nodded. "Minutes before you landed we re-ceived word they were rescued by a local tribe of Indians and are on their way to a local hospital."

Micki sank down into a passenger seat and sighed. "Then it's over."

Henry sat on an armrest and took her hand in his. "This is for us," he said gently. "From now on we'll live the rest of our lives together as a pair of old teachers in university with vine-covered walls."

She looked up at him. "Is that so terrible?"

"No," he said, kissing her lightly on the forehead, "I think we can handle it."

36

PITT WAS SURPRISED TO FIND THAT HE DIDN'T FEEL OVERLY weak from loss of blood. He unclipped from his forearm the flashlight that Giordino had given him after their drop over the falls, switched it on, and propped it in the sand so the beam was aimed at his upper torso. He unzipped his wet suit jacket and tenderly probed the wound in his shoulder. The bullet had passed through the flesh and out his back without striking the scapula or the clavicle. The neoprene rubber on his shredded but still nearly skintight wet suit had helped seal the opening and restrict the flow of blood. Relieved that he did not feel as drained as he thought he would, he relaxed and took stock of his situation. His chances of survival were somewhere beyond impossible, with 100 kilometers (62 miles) of unknown rapids, sharp cascades, and extensive river passages that passed through caverns completely immersed with water. Even if he had air passages the entire way, there was still the distance from the opening of the subterranean channel to the surface of the Gulf.

Most other men who found themselves darkness deep within the earth with no hope of escape would have panicked and died tearing their fingers to the bone in a vain attempt to claw their way to the surface. But Pitt was not afraid. He was curiously content and at peace with himself.

If he was going to die, he thought, he might as well get comfortable. With his good hand he dug indentations in the sand to accommodate his body contour. He was surprised when the flashlight beam reflected from a thousand golden specks in the black sand. He held up a handful under the light.

"This place is loaded with placer gold," he said to himself.

He shone the light around the cavern. The walls were cut with ledges of white quartz streaked with tiny veins of gold. Pitt began laughing as he saw humor in the implausibility of it all.

"A gold mine," he proclaimed to the silent cave. "I've made a fabulously rich gold strike and nobody will ever know it."

He sat back and contemplated his discovery. Someone must be telling him something, he thought. Just because he wasn't afraid of the old man with the scythe didn't mean he had to give up and wait for him. A stubborn resolve sparked within him.

Better to enter the great beyond after an audacious attempt at staying alive than to throw in the towel and go out like a dishrag, he concluded. Perhaps other adventurous explorers would give up everything they owned for the honor of entering this mineralogical sanctum sanctorum, but all Pitt wanted now was to get out. He rose to his feet, inflated the buoyancy compensator with his breath and walked into the water until he was adrift in the current that carried him along.

Just take it one cavern at a time, he told himself, flashing the light on the water ahead. There was no relying on eternal vigilance. He was too weak to fight rapids and fend off rocks; he could only be calm and go wherever the current took him. He soon felt as if he had been cruising from one gallery to another for a lifetime.

The roof of the caverns and galleries rose and fell with monotonous regularity for the next 10 kilometers (6.2 miles). Then he heard the dreaded rumble of approaching rapids. Thankfully, the first chute Pitt encountered was of medium roughness. The water crashed against his face and he went under churning froth several times before reaching placid water again.

He was granted a comfortable reprieve as the river turned smooth and ran through one long canyon in an immense gallery. When he reached the end nearly an hour later, the roof gradually sloped down until it touched the water. He filled his lungs to the last crowded millimeter and dived. Able to use only one arm and missing his swim fins, the going was slow. He aimed the flashlight at the jagged rock roof and swam on his back. His lungs began to protest the lack of oxygen, but he swam on. At last the light revealed an air pocket. He shot to the surface and mightily inhaled the pure, unpolluted air that had been trapped deep beneath the earth millions of years ago.

The small cave widened into a large cavern whose ceiling arched beyond the beam of the flashlight. The river made a sweeping turn where it had formed a reef of polished gravel. Pitt crawled painfully onto the dry area to rest. He turned off the light to prolong the life of the batteries.

Abruptly, he flicked the flash on again. Something had caught his eye in the shadows before the light blinked out. Something was there, not 5 meters away, a black form that revealed a straight line aberrant to natural geometrics.

Pitt's spirits soared as he recognized the battered remains of the *Wallowing Windbag*. Incredibly, the Hovercraft had come through the horrific fall over the cataract and had been cast up here after drifting nearly 40 kilometers. At last a gleam of hope. He stumbled across the gravel beach to the rubber hull and examined it under his light.

The engine and fan had been torn from their mountings and were missing. Two of the air chambers were punctured and deflated, but the remaining six still held firm. Some of the equipment was swept away, but four air tanks, the first-aid kit, Duncan's plastic ball of colored water dye tracer, one of Giordino's paddles, two extra flashlights, and the waterproof container with Admiral Sandecker's thermos of coffee and four bologna sandwiches had miraculously survived.

"It seems my state of affairs has considerably improved," Pitt said happily to nobody but the empty cavern.

He began with the first-aid kit. After liberally soaking the shoulder wound with disinfectant, he awkwardly applied a crude bandage on it inside his tattered wet suit. Knowing it was useless to bind fractured ribs, he gritted his teeth, set his wrist and taped it.

The coffee had retained most of its heat inside the thermos, and he downed half of it before attacking the sandwiches. No medium-rare porterhouse steak tasted better than this bologna, Pitt decided. Then and there he vowed never to complain or make jokes about bologna sandwiches ever again.

After a brief rest, a goodly measure of his strength returned and he felt refreshed enough to resecure the equipment and break open Duncan's plastic dye container. He scattered Fluorescein Yellow with Optical Brightener into the water. Under the beam of his flashlight he watched until the dye stained the river with a vivid yellow luminescence. He stood and watched until the current swept it out of sight.

"That should tell them I'm coming," he thought aloud.

He pushed the remains of the Hovercraft out of the

allows. Favoring his injuries, he awkwardly climbed ⬤oard and paddled one-handed into the mainstream.

As the partially deflated *Wallowing Windbag* caught ⬤e current and drifted downriver, Pitt leaned back ⬤mfortably and began humming the tune to "Up a Lazy ⬤iver in the Noonday Sun."

The patrol vessel entered the breakwater of San Felipe ⬤d tied up alongside the *Alhambra*.

As Pitt had suspected, after reaching shore in the life ⬤ft, Gordo Padilla and his crew had gone home to their ⬤ives and girlfriends and celebrated their narrow escape ⬤y taking a three-day siesta. Then, under the watchful ⬤e of Cortina's police, Padilla rounded everyone up and ⬤itched a ride on a fishing boat back to the ferry. Once ⬤n board they raised steam in the engines and pumped ⬤ut the water taken on when Amaru opened the sea-⬤cks. When her keel was unlocked by the silt and her ⬤ngines were fired to life, Padilla and his crew sailed the ⬤lhambra back to San Felipe and tied her to the dock.

To the crew of the patrol vessel, looking down from ⬤eir bridge, the forward car deck of the ferry looked like ⬤e accident ward of a hospital.

Loren Smith was comfortably dressed in shorts and ⬤alter top and exhibited her bruises and a liberal assort-⬤ent of small bandages. Giordino sat in a wheelchair ⬤ith both legs propped ahead of him in plaster casts.

Missing was Rudi Gunn, who was in stable condition ⬤n the El Centro Regional Medical Center just north of ⬤alexico, after having survived a badly bruised stomach, ⬤ix broken fingers, and a hairline fracture of the skull.

Admiral Sandecker and Peter Duncan, the hydrolo-⬤ist, also stood on the deck of the ferryboat, along with ⬤hannon Kelsey, Miles Rodgers, and a contingent of ⬤ocal police and the Baja California Norte state coroner. ⬤heir faces were grim as the crew of the navy patrol ship

lowered the stretcher containing the body onto t
Alhambra's deck.

Before the coroner and his assistant could lift the bo
bag onto a gurney, Giordino pushed his wheelchair up
the stretcher. "I would like to see the body," he sa
grimly.

"He is not a pretty sight, señor," Lieutenant Carl
Hidalgo warned him from the deck of his ship.

The coroner hesitated, not sure if under the law I
could permit foreigners to view a dead body.

Giordino stared coldly at the coroner. "Do you wa
an identification or not?"

The coroner, a little man with bleary eyes and a gre
bush of gray hair, barely knew enough English to unde
stand Giordino, but he nodded silently to his assista
who pulled down the zipper.

Loren paled and turned away, but Sandecker move
close beside Giordino.

"Is it . . ."

Giordino shook his head. "No, it's not Dirk. It's th
psycho creep, Tupac Amaru."

"He looks as if he was churned through an empt
cement mixer."

"Almost as bad," said Duncan, shuddering at th
ghastly sight. "The rapids must have beat him agains
every rock between here and Cerro el Capirote."

"Couldn't happen to a nicer guy," Giordino muttere
acidly.

"Somewhere between the treasure cavern and th
Gulf," said Duncan, "the river must erupt into a ram
page."

"No sign of another body?" Sandecker asked Hidalgo

"Nothing, señor. This is the only one we found, but w
have orders to continue the search for the second man."

Sandecker turned away from Amaru. "If Dirk hasn'
been cast out into the Gulf by now, he must still be
underground."

"Is there any hope for Dirk?" Loren pleaded. "Any hope at all?"

Duncan looked from Giordino to Sandecker before answering. All eyes reflected abject hopelessness and their faces were etched with despair. He turned back to Loren and said gently, "I can't lie to you, Miss Smith." The words appeared to cause him great discomfort. "Dirk's chances are as good as any badly injured man's of reaching Lake Mead outside of Las Vegas after being cast adrift in the Colorado River at the entrance to the Grand Canyon."

The words came like a physical blow to Loren. She began to sway on her feet. Giordino reached out and grabbed her arm. It seemed that her heart stopped, and she whispered, "To me, Dirk Pitt will never die."

"The fish are a little shy today," said Joe Hagen to his wife, Claire.

She pushed her sunglasses on top of her head and laughed. "You couldn't catch a fish if it jumped up and landed in the boat."

He laughed. "Just wait and see."

"The only fish you'll find this far north in the Gulf is shrimp," she nagged.

The Hagens were in their early sixties. Together they ran a family auto dealership in Anaheim specializing in clean, low-mileage used cars.

After Joe bought a 15-meter (50-foot) oceangoing ketch, and named it *The First Attempt,* out of Newport Beach, California, they began leaving the management of their business to their two sons. They liked to sail down the coast and around Cabo San Lucas into the Sea of Cortez, spending the fall months cruising back and forth between picturesque ports nestled on the shores.

"Aha, they laughed at all the great geniuses," said Joe as he felt a tug on his trolling line. He reeled it in and discovered a California corbina about the length of his arm on the hook.

Claire shaded her eyes with one hand. "He's too pretty to keep. Throw the poor thing back."

"That's odd."

"What's odd?"

"All the other corbinas I've ever caught had dark spots on a white body. This sucker is colored like a fluorescent canary."

She came astern to have a closer look at his catch.

"Now this is really weird," said Joe, holding up one hand and displaying palm and fingers that were stained a bright yellow. "If I weren't a sane man, I'd say somebody dyed this fish."

"He sparkles under the sun as if his scales were spangles," said Claire.

Joe peered over the side of the boat. "The water in this one particular area looks like it was squeezed out of a lemon."

"Could be a good fishing hole."

"You may be right, old girl." Joe moved past her to the bow and threw out the anchor. "This looks as good a place as any to spend the afternoon angling for a big one."

37

THERE WAS NO REST FOR THE WEARY. PITT WENT OVER FOUR more cataracts. Providentially, none had a steep, yawning drop like the one that almost killed him and Giordino. The steepest drop he encountered was 2 meters (6.5 feet). The partially deflated *Wallowing Windbag* bravely plunged over the sharp ledge and successfully ran an obstacle course through rocks hiding under roaring sheets of froth and spray before continuing her voyage to oblivion.

It was the boiling stretches of rapids that proved brutal. Only after they extracted their toll in battering torment could Pitt relax for a short time in the forgiving, unobstructed stretches of calm water that followed. The bruising punishment made his wounds feel as if they were being stabbed by little men with pitchforks. But the pain served a worthy purpose by sharpening his senses. He cursed the river, certain it was saving the worst for last before smashing his desperate gamble to escape.

The paddle was torn from his hand, but it proved a small loss. With 50 kilograms (110 pounds) of equipment in a collapsing boat in addition to him, it was useless to attempt a sharp course change to dodge rocks that loomed up in the dark, especially while little more paddle with one arm. He was too weak to d

than feebly grasp the support straps attached to t‍
interior of the hull and let the current take him where ‍
might.

Two more float cells were ruptured after colliding wi‍
sharp rocks that sliced through the thin skin of the hu‍
and Pitt found himself lying half-covered with water ‍
what had become little more than a collapsed air ba‍
Surprisingly, he kept a death grip on the flashlight wit‍
his right hand. But he had completely drained three ‍
the air tanks and most of the fourth while dragging th‍
sagging little vessel through several fully submerge‍
galleries before reaching open caverns on the other sid‍
and reinflating the remaining float cells.

Pitt never suffered from claustrophobia but it woul‍
have come easy for most people in the black neve‍
ending void. He avoided any thoughts of panic b‍
singing and talking to himself during his wild rid‍
through the unfriendly water. He shone the light on hi‍
hands and feet. They were shriveled like prunes after th‍
long hours of immersion.

"With all this water, dehydration is the least of m‍
problems," he muttered to the dank, uncaring rock.

He floated over transparent pools that dropped dow‍
shafts of solid rock so deep the beam of his lamp coul‍
not touch bottom. He toyed with the thought of tourist‍
coming through this place. A pity people can't take th‍
tour and view these crystallized Gothic caverns, h‍
thought. Perhaps now that the river was known to exist‍
a tunnel might be excavated to bring in visitors to stud‍
the geological marvels.

He had tried to conserve his three flashlights, but one‍
by one their batteries gave out and he dropped them over‍
the side. He estimated that only twenty minutes of light‍
‍‍‍ained in his last lamp before the gloom returned for‍

Running rapids in a raft under the sun and blue sky is‍

lled white-water rafting, his exhausted mind deliber-
ed. Down here they could call it black-water rafting.
he idea sounded very funny and for some reason he
ughed. His laughter carried into a vast side chamber,
choing in a hundred eerie sounds. If he hadn't known it
ame from him, it would have curdled his blood.

It no longer seemed possible that there could be any
lace but this nightmare maze of caverns creeping tortu-
usly end on end through such an alien environment. He
ad lost all sense of direction. "Bearings" was only a
ord from a dictionary. His compass was made useless
y an abundance of iron ore in the rock. He felt so
isoriented and removed from the surface world above
hat he wondered if he had finally crossed the threshold
nto lunacy. The only breath of sanity was fueled by the
tupendous sights revealed by the light from his lamp.

He forced himself to regain control by playing mind
ames. He tried to memorize details of each new cavern
nd gallery, of each bend and turn of the river, so he
ould describe them to others after he escaped to sun-
ght. But there were so many of them his numbed mind
ound it impossible to retain more than a few vivid
mages. Not only that, he found he had to concentrate on
eeping the *Windbag* afloat. Another float cell was
issing its buoyancy away through a puncture.

How far have I come? he wondered dully. How much
arther to the end? His fogged mind was wandering. He
ad to get a grip on himself. He was beyond hunger; no
houghts of thick steaks or prime rib with a bottle of beer
looded through his mind. His battered and spent body
ad given far more than he expected from it.

The shrunken hull of the Hovercraft struck the cav-
rn's roof which arched downward into the water. The
raft revolved in circles, bumping against the rock until
t worked off to one side of the mainstream of the river
nd gently grounded on a shoal. Pitt lay in the pool that

half-filled the interior, his legs dangling over the side
too played out to don the last air tank, deflate the cra.
and convey it through the flooded gallery ahead.

He couldn't pass out. Not now. He had too far to g
He took several deep breaths and drank a small amou:
of water. He groped for the thermos, untied it from
hook and finished the last of the coffee. The caffei:
helped revive him a bit. He flipped the thermos into t]
river and watched it float against the rock, too buoya:
to drift through to the other side.

The lamp was so weak it barely threw a beam. H
switched it off to save what little juice was left in th
batteries, lay back, and stared into the suffocating blacl
ness.

Nothing hurt anymore. His nerve endings had shu
down and his body was numb. He must have bee
almost two pints low on blood, he figured. He hated t
face the thought of failure. For a few minutes he refuse
to believe he couldn't make it back to the world abov(
The faithful *Wallowing Windbag* had taken him this fa:
but if it lost one more float cell he would have t
abandon it and carry on alone. He began concentratin
his waning energies on the effort that still lay ahead.

Something jogged his memory. He smelled something
What was it they said about smells? They can trigger pas
events in your mind. He breathed in deeply, trying not t(
let the scent get away before he could recall why it was s(
familiar. He licked his lips and recognized a taste tha
hadn't been there before. Salt. And then it washed ove
him.

The smell of the sea.

He had finally reached the end of the subterranea:
river system that climaxed in the Gulf.

Pitt popped open his eyes and raised his hand until i
almost touched the tip of his nose. He couldn't distin
guish detail, but there was a vague shadow that shouldn'
have been there in the eternal dark of his subterranea:

orld. He stared down into the water and detected a
urky reflection. Light was seeping in from the passage
ead.

The discovery that daylight was within reach raised
mensely his hopes of surviving.

He climbed out of the *Wallowing Windbag* and consid-
ed the two worst hazards he now faced—length of dive
 the surface and decompression. He checked the pres-
re gauge that ran from the manifold of the air tank.
ight hundred fifty pounds per square inch. Enough air
r a run of maybe 300 meters (984 feet), providing he
ayed calm, breathed easily, and didn't exert himself. If
rface air was much beyond that, he wouldn't have to
orry about the other problem, decompression. He'd
rown long before acquiring the notorious bends.

Periodic checks of his depth gauge during his long
urney had told him the pressure inside most of the air-
led caverns ran only slightly higher than the outside
tmospheric pressure. A concern but not a great fear.
nd he had seldom exceeded 30 meters of depth when
iving under a flooded overhang that divided two open
alleries. If faced with the same situation, he would have
 be careful to make a controlled 18-meter- (60-foot-)
er-minute ascent to avoid decompression sickness.

Whatever the obstacles, he could neither go back nor
tay where he was. He had to go on. There was no other
ecision to make. This would be the final test of what
ttle strength and resolve was still left in him.

He wasn't dead yet. Not until he breathed the last tiny
it of oxygen in his air tank. And then he would go on
ntil his lungs burst.

He checked to see that the manifold valves were open
nd the low-pressure hose was connected to his buoyan-
y compensator. Next, he strapped on his tank and
uckled the quick-release snaps. A quick breath to be
ure his regulator was functioning properly and he was
eady.

Without his lost dive mask, his vision would 1
blurred, but all he had to do was swim toward the ligl
He clamped his teeth on the mouthpiece of his breathi
regulator, gathered his nerve, and counted to three.

It was time to go, and he dove into the river for the la
time.

As he gently kicked his bare feet he'd have giv
anything for his lost fins. Down, down the overha
sloped ahead of him. He passed thirty meters, then fort
He began to worry after he passed fifty meters. Whe
diving on compressed air, there is an invisible barri
between sixty and eighty meters. Beyond that a div
begins to feel like a drunk and loses control of his ment
faculties.

His air tank made an unearthly screeching sound as
scraped against the rock above him. Because he ha
dropped his weight belt after his near-death experienc
over the great waterfall, and because of the neoprene i
his shredded wet suit, he was diving with positi
buoyancy. He doubled over and dove deeper to avoid th
contact.

Pitt thought the plunging rock would never end. H
depth gauge read 75 meters (246 feet) before the currer
carried him beneath and around the tip of the overhan
Now the upward slope was gradual. Not the idea
situation. He'd have preferred a direct ascent to th
surface to cut the distance and save his dwindling ai
supply.

The light grew steadily brighter until he could read th
numbers of his dive watch without the aid of the dyin
beam from the lamp. The hands on the orange dial rea
ten minutes after five o'clock. Was it early morning o
afternoon? How long since he dove into the river? H
couldn't remember if it was ten minutes or fifty. Hi
mind sluggishly puzzled over the answers.

The clear, transparent emerald green of the river wate

urned more blue and opaque. The current was fading and his ascent slowed. There was a distant shimmer above him. At last the surface itself appeared.

He was in the Gulf. He had exited the river passage and was swimming in the Sea of Cortez. Pitt looked up and saw a shadow looming far in the distance. One final check of his air pressure gauge. The needle quivered on zero. His air was almost gone.

Rather than suck in a huge gulp, he used what little was left to partially inflate his buoyancy compensator so it would gently lift him to the surface if he blacked out from lack of oxygen.

One last inhalation that barely puffed out his lungs and he relaxed, exhaling small breaths to compensate for the declining pressure as he rose from the depths. The hiss of his air bubbles leaving the regulator diminished as his lungs ran dry.

The surface appeared so close he could reach out and touch it when his lungs began to burn. It was a spiteful illusion. The waves were still 20 meters away.

He put some strength into his kick as a huge elastic band seemed to tighten around his chest. Soon, the desire for air became his only world as darkness started seeping around the edges of his eyes.

Pitt became entangled in something that hindered his ascent. His vision, blurred without a dive mask, failed to distinguish what was binding him. Instinctively, he thrashed clumsily in an attempt to free himself. A great roaring sound came from inside his brain as it screamed in protest. But in that instant before blackness shut down his mind, he sensed that his body was being pulled toward the surface.

"I've hooked a big one!" shouted Joe Hagen joyously.

"You got a marlin?" Claire asked excitedly, seeing her husband's fishing pole bent like a question mark.

"He's not giving much fight for a marlin," Joe panted as he feverishly turned the crank on his reel. "Feels more like a dead weight."

"Maybe you dragged him to death."

"Get the gaff. He's almost to the surface."

Claire snatched a long-handled gaff from two hooks and pointed it over the side of the yacht like a spear. "I see something," she cried. "It looks big and black."

Then she screamed in horror.

Pitt was a millimeter away from unconsciousness when his head broke into a trough between the waves. He spit out his regulator and drew in a deep breath. The sun's reflection on the water blinded eyes that hadn't seen light in almost two days. He squinted rapturously at the sudden kaleidoscope of colors.

Relief, joy of living, fulfillment of a great accomplishment—they flooded together.

A woman's scream pierced his ears and he looked up, startled to see the Capri-blue hull of a yacht rising beside him and two people staring over the side, their faces pale as death. It was then that he realized he was entangled in fishing line. Something slapped against his leg. He gripped the line and pulled a small skipjack tuna, no longer than his foot, out of the water. The poor thing had a huge hook protruding from its mouth.

Pitt gently gripped the fish under one armpit and eased out the hook with his good hand. Then he stared into the little fish's beady eyes.

"Look, Toto," he said jubilantly, "we're back in Kansas!"

38

COMMANDER MADERAS AND HIS CREW HAD MOVED OUT OF San Felipe and resumed their search pattern when the call came through from the Hagens.

"Sir," said his radioman, "I just received an urgent message from the yacht *The First Attempt.*"

"What does it say?"

"The skipper, an American by the name of Joseph Hagen, reports picking up a man he caught while fishing."

Maderas frowned. "He must mean he snagged a dead body while trolling."

"No, sir, he was quite definite. The man he caught is alive."

Maderas was puzzled. "Can't be the one we're searching for. Not after viewing the other one. Have any boats in the area reported a crew member lost overboard?"

The radioman shook his head. "I've heard nothing."

"What is *The First Attempt*'s position?"

"Twelve nautical miles to the northwest of us."

Maderas stepped into the wheelhouse and nodded at Hidalgo. "Set a course to the northwest and watch for an American yacht." Then he turned to his radioman. "Call this Joseph Hagen for more details on the man they pulled from the water and tell him to remain at his present position. We'll rendezvous in approximately thirty-five minutes."

The Hagen broadcast was picked up by a Mexican navy radio station in La Paz. The radio operator on duty asked for confirmation, but Hagen was too busy jabbering away with other yacht owners and failed to reply. Thinking it was another of the wild parties in the boating social swing, he noted it in his log and concentrated on official navy signals.

When he went off duty twenty minutes later, he casually mentioned it to the officer in charge of the station.

"It sounded pretty loco," he explained. "The report came in English. Probably an intoxicated gringo playing games over his radio."

"Better send a patrol boat to make an inspection," said the officer. "I'll inform the Northern District Fleet Headquarters and see who we have in the area."

Fleet headquarters did not have to be informed. Maderas had already alerted them that he was heading at full speed toward *The First Attempt*. Headquarters had also received an unexpected signal from the Mexican chief of naval operations, ordering the commanding officer to rush the search and extend every effort for a successful rescue operation.

Admiral Ricardo Alvarez was having lunch with his wife at the officers' club when an aide hurried to his table with both signals.

"A man caught by a fisherman." Alvarez snorted. "What kind of nonsense is this?"

"That was the message relayed by Commander Maderas of the G-21," replied the aide.

"How soon before Maderas comes in contact with the yacht?"

"He should rendezvous at any moment."

"I wonder why Naval Operations is so involved with an ordinary tourist lost at sea?"

"Word has come down that the President himself is interested in the rescue," said the aide.

Admiral Alvarez gave his wife a sour look. "I knew that damned North American Free Trade Agreement was a mistake. Now we have to kiss up to the Americans every time one of them falls in the Gulf."

So it was that there were more questions than answers when Pitt was transferred from *The First Attempt* soon after the patrol vessel came alongside. He stood on the deck, partially supported by Hagen, who had stripped off the torn wet suit and lent Pitt a golf shirt and a pair of shorts. Claire had replaced the bandage on his shoulder and taped one over the nasty cut on his forehead.

He shook hands with Joseph Hagen. "I guess I'm the biggest fish you ever caught."

Hagen laughed. "Sure something to tell the grand-kids."

Pitt then kissed Claire on the cheek. "Don't forget to send me your recipe for fish chowder. I've never tasted any so good."

"You must have liked it. You put away at least a gallon."

"I'll always be in your debt for saving my life. Thank you."

Pitt turned and was helped into a small launch that ferried him to the patrol boat. As soon as he stepped onto the deck, he was greeted by Maderas and Hidalgo before being escorted to the sick bay by the ship's medical corpsman. Prior to ducking through a hatch, Pitt turned and gave a final wave to the Hagens.

* * *

Customs Agent Curtis Starger got the word in Guaymas that Pitt had been found alive. He was searching the hacienda used by the Zolars. The call came in over his Motorola Iridium satellite phone from his office in Calexico. In an unusual display of teamwork, the Mexican investigative agencies had allowed Starger and his Customs people to probe the buildings and grounds for additional evidence to help convict the family dynasty of art thieves.

Starger and his agents had arrived to find the grounds and airstrip empty of all life. The hacienda was vacant and the pilot of Joseph Zolar's private plane had decided now was a good time to resign. He simply walked through the front gate, took a bus into town, and caught a flight to his home in Houston, Texas.

A search of the hacienda turned up nothing concrete. The rooms had been cleaned of any incriminating evidence. The abandoned plane parked on the airstrip was another matter. Inside, Starger found four crudely carved wooden effigies with childlike faces painted on them.

"What do you make of these?" Starger asked one of the agents, who was an expert in ancient Southwest artifacts.

"They look like some kind of Indian religious symbols."

"Are they made from cottonwood?"

The agent lifted his sunglasses and examined the idols close up. "Yes, I think I can safely say they're carved out of cottonwood."

Starger ran his hand gently over one of the idols. "I have a suspicion these are the sacred idols Pitt was looking for."

Rudi Gunn was told while he was lying in a hospital bed. A nurse entered his room, followed by one of Starger's agents.

"Mr. Gunn. I'm Agent Anthony Di Maggio with the
'ustoms Service. I thought you'd like to know that Dirk
itt was picked up alive in the Gulf about half an hour
go."

Gunn closed his eyes and sighed with heavy relief. "I
new he'd make it."

"Quite a feat of courage, I hear, swimming over a
undred kilometers through an underground river."

"No one else could have done it."

"I hope the good news will inspire you to become
nore cooperative," said the nurse, who talked sweetly
vhile carrying a long rectal thermometer.

"Isn't he a good patient?" asked Di Maggio.

"I've tended better."

"I wish you'd give me a pair of pajamas," Gunn said
aastily, "instead of this peekaboo, shorty nightshirt."

"Hospital gowns are designed that way for a purpose,"
he nurse replied smartly. "You rest now," she ordered.
'I'll be back in an hour with your medication."

True to her word, the nurse returned in one hour on
he dot. But the bed was empty. Gunn had fled, wearing
1othing but the skimpy little gown and a blanket.

Strangely, those on board the *Alhambra* were the last
to know.

Loren and Sandecker were meeting with Mexican
Internal Police investigators beside the Pierce Arrow
when news of Pitt's rescue came from the owner of a
luxurious powerboat that was tied up at the nearby fuel
station. He shouted across the water separating the two
vessels.

"Ahoy the ferry!"

Miles Rodgers was standing on the deck by the wheelhouse talking with Shannon and Duncan. He leaned
over the railing and shouted back. "What is it?"

"They found your boy!"

The words carried inside the auto deck and San decker rushed out onto the open deck. "Say again!" h yelled.

"The owners of a sailing ketch fished a fellow out c the water," the yacht skipper replied. "The Mexica navy reports say it's the guy they were looking for."

Everyone was on an outside deck now. All afraid t ask the question that might have an answer they dreade to hear.

Giordino accelerated his wheelchair up to the loadin ramp as if it were a super fuel dragster. He apprehen sively yelled over to the powerboat. "Was he alive?"

"The Mexicans said he was in pretty poor shape, bu came around after the boat owner's wife pumped som soup into him."

"Pitt's alive!" gasped Shannon.

Duncan shook his head in disbelief. "I can't believe h made it through to the Gulf!"

"I do," murmured Loren, her face in her hands, th tears flowing. The dignity and the poise seemed tc crumble. She leaned down and hugged Giordino, he cheeks wet and flushed red beneath a new tan. "I knev he couldn't die."

Suddenly, the Mexican investigators were forgotten as if they were miles away and everyone was shouting and hugging each other. Sandecker, normally taciturn and reserved, let out a resounding whoop and rushed to the wheelhouse, snatched up the Iridium phone and excit- edly called the Mexican Navy Fleet Command for more information.

Duncan frantically began poring over his hydro- graphic charts of the desert water tables, impatient to learn what data Pitt had managed to accumulate during the incredible passage through the underwater river system.

Miles reflected genuine joy at the news, but Shannon's eyes seemed unusually thoughtful. She stared openly at

Loren, as a curious envy bloomed inside her that she couldn't believe existed. She slowly became aware that perhaps she had made a mistake by not displaying more compassion toward Pitt.

"That guy is like the bad penny that always turns up," said Giordino, fighting to control his emotions.

39

THE SMALL PORT OF SAN FELIPE WORE A FESTIVE AIR. THE dock was crowded with people. Everywhere there was an atmosphere of excitement as the patrol boat neared the entrance to the breakwaters forming the harbor.

Maderas turned to Pitt. "Quite a reception."

Pitt's eyes narrowed against the sun. "Is it some sort of local holiday?"

"News of your remarkable journey through the earth has drawn them."

"You've got to be kidding," said Pitt in honest surprise.

"No, señor. Because of your discovery of the river flowing below the desert, you've become a hero to every farmer and rancher from here to Arizona who struggles to survive in a harsh wasteland." He nodded at two vans with technicians unloading television camera equipment. "That's why you've become big news."

Pitt groaned. "All I want is a soft bed to sleep in for three days."

Pitt's mental and physical condition had improved considerably upon receiving word over the ship's radio from Admiral Sandecker that Loren, Rudi, and Al were alive, if slightly the worse for wear. Sandecker also

370

rought him up to date on Cyrus Sarason's death at the
ands of Billy Yuma and the capture of Zolar and Oxley,
long with Huascar's treasure, by Gaskill and Ragsdale
ith the help of Henry and Micki Moore.

There was hope for the little people after all, Pitt
nought stoically.

It seemed like an hour, though it was only a few
minutes before the *Porquería* tied up to the *Alhambra* for
ne second time that day. A large paper sign was un-
olded across the upper passenger deck of the ferryboat,
ne letters still dripping fresh paint. It read, WELCOME
ACK FROM THE DEAD.

On the auto deck a Mexican street band was lined up,
laying a mariachi version of "Waiting for the Robert E.
.ee." Loren stood among the throng that had mobbed
n board the ferry and waved wildly. She could see Pitt
earch the crowd until he found her and happily waved
ack.

She saw the dressing wrapped around his head, the left
rm in a sling, and the cast on one wrist. In his borrowed
horts and golf shirt he looked out of place among the
iniformed crew of the Mexican navy. At first glance, he
ppeared amazingly fit for a man who had survived a
ourney through a black abyss. But Loren knew Pitt was
master at covering up exhaustion and pain. She could
ee them in his eyes.

Pitt spotted Admiral Sandecker standing behind Giordino in his wheelchair. His wandering eyes also picked
out Gordo Padilla with his arm around his wife, Rosa.
Jesus, Gato, and the engineer, whose name he could
never remember, stood nearby brandishing bottles in the
air. Then the gangplank was down, and Pitt shook hands
with Maderas and Hidalgo.

"Thank you, gentlemen, and thank your corpsman for
me. He did a first-rate job of patching me up."

"It is we who are in your debt, Señor Pitt," said
Hidalgo. "My mother and father own a small ranch not

far from here and will reap the benefits when wells a
sunk into your river."

"Please make me one promise," said Pitt.

"If it's within our power," replied Maderas.

Pitt grinned. "Don't ever let anyone name that riv
after me."

He turned and walked across to the auto deck of th
ferry and into a sea of bodies. Loren rushed up to hir
and as the tears flowed, she smiled and said, "Welcom
home."

Then the rush was on. Newsmen and TV camerame
from both sides of the border swarmed around as Pi
greeted Sandecker and Giordino.

"I thought sure you'd bought a tombstone this time,
said Giordino, beaming like a neon sign on the Las Vega
strip.

Pitt smiled. "If I hadn't found the *Wallowing Wina
bag,* I wouldn't be here."

"I hope you realize," said Sandecker, faking a frown
"that you're getting too old for swimming around i
caves."

Pitt held up his good hand as if taking an oath. "S
help me, Admiral, if I ever so much as look at anothe
underground cavern, shoot me in the foot."

Then Shannon came up and gave Pitt a long hug tha
had Loren fuming. When she released him, she said, "
missed you."

Before he could reply, Miles Rodgers and Peter Duncan were pumping his uninjured hand. "You're one
tough character," said Rodgers.

"I busted the computer and lost your data," Pitt said
to Duncan. "I'm genuinely sorry."

"No problem," Duncan replied with a broad smile.
"Now that you've proven the river runs from Satan's
Sinkhole under Cerro el Capirote and shown where it
resurges into the Gulf, we can trace its path with floating

onic geophysical imaging systems along with transmit-
ing instrument packages."

At that moment, unnoticed by most of the mob, a
dilapidated Mexicali taxi smoked to a stop. A man
jumped out and hurried across the dock and onto the
auto deck wearing only a blanket. He put his head down
and barreled his way through the mass of people until he
reached Pitt.

"Rudi!" Pitt roared as he wrapped his free arm around
the little man's shoulder. "Where did you fall from?"

As if he'd timed it, Gunn's splinted fingers lost their
grip on the blanket and it fell to the deck, leaving him
standing in only the hospital smock. "I escaped the
clutches of my nurse to come here and greet you," he
said, without any sign of embarrassment.

"Are you mending okay?"

"I'll be back at my desk at NUMA before you."

Pitt turned and hailed Rodgers. "Miles, you got your
camera?"

"No good photographer is ever without his cameras,"
Rodgers shouted over the noise of the crowd.

"Take a picture of the four battered troopers of Cerro
el Capirote."

Rodgers got off three shots before the reporters took
over.

"Mr. Pitt!" One of the TV interviewers pushed a
microphone in front of his face. "What can you tell us
about the subterranean river?"

"Only that it exists," he answered smoothly, "and that
it's very wet."

"How large would you say it is?"

He had to think a moment as he slipped his arm
around Loren. "I'd guess about two-thirds the size of the
Rio Grande."

"That big?"

"Easily."

"How do you feel after swimming through underground caverns for over a hundred kilometers?"

Pitt was always irritated when a reporter asked how mother or father felt after their house burned down with all their children inside, or how a witness felt who watched someone fall from an airplane without a parachute.

"Feel?" stated Pitt. "Right now I feel that my bladder will burst if I don't get to a bathroom."

EPILOGUE

HOMECOMING

November 4, 2005
San Felipe, Baja California

40

TWO DAYS LATER, AFTER EVERYONE GAVE DETAILED STATE-
ments to the Mexican investigators, they were free to
leave the country. They assembled on the dock to bid
their farewells.

Dr. Peter Duncan was the first to leave. The hydrologist slipped away early in the morning and was gone
before anyone missed him. He had a busy year ahead of
him as director of the Sonoran Water Project, as it was to
be called. The water from the river was to prove a
godsend to the drought-plagued Southwest. Water, the
lifeblood of civilization, would create jobs for the people
of the desert. Construction of aqueducts and pipelines
would channel the water into towns and cities and would
turn a dry lake into a recreational reservoir the size of
Lake Powell.

Soon to follow would be projects to mine the mineral
riches Pitt had discovered on his underground odyssey
and to build a tourist center beneath the earth.

Dr. Shannon Kelsey was invited back to Peru to
continue her excavations of the ruins in the Chachapoyan cities. Where she went, Miles Rodgers followed.

"I hope we meet again," said Rodgers, shaking Pitt's
hand.

"Only if you promise to stay out of sacred sinkholes,'
Pitt said warmly.

Rodgers laughed. "Count on it."

Pitt looked down into Shannon's eyes. The determination and boldness burned as bright as ever. "I wish you
all the best."

"So long, big guy. Don't forget me."

Pitt nodded and said simply, "I couldn't if I tried."

Shortly after Shannon and Miles left in their rented
car for the airport in San Diego, a NUMA helicopter
dropped out of the sun and touched down on the deck of
the *Alhambra*. The pilot left the engine idling as he
jumped down from the cargo hatch. He looked around a
moment and then, recognizing Sandecker, approached
him.

"Good morning, Admiral. Ready to leave, or should I
shut down the engine?"

"Keep it running," answered Sandecker. "What's the
status of my NUMA passenger jet?"

"Waiting on the ground at the Yuma Marine Corps Air
Station to fly you and the others back to Washington."

"Okay, we're set to board." Sandecker turned to Pitt.
"So, you're going on sick leave?"

"Loren and I thought we'd join a Classic Car Club of
America tour through Arizona."

"I'll expect you in one week." He turned to Loren and
gave her a brief kiss on the cheek. "You're a member of
Congress. Don't take any guff from him and see that he
gets back in one piece, fit for work."

Loren smiled. "Don't worry, Admiral. My constituents want me back on the job in fighting shape too."

"What about me?" said Giordino. "Don't I get time
off to recuperate?"

"You can sit behind a desk just as easily in a wheelchair." Then Sandecker smiled fiendishly. "Now, Rudi,
he's a different case. I think I'll send him to Bermuda for
a month."

"Whatta guy," said Gunn, trying desperately to keep a straight face.

It was a charade. Pitt and Giordino were like sons to Sandecker. Nothing went on between them that wasn't marked with a high degree of respect. The admiral knew with dead certainty that as soon as they were sound and able, they'd be in his office pressuring him for an ocean project to direct.

Two dockhands lifted Giordino into the helicopter. One seat had to be removed to accommodate his outstretched legs.

Pitt leaned in the doorway and tweaked one of the toes that protruded from the cast. "Try not to lose this helicopter like all the others."

"No big deal," Giordino came back. "I get one of these things every time I buy ten gallons of gas."

Gunn placed his hand on Pitt's shoulder. "It's been fun," he said lightly. "We must do it again sometime."

Pitt made a horrified face. "Not on your life."

Sandecker gave Pitt a light hug. "You rest up and take it easy," he said softly so the others couldn't hear above the beat of the rotor blades. "I'll see you when I see you."

"I'll make it soon."

Loren and Pitt stood on the deck of the ferryboat and waved until the helicopter turned northeast over the waters of the Gulf. He turned to her. "Well, that just leaves us."

She smiled teasingly. "I'm starved. Why don't we head into Mexicali and find us a good Mexican restaurant?"

"Now that you've broached the subject, I have a sudden craving for huevos rancheros."

"I guess I'll have to do the driving."

Pitt lifted his hand. "I still have one good arm."

Loren wouldn't hear of it. Pitt stood on the dock and guided her as she competently drove the big Pierce Arrow and its trailer up the ramp from the auto deck of the ferryboat onto the dock.

Pitt took one last, longing look at the walking beams of the old paddlesteamer and wished he could have sailed it through the Panama Canal and up the Potomac River to Washington. But it was not meant to be. He gave a forlorn sigh and was slipping into the passenger seat when a car pulled up alongside. Curtis Starger climbed out.

He hailed them. "Glad I caught you before you left. Dave Gaskill said to make sure you got this."

He handed Pitt something wrapped in an Indian blanket. Unable to take it with both hands, he looked helplessly at Loren. She took the blanket and spread it open.

Four faces painted on clublike prayer sticks stared back at them. "The sacred idols of the Montolos," Pitt said quietly. "Where did you find them?"

"We recovered them inside Joseph Zolar's private plane in Guaymas."

"I'd guessed the idols were in his dirty hands."

"They were positively identified as the missing Montolo effigies from a collector's data sheet we found with them," explained Starger.

"This will make the Montolos very happy."

Starger looked at him with a crooked smile. "I think we can trust you to deliver them."

"I promise to drop the idols off in the Montolo village on our way to the border."

"Dave Gaskill and I never nourished a doubt."

"How are the Zolars?" Pitt asked.

"In jail with every charge from theft and illegal smuggling to murder hanging over their heads. You'll be happy to learn the judge denied them bail, dead certain they would flee the country."

"You people do nice work."

"Thanks to your help, Mr. Pitt. If the Customs Service can ever do you a favor, don't hesitate to give us a call."

"I'll remember that, thank you."

* * *

Billy Yuma was unsaddling his horse after making the daily rounds of his small herd. He paused to look over the rugged landscape of cactus, mesquite, and tamarisk scattered through the rock outcroppings making up his part of the Sonoran Desert. He saw a dust cloud approaching that slowly materialized into what looked to him to be a very old automobile pulling a trailer, both vehicles painted in the same shade of dark, almost black, blue.

His curiosity rose even higher when the car and trailer stopped in front of his house. He walked from the corral as the passenger door opened and Pitt stepped out.

"A warm sun to you, my friend," Yuma greeted him.

"And clear skies to you," Pitt replied.

Yuma shook Pitt's right hand vigorously. "I'm real glad to see you. They told me you died in the darkness."

"Almost, but not quite," said Pitt, nodding at the arm held by the sling. "I wanted to thank you for entering the mountain and saving the lives of my friends."

"Evil men are meant to die," said Yuma philosophically. "I'm happy I came in time."

Pitt handed Yuma the blanket-wrapped idols. "I've brought something for you and your tribe."

Yuma pulled back the top half of the blanket tenderly, as if peeking at a baby. He stared mutely for several moments into the faces of the four deities. Then tears brimmed in his eyes. "You have returned the soul of my people, our dreams, our religion. Now our children can be initiated and become men and women."

"I was told those who stole them experienced strange sounds like children wailing."

"They were crying to come home."

"I thought Indians never cried."

Yuma smiled as the joyous impact of what he held in his hands washed over him. "Don't you believe it. We just don't like to let anyone see us."

Pitt introduced Loren to Billy's wife, Polly, who insisted they stay for dinner, and would not take no for an answer. Loren let it slip that Pitt had a taste for huevos rancheros, so Polly made him enough to feed five ranch hands.

During the meal, Yuma's friends and family came to the house and reverently looked upon the cottonwood idols. The men shook Pitt's hand while the women presented small handcrafted gifts to Loren. It was a very moving scene and Loren wept unashamedly.

Pitt and Yuma saw in each other two men who were basically very much alike. Neither had any illusions left. Pitt smiled at him. "It is an honor to have you as a friend, Billy."

"You are always welcome here."

"When the water is brought to the surface," said Pitt, "I will see that your village is at the top of the list to receive it."

Yuma removed an amulet on a leather thong from around his neck and gave it to Pitt. "Something to remember your friend by."

Pitt studied the amulet. It was a copper image of the *Demonio del Muertos* of Cerro el Capirote inlaid with turquoise. "It is too valuable. I cannot take it."

Yuma shook his head. "I swore to wear it until our sacred idols came home. Now it is yours for good luck."

"Thank you."

Before they left Canyon Ometepec, Pitt walked Loren up to Patty Lou Cutting's grave. She knelt and read the inscription on the tombstone.

"What beautiful words," she said softly. "Is there a story behind them?"

"No one seems to know. The Indians say she was buried by unknown people during the night."

"She was so young. Only ten years old."

Pitt nodded. "She rests in a lonely place for a ten-year-old."

"When we get back to Washington, let's try to find if ⎽e exists in any records."

The desert wildflowers had bloomed and died so ⎽oren made a wreath from creosote bush branches and ⎽id it over the grave. They stood there for a while ⎽oking over the desert. The colors fired by the setting ⎽un were vivid and extraordinary, enhanced by the clear ⎽lovember air.

The whole village lined the road to wish them *adios* as ⎽oren steered the Pierce Arrow toward the main high-⎽ay.

Pitt stared through the windshield at the road ahead ⎽r a long time. Finally, he said, "How far to Wash-⎽ngton?"

"About five thousand kilometers. Why?"

He pulled the sling off his arm, threw it in the backseat ⎽nd put his arm around her shoulder. "Let's take the ⎽ong route—and promise me one thing?"

"And what is that?" Loren asked.

Pitt smiled slyly and his green eyes twinkled. "That we ⎽o *nowhere* near water until we reach the banks of the ⎽otomac."

POSTSCRIPT

THE WALLS IN THE WAITING ROOM OUTSIDE SANDECKER'S
private office in the NUMA headquarters building are
covered with a gallery of photographs taken of the
admiral hobnobbing with the rich and famous. The
subjects include five presidents, numerous military leaders and heads of state, congressmen, noted scientists,
and a sprinkling of motion picture stars, all staring at the
camera, lips stretched in predictable smiles.

All have simple black frames. All except one that
hangs in the exact center of the others. This one has a
gold frame.

In this photograph Sandecker is standing amid a
strange group of people who look as if they have just
been in some kind of spectacular accident. One short,
curly-headed man sits in a wheelchair, his legs in plaster
casts, jutting toward the cameraman. Beside him is a
small man wearing horn-rimmed glasses, with his head
encased in a bandage and splints on several of his fingers,
wearing what appears to be a flimsy untied hospital
smock. Then there is an attractive woman in shorts and
a haltertop who looks as if she belongs in a safe house for
battered wives. Next to her stands a tall man with a
bandage on his forehead and one arm in a sling. His eyes

have a devil-may-care look and his head is tilted back
robust laughter.

If, after being ushered into the admiral's office, y
casually ask about the unusual characters in the pho
graph with the gold frame, be prepared to sit and list
attentively for the next hour.

It is a long story, and Sandecker loves to tell how t
Rio Pitt got its name.

37065

PB
Cussler, Clive
Inca gold

DATE DUE

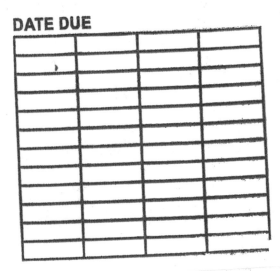